THIN LINE

THE JACK NOBLE SERIES™ BOOK THREE

L.T. RYAN

LIQUID MIND MEDIA

For information contact:

Contact@ltryan.com

http://LTRyan.com

https://www.facebook.com/JackNobleBooks

THE JACK NOBLE SERIES

For paperback purchase links, visit:
https://ltryan.com/pb

CHAPTER 1

December 31, 2006

"THE TARGET'S NAME is Brett Taylor, and this'll be your toughest assignment yet."

Frank Skinner set the blue folder in front of me, opened to Taylor's service record. A paper clip held a small photo to the upper left side of the folder. A head shot of a face chiseled from stone, with eyes that gave a glimpse into a heart made of ice. I read over the file, then glanced at the picture again. I might as well have been looking into a mirror. There were a few similarities between me and the target. Physically we were identical: 6'2", 220. We'd both enlisted in the military at the age of eighteen. He went into the Army; I became a Marine. We had both been selected for special assignment during boot camp.

I turned to the next page. It was blank. Every single one that followed was as well. There were only a few reasons for that.

"I'm not kidding, Jack," Frank continued. He pushed off the desktop and rolled backward. A rusted wheel squeaked until his chair collided into the wall with a soft thud. "This guy makes you look like a teddy bear. While you were off playing with the CIA guarding doors in Baghdad and whatnot, Taylor was doing black ops so insidious that any record indicating they'd ever even been thought of has been incinerated. When you were playing anti-terrorist agent along with me, he was taking down cell leaders before they even knew that they wanted to blow something up. He's the ultimate government weapon. And my understanding is that lately those hostile to the Nation's interests were not his only targets."

I looked up from the documents and met Frank's stare. His dark eyes didn't waver. I saw fear, perhaps. Anytime we had one of these meetings, Frank looked serious. Lips, nose, jaw, eyebrows, all could be manipulated. But his tone and gestures conveyed more concern than I'd ever seen from him. And we had a history that went back nearly five years to the summer of 2002, when he had hand-selected me to join him as his partner in the SIS. Together, we'd faced our share of men who had no regard for the welfare of others - so many that Frank's warning list read like the back of a cereal box.

What was so different about Brett Taylor?

"Can you give any examples?"

Frank leaned back in his chair and placed both hands behind his shaking head. "You know I can't do that."

"A hint, then?"

Frank said nothing. He bit at his bottom lip - a tell that he was considering revealing more than he should. I had to press.

"Hell, give me a country, Frank. I can take it from there."

For guys like us, news headlines read like a *Who's Doing What* in the espionage and assassin community. Nothing was ever as tidy as they made it sound in the papers and on TV.

Frank shook his head. "Can't do it. Not yet, at least. You live to finish the job, then we'll talk."

I closed the folder, pushed it toward Frank. "Nothing but a bunch of blank pages in there."

"That's to make a point."

"Which is?"

"Don't underestimate this guy. Every single one of those blank pages, and there's at least fifty, could be filled with details of the assignments this guy has completed."

"I get it. He's a badass. Jesus, Frank. How long have I been doing this?" I rose and shoved the chair to the side with my leg, and then leaned back against the glass wall and shoved my hands in my pockets. The glass felt cold against the back of my arms.

Frank remained silent. Thick jaw muscles rippled at the corners of his face as he stared me down. There was plenty about Taylor, and the job, that he wasn't willing to share. Or had been prohibited from revealing. At times, things worked that way. We'd all become accustomed to it. And it was beneficial. The less I knew about a target, the easier it was to complete the assignment. The less Frank knew, the less guilt there might be over handing it over to me. I operated with the general understanding that if a government agency signed off on an order and sent me to someone's door, there was a pretty good reason. The justice I was dispatched to enforce was quick and generally merciful.

We should all be so lucky.

So, Brett Taylor, while he provided service to his country for over a decade, must've done something pretty heinous for me to be sitting across from Frank, staring at a blank service record.

I sat down, placed my arm on the desk, leaned forward. "Where and when?"

"New York," he said. "Brooklyn. Close to Prospect Park. He's due back ten days from now, on Tuesday, the ninth."

I had a place in New York. A few friends there, too. It'd be better if they didn't know I was coming into town, though. Not for something like this.

"Know his itinerary?" I said.

"Not yet, but we'll get it."

"He in the States now?"

"Coming in international."

"From where?"

"Not sure yet."

"I'll have Bear tail him."

Frank pressed his lips together so tightly they turned white. He'd never been a fan of my partner, Riley "Bear" Logan, whose nickname suited the guy in more ways than one. The big man and I had been best friends since boot camp. After I left the SIS, we went into business for ourselves. I trusted him with my life, and I didn't care what any of my contacts thought. Bear handled himself and got results. We were a great team.

Better than Frank and I ever were.

"He's in," I said. "Or I'm out."

Frank took a few deep, ragged breaths, and then nodded. "I'll make sure you have the flight info in time. I'm waiting on additional details of Taylor's offices, residences, and so on, in case there are alternatives. I'll fax them over as soon as I get them. Meanwhile, limit how many sources you reach out to. As you can imagine, if something this high-profile leaks, we'll all go down for it."

"Got it." I rose, turned, grabbed the door handle and pulled it open an inch. The air from the overhead vent shot past me on the path of least resistance.

Take one more shot at it, I thought.

Letting the door fall closed, I turned around. "What'd this guy do?"

Frank diverted his focus to his computer monitor and shook his head.

"Come on, Frank. Just between you and me."

A single laugh escaped past his pursed lips. He shuffled his mouse around on a gray square pad, clicking the left and right buttons. "You know people end up on these lists at times because of conversations that go too far. If I say anything more, it'll be someone like Brett Taylor paying a visit to both of us."

"Fair enough." I turned my back to him.

"Jack."

I didn't look back. "Yeah?"

"Close this one out, and maybe I'll tell you everything over a pitcher or three. In the meantime, happy New Year."

CHAPTER 2

L OCATED ON 4TH Street between 6th and 7th Avenue, the five-story brownstone loomed like weathered ruins amid the surrounding rehabbed and renovated buildings. The owner had received multiple unsolicited offers to purchase for reasonable sums, but he had refused to sell. The building held too much value for him. Presumably Brett Taylor didn't care that the building was in shambles, or that nine of the ten apartments inside matched the rough exterior. I guess everything he needed existed in that tenth pristine apartment.

Between Frank and one of my sources, I had a five-year history on the building as well as the day-to-day nuances of life within its walls.

When the block showed no human activity, I crossed the street and forced my way inside the brownstone. A combination of human waste, sweat, mildew, and cigarette smoke pelted me, and I nearly gagged at the overwhelming stench. After a few moments I adjusted, and then continued past the entrance hall, which branched in two, one passage leading east and the other west.

The first floor had four apartments. From the looks of things, transients and homeless occupied these units when Taylor wasn't there. Same with the two units on the second floor. The fourth and fifth floors contained a single residence each. For whatever reason, Taylor had chosen to forgo the supposed prestige of a penthouse, and lived in an apartment on the third floor.

I started my search in the west hall. My primary concern was security equipment - anything that would give our position away or record our actions when Bear and I returned to complete the job. I saw no cameras on the outside, and none at the entrance. Presumably, Taylor had some sort of a monitoring system in place. Men in his position had to.

The apartments on the first floor had all been occupied recently, although they were empty at the moment. Leftover cellophane wrappers, soda cans, and liquor bottles were strewn about. Body odor lingered, a stench nearly as foul as that at the main entrance.

At the end of the east hall was a door that opened up to stairs leading to the basement. I followed them down, sticking to the edges to minimize squeaking. The room below the building was wide open from foundation wall to foundation wall, aside from evenly spaced support columns that resembled an old man's bowed legs. An old furnace sat dormant in the middle of the rear wall, the bricks surrounding it several shades darker than the rest. The floor was covered in an inch of soot and dust. Pristine. No footprints. Clearly no one ventured into the brownstone's basement these days. I walked along the perimeter of the room and remained on the lookout for electrical wires and communication lines. Only thing I found was brick and mortar and dust.

Satisfied that the basement was just that, I hiked back up the stairs, bypassing the first floor landing, and made my way through the building's second level.

Again, I found the rooms looking recently occupied, but currently empty. Perhaps Taylor had a system of letting the homeless that frequented his building know when he'd return. *Use my place, but don't dare be there when I get back.* Perhaps his way of repenting for the sins he committed for our government.

I made the journey from the second floor to the third with more trepidation. So far, there were no signs of security. That had to change. Still, I didn't find anything.

Of the two units on the third floor, one was used by Taylor.

I searched the unoccupied third floor apartment first. Unlike the units of the first two levels, no one had been inside this space for quite some time. Maybe not since the last tenant, who might even have died in the room. Cobwebs hung from the ceiling and draped the walls. Roaches scattered as light penetrated the space for the first time in perhaps years. I couldn't see them, but their thin legs scratched the hardwood floor with a sound like someone clawing their way out of a wooden box.

The place was fully furnished. The furnishings had to be sixty or seventy years old, with a few turn-of-the-century pieces. The kind of stuff my mother had, but never let me or my brother or my sister sit on. *And don't let your friends near it, Jack!* Antique picture frames housed yellowing photographs. A young woman. A young man. A young couple, together. Her in her wedding dress, him in his suit. Her perched on his lap. A baby. A child. A teenager. The sequence was repeated at the other end in reverse. One boy, one girl. One happy couple aging decades in a series of photographs perched on the mantle. A casket cross etched with the name "Robert." He died first. She remained in the apartment, loyal to him, waiting to return to him, until her final day passed.

I returned to the hallway. Examined the area surrounding the front door of Taylor's apartment. Again, I found nothing. He'd concealed his security and monitoring devices well. When Bear and I returned, we'd have to bring equipment to aid in our search, and disrupt any communications equipment he had on site.

The search concluded with a quick tour of the fourth and fifth floors. These were big hollow spaces void of furnishings. After passing through the fourth floor, I expected the top level to be full of computers or weapons or an army, even. None of that. And no signs anyone had been up there in some time. A fine layer of dust coated the hardwood floors, and cobwebs lined the walls, though not to the extent of the third floor apartment. Perhaps my intel was wrong. Maybe these spaces were used regularly. That, or someone must regularly be cleaning the space on the upper levels.

The narrow hallway on the top floor had roof access. An old rusted ladder mounted to the rear wall. I climbed it and popped the hatch to the roof. Strong gusts of wind passed by. A steady stream pelted down on me. The cold wormed its way into my clothing. I performed a quick recon of the roof's perimeter and determined there was no way off unless one was willing to risk a drop of seventy feet or so to the concrete below by attempting a ten-foot jump to the next building.

I double-checked every room on the way down. All except Taylor's. I wasn't looking for signs of life. Instead, I wanted to root out any possible escape routes. Iron bars on the upper level windows made any attempt from there impossible. The fire escapes on the second and third floors had been removed. Heavy bolts stuck out of the wall as a reminder they had once been attached. An alley around the length and width of the Brownstone, but there was no outlet. It formed a U that originated and terminated on 4th Street.

So that left one way in and out of the building: the front door. And once we saw Brett Taylor enter through it, that spelled game over.

CHAPTER 3

I SAT AT a wrought-iron bistro table, across from Bear, on the frigid and desolate terrace of a small Brooklyn café, a block east of the brownstone and two blocks west of Prospect Park. Dead leaves skated along the herringbone brick pavers, the first traffic we'd seen pass by.

Gray clouds raced overhead. Along with them came the promise of a winter storm. The temperature had already dropped ten degrees since the high of thirty-one at 8:00 that morning. Wouldn't be long until the storm hit. I had to wonder if Bear and I would manage to get out of the city today.

I pinched the handle of a mug that had once been hot between my thumb and forefinger. The dark roast emitted a bitter odor. Inches from my mouth, the rising steam mingled with my chilled breath. A smoky veil lifted into the air between Bear and me. I stared through it past the big man and scanned the street and sidewalk that stretched beyond the empty terrace. I took a sip. I'd waited four and a half minutes too long to do so. Might as well have been sucking on unbrewed grounds.

Bear stared at a newspaper pinned to the table by his large hands. His laughter broke the monotony of distant traffic. I glanced down and saw him reading an op-ed piece about our involvement in Iraq.

I decided it was a good time as any to kill a few minutes with mind-numbing conversation, so with the mug covering my mouth, I said, "Good and evil."

Bear's forehead wrinkled as he shifted his gaze from the paper to me without moving his head. "What about it?"

"That's the wrong question."

"Then what's the right question?"

"What's the difference?"

Bear shrugged, said nothing, redirected his focus to the op-ed piece.

"The difference," I said, "is that both halves sit on a line so thin I don't believe it exists."

Without looking up, Bear offered a half-hearted chuckle as he hiked his thumb over his shoulder toward the cop who was leaning against a light post on the opposite side of the intersection. The officer wore a ski mask with a full oval cutout for his face. This resulted in the man's nose and cheeks turning bright red. The cop brought his hands to his face, lifted the elastic bands on his gloves, and blew into them. I doubted the effect would last long.

"Why don't you go tell Johnny Law over there about your theory?" Bear said.

I wasn't sure how he'd spotted the cop; the man had arrived after we sat down. I resisted the urge to check the glass behind me.

"He'd agree with me," I said. "Think about everything he's seen working in Brooklyn. It ain't Iraq, but it sure as hell isn't a theme park either."

"Nonsense." Bear leaned forward and dropped a thick forearm on the table. Its legs creaked as my side rose up an inch or two. "Just like you learned in Sunday school as a kid, there's right and wrong and laws and consequences that most people abide by. You can say they do it blindly, or willingly, or unwillingly but out of fear of retribution. Doesn't matter. Without those laws, chaos would ensue." He tapped on the table with two fingers and added, "To me, that's a pretty thick line."

"Yet at times, the two of us are given a pass to break those laws if it's good for the government and the welfare of those law-abiding citizens who went to Sunday school and do everything they're told. Besides, I didn't say 'right and wrong.' I said 'good and evil.' The difference between them might as well be as wide as the Grand Canyon - at that spot a half-inch or less before the two sides finally meet. According to some, and I'm talking people high up the black ops food chain, if we take out a target on a hit they sanctioned, then we did something right. Makes us good guys for doing our job. But there are others, most likely our targets' loved ones, and presumably *our* targets, who'd say we are the face of evil in its purest form."

"Face of evil." Bear waved me off. "You know who that is."

"And yet, if you didn't know what they'd done, you wouldn't be able to tell them apart from anyone else."

"A thin line, eh?"

"So thin your vision would blur trying to focus on it."

Bear worked his hands against each other. "Hurry up with that coffee, Jack. I don't feel like sitting out here anymore."

"Got somewhere you have to be?"

"We both do. Or did you forget that, while you were philosophizing over your now-chilled java?"

I tilted the mug to my mouth and drained the remainder, now cooled to a temperature just above freezing.

"This stuff hasn't changed in thousands of years, Bear. My stance in 250 B.C. would be no different than it is now in 2007."

Bear stared at me without speaking for a few moments, then turned away, stared down the street toward the brownstone.

I said, "Does this make you uncomfortable?"

The big man shrugged and said nothing.

"You brought me into this line of work. Remember?"

Slowly, Bear swung his head around and nodded. "Yeah, I remember, Jack. And, like I've said a hundred times, I don't like thinking about what we do outside of the times we're actually doing it. Right up till that moment, it's like a game to me. And then I can block out those few minutes where we neutralize our targets. In the end, it's just a way to make a living. Hell, you wanna talk about a line? I'm straddling that line every day. Besides, you know the stories on most of the dudes we take out. It ain't like they're heroes or Roy Rogers wannabes. These bastards deserve what they get. Every last one of them."

I'd managed to get him worked up. But I couldn't relish the moment for too long. The cop across the street was talking into his shoulder-mounted radio. Dark sunglasses now hid his eyes, and he had repositioned himself to face us.

I brought the empty mug up and hid my lips with it. "Don't look, but that cop seems awfully interested in us. You didn't do anything to get your ugly mug painted on a wanted sign, did you?"

Bear looked past me - at the window, I presumed. He pushed back from the table and rose. "If I did, then so did you. Just go easy if he tries, man. We'll be out in an hour."

"And we'll lose our guy. Think about the sacrifice you've made for this. Been up for over twenty-four hours. Haven't showered. Changed your clothes. I've been trying to figure out if that's the sewer or you I've been smelling."

"Not now, Jack."

"We get hauled in, and the clock on Taylor resets to zero. For us, at least. We'll be off the job and out of the time we spent on this."

Bear said, "I'll go over the fence. You go through the cafe, then head down to the park, come back down 5th. You know where to meet from there."

I nodded, rose, dropped a twenty on the table, and set the mug on top to keep the bill from blowing away in the gusts. By the time I looked up, Bear had cleared the fence and was on his way toward the brownstone. I tossed a quick glance at the cop, who remained in the same place, but was obviously watching me as I turned and pushed past the door leading inside the café.

A blonde-haired woman in her early twenties looked up from her crossword puzzle as I entered. She started to get up. I gestured for her to remain seated.

"There's a cop out there," I said. "What's he doing?"

Again, she leaned forward to stand.

"Just turn your head toward the door and cough," I said.

She lowered her eyebrows and then did as instructed. Looking back toward me, she said, "He's bouncing from one foot to the other."

"Where?"

"On the sidewalk."

"This side of the street, or the other?"

"The other."

"Thanks." I scanned the small dining room. "Got a back way out of here?"

"Are you in trouble?"

"Would it make a difference if I were?"

She smiled and tilted her head to the side. Blonde ringlets with pink highlights splayed over her right shoulder. She reached up and twirled a tendril. "Maybe."

I glanced at the colored tattoos that lined the exposed skin of her forearms and neck. She'd be more inclined to help me, I figured, if the cop wanted something with me.

"You got a back door or not?"

She gestured with her head toward the counter. "That door leads to the storeroom. Just head to the back and through the emergency door. Don't worry, it won't trigger the alarm. Been dead as long as I've worked here. You'll end up in an alley that runs between 4th and 5th. It meets up with the cross streets."

I nodded, turned and headed for the storeroom.

"Hey," she called out.

I glanced back. "Yeah?"

"What'd you do?"

"If I told you I killed someone, would you believe me?"

The curious grin on her face spread. "No."

CHAPTER 4

I TOSSED ONE final glance past the café's windows and saw an empty street. The cop was no longer positioned outside. Had he followed Bear? Perhaps he'd crossed the street and stood against the brick exterior of the building, out of view, waiting for me to exit.

It didn't matter. I raced through the storeroom, past the non-emergency exit, and into the brick-lined walled canyon behind the café. One side of the asphalt was slick with runoff. Overflowing dumpsters butted up to the buildings. I caught hints of grease and fish and rotting meat.

No one hung out back there, except for a half-dozen feral cats. They lay out on any spot that gave them respite from the winds that barreled through the narrow alley. I remained cautious as I passed each door, each crevice that led from the street to my position. Gusts continued to pummel me as I walked. Might as well have been inside a wind tunnel in an underground government testing facility.

If they existed, of course.

I flipped my collar up and shoved my hands in my pockets. Didn't help. The cold air had made a home there already. My hand brushed against the handle of my Beretta, holstered securely in my waistband.

The worst thing the cop could do would be to show up here and now.

Though targets were limited to those identified by the government, I had the autonomy to do whatever I deemed necessary to remain alive.

Surprisingly to some, I'd never discharged a round at a cop. And I didn't want my first time to be today, either. It was a moot point. If taken into custody, a single call would get me out, no matter what I did. But it was looked down upon, and might result in me losing a fair amount of work. Too much paperwork. Too much cover-up. Employers didn't want to have to deal with that. Best thing to do was not get caught.

At 8th Avenue, I traveled a half-block south, then continued east on 5th. A few minutes later, I stood on the pitted curb of Prospect Park West.

The scene was ordinary for a freezing day, if not a little more congested than the view from the café terrace. A few people scurried along the sidewalk, wrapped in heavy coats and scarves and wool hats, under the skeletal branches that hung overhead. None of them were a threat. The cop from the café was nowhere to be seen, and it didn't appear that he had called in back-up. The thought that the officer had followed Bear lingered in the back of my mind. I shoved it aside on grounds of paranoia.

I reached into my jeans pocket and retrieved my cell phone, then used it to call Bear. The big man didn't answer. A second call yielded the same results. I closed the phone and stuffed it inside my coat pocket for quicker access should Bear call me back. I resumed my trek, heading one block south before turning west on 6th Street.

Ten minutes later, I was a block from the brownstone. I'd called Bear twice during the walk and received no answer each time. Concern grew that the cop had picked him up. Could have been for any number of reasons, none of which would sound pretty at booking.

I took a chance on the front door of an apartment building situated on the opposite side of the street. The door was locked, but had been left open a crack. Maybe the wind had kept it from shutting. Or the cold air had bent the frame, making it hard to shut. Whatever, didn't matter.

Warm air welcomed me as I stepped in from the cold. Light traveled through a rectangular window covered with a film of grime. Disturbed dust kicked up into the air and reflected the filtered light as it settled back toward the floor. A few feet past the entryway, a stairwell cut through the middle of the hall. I took the stairs two at a time to the third floor. There, I took position at a window overlooking the road below and the brownstone's entrance.

The sidewalks were void of life except for two women who appeared to earn their living through dubious means. They walked toward me, coming from the direction of the café. Despite the cold, they wore skirts short enough to reveal the goods they had to offer to potential buyers. Their worn faces indicated weather conditions would not dictate their work schedule. Had they passed the cop? Had the cop spotted the women while Bear and I mused about life as we drank bitter coffee on a frigid patio? Were two old hookers the reason the cop received the call?

In this city? Not likely.

Presumably, the call had no bearing on me, or the prostitutes. The cop could've been checking in. Nothing more.

The women passed, and the only other traffic I spotted raced by on four wheels. After a quick glance around the dim corridor, I pulled out my phone and called Bear.

"Hello?" a woman said.

"Who's this?" I backed away from the window.

"Alexis," she said. "Are you the big guy who was drinking coffee out in the cold?"

"No. I'm the tall, good-looking guy that was with him."

"Haven't had anyone here that matches that description today, sir." Her smile resounded in the playfulness of her voice.

"You're right. Can you keep the phone behind the counter? We'll be back this afternoon to get it."

"Yeah, sure, but come before five. OK?"

"Why five? You close then?"

"No. I leave then."

I ended the call and tucked the phone away. The woman's proximity to our target left me uneasy. She was ten years younger than Taylor, and came across as too interested. The likelihood of her having anything to do with the man we were to assassinate was virtually nil. But to me, that meant there was a chance.

And that gave me reason to pause.

Over needless worrying.

I pulled the phone out once again. Removed the battery and SIM card. I thought about breaking it in two and discarding the pieces in different locations, but instead shoved it back in my pocket.

A large man crossing the street in front of the brownstone caught my attention. It was Bear, and he wasn't being followed. The big man walked past the target's building and continued toward me. By this point, Bear was likely aware of his missing phone and now was keeping himself visible.

I descended the stairs and exited the building. Bear spotted me as I came down the entryway steps. I nodded. We continued walking on opposite sides of the street, toward the brownstone.

CHAPTER 5

F ROM A SPOT under a sycamore tree on the other side of the street, I watched Bear's silhouette disappear behind the frosted panes of the building's front doors. There was no sign of movement from the darkened windows that lined the structure in uniform fashion. Hard to tell. Years of neglect had left them covered with dirt and grime. Aside from our target, the intel indicated no one had lived in the place since the mid-nineties. Only the homeless and transient, a constant stream of in-and-out, and not the folks one would expect to tidy up on their way out. They also weren't big on washing windows. These days, most of them knew their stay at the brownstone wouldn't be a long one. When the main tenant returned, he'd run the remaining squatters out of the building.

I'd determined earlier that the exterior showed no signs of being fitted with surveillance equipment. Didn't mean it wasn't there, but I couldn't see it. We found it odd. Brett Taylor was a top agent. And from what we'd been told, he'd been involved in some shady dealings recently. At the very least, his instincts should have told him someone would come to pay him a visit sooner rather than later. He possessed the skills and had the resources to outfit the building with not only cameras, but a defense system as well.

Heightened awareness was the buzzword for the day.

A second floor window sat right of center, opened wider than a crack.

Through the crevice, Bear gave me an OK sign. After a quick check of my surroundings, I stepped to the curb. A late-model white Chrysler driven by a woman who could barely see over the steering wheel passed in front of me. I stepped into the exhaust and crossed the street. Bear had left the front door open. I tapped it with the toe of my shoe and stepped over the threshold.

Cool, stale air coated with the same disgusting odors from earlier greeted me. I didn't react the same way. Guess I'd adjusted. Maybe it had aired out a bit.

The cone of light spread out in front of me dwindled to a line as the door closed behind me. I pulled a pen light from my coat pocket and scanned the floor ahead. It would have been a waste of time to focus on things that had obviously been left behind by recent guests. Instead, I picked a path and moved toward and up the stairs, using the light to scan the walls and ceiling for cameras. Stripped wires hung down a foot or so along the wall in a few spots. Maybe there was no surveillance because it never lasted. When Taylor was out of town, uninvited guests took anything they could get their hands on.

The ones that didn't want to be invited back, at least.

Bear waited at the top of the stairs. He held an RF scanner in his left hand and a pistol in his right.

"Anything?" I said.

"Flat," he said. "What floor is this guy supposed to be on?"

"Third." The front door whipped open and slammed shut. I switched off the light, retrieved my pistol and crouched down to get a view. The door jerked open and closed a few more times.

"Front must've come through."

I nodded. "Earlier than I thought."

"Hope the snow holds off a little longer. Don't want to stay in the city tonight."

"You know our luck."

"Unfortunately, I do."

"Anyway, been up yet?"

He shook his head, said nothing.

"Let's go, then."

Bear stepped aside and waited for me to take the lead. I panned the pen light floor to ceiling. My pistol followed. There were more bare wires hanging from the walls. I checked the area in front of me before every step. We had to watch out for any trigger that could set off an explosive. I remained vigilant despite the fact that I had been through the building earlier; failure to act otherwise could have terminal results.

The RF detector beeped twice. The green light on the meter flashed red at the same time. We stopped two steps from the third floor. I cut the flashlight. Darkness fell upon us. Not a single trace of light permeated from the cracks surrounding doors or the gaps underneath. The device in Bear's hand beeped again, its red light casting a quick, ominous glow over my partner's face.

"It's the door in front of us," he whispered.

I switched the flashlight on and scanned the door and wall. There was nothing on or surrounding it. Same as earlier. I thought back to the building plans Frank had shown us a week ago. The apartment had a simple floor plan. No hallway or foyer. The only room closed off from the rest was the bedroom, which had an attached bathroom. There would be little guesswork once we were inside. That made the job easy. What made it difficult was the target.

I recalled my initial meeting with Frank Skinner. The documents I'd reviewed in his office. Brett Taylor was more than a killer; he could infiltrate any group, get close to any person. And when he'd earned their trust, they died. He had never failed. Overconfidence had gotten the better of him, though, and he'd handled things too loosely in his latest dealings. The government takes care of those who do its dirty work. But don't ever cross that line.

If Taylor knew we were outside his door, then we were dead men walking. Didn't matter if we turned around to leave. Best-case scenario was one of us would get out alive. The reason we'd sat on the job for ten days was because we wanted to do this at a time when it was to our advantage. Taylor had spent close to twenty hours traveling to get home. Bear had followed him the last eight, then watched him enter the building. The assumption was that while we were drinking sub-lukewarm coffee, our target was relaxing, getting comfortable in the only place he could, and falling asleep.

Now we had to find out if our assumption had turned out the way assumptions normally do.

I took point and moved to the door. The air in the hallway was cooler than the stairwell, moving from left to right. I traced the door where it met the frame. Taylor hadn't left a marker. Some guys might leave their apartment or hotel room and use a piece of tape on the door and frame, or tape a piece of hair there, or place something over the knob. If the door was opened while they were out, the tape would break, the hair would snap, whatever they put on the doorknob would be on the floor, and they'd know their location had been compromised. Such a device would tell us that Taylor had left or was waiting elsewhere for us.

I found nothing, and it didn't ease my nerves.

Holding the flashlight between my teeth, I reached out and turned the doorknob. It gave with ease. I gestured for Bear to join me before turning the knob completely and inching the door open.

Warm air laced with lemon-scented disinfectant flooded into the hallway. It washed over my face, neck, and hands. The chemical odor singed my throat and lungs. Overhead lights cast a warm yellow glow throughout the space. The only thing obstructing my view was a wide leather couch, but unless Taylor was on it, or lying on the floor on the other side of it, he wasn't in the room.

With a nod to Bear, I crouched down, pushed the door open further and entered. Knowing that the big man had my back made the effort easier.

The apartment opened to a kitchen lined with modern cabinets and stainless steel appliances. The clocks on the stove and microwave flashed the time, which was off by an hour and change. It wasn't uncommon for the power to go out in a building this old during a cold spell. But I had doubts that the city's electrical grid had caused the disruption that led to the clocks resetting.

I gestured for Bear to enter and covered him as he did so. He moved past the kitchen into the living room. I focused on the bedroom door while he circled the furniture and checked the windows. There was no draft inside, so I didn't expect them to be open. After he finished, we both focused on the bedroom door. Bear performed the same checks I had made on the front door, and then motioned me forward.

On a silent count of three, Bear threw the door open. I stepped forward and swept the room, finally settling on the motionless body lying on the bed.

CHAPTER 6

A PILLOW COVERED the man's face. The sheets underneath were soaked in crimson. The guy had been stripped of his clothes. Cuts along his legs indicated his pants had been cut off hastily. Someone had been concerned their DNA had been left behind. The smell of disinfectant was stronger in here than the other room.

Bear stepped past me and walked to the side of the bed. He stared down at the corpse. "Somebody already did him in?"

"Let's check the bathroom."

I covered Bear as he kicked the door open. The restroom was clean, compact, and empty.

We turned back to the bed, and Bear said, "You gonna do the honors, or should I?"

I shrugged. "You're closer."

Bear reached down and grabbed the pillow. He took a deep breath, then pulled it off.

"Christ," he said.

"That's not our guy," I said.

"Not even close."

There was a single hole in the man's forehead. Blood coated the skin around it and had trickled down either side of his head and pooled in his blond hair and on the sheets. I didn't have to lift his head to know the back of his skull had been blown out.

I touched the guy's chest with the back of my hand. "Still warm."

"Wasn't even two hours ago I saw our guy enter the building. We've maintained a visual on it every minute since?"

"Every room, Bear. I found no way out. I checked every single room, except this one. There's gotta be a way out in here."

"Or Taylor hasn't left. Maybe he...hell, I don't know, man. Think he knows?"

I shook my head. "No way he's still here, not leaving a mess like this behind, and especially not if he knows about us."

Bear said nothing when I turned toward him.

"This was him letting us know he was aware we were coming for him."

"Think he spotted me?"

"Probably."

"If he's got any connections, it won't take him long to figure out who I am."

"Most likely."

"Then he'll figure out who you are, Jack."

"Undoubtedly."

Bear leaned forward. "So who's this guy?"

"A bum that didn't get out in time? Best guess, anyway." I turned and walked toward the living area. "And I'd put money down that Taylor saw us enter. I wouldn't doubt that he either has someone waiting for us outside, or they're on their way."

We wiped down any surfaces we might have come into contact with inside the apartment. Didn't bother with the rest of the building with the exception of the handrail leading to the third floor. Below that was a breeding ground of fingerprints and DNA.

Outside the building, a sheet of white limited our visibility. The moment was rife with tension. Anyone could be across the street, in an apartment, window cracked, rifle aimed at our chests. The reduced visibility made it impossible to verify the safety of our surroundings. It'd be nice if it worked both ways, and to an extent it did. But all the shooter had to do was verify that the door opened.

Remove any threat regardless of the danger the actions presented to the public.

The first hundred feet were the worst. My heart pounded against my chest like a pent-up bull ready to explode through the gate. I searched through the white veil, but the exercise was pointless. To make it worse, Bear had crossed the street and was walking opposite me.

Recalling maps I studied earlier, I knew that none of the alleys running between the buildings would offer us an escape route. So we hurried toward 6th Avenue, and turned north. After traveling another block, I crossed the street and met up with Bear.

Few cars were out, but the sidewalks grew thick with people eager to beat the brunt of the storm home. While the snow accumulated quickly on the sides of the road, the sidewalk was a pile of slush.

We were far enough removed from the brownstone that I started to feel confident we would not be followed. As an added measure of security, I pulled the battery from my cell phone, broke the device in two, then tossed the three components into three different trash cans. We wouldn't return to the café to pick up Bear's cell either. That wasn't an option. And it didn't matter. These were throw-away phones, good for no more than a day or two.

Bear pointed at a diner fifty feet ahead. "Hungry?"

I wasn't, but recalling the scene at the brownstone and the condition of most of the building left me with a desire to wash my hands.

And I could always go for a cup of coffee.

We entered the empty diner and took a seat at a table that had a wrap-around booth in the corner of the dining room. It offered a view of the diner and the street, and we both could take advantage of it without having to sit side by side. They didn't make seats big enough for that. I left Bear with instructions to order me a coffee and then slipped into the bathroom to clean up. Not long after I returned to the table, a dark-haired waitress dropped off a water and a steaming mug of java.

Bear soaked in the scene. His gaze traveled from empty table to empty table, lingered on the members of the waitstaff that were visible, then finally passed me over and settled on the street. "Thoughts or theories?"

I shrugged. "Just a matter of how he knew. Was he tipped off by the sight of you, or did someone tell him?"

"Who would've done that?"

"Your guess is as good as mine."

"Problem is we don't know who all knows about the job. Your guy got it from someone who might've got it from someone else. They could've offered it to another group, who turned it down for whatever reason, one of those reasons possibly being a working relationship with the target. In which case, they told him, so he knew it was coming. All it took was one 6'6" guy to look out of place."

"Then a homeless guy is dead. But why? If he could disappear, why not just disappear? I mean, what would you do?"

Bear leaned back, one arm over the top of the booth, hand dangling behind it, out of sight. He considered the question for a moment. "Guess it depends on what I thought of that bum. Maybe the guy was royal pain. Kill two birds with one stone. You get rid of the guy, and you tell your newly acquired enemies that you don't play games."

"By playing the ultimate game."

That was the issue with our work. We had a single contact within each of the agencies, at the Pentagon, Langley, so on. That's who reached out to us with contract work. I knew each of them either by name or alias, but none like Frank Skinner. At one time, he and I had been partners. Agents in the SIS. But even when the job came from him, we never knew the identities of the players behind the contracts, or how high up the command came from. And it never mattered. Bear and I continued to play the part of the good soldiers. We did as requested without asking questions or demanding proof. Both of us felt that if we were sent to terminate a target, there was a good reason why.

Bear said, "You wanna tell Frank?"

I nodded. "As soon as we get back to our place."

"We staying?"

I tapped on the glass. "We're not getting out in this mess. Not today."

Bear stuffed half a pancake in his mouth and nodded.

Ten minutes later, we paid for the meal and left the diner. Despite the weather, cabs were still running. Bear flagged one down and we slogged through the gathering snow to Manhattan. We both lived in D.C., but spent enough time in New York and flying out of JFK that it made sense to keep an apartment. It wasn't much, less than eight hundred square feet, but it offered a base away from home. We purchased it under a friend's name. No one knew about it. Not even Frank. At least, as far as I knew.

I had a feeling that theory was about to be put to the test.

CHAPTER 7

FIVE FLIGHTS OF stairs waited for us. The elevator had been broken since before we bought the place eighteen months ago. Every time we visited, we trudged up and down those stairs. It was a good way to meet people. Problem was, we didn't care to meet anyone. It was bad for us, and dangerous for them. Since we were only there once or twice a month, it wasn't a big deal. I imagined the other residents felt the same way.

Our heavy footsteps echoed through the chamber. There was little to fear in the building. There was also little point in taking unnecessary risks. I held my pistol and draped my jacket over my arm to conceal the weapon. Bear pulled the reinforced steel door that barricaded the fifth floor from the stairwell. He held it open long enough for me to enter, then pushed past me and stepped into the empty corridor, which smelled like it had been shampooed recently. Our condo fees in action.

We passed two doors on the left and right and stopped in front of our unit. I couldn't remember if I'd set a marker last time we were there. If so, it was gone.

Bear leaned into the dimpled red door. "You leave the television on this morning?"

"I wasn't here this morning," I said.

"Then someone's in there." His big fingers swallowed the doorknob and inched to the right. He looked at me. "Unlocked."

We hesitated and stared at each other for a few moments. Could Taylor have found our location that quickly? If he was going to do something, it would have been in his building, on his turf, where he had control. Perhaps someone else had found out about the condo. We worked with people in the business of knowing everything, so I couldn't discount the possibility.

I pushed Bear to the side and grabbed the knob, turned it slowly, pushed the door open. And when I saw who was sitting there, I wished it had been related to the job.

"Weren't gonna bother telling me you were in town?"

Clarissa Abbot. A beautiful redhead with the temper to match. I'd known her for over ten years, back when she was a gangly pre-teen who played baseball and watched wrestling. She had lost her mother young, and her father had done the best he could. He was the connection we shared. Colonel Abbot had been my CO during my time in the Marines. When he was murdered, I took over as her guardian, although she was over eighteen at the time. She and I had been dating for four months. I had almost eight years on her. She was too beautiful for me.

The whole thing was a disaster in the making, and both of us signed up for front row seats.

I took a few steps inside and scanned the room before focusing on her. "I like your hair like that. You lighten it up a bit since I last saw you?"

"Don't even try it, Jack." She rose from the couch, turned, and walked toward the back window. She stood there for a moment, silent, then peeled back the curtains, letting the snow-soaked light in.

"I'm here for work," I said. "Thought it was going to be a quick in-and-out kind of deal. Things didn't go smoothly, so we stopped by here to regroup and refocus."

She looked over her shoulder, past me, toward the door. "Hello, Riley."

Bear held up both hands in retreat and said, "I can wait in the hall."

Clarissa shrugged. "Don't matter to me. I'm leaving."

I intercepted her as she made for the door. With my hands on her shoulders, I thought she might take a moment and think it through.

Instead, she pulled away from my grasp and drove her shoulder into mine as she passed.

"How'd you even find out I was here?" I said.

"For someone who needs to remember faces in order to stay alive, you're pretty inept. You know that, Jack?"

Aside from a few homeless guys and cab drivers and maybe the aging prostitutes, I hadn't run into anybody she might have known.

Shaking her head, she said, "You remember Alexis?"

I didn't, but decided against admitting to the fact.

"One of my friends. You met her before we started dating."

I shrugged, said nothing.

"Jesus, Jack. Blonde, sometimes with weird highlights in her hair. About my age. Shorter than me. Works in a coffee shop. Any of that ring a bell?"

"The woman from the café this morning?"

Clarissa nodded and folded her arms over her chest. The look on her face reeked of attitude. And it wasn't an act. She was tough as nails.

"You might want to have a talk with her, because she was all over me."

"All you guys are the same. Overconfident, egotistical maniacs. Once she realized you didn't recognize her, she tried to trap you. She didn't realize you left the phone behind simply because you're dumb."

I pointed at Bear. "That was him. And, hey, at least I've got you to knock me down a peg or two when my head swells up like a football."

"Shut up, Jack." She looked away.

Bear laughed from the doorway.

"You too," she said with a look that caused the big man to take a step back.

Bear said, "I don't think I've ever seen you this mad."

"This is nothing," I said.

"I'm leaving. Don't bother calling me next time you're in town."

Bear stepped into the apartment so she could get out. The steel door to the stairwell slammed against the concrete wall and banged shut.

"Sorry about that," Bear said.

I shrugged. I'd seen it before. "She'll cool off. Might be worth me staying around an extra night to make peace with her."

"You know Frank won't let you do that while the target's on the run."

"Let's find out."

I pulled a Winslow Homer knock-off down from the wall. The safe it hid had a ten-digit number pad. I punched in the code and pulled the door open. Inside was ten thousand in cash, mostly twenties and fifties, three false passports and matching drivers' licenses, a back-up Beretta and extra ammunition, and seven clean and disposable cell phones.

The safe served as my own safe deposit box. And I didn't have to show my face on camera to access it. A second safe located in the bedroom closet contained Bear's belongings. I assumed they were similar to mine. Hadn't ever looked to verify.

I flipped the phone open. Frank's number was on speed dial. I pressed the button, then switched the call to speaker so Bear could listen in when he returned from the bedroom.

Frank answered on the second ring. "What the hell happened this morning?"

I looked up at Bear, who had just stepped into the room carrying a black bag. He shrugged. Guess I was on my own for the explanation.

"Well?" Frank said.

"I take it you heard."

"Yeah, I heard. So far, I've been able to contain it."

"How'd you find out?"

"Don't you worry about that, Jack. What you and that overgrown partner of yours need to do is figure out where this guy went and then go get him."

"He was an hour ahead of us."

"How do you know that?"

"The body in his bed was still warm."

"You're kidding," Frank said. "Anybody we know?"

"Only people that knew this guy were other homeless and maybe a package store purveyor."

Frank exhaled loudly. It sounded like wind blasting through a tunnel. "I need you back in D.C., but that isn't going to happen today with this monster storm passing through. They've been canceling flights left and right. Do what you can from there, and I'll be in touch soon."

"Frank?"

There was a pause, then he said, "Yeah?"

"Any idea how this guy knew we were coming?"

"You tail him, or Riley?"

"Bear did."

"That's probably how, then."

"Bear's good at what he does. You know that."

"Yeah, I know. I'm not sure, Jack. Hopefully I'll have some answers by the time you get back. In the meantime, hit the streets around his building and see if anyone saw or knows anything. I'll keep working my angles."

"Ten-four." I flipped the phone shut and set it down on the counter. I'd have to get a new cell to replace this one, as it was now known.

"What do you think?" Bear said.

"I'm thinking that I hope this guy doesn't know it was us after him. He's got friends. Same type of friends you and I have. Maybe worse."

"Can't get much worse than the people you and I know."

"Never say that. If he goes to them, and gets them to come after us, not even Frank is gonna stick his neck out to help."

Bear placed his forearm on the counter and leaned over it. "You scared, Jack?"

I shook my head. "Not scared. Concerned."

CHAPTER 8

A FOOT OF snow left travelers stranded at the airports. All flights in and out had been canceled by three that afternoon. The news showed footage of people fighting over empty seats at the gates, each of which was packed so tight that people had resorted to sitting and sleeping on the floor, using luggage as makeshift furniture and pillows. Lines for the fast food joints snaked down the terminal aisles. In short, a total mess.

With the airport a no-go and less than no chance we'd take a bus, our only other option was to take one of the cars. That would have been more frustrating than sleeping on the worn corn chip-scented airport terminal floor. Driving ten miles per hour, packed tight on the iced-over south-bound lanes of I-95 held little appeal. In a day it'd be as though the storm had never happened. For now, though, the city was at a standstill.

So we stayed. And Bear and I worked our phones and called our contacts until five that afternoon. None of our sources knew anything. We were hamstrung with most. We couldn't mention the target by name. We spoke in generalities. The results received were proportionate to the information we gave them.

Perhaps Frank was having better luck. The man had contacts in every agency, every branch of the military. The DOD. DOJ. Congress. Even the people he'd pissed off in the past would go out of their way to help the guy. I hoped for good news from him. He'd let us know soon enough.

The storm had toned down to something between flurries and snow-fall, so we decided to head out for a while to grab a bite to eat. Three-quarters of the city might've been shut down, but there'd be places open. Some guys, like Frank, would never venture out under the current circumstances. Not the storm; rather the imminent danger of a target potentially knowing our identities. Neither of us cared.

The faintest trace of sunset lingered to the west. The sky above and beyond the concrete landscape tinged pink, for a few minutes at least. Snow banks rose six feet high in some places. A slushy path maybe four feet wide had been worn down the center of the sidewalk. Along the edges, the snow was gray, but the rest was virgin white. It wouldn't last long once the vehicles returned en masse. Then leftover precipitation along the sides of the road would turn black with dirt and exhaust. But for now, with only the occasional cab or NYPD cruiser passing by, it was safe.

Bear pointed to an unassuming bar with a weathered front door sunken from the sidewalk. "How about there?"

I stopped. "I don't know."

"Think about the walk back, Jack. This might be the only pub open this close."

"Yeah." I covered my brow and scanned the street.

"What is it?"

"You know what it is."

He shrugged. "So what? They can't kick us out. It'd be discrimination."

"On what grounds?"

"We're too tall?"

"I don't want her to think I'm in there because of her."

"So what if she does? You two'll make up soon enough anyway. Let the healing start tonight, Jack. And let a thick rib-eye and a beer or two be the catalyst."

The longer I stood still, the colder my toes and fingers became. Taking refuge inside, no matter who might be in there, was worth it. So I shrugged, shook the snow off my head, and extended a hand toward the door. "Lead the way, big man."

The white reflecting off the black-tinted glass entrance door transitioned to a mirror image of Bear as he pulled the door open. Stepping in from the almost-blinding snow-covered street, the pub's interior seemed as though it was mired in a thick black fog. A few seconds later my eyes adjusted to the dim pendant lighting. Normally, I'd perform a scan of the establishment to rank every patron's possible threat level. But right then there was only one threat I was concerned with.

And she wasn't behind the bar.

Bear walked past me, shrugged his coat off, and took a seat on a stool at the far end of the room, his back to the bar area. His gaze swept the place, then settled on me. He gave me a nod before spinning on his stool and knocking on the wooden bar top. A guy I didn't recognize stepped out from the kitchen and poured Bear a beer. A few seconds later the smell of the grill hit me and my stomach tightened.

I joined Bear at the bar and ordered a shot of whiskey. It went down fast and hot. So did the second. I could continue and numb everything, including my wits. So I eased off.

The place was quiet. I'd been in there a few times before and each time there had been a decent-sized crowd. If there was one group I didn't think would be affected by the storm, it was the regular patrons of establishments that served alcohol. Yet they weren't present. Perhaps it was too early.

Bear and I said little. What were we going to talk about? The events of the day? Not in public. It didn't matter. This wasn't a strategy session. We were here to recoup.

"You know that big guy over there?" Bear said.

I looked at Bear in the mirror. "Which one?"

"The one with the giant head and fists to match."

I shifted my gaze to the right and saw the man matching the description. "What about him?"

"He was pointing over here a few seconds ago. I don't recognize him."

"I do. His name is Charles something-or-another. Some low-life criminal that works for the Old Man. Well, was low-level, but recently received a promotion."

"How do you know all this?" Bear said.

I shrugged and looked away. "I know people now."

"Well, get ready to introduce us. He just got up and is on his way over."

Heel-to-toe, Charles's footfalls grew nearer. I continued to look away. Once the reverberation in my stool stopped, I knew he had too.

"Jack Noble, right?"

I ignored him.

Two thick fingertips pelted my right shoulder blade. "I'm talking to you. Be best for you to answer me."

Charles's rise in the Old Man's organization meant he had some clout behind him. But he also had something to prove. According to some, a lot to prove. He was a new captain, hustling out on the street to show his dominance, that he was the alpha in all situations now.

I turned toward Bear, looked over my shoulder, and nodded without making eye contact.

Charles looked me up and down. "Don't bother getting up or anything."

"I won't." I spun forward and picked up my drink.

"Maybe you don't know who I am?" Charles asked.

Before I could reply, Bear hopped off his stool and placed himself between Charles and me. It was like watching two grizzlies belly up to each other. Between the two of them, they had to weigh over six hundred pounds and were at least thirteen feet tall combined. I wasn't sure the floor would be able to withstand the impact if they went to the ground.

"Maybe you don't know who we are," Bear said, as he delivered a pointed finger to Charles's sternum the way cops like to do. "And I guarantee if you try to find out, you won't like the results you get."

By this time, I was off my stool and attempting to wedge a hand in between the two Goliaths. Across the room, the three guys who'd accompanied Charles into the bar were on their feet and moving toward us. Each had one hand concealed, presumably wrapped around a pistol grip, or a knife, or a blackjack. Though I didn't relish the idea of facing any of the weapons, I preferred a man with a knife in this situation. Meant he'd have to get close to do any damage.

Charles lips parted and spread, a strand of saliva trapped between. He lifted both arms, took a step back. He never diverted his stare from Bear.

"Easy, everyone. Easy."

On their boss's order, the men stopped halfway between their table and the bar. Hands remained inside jackets. I kept mine visible. No need to give anyone a reason to act due to panic or uncertainty.

Yet.

Charles, still staring at Bear, said, "Jack, I just came over to introduce myself. I thought maybe you and I could help each other out. You know, a business opportunity."

"What would I need your help for?"

He smiled and shrugged. "I heard you ran into some trouble this morning."

"Is that right? Where'd you hear this?"

"I hear things, Jack. I dunno. Hell, what do I know? Maybe something that helps you."

"In what way would you be able to assist with any trouble I might have had this morning?"

For the first time, Charles looked directly at me. "I know things. I know people. We might even know some of the same people, and the identities of those individuals would probably surprise you."

"Nothing surprises me."

"Then accept my offer to help you."

"Why would you offer that help to us?"

He glanced at Bear, then back to me. "I help you, then maybe you do a favor for me."

"Maybe, huh?"

Charles shrugged again, said nothing.

"I'm afraid I don't delve into your line of business, Charles," I said. "We tend to stick to things on the up and up."

"There's not much difference between what you do and what I do, Noble. But I didn't come here to argue that. I really do want to help you out, and so does my boss. And, if it makes a difference, he can sweeten the offer by tossing in a hundred grand. You two can split that up any way you want."

"Won't be nothing to split up," Bear said. "My partner told you to piss off, so why don't you and your band of merry hooligans over there get lost?"

Most men backed off when a guy the size of Bear told them to get lost. Charles didn't, though. A smile crossed the criminal's face.

"I know you think you're a bad dude," Charles said to Bear. "But you don't know me. And you better pray to God you never get to know me in an intimate manner, because I will use your nuts as bobbers and your dick as bait."

Bear took a step forward. He'd rolled his sleeves up after shedding his coat earlier. His forearm muscles rippled as he clenched his fists.

The tension rose like heat from fresh lava. The guys midway across the room sensed it, too. They grew edgy, shifting from foot-to-foot, waiting for the inevitable fight to break out. Only they wouldn't jump in with fists and boots. They'd bust out their weapons and put a quick end to the ordeal.

And to me and Bear.

CHAPTER 9

WITH THE DIVIDE between Charles and Bear shrinking, a familiar voice drove a wedge between the two large men.

"I thought I told you to stay out of here, Charles." The kitchen door swung out and banged against the wall as Clarissa stepped through. "And your boss knows why, and he agrees with me."

I leaned forward, whispered, "Big guy like you lets a little thing like her push you around?"

"You can shut up, Jack," she said. "I don't know what the hell you're doing in here either. I'm liable to let old Chucky-boy carry you out with him."

"That won't be necessary." Charles took a few steps back, held his hands up. "We're taking off." He motioned his guys toward the door, then added, "Think about what I said, Jack. We could use a guy like you. Him, too."

Bear chuckled as he turned toward the bar. Clarissa met him on the other side. He asked her for an update on his steak. The place smelled of seared meat. It was killing the big guy.

Frigid air and wafts of snow knifed through the establishment as the door closed in the wake of the men. With Charles and his guys gone, there were only two other groups of people remaining. They did their best to ignore me as I looked over them. In time, they'd get up and make their way out, too, with as little disturbance as possible. People hate conflict, and hate being around those likely to cause it.

"Why are you getting involved with a guy like Charles?" Clarissa asked.

I swung my right leg over the bar stool and sat down. "Money sounds good."

"You realize the things they're into? You'll have every agent you used to work with camping out in your hallway, waiting to bust you two idiots."

Apparently she'd cooled off. Her concern seemed genuine.

I said, "We aren't considering doing anything with Charles, or his boss. That's not our gig. You know that. He approached me just now. And you saw how that turned out."

"All I know is what you tell me, and there are times I don't think your words are grounded in the reality that most of us share."

"I tell you everything I'm allowed to, Clarissa. If that's not good enough, then I don't know where to point you for better explanations."

"Don't patronize me." She poured me another drink, then exited through the kitchen door. It flapped in and out, sending wave after wave of wood-smoke-laden air in our direction.

The hum from the television blended with the sounds of conversation from the tables behind us. The white noise provided welcome respite.

After a few minutes, Bear said, "You think that Charles guy is gonna take this personally?"

I shrugged. "I suppose, but frankly, I don't care, man. We've got a bigger problem. Presumably one that can inflict more harm on us than Charles."

"What about the guy he works for?"

"Taylor?"

Bear shook his head. "Charles."

"Don't know too much about him. No one does. Goes by the moniker of Old Man to most. Runs his organization from the dark. Into a lot of things, from what I gather. Some of which crosses paths with our line of work. I've heard of a few politicians having dealings with him. Maybe a person or two in the Pentagon."

"Really?"

I shrugged again. "That's what I hear."

"Sounds like the pay's better."

"You considering it?"

"Thin line, right? Maybe money is what makes it fade."

I had to smile after Bear sprang the comment back on me. But before I could mount a response, Clarissa emerged from the kitchen carrying two plates loaded with meat and vegetables. She set them down in front of us, disappeared into the kitchen again, then returned with a rack of glass mugs.

"We're shutting down in thirty," she said on her way past us. "Order up if you want anything else."

I got up and joined her at the other end of the bar. A risky move, considering Bear had already devoured half his meal.

"We all right?" I said.

"No, Jack, we aren't."

"Look, I told you we were up here on business. If it weren't for this storm, we'd have been gone by now."

Clarissa said nothing. She flipped each mug in her hand and slid them upside down on the rack perched over the bar.

"Why don't you come back to the apartment with us?" I said. "It's closer than your place. The streets are a mess. Not many cabs running."

"I've got no interest in hanging out with you two drunks tonight in that matchbox you call an apartment."

"Clarissa-"

"It's time to quit playing dress-up." She looked up and set the hand towel she'd been drying the glasses with on the counter between us. "You're great, Jack, but together, we're not."

I reached for the towel and said nothing.

She turned and made her way toward the kitchen, stopping to pour the final round of drinks before pushing through the door that divided us. The door thumped against the frame with each pass until it came to rest, slightly off-center.

I returned to the stool and sat down next to Bear.

"She had tears in her eyes," he said.

I nodded, said nothing.

"Wanna talk about it?"

"Nothing to talk about."

Bear stuffed the last bite of steak into his mouth. He glanced down at my plate. "You gonna eat that?"

I was no longer hungry, so I slid the plate in front of him. A few seconds later, my cell phone reverberated against the bar top. I flipped it open. Frank was calling.

"Yeah?" I said.

"You guys alone?"

I glanced up at the panoramic mirror and saw three patrons remaining, seated at the booth in the corner. "Yeah, we're alone."

"I've got you on a charter out of there at eleven tomorrow morning. Think you can get to Long Island? Place called Republic Airport."

"Should be able to do that. Where's the flight heading?"

Bear glanced at me in the mirror, a piece of steak fixed in front of his face to the fork. I held up a finger in response.

Frank said, "D.C. area."

"Just the area? No place specific?"

"You'll see when you get there."

"It's cool with me as long as I get to depart from the plane under my own power and won't be walking into a hornet's nest."

"Nothing to worry about, Jack. It's on the up-and-up, and I've got some stuff to show you." He paused, and I said nothing. "I'll meet you on the runway."

I set the phone down on the bar and grabbed the last roll out of the basket between Bear and me. It was slick with butter and laced with garlic. If Bear hadn't eaten the others, a single bite would have led me to devouring the entire basket.

"What's the deal?" Bear said.

"We're on a charter tomorrow morning. Leaves at eleven out of a private airstrip called Republic Airport on Long Island."

"Peachy." He lifted his mug to his mouth and tilted his head back, draining the remaining liquid. "We get to show up to God-knows-where unarmed."

"Won't be the first time."

Bear set his mug down. It clanked against the bar top. "And hopefully not the last."

CHAPTER 10

THE SNOW HAD stopped by midnight. Crews worked tirelessly throughout the night, clearing the streets and sidewalks. Finding an unoccupied cab outside our condo building had been the toughest part of leaving Manhattan that morning.

The charter departed fifteen minutes after our arrival at Republic Airport. We were the only ones on board. Takeoff was quick and effortless. Bear had his typical bout of anxiety during our initial ascent, but seemed to do well after the plane leveled off. I did my best to distract him by discussing the playoffs. I never held the fact that he was a Cowboys fan against him. They'd already been knocked out anyway.

The altitude thwarted my attempts at keeping track of our location. The plane flew over an endless patch of thick white clouds. We traveled in a southwest direction, which was to be expected if we were going to D.C. It wasn't until moments before we landed, ninety minutes after takeoff, that I recognized where we were.

Halfway between D.C. and Charlottesville, Virginia.

Tall pines surrounded the airstrip for at least a mile in every direction, ringed by a ten-foot security fence about a quarter-mile out. The barren patch of land that snaked through the forest had been visible from the air. A narrow gravel path wide enough for a large SUV led from the runway to the nearest access road. It passed a guard station positioned at the gate and manned twenty-four hours a day.

Several agencies had access to the runway. Most used it when they had to bring in a guest they wanted no one to know about, or when an agent returned home from a clandestine operation, or when someone had to get out of the country and security was at a premium.

The first time I'd been diverted to the runway was because I was coming in hot. Two and a half years ago, I got into trouble across the border while working with the SIS. Two of our agents had been kidnapped while scouting a drug cartel. One of them didn't make it out alive. I rescued the other, and in doing so, made myself a target. The cartel had reach, and Frank knew that they'd have a man positioned at every possible destination airport looking for me. We hopped on a puddle jumper to the Caymans, then a charter to this same airstrip.

Bear hadn't been around for that operation. He was finishing his stint in the Marines. After he retired from the military and I left the SIS, we formed our contracting company. It'd led us around the world.

And back to that same airstrip.

I didn't want to speculate why. Who might be after us. Frank could explain all that when we saw him. If we saw him, I figured.

The cabin door opened and one of the flight crew stepped out. He was a tall man, rail thin. His voice was twice as deep as Bear's.

"You guys can exit now. Your ride is already here."

Bear rose and headed toward the front of the plane as the man opened the door and lowered the stairs. I got up and stopped halfway. Once Bear reached the opening, he surveyed the scene, then signaled that it was OK to depart.

A cold gust, laced with jet-fuel fumes, smacked me in the face as I emerged from the fuselage. My eyes burned and watered. Brown grass surrounded the strip. The storm had apparently missed the area. Over-head, the sun fragmented the clear blue sky. I reached out for the frigid stair railing and descended to the ground.

Frank stood next to a black full-sized Chevy SUV. He had on a heavy black overcoat and black leather gloves. Practically blended in with the vehicle. He nodded at me and opened the back driver's side door.

Bear walked up to the man. They exchanged words, and then both looked toward me. Neither trusted the other. Each could do without the other. It had been like that since I started working with Frank at the SIS.

"Good to see you, Jack," Frank said as I approached.

I nodded, left my hands in my pockets. "You too."

Neither of us meant it.

The three of us stood outside the SUV for several seconds, freezing in the blustery cold. No one spoke.

"We gonna talk out here, or you got somewhere to take us?" Bear said.

"Yeah, get in," Frank said. "One of you sit up front."

"I'm good in back," Bear said, halfway into the SUV's middle row.

Behind me and next to Bear sat another man neither of us had seen before. His hair was neat and brown and short, his cheeks slightly red. His dark suit wasn't cheap, wasn't expensive. He'd spent some money on the overcoat, though. I figured the same would be true of his shoes, if I could see them.

Frank slid in and said, "Let me introduce you guys to Joe Dunne. Joe's been working on a related case for at least a year. When I started pulling information up, it was flagged for me to contact him."

"Who's he work for?" I asked.

"He's right there, Jack. Why not ask him?"

I glanced up at the mirror positioned in the middle of the visor. "Well?"

"FBI."

"What the hell is going on over there, Frank? I leave, and now you're cutting deals with the Feebs?"

"Jack."

"Frank."

"Listen," Joe Dunne said from the backseat. "I don't care about interagency pissing matches. Doesn't matter to me whose is longer. I've forgotten the two incidents where I was bumped off a case due to SIS involvement."

Frank coughed. "Enough. Christ. What is this? High school? Cut it out, Jack. We've got some serious stuff to discuss here."

We pulled away from the airstrip. The cabin quieted to a hum. Occasionally, a stray piece of gravel pelted the undercarriage. I glanced over my shoulder. Bear leaned against the door and had his eyes closed. Guess that meant all the talking, and explaining, and arguing, would be left up to me.

We stopped at the security station. Frank showed his credentials to the man. A moment later, the gate parted and let us out.

Frank said, "So, what happened in the city?"

"How much can I say?" I stared at Joe Dunne in the mirror.

"I've read him in. He understands the penalty that can be incurred for repeating anything you say here."

"He had the drop on us." I adjusted the vent so the heat blew on my face.

Frank glanced from the narrow road to me, then back. "You gotta do better than that, Jack."

"What do you want me to say?" I looked into the visor mirror. Dunne looked away. I turned to face my window. The trees passed by in slow motion. "I got up there around four in the morning. You know Bear arrived on the same flight as the target, who gave no indication that he knew who Bear was or what he was doing there."

"You're sure about that?"

"You think Taylor would have led Bear to his building if he knew he was being followed?"

Frank shrugged. "Hard to tell with this guy. Battle-tested doesn't begin to describe him."

Sweat formed on my brow. I directed the flow of air toward the window. "Anyway, Bear watched the target enter his building, and after that he never took his eyes off it. We met a block away. Sat outside. Stayed there long enough to give the guy time to fall asleep."

"Nothing happened between then and when you entered the building?"

"There was a cop..."

"A cop?"

"It was nothing. We split up for a few minutes. Bear maintained visual contact with the building at all times. I looped around and was there in time to watch Bear enter, then went in myself."

"Any way out? A back door?" He placed his left hand on the wheel and moved his right to his lap.

"You tell me, Frank."

"I wasn't there, Jack."

"I checked the place out that morning. Every apartment but his. The roof. The basement. It was dark, and it stank like human waste and vomit in there. I didn't find a way out. The intel we had said there was no way out."

"But you never saw him leave."

"That's right."

"Well?"

"Maybe he scaled the walls. Christ, Frank, I don't know."

"And the guy you found in his bed, didn't recognize him?"

I recalled the image of the naked man, hole in his head, blood streaking through his blond hair and pooling underneath his neck and shoulders.

"Right," I said. "Probably some homeless guy that didn't get out of the building in time."

"Sure about that?" Dunne said.

"Getting sick of this questioning."

"Just answer," Frank said.

"How can I be sure? Did I recognize the guy? No. Can I tell you with one hundred percent certainty that he was homeless? No."

Frank pointed at the glove box.

"What?" I said.

"In there," he said.

"What about it?"

"Check the file."

I looked up at the rear-view mirror. Bear had shifted in his seat and was now leaning forward. Joe Dunne hadn't moved. Presumably he already knew the contents. I opened the glove box and pulled out a light blue folder. My stomach knotted as I opened the document.

"Christ," I said.

"What is it?" Bear said.

I held the folder up so he could see the six-by-nine picture taped to the first page of what looked to be an Army service record.

"Is that the guy?" Bear said.

"Yeah," I said. "The one we found dead in Taylor's bed."

CHAPTER 11

T HE ODOR THAT rose from the folder indicated someone had stuffed it in a box and stuck it in the back of a warehouse. I figured Joe Dunne had something to do with it ending up in Frank's possession.

Hollow eyes stared back at me from within the pages. The guy looked about ten years younger in the picture. Unmistakable, though. It was him, minus the hole in his head. Maybe a little more hair around the temples and at the top of the forehead. It'd be easy to call the entire thing a coincidence. But then, Frank wouldn't have made such a big deal of me opening the glove box and making the discovery.

Aside from the picture, there was little on his record. The scant information told me that the dead guy's name was Neil McLellan. He was thirty years old. Same as me. Same as Brett Taylor. And like Taylor, Neil had enlisted in the Army at the age of eighteen.

And like Taylor's file, when I turned the page, there was nothing. Only blank paper added to give the folder some heft. Made it look legit should someone come looking around. There had to be a handful of guys in the country who had jackets like this. What were the odds I'd see two in less than a week?

"Frank, is he...?"

Frank lifted his right hand off the steering wheel as if to cut me off. "We're working on it."

"Did this guy know Taylor beforehand? Did they serve together?"

"Like I said, Joe and I are working on it, but you can look at the dates there and put two and two together."

"Yeah, well, with what I've got here and what I've seen, I'm coming up with five as the sum."

Bear said, "Something stinks about this."

I said, "Someone else is involved in this, and one side is playing the other."

Frank said, "You think we're on the losing end, don't you?"

"Figure it out." I closed the folder and passed it back to Bear. "Here we were concerned that Taylor got the drop on us and bailed, leaving behind a dead body. Initially, I presumed he did so either to frame us, fool us, or scare us. But now I'm thinking that he didn't even know about us. McLellan arrived first, otherwise we would have spotted him entering. Unless there's a way in we don't know about."

Bear grabbed my seat and pulled back. "You saw the same plans I did. Not only that, you walked the building. No way in or out of that building other than the front door."

"Right, I verified it myself. So this guy was there early, and either in Taylor's apartment or hiding somewhere. Why, though? Paying a visit to his old Army buddy? Could be, right? But then, why does McLellan end up dead? It's possible they got into an argument over something stupid that quickly escalated."

"He wouldn't leave the corpse in his bed and flee," Bear said.

"That's right," I said. "He wouldn't. Unless he panicked."

"Guys like Taylor don't panic, Jack," Frank said. "You know that. You're a guy like Taylor."

"If I killed Bear, I might panic."

"Only because I'd rise from the dead."

The three of us shared a quick tension-easing laugh. Joe didn't crack a smile.

Bear said, "What if McLellan was dead already?"

"Body was still warm," I said, "but the apartment was heated. Under those conditions, it'd lose one degree, maybe one-and-a-half per hour.

Without knowing the exact temperature, it's hard to tell. I'd guess he'd been killed within two hours of us discovering him."

"Which means it could have been before Taylor got there," Bear said. "That might explain why he bolted."

I nodded. "Or someone was already there. Maybe McLellan was being used as a bargaining chip, and when Taylor called the third party's bluff, McLellan was terminated."

"Then what happened to Taylor?" Frank said.

"Left with the third party maybe." I thought it over for a second, then added, "We didn't see Taylor leave, so it's possible he wasn't alone when he did."

"And how'd they leave if you guys had the door covered?" Frank asked.

"Gotta be another way out," Bear said.

The car's cabin was quiet for several minutes as we each worked through the various scenarios.

"And then there's the other possibility," Frank said.

"That someone else wanted Taylor dead," I said. "And McLellan was sent to do the job, and failed."

Frank nodded, said nothing. If someone else wanted Taylor dead, Frank should have known. Now he'd have to find out who the guy worked for, and what he was doing inside Taylor's apartment.

The community of assassins was larger than most believed. Some operated within a single agency or organization, others, like Bear and me, contracted our services out, and still others operated with a great deal of moral ambiguity and took job offers from anyone and everyone, and often from the highest bidder. We had to find out who'd sent McLellan to determine the reason he was there and what kind of man he was. That wouldn't be an easy task, either. Frank would have to call in some big favors; and even then, he might not receive verification that McLellan had ever existed.

"You've been awfully quiet during this segment, Joe," I said.

He nodded, said nothing.

"What's your input?"

"I'm trying to sort it out myself. I lost track of McLellan a couple months ago."

"Well, what can you tell us about his past?"

"You saw the folder. That's what I have."

"Jesus Christ. Frank, why am I putting up with this?"

Frank said, "He's working an investigation too, Jack. We're gonna share. Joe's taking the angle on McLellan in an effort to piece together the guy's moves the last couple months. If we're lucky, together you two will figure out why those two were destined to be at the same place on the same day, and why the wrong one came out dead."

We pulled into a shopping center parking lot and stopped next to a dark sedan.

Joe Dunne handed Frank a business card and dropped another on his seat. I presumed it was meant for me. "I'll be in touch. If you get anything on McClellan, call me immediately."

The door shut, and Frank pulled away. My initial reaction was to light him up over bringing in the FBI. Then my gut said don't bother.

We were sixty miles out of D.C. An hour, at least, not taking traffic into consideration. I wouldn't be able to stay there for long.

"I need to get back to New York."

"Why?" Frank said.

"I missed something in that building."

"The escape route," he said.

"Maybe I can find a homeless who's familiar with the place. Get him to lead me to it."

"What do you think you'll find?" Bear said.

"Don't know if I'll find anything. I have to determine how he, or they, got out. I missed something, and that's unacceptable. It put the job at risk. And that put us at risk."

The thought that I'd led Bear into a potential trap ate away at me. We'd had each other's backs since we were eighteen. He'd never let me down.

"So we'll head back up tonight," Bear said.

"No," I said. "I'll head back up. You stay and follow up on any leads Frank comes up with. Check with your sources, too, and see what they have to say."

Frank said, "Don't speak a word of this with anyone else. I'm serious. The wrong person gets wind of this and we'll all be screwed."

I turned away, stared out the window. "We're already screwed, Frank."

CHAPTER 12

FIVE HOURS LATER I pulled into a multi-level garage four blocks from the apartment and parked in a vacant spot that cost me over five hundred dollars a month. It was one of two that we leased. We always left a car parked at the other location, though not always the same vehicle. Paranoia prevented me from doing so. I'd spend too much time wondering if anyone noticed the car that never left.

I headed to the apartment first. Though the snow had stopped falling the night before, the trek wasn't any easier because of it. A thin layer of uneven ice coated the sidewalk. Felt worse than an ice rink. I slipped a half-dozen times. Managed to keep from falling.

When I reached the building, I half-expected to find Clarissa waiting there. She had no idea I'd left. Probably didn't care. That, or she'd ream me for not letting her know. We'd tried dating once before. The relationship had lasted three months before we decided it wouldn't work. Don't know what made us think this time would be any different. She'd grown. I'd grown. We'd grown apart.

I entered the condo slowly and cautiously. Clarissa wasn't there. No one else was, either.

I pulled a fresh cell phone from the safe and placed a call to an old contact from my days on loan to the CIA. If anyone could dig up the details of Brett Taylor and Neil McLellan's relationship, it was Brandon Cunningham.

"How's life in Madison, Wisconsin?" I said.

Brandon laughed. "Not even close."

It had become a running joke that every time I called, I'd name a random place in an attempt to throw off anyone who was listening. Only a few people knew his real location outside Harrisburg, Pennsylvania. Fewer knew the man's past and his current affiliations. I wasn't among those who did. All I cared about was that he remained affiliated with me.

"What d'you need, Jack?"

"Without going into much detail, I'm trying to tie together what relationship, if any, two guys who entered the Army at roughly the same time twelve years ago had then, and currently have now."

"Can't you tell by their records?"

"Would I be calling you if I could? It'd be nice if it was that easy. Unfortunately, it isn't this time."

"So I guess my follow-up question is unnecessary."

"Probably."

"You got names?"

I gave him the names and waited while he tapped at his keyboard. He must've pinned the phone between his shoulder and face because his heavy breaths surrounded the occasional grating of his stubble against the mouthpiece.

"You're not gonna like this, Jack."

"What is it?"

"I ain't got nothing, man. These guys are ghosts."

I walked toward the window and positioned myself so I could see down the concrete corridor. More storm clouds had rolled in. Even the snow on the ground had taken on the sky's gray appearance.

"I'll have to dig a little deeper," Brandon said.

"You do that. Get back to me on the standard number."

"Will do." He paused, then added, "Working alone on this one?"

"Alone enough." Leaving the door open a crack for outside involvement would spook Brandon. I knew that. But it might also get him thinking of other avenues to investigate.

"Who else is involved?"

"Let me worry about that, Brandon. You know it's best that way. Focus on getting me anything and everything you can on those two guys and what they've been up to."

"How far back?"

"If it's relevant? Birth."

We ended the call. After pulling the battery, I snapped the phone in two. One half would go in the dumpster, the other in the middle of the road. A random trashcan would be suitable for the battery. I trusted Brandon, but only to a point. If given enough incentive, he'd turn on me in a heartbeat. I couldn't take the chance that he'd track me through the cell. When he called back, he'd do so on a generic number that I had routed through six servers. His call would travel halfway around the world and back before it reached me.

I turned back to the window. Light was fading fast. The gray glow would turn to artificial orange and yellow soon. I decided this was a good time to head over to the brownstone and poke around. The type of people I needed to question would be there. Fewer of those who wanted to question me would be around.

A cab dropped me off across the street from the café Bear and I had sat in front of a day earlier. The interior lights were off. I had half-hoped they'd be open so I could give a little grief to Alexis, the woman who sold me out to Clarissa. That'd get back to Clarissa, though, so it was better that the establishment wasn't open. I took one look inside after crossing the street and confirmed the place was empty.

Despite the frozen sidewalks and frigid air, the sidewalk teemed with enough activity to keep me on my toes. I walked with my head on a swivel. The crowd contained a mix of regular folks out for a walk or perhaps out for dinner and plenty of street people. Those were the ones I had to watch. Any of them could be dumb enough to target me. And worse than that, one of them could be an undercover. Asking about the scene inside the brownstone would give a cop enough of an excuse to pull me aside.

Nothing good would come from that.

I found shelter from the biting wind on a covered stoop. There I surveyed the area. Piles of snow rose and fell like a tattered seawall along the side of the road. None of it was white. Ice covering north-facing windows reflected the streetlights, which cast orange pools of light on the ground below. The poles had been spaced close enough that little of the ground remained in the dark. Only the rare tree that broke through the concrete floor provided respite from the glow. Surprisingly, the entrance to the brownstone was undisturbed and unaltered. I saw no yellow police tape strung across the door.

Did anyone know what had happened inside the day before?

I studied the faces that passed by. Few, if any, even noted my presence.

Half an hour passed with little change in the scenery. Gusts of wind whipped up clouds of snow. The powder settled again on the street, only to spiral back to the curb in a violent torrent from the next car that passed. The people who walked by did not linger. I isolated three potential witnesses. All had been there when I had arrived. One was a prostitute, presumably, who hung back close to an alley opening. The second was a young Hispanic drug dealer. You wouldn't think it to look at him, but the fact that he was camped out on the sidewalk and had people stop by at odd intervals gave him away. The most promising prospect was leaning back against Taylor's building, wrapped up in a flannel blanket. He hadn't been there the day before, but I had a feeling he frequented the spot. I'd start with him. The other two were always on the lookout for something. A client. The cops. Whatever.

The homeless man had nothing better to do than observe it all.

I lifted my collar and pulled it tight across my neck and under my chin, then vacated the stoop and turned in the direction of the liquor store located two blocks to the west. An offering of whiskey would produce results faster and easier than strong-arming the guy camped out in front of the brownstone. It'd also be cheaper than the cost associated with getting stories out of the other two possible witnesses.

When I returned fifteen minutes later, the drug dealer was gone. Perhaps he'd had enough of the arctic blast and closed shop for the day. Or maybe sales had been stronger than normal since everyone was stuck with nothing to do, and he had to restock his supply. Also gone was the hooker. I didn't bother to check the alley. That she wasn't there was good enough for me.

The homeless man didn't acknowledge me as I cut across the icy street diagonally toward him. His face was hidden under a gray hood. I couldn't see his eyes.

The snow was piled up high enough that I had to kick through it to cross the asphalt-to-concrete threshold. My foot hit the ground and slid six inches or so on the ice. I threw my arms out to regain my balance and nearly dropped the whiskey peace offering.

The brief ice show caught the man's attention. He unburied his chin from his chest, and the hood fell back a couple inches. His face hadn't seen a razor in the better part of a year. Frost covered the hairs that draped over his lips. His eyebrows where thick and wily, covering eyes that showed no fear of me. He was short, stocky, and despite his age, could still hold his own. From six feet away, the stench of the man hit me. I fought back the urge to let him know and stopped there. His gaze darted from me to the unmistakable sight of a liquor bottle in a brown bag. His tongue shot out, wetting cracked lips.

"How long did you serve?" I said.

His gaze lifted from the liquid devil in my hands to my eyes. "Twelve years."

"When?"

"Eighties."

"Any action?"

"Place called Panama."

"A lot of tough men went to Panama in the eighties."

He shrugged. "They said it was for a 'just cause,' but I'd have gone for any cause."

The man, though disheveled, was a SEAL. A former SEAL, but a SEAL nonetheless. What were the odds?

"Are you braving the frigid conditions to talk war with an old vet? Or is there some other reason you're standing there with my favorite drink at dusk when the temperatures are barely in the teens?"

I held the bottle out in front of me. "How do you know it's your favorite?"

He reached for the bottle, smiled, said, "They're all my favorite."

I didn't let go after he wrapped his gloved hand around the sheathed bottle. "Consider this payment in advance."

"For what?" His posture changed, became defiant.

"Answers."

"To what kind of questions?"

"The kind I'm going to ask."

"What if I can't help you?"

"I only ask that you try."

"Fair enough."

I let go of the bundle, then gestured toward empty brownstone's door. "Let's go inside."

CHAPTER 13

THE BUILDING'S FOYER was warmer than outside, but not by much. Steam rose in front of me with every exhalation. Light peeked through the crack between the closed door and the frame. A myriad of footprints littered the dusty floor, going this way and that. They could have belonged to shoes that adorned the feet of other homeless, or cops, or government agents.

The plastic seal that held the cap to the liquor bottle ruptured with the sound of a mini-thunder clap. The man discarded the cap. It bounced and clattered across the hardwood floor, leaving a trail through the dust. He took three solid gulps, then inhaled sharply. His face pinched inward like a catcher's mitt closing. A few seconds passed, and then he let out a strained exhale.

"So, what'd you want to know?"

I held up my hand with my forefinger, pointing toward the ceiling. His gaze followed the trajectory upward. It was impossible to tell if the building was occupied, but I figured if someone was there, they would react to the man's voice. He cocked his head to the side and lifted his wool cap over his ears, seemingly understanding my silent message.

The brownstone was like an old man. It creaked and groaned and moaned and bowed and sagged. If I closed my eyes, I could feel it teetering from one side to the other, trying to maintain its balance in the face of the arctic blasts that pelted its weathered exterior.

Aside from the sounds of the building and the sound of the wind, there was nothing else. That didn't mean we were alone, of course, but I felt better.

"How well you know this building?" I asked.

The guy shrugged. "Been in here a time or two."

I pulled a small LED flashlight out of my pocket, flicked it on, and shined it toward the east hall. "Know what's down there?"

He nodded.

"Lead the way."

He lifted the bottle to his lips and took a long slow draw. His gaze seared past the light and settled on my eyes. There was a quiet confidence about the guy. *Don't let my looks deceive you,* I could see him saying. *I still got it.*

And I'm sure he did.

In his prime, he would've been the kind of guy who could kill another man with his bare hands a dozen different ways in seven seconds or less. His thumbs were more dangerous than the average guy holding a Glock. In the old building, dark and dusty and confined, he probably felt he had a fifty-fifty shot against me. I'd put it closer to twenty-eighty, but that still left a chance. Plus, I didn't know if he was armed. I'd bet money he assumed I was. And he would've been right.

The first door we came to was a quarter of the way open. He stopped in front of it, reached out with his foot, and kicked it inward. It creaked on old hinges that sounded as if they were about to pull free from the rotten frame. I panned the light across the room. It was empty, but there was plenty of evidence that people had occupied it recently. A couple of old sleeping bags on the floor. Paper wrappers that had once surrounded hamburgers. Empty beer and soda cans.

"I don't like this room," the man said.

"Why not?"

He turned and walked away without replying.

I followed him to the next room. The door was closed. He hesitated in front of it.

"You armed?" he asked.

"Maybe."

"If someone's behind this door, then there's a chance they're armed, too. If we open it, they're gonna start firing without bothering to see who it is they're shooting at."

"Then knock."

He looked at me like I'd grown horns and a tail. But he reached out anyway and turned the knob. I stepped forward and shined the light into the room. The move was quick enough that anyone inside would assume it was the police and not some random homeless or petty thief.

"Empty," I said.

"Let's go in," he said.

"You first."

He stepped in, and as he did so, I retrieved my pistol and moved it to my coat pocket. I let the door fall shut. I kept my hand in my pocket, gripping the sidearm. The guy perched himself on the windowsill. He parted the blinds and stared out at the street, leaning far to the right and then the left to get as broad a view as possible. Not once since we entered the room did he glance back at me. Either he trusted me, or he figured he was dead no matter what. I knew when the time came, he'd put up a good fight. Fortunately for him, and maybe for me, that time wouldn't be today.

"Now tell me, what is it you want to know?" He rose from the windowsill and leaned back against the wall next to the window. Thin horizontal lines of yellow light spread across his body.

"To start, what do you know about the guy that lives in this building?"

"Lots of guys live in this building."

"That may be true, but only one can call this his residence, and that's who I want to know about."

The man shrugged and the yellow lines squiggled across his chest and shoulders.

"You've never seen him or heard of him?" I said.

"Didn't say that," he said.

"Then tell me what you know."

"You a cop?"

"No."

"Sure?"

"Mostly."

His head was cocked sideways, a grin splayed across his face. "Don't know much about him. He comes and goes. Gone for weeks at a time, sometimes. When he's here, no one will enter the building. When he gets back, people scatter like roaches suddenly exposed to light. But he don't mess with no one right away. He gives them a little time, maybe thirty minutes, to get out. Nobody goes past the second floor or touches his apartment. It's like some unwritten rule, you know? Word is that a group of four or five guys, young guys, tried to take advantage of him once. They stayed up on the fourth floor and didn't leave after he got back. After a few hours, they forced their way into his apartment."

"What happened?"

"He let one live, but cut the dude's tongue out and severed his fingers. So no one knows exactly what happened."

"Can you tell me what he looks like?"

"You sure you're not a cop?"

"Would it matter at this point if I was?"

"Not really."

We faced off in silence for close to a minute.

He said, "He's about your height. Close-cut hair. Good shape, physically. Carries himself like a soldier. You can tell when he enters a room, he knows he's the baddest dude in there. Especially here."

"Even when you're inside?"

"I make it a point to not be inside."

"So you're saying you have inside info on when he comes and goes?"

The man said nothing. He turned toward the window and stared out at the empty street.

"One last thing," I said.

"What's that?"

"How many ways are there to leave the building?"

He leaned his head back and looked up toward the ceiling. A band of light turned the whites of his eyes yellow. "I guess the front door plus however many windows there are."

"So no other way out."

His gaze lingered on the ceiling. "Right."

I didn't believe him. There had to be something I'd missed my first time here. Perhaps down in the basement, a tunnel or hidden door.

"We done now?" he said.

"Getting antsy?"

He shrugged. "Just figure the cops will be by here soon, with the murder and all."

"What do you know about that?"

The man hopped off the window sill and walked past me with the grin still plastered on his face. "You already said last question."

I waited in the dark room until his footsteps faded down the hallway. The smell of the mildew seemed stronger than when we first entered. I crossed the room, peered through the slits in the blinds at the street. The blinds were coated with dust. The wind blew loose snow into the air and across the road. The man wasn't anywhere to be seen. Maybe he hadn't left the building.

I stepped into the hallway and went back to the foyer. There, I stopped and listened. The building's bones creaked and popped and groaned. Given the guy's history, he could have been within ten feet of me and I wouldn't spot him if he didn't want me to.

The wind picked up and tore through the first floor, sounding like a wolf howling. Frigid air knifed through me. Finally, the latch gave way and the door burst open. A solitary figure stood on the stoop out front.

And it wasn't the ex-SEAL I had just questioned.

CHAPTER 14

"WHAT THE HELL are you doing in here?"

I couldn't make out her face, or the color of her hair, only that it was pulled back, and that didn't matter in the gusts. Tendrils whipped around her head and danced on her cheeks, jawline, and neck. A dark jacket was zipped up to her collar. She wore tight blue jeans. One hand held a cell phone, the other gripped the butt of her pistol.

"Answer me," she said.

The tone of her voice. Decisive. Direct. There was no doubt she was a cop. And I knew there was only one reason for her to be there.

"Name's Golston," I said. "I'm a special investigator for the government."

"So the rumors are true?" She left her hand on her pistol and took a step forward. "This wasn't a random murder."

I said nothing.

"How'd you find out about it?" she said. "We haven't put anything out yet. Other than the kid that called the cops, and the few people outside at two in the morning on a ten-degree night, no one even knows anything happened here."

"We have our ways."

She clicked on her flashlight and aimed it at me. "Identification?"

"I'll ask for the same."

Like gunslingers, we both reached for our credentials. I had used the name that matched the government ID I carried. It said my name was Lawrence Golston, and revealed little else. I held it out. She shined her light and glanced from the picture to my face and back.

"How do I know that's legit?"

"Have to trust me, I guess."

"Maybe I should bring you to the precinct, and we can make a call and get it sorted."

"Officer ...?"

"Detective," she said, extending her ID toward me. "Detective McSweeney."

It looked to be a recent picture, at least as much as I could tell in the dim lighting. She hadn't prepped for it - it was as though she'd taken a moment between interrogations to have the photo snapped. Her hair was pulled back, like it was now. Her blue shirt was buttoned two from the top. She failed to smile.

"Detective, if you follow through with that plan, you'll be directing traffic in Harlem for the next five years."

She smiled briefly, then stepped forward. "So, are you here for the man that lives in this building, or the dead guy?"

"I can't get into that, detective."

"Come with me."

She pushed past me and took the stairs, two steps at a time. The muted smell of her perfume replaced the musty odor that had been present since I entered the building. I caught up to her at the first landing. We climbed the stairs side by side to the third floor.

Police tape crossed like an x in front of Brett Taylor's apartment door. It seemed the cops were also OK with vagrants squatting in the building, so long as they stayed out of Taylor's apartment.

"We didn't want to draw unnecessary attention to the building," she said, as though she had read my thoughts. She reached into her coat pocket and pulled out a set of keys. Fingering them, she settled on one and went to the door. After pulling down the tape, she stuck the key into deadbolt.

"How'd you get those?" I asked.

"Didn't," she said. "We changed the locks in case someone had made a set while he was away."

I wondered how much she knew about the man that lived in the building. Had Taylor been on the NYPD's radar? If so, they likely would have had the brownstone under surveillance, in which case, they might have seen Bear and me enter. I had to find out.

"What do you know of the events on the day the man died?" I said.

"Little to nothing. We got an anonymous tip."

"That said what?"

"That there was a dead guy in an apartment in this building." She pushed the door open and gestured for me to follow her inside.

Once again, I stepped into her perfume trail. My fingers grazed the rough exterior of the door, which belied the apartment it protected.

Nothing had been disturbed; not that Taylor had left anything of importance behind. I doubted he'd kept much in the apartment to begin with. Like me, he worked in a manner that made it possible for him to move at a moment's notice. Any systems he had were no doubt easily transportable so that he could disappear before anyone would go looking for him.

Finding a dead guy in his bed, or putting the man there, would qualify as a reason to go to ground.

We continued into the bedroom. The sheets had been stripped from the bed. A dark crimson pool of dried blood stained a quarter of the mattress.

"We found him in here," she said. "Cause of death was a bullet in the head. We don't have an identity yet, and it's too early for DNA results."

All along, I had feared they knew the identity of the man. If they did, she wasn't letting on. I operated under the assumption McSweeney was trying to play me, however.

"I'm hoping you can help with the ID," she said, looking up from the remnants on the mattress. "The morgue is only a few blocks away."

I nodded. Refusing to help would only draw unwanted attention, and that would make finding Brett Taylor and finishing the job impossible even if he remained in or anywhere near New York. I doubted he did, but this wasn't the time to make that kind of assumption.

We exited the brownstone together. The arctic air continued to blow, whipping directly in our faces. I blinked several times to clear the tears from my eyes. I glanced around for familiar faces. Saw none. The man I had questioned earlier had left the block or was hiding in one of the alleys. The perfect place for a predator on a dark night. There was no one else outside. Chances were they all knew McSweeney, or made her as a cop on sight. A life on the street made them adept at spotting the law.

"I'm parked over there." She pointed to her unmarked cruiser.

"I prefer to walk."

"It's freezing."

I shrugged. "Doesn't bother me."

"Don't be stupid. Let's take my car."

"I hope you don't take this the wrong way, but I'm not inclined to get in the car with a detective I just met."

She shook her head. "Suit yourself then. I'll drive slow. Make sure you keep up, or I'll find some reason to bring you in."

She shoved her hands in her coat pockets as she crossed the road toward her car. Streetlights shimmered off the ice that coated the asphalt. She nearly fell twice. The sidewalks would be even more treacherous.

I called out to her as she pulled open her door. "I'll ride with you."

She got in and revved the engine. Light from her headlights washed over the street as she pulled away from the curb, drove past me, and made a sweeping U-turn.

The front passenger seat was empty. Tinted windows prevented me from seeing inside the rear of the vehicle. She could have had a partner back there, waiting for me to enter. I knocked on the window. She rolled it down.

"Roll down the back ones, too."

Shaking her head and muttering something indecipherable, she complied with my request. The backseat was empty. Satisfied we were alone, I pulled the passenger door open and climbed inside.

The seat was cold and vinyl, and it sank under my weight. The vents blew hot, stale air into my face. My eyes felt dry. I glanced around the dash, looking for anything that might be related to the case.

She pulled away from the curb, driving slowly along the icy road.

"Thanks for coming," she said.

"Didn't think you were going to leave me with much choice."

"Don't feed me that line. You know I'm powerless. Even if I bring you in, you'll call your people, who will show up and give my people a reaming, and then my people will make sure I feel the same pain. In the end, I'm the loser."

"Sounds like you've done this before."

She nodded, looked at me. "It's pointless dealing with you Feds and Feebs."

"I'm not FBI."

"Didn't say you were, only that I've dealt with them before. They're the worst. More demanding than any prick of an ex I've ever had." She smiled, and then continued when I didn't return the gesture. "Anyway, yeah, I've been down that road before. Figured when I saw your ID that you were going to freeze me out right there."

"Too soon," I said. "Might still need your help."

"The feeling is mutual."

We fell into silence. She turned left, went a block, then turned right. Above streetlight level, darkness pervaded, interrupted only by the occasional glow of a night owl's television lighting up a window or two. She pulled into the emergency room parking lot of the hospital, rounded the structure, and parked in the rear.

"That's it." She aimed her finger in the direction of an unmarked and unassuming door.

We exited the car and trudged through the packed snow that covered the sidewalk. Someone had thrown down salt in front of the morgue entrance, which left it strangely barren compared to the rest of the city. McSweeney entered first. Inside, she rapped her knuckles against a Plexiglas window and grabbed a clipboard that held a sign-in sheet.

I expected her features to look hardened in the light. Twenty years on the street could age you thirty. There was a softness about her face, though. No wrinkles. Tight skin. She was around my age. Maybe a couple years older. She had a kindness about her eyes, like they hadn't been witness to hundreds of crime scenes and corpses.

"Can I put you down on here, Golston?"

"Better if you didn't."

A balding man wearing glasses appeared behind the window. "Detective," he said, and then his gaze shifted toward me. "Who's this?"

"He's with the Feds."

The man glanced down at the sign-in sheet. "He needs to be on here."

"He won't sign, but he might be able to help us with an identification. Can you turn your head this one time?"

The man said nothing. He shook his head slightly and reached under the counter. The door buzzed and clicked and cracked open.

"Thank you, Harold," McSweeney said.

We followed the slight man down a bright hallway. He waved a card in front of a magnetic reader and pulled open a thick door.

"Welcome to the morgue," he said. "Please do not touch, talk to, feed, or in any other way disturb our guests while they enjoy their slumber."

I looked at McSweeney. She shook her head and shrugged.

"OK," Harold said. "You're here for John Doe number four."

"You've got four John Does in here?" I said.

"No," he said. "Six. And if it gets any colder, I imagine we might climb into double digits. Oh, what fun that would be."

"You don't get out of here much, do you?" I said.

He ignored me, and instead traced his finger along a sheet of paper affixed to the wall and stopped on a line near the bottom. Mumbling, he tapped the line a couple times, then turned and walked away from us toward a set of chilled lockers.

"Sorry," McSweeney said. "They're a bit odd down here."

"Not my first time in a morgue, detective."

"Here's your guy," Harold said.

McSweeney and I walked over to where the covered corpse of Neil McLellan was stored.

"Any personal affects?" I asked, knowing the answer.

"Nothing," she said. "Found him naked."

I nodded, said nothing.

Harold pulled back a sheet covering the cold and ashen corpse. "Recognize him?"

Prepared to lie, I took a step to the left and leaned over the lifeless shell of bone and flesh laid out on the steel table. Then I told the truth.

"Never seen him before."

CHAPTER 15

MCSWEENEY AND I exchanged contact information outside the morgue. She gave me her card. I gave her a forwarding number that pointed to my personal cell phone. She offered me a ride. I declined and told her I preferred to walk so I could see the rising sun. The truth was I needed to get rid of her so I could call Frank and let him know that Neil McLellan's body wasn't where it should be, and in its place was a true-to-life John Doe.

She slipped into her unmarked cruiser and shot me a quick smile. The engine turned over slowly after her first few attempts before roaring to life. A belt whined against the cold. Her door swung open and she stepped out.

"Golston," she said.

"Yeah?"

"Don't cut me off, OK?"

"You'll be the second person I call if I hear anything."

She turned her head slightly to the left. "Who'll be the first?"

I shrugged, smiled, said, "You know I can't tell you that."

She dipped down and closed her door. The transmission groaned into reverse. Tires spun on icy asphalt. A minute later McSweeney's taillights faded out of sight.

I didn't want to compromise my personal phone, so I hurried around the front of the hospital and stopped inside the first drug store I found. There I purchased a disposable cell and called Frank from outside the store.

"Got trouble here," I said.

He exhaled into the receiver, then said, "Don't dance around it."

I told him everything, starting from the homeless ex-SEAL and stopped after telling him it wasn't McLellan's body in the morgue.

"The homeless guy, you sure he's a former SEAL?"

"Maybe. He looks the part, just a bit dirty. Talked about Panama like he was there."

"I want to keep you on the ground in New York for a bit longer, Jack. See if you can track that guy down and find out what he saw. If he insists he knows nothing, then get him to introduce you to others who frequent the building. Someone had to have seen something. Also, check with your detective friend and get her to tell you what time the first responder arrived at the scene. There's a gap, and during that time, somebody went back in and retrieved the body. Was it McLellan's boss, someone else involved, or did Taylor take care of it? For all we know, he was there the whole time."

"Any luck on your end determining who sent McLellan in?"

"Still working on it." Frank paused, and then asked, "Any clue who the John Doe is?"

"Never seen him before in my life."

"Same cause of death?"

"By all appearances."

"So we've got someone replacing the body of a government assassin with an unlucky schmuck off the street."

"It'd help to have a time and cause of death on the body. Maybe the bullet was added postmortem." I couldn't get in to see the medical examiner, but I might be able to find him after work. "I can double back and check with the ME."

"Wait on that." I heard Frank tap on his keyboard. "Let me see what strings I can pull there. It's probably better that we don't send you back in, but I'm betting I can get my hands on that report."

"Remember, he's a John Doe to them. Guy called him J.D. number four."

"Is that everything?"

"Yeah." I glanced back at an approaching cab and held up my free hand. "You hear from Bear?"

"Was gonna ask you the same thing. Let me know if you do."

"Same."

The cab came to a stop in front of me. I hopped in and gave the driver an address three blocks from my apartment. Once seated on the hard seat, I ignored his advances at conversation. There was too much to consider to be bothered with small talk. I scratched at a tear in the vinyl and gazed out the window.

More people cluttered the sidewalk today, even at the early hour. An eclectic mix of everything from tourists to nuns to businesspeople headed in each direction. The morning sun had burned off a layer of ice from the sidewalks and the snowbanks piled high at the curbs, and trickles of runoff streamed toward the sewers. If temperatures continued to climb, everything not hidden by shadows all day would melt away.

My thoughts turned to Brett Taylor. I knew little about the guy, but what I did know told me he could be anywhere by now. I had to assume that he was in the crosshairs, and I wasn't the only one after him. A guy like him would have an advanced support network in place across the country, and maybe around the globe, in the event he had to go to ground. It was entirely possible we'd never find him. I felt that our initial focus had to be on Neil McLellan. Who was he? Who had employed him? Why was he inside Taylor's apartment?

I let a laugh slip out. The cabbie looked up into the rear view and lifted his eyebrows, inviting me to share whatever thought had elicited the laugh.

I looked toward the side window. I couldn't share anything. Only two people could hear the thought running through my mind. And only one of them could answer.

What the hell did Taylor do to warrant an attempt on his life?

Frank had claimed ignorance on this. I knew better. He didn't accept a job without knowing the details. Not that his intentions were altruistic; it was a measure to cover himself in the event the job could come back to harm the agency. He lived and breathed the SIS. The fact that he'd called on me and Bear to do the work meant it was shady. Just not enough for him to turn down entirely.

Or it had one hell of a payout.

The cab came to a stop two blocks away from the address I had given the driver. A line of cars, all stopped, extended as far as I could see. There was no point in trying to get him to take me any further. I reached across the seat with a twenty in hand, then exited into a pile of snow. After climbing the embankment, I joined a line of people trekking down the middle of the sidewalk. Those that had come before us had worn a path into the ice, leaving sure footing for all who followed.

I didn't mind the extra walking it took to reach the apartment. The cold air refreshed me and cleared my head. I was close to deciding to get on a plane back to D.C. to confront Frank over the source of the job and the reason behind it. Instead, in less than half a block of walking, I decided to stay put for now. There were answers here.

I looked up and noticed Clarissa's bar a few steps ahead. It was early, but through the tinted front door, I saw her inside. She held a clipboard in one hand and a pencil clamped between her teeth. She looked and reached upward, and appeared to be counting with her free hand.

I took a step back and grabbed the door handle. To my surprise, it was unlocked. Warm air rushed out as I pulled the door open. Clarissa didn't notice me standing in the entryway.

"You didn't have to wait up for me," I said.

She glanced at me. Her cheeks turned red, a sure sign she was still angry with me. As quickly as she looked in my direction, her gaze returned to the bottles she had been counting.

The door fell shut behind me. Bells strung vertically rang and jingled as they bounced off the wood. They hadn't been there the night before. Perhaps she only strung them up there during the day. I hopped over the bar, grabbed a bottle of whiskey, and poured myself a drink.

Clarissa still said nothing. She continued counting inventory.

I leaned my head back and let the whiskey do its trick. Then I poured another one and returned the bottle to its place on the shelf.

"What are you doing here, Jack?"

I lifted the glass in a mock toast toward her. "Getting a drink."

She set her clipboard down and placed the pencil on top of it. The pencil rolled off and traveled along the bar top before falling onto the spill ledge and rolling to a stop. Clarissa turned toward me, crossed her arms over her chest. Her head was tilted to the side. Strands of red hair fell across her face. The dim lighting muted her eyes. Instead of their regular emerald green, they looked brown.

"I don't think I can keep doing this," she said.

"Doing what?" I grabbed the bottle again and poured a third drink. She reached up, retrieved a glass and set it in front of me. I splashed a couple inches of whiskey into it for her. "We don't have to make this so difficult."

"That's the thing, though, right?" She took a sip, bit her bottom lip. "We do make it difficult. You're never around, Jack. And when you are, it seems all we do is argue. Just like before."

I set my glass down and stepped toward her. She didn't block my advance. With my hands on her shoulders, I leaned forward so that we were eye to eye.

"Things are a little out of control with this job," I said. "But I promise, once this one is done, I'm taking a break for a few months. We can go anywhere you want during that time. The Keys, Antigua, anywhere. You and me. No phones. No friends. Us."

She closed her eyes and exhaled deeply. The hair hanging to the side of her mouth puffed up and fell again like dying fireworks.

"What do you say?" I said.

She nodded, then leaned forward and kissed me. Pulling back, she asked, "Did you lock that door?"

I shook my head. Then I hopped over the bar and crossed the room. By the time I'd switched the latch, cut the lights, and turned back toward her, Clarissa had her shirt off. I met her behind the bar once again, traced the curves of her soft flesh. And we sank to the floor and into one another.

A while later, I pulled the front door open. The smell of the city rode in on a cold gust. It might have been an improvement from the moldy entryway. Clarissa's footsteps rose over the sounds of the street. I turned to see her standing a couple feet away.

"Will you be around tonight?" she said.

"If I am, I'll come by. What time are you working till?"

"I'll be back here at six and am staying until closing, or whatever time I kick the last loser out."

I smiled, kissed her, and then merged onto the crowded sidewalk, thinking I'd make it the next few blocks back to the apartment undisturbed.

I was wrong.

CHAPTER 16

THE BLACK CADILLAC that pulled to a stop ten feet in front of me had a deep dent in the fender and a series of scratches that continued past the front door. Three men sat inside. They ranged from size extra-large to behemoth. The driver's door swung open and a guy wearing dark sunglasses and a leather trench coat stepped out. His boot-covered left foot sunk into a slushy pothole. He didn't seem to care. Foot fully extracted, he peeled back one side of his coat and revealed a pistol sunk into his waistband.

About that time, the front and rear passenger doors opened. One of the men looked like the first. I recognized the third guy.

"Don't bother running, Jack," Charles said. He glanced over the roof of the car and nodded at the driver, who took a step forward, reached out, and opened the back door.

"I'll pass," I said. "Only a couple blocks to go."

"Get in," Charles said.

Taking my eyes off of the men would be the worst thing I could do at that moment.

I did it anyway.

The bar's door remained closed. The blinds were drawn over the windows. Clarissa had no idea what was happening a few feet away from her establishment.

By the time I turned around, Charles's second henchman had rounded the trunk and was heading toward me.

"Don't think about it," Charles said at the same time my reflexes kicked in. "You may get him, but we'll get you. And not a single person out here will admit to seeing anything."

I said nothing.

"I can see you're thinking hard on this. Let me make it easy for you, Jack. My boss wants to meet you. He's heard good things. I tried to dissuade him and told him what a piece of trash you are. Despite that, he still wants to meet you. And he gave me the unfortunate displeasure of coming out here to get you."

It was difficult to get a read on the man. His eyes were hidden behind mirrored sunglasses, and a thick layer of stubble covered his chin and cheeks. He stuck his right arm over the roof and motioned toward his driver, who turned and slid into the car to his position behind the wheel. The guy who'd come toward me from the rear of the vehicle also spun around and went back to his seat.

"See, Jack," Charles said. "Just come along for the ride. If you like what the Old Man has to say, you can cut a deal with him. If you don't, you'll be free to walk out, and walk back home." He glanced at my waist, then back up. His gaze drifted past me. "You can keep your piece on you until we get to the compound. Fair enough?"

As far as choices went, I had one. Go with him. It was obvious where I had been. They had probably been parked a block away waiting for me to leave the bar. Perhaps she'd tipped them off. Or maybe they'd been watching me all morning.

A group of grade school kids approached, led by their teacher. I waited until they passed, then I stepped off the sidewalk, over a pothole full of ice and water, and slipped inside the vehicle, taking a seat in the back next to henchman number two. It smelled like three sweaty guys and bagels in the cabin.

Charles sat down a moment later. The vehicle dipped to the right under his weight. The driver pulled away from the curb before the big man had managed to slam his door shut.

"Guys," he said, "this is Jack. Jack, these are my guys."

No one spoke.

"Glad you listened to reason," Charles continued. "I don't know what you've heard about the Old Man, but I can tell you, his reach is long and wide these days. In fact, I bet he knows a lot of the same people as you. You'd be surprised how much influence he has in certain circles."

Our stares met in the mirror centered in the sun visor. He lifted an eyebrow, inviting me to speak.

I didn't.

The route took us through Long Island City, to Sunnyside, and finally to Blissville. We entered a part of the city I'd never seen before, except maybe from the air, and even then I wouldn't have been looking for it. The area we drove through was residential that bled into a warehouse district. The driver navigated to the heart of the neighborhood. I spotted a few guys hanging on street corners. Some might figure them to be drug dealers, or perhaps spotters for the dealers. They weren't. These guys had a look about them, the same look I'd seen on men I'd worked with while in the Marines and SIS.

These guys were trained killers. Some might have been ex-Special Forces. Some former soldiers who'd done time in Iraq or the 'Stan. Work was work, and it wasn't uncommon to take whatever job came along.

"You spotted them," Charles said.

I nodded without looking in his direction. "Guess we're close."

"Yup."

The compound rose in front of us. It was two stories high, and between the structure and the land, it occupied an entire block. I wondered how they'd managed to accomplish building something so massive in the area. How many people had they displaced to do so? A block this size could have housed fifty or so families. The Old Man had connections, that much I knew. He must've called in more than a few favors to get the plans approved.

A black wrought-iron gate slid open, parting at the middle. The Cadillac bounced as it crossed from asphalt to concrete. Two men were positioned on either side inside the fence. They were not bashful about putting their HK MP5s on display.

I swept the visible area looking for additional sentries and surveillance equipment. I found some of each: men positioned by the doors, on the roof, and on the lawn; cameras mounted along the roof every twenty feet.

It was safe to assume that the Old Man was paranoid and believed in security. And, presumably, he had plenty of enemies, as well as friends who couldn't be trusted.

We followed the driveway toward the rear of the house and came to a stop in front of a four-car garage. The driver cut the engine, and Charles stepped out. The man in the back next to me remained seated. His gaze was fixed on the headrest in front of him. *Good doggie. Here's your treat.* Charles disappeared behind the Cadillac. In my peripheral vision, I saw his meaty hand appear, then the door pop open.

"Let's go," Charles said.

I stuck one foot on the ground. Then someone grabbed hold of my elbow and pulled. I rotated my arm outward, clockwise, grabbed their forearm, and continued in a clockwise motion. Whoever had grabbed my arm groaned in pain and released their grasp. I didn't give up so easy, though. I continued until the guy was on his knees, face planted against the blanched concrete.

"That's enough," Charles said. "You don't need to be making enemies on your first day, Jack."

I released the man's arm and rose. The take-down had drawn the attention of several of the Old Man's sentries. I ignored the barrels aimed in my direction.

"Follow me." Charles waved toward the door. "They're going to pat you down inside." He glanced over his shoulder at me and smiled, then added, "It won't be the first time, I'm sure. Just let them take your weapon. They'll lock it up and hold it until you leave. Any questions?"

I said nothing. Caught up with Charles on the walkway.

He stopped short of the door. It opened. A thick black man took its place. The guy was even bigger than Charles. After a big dinner they'd likely need to grease him down to get him out. He was armed with an HK MP5, like everyone else, it seemed. He motioned me forward with the barrel of his submachine gun.

As I crossed the threshold, two sets of hands grabbed and pulled me in. I offered no resistance. There was no point. I'd been through the drill before. These guys used more intimidation, but I didn't let it get to me. The less I resisted, the rougher they got. They kicked my legs wide. Twisted on my arms until I submitted and planted my face against the wall. They did as Charles said, and confiscated my Beretta and locked it up.

Charles had come in while they were patting me down. He waited halfway down the hall. He turned and walked away the moment the large black man shoved me forward.

"Hope to return the favor one day," I said to the trio who remained by the door.

"Bet that was the best date your ugly mug has had in quite a while," Charles said after I'd caught up to him. "Probably better looking than that skank you hang out with at the bar."

I ignored his goading. In here, unarmed, a swing at him was all it would take for me to get fitted for concrete boots. I had no doubt an underground tunnel led out of the compound and came up more than a few blocks away.

"Guess you're in agreement with my assessment of the bartender," he said.

"Don't use big words," I said. "Just makes you look even dumber."

He chuckled. "I think you and I are gonna be good friends, Jack."

"Don't count on it."

He stopped in front of paned French doors. Curtains on the inside blocked the view of the room behind.

"I'm not, Jack." Charles wrapped a hand around my shoulder. "You can count on that."

He rapped on the door with the thick knuckles of his left hand. They were scarred and permanently swollen, probably from years of cracking heads and turning wrenches.

"What?" a thin voice called from inside the room.

"It's Charles, Boss. I brought Jack Noble in to see you."

I heard the sound of a cup or mug being set down on a table. The floor reverberated slightly, matching the footsteps I heard approaching from the other side of the room. The doors swung inward. A slim Asian man in an Armani stood before me. He smiled, revealing crooked yellow teeth. The color matched the whites of his eyes. His irises were clouded over. Spots adorned his cheeks. A Marlboro burned at the end of his fingertips, the smoke rising up his arm and circling his neck and head.

"Jack Noble," he said, extending a bony hand. "What a surprise."

CHAPTER 17

THE ONLY SURPRISE was that a plastic sheet hadn't been spread across the floor in anticipation of my visit.

The Old Man took a step back. His grin widened as he opened his arms and gestured me inside the room. Charles slid his hand to the middle of my back. The shove he gave me knocked me off balance for a second. I had to step forward to regain it, placing me inside the room before I had a chance to survey the entire space.

"Have a seat, Mr. Jack," the Old Man said. He aimed a bony finger toward an overbearing mahogany desk, the kind of thing you'd expect to see in a monarch's study.

Before I took a step, he turned his back on me and crossed the room. The doors shut. I glanced back over my shoulder. Charles had gone, leaving me alone with the Old Man. I felt my chances of survival rise by a few notches.

"Sit, sit," he said, already settled into a plush leather chair.

I pulled back a seat and sank into it. It'd take me twice as long to get out of it should danger present itself. That was likely the purpose. It also allowed the Old Man to sit almost a head higher than anyone across the desk from him.

"I'm sure you're wondering why I brought you here," he said.

"You want me to work for you."

Smiling, he grabbed a stack of papers and evened them out by tapping the edges against his desktop. The blank sides faced me. I couldn't tell what was written on them. He set them to the side and placed his hands on the desk, palms down, tips aimed at me.

"I can get anyone to work for me, Mr. Jack. What I need is someone who can kill for me. And not just kill - because, as you can see, I have plenty of firepower at my disposal, including men who have killed for a living as long as you've been alive." He cocked his head and narrowed his eyes. "Thirty, right?"

"Just turned."

"Congratulations." His smile lingered for a moment. He continued. "I need someone who can get in and out, neutralize any target, and do so without leaving a trace of evidence behind."

"I'm not your man."

"Someone who is self-sufficient, can cross borders, and has or can get contacts in those countries."

"I'm not your man."

He smiled, briefly, and diverted his eyes to the stack of papers. He looked up, said, "You're having trouble locating a target. Isn't that correct?"

I said nothing.

"Not only that," he continued, "but you also lost a corpse. One that has been determined to also dabble in the art of black operations. Dreadful."

I said nothing.

"I'll take your silence as an affirmative response."

Murmurs from the hall found their way into the room. The whispers didn't seem to distract the Old Man. He kept his focus on me. I couldn't flinch without him reacting.

"I may be able to help you, Mr. Jack. Of course, in doing so, I'll expect something from you as well."

"Of course."

His smile returned. Those yellow teeth were the gatekeepers to a calloused heart. There was ice behind his cloudy eyes. He was as comfortable in his two-thousand-dollar suit as he would be in sweats, issuing commands to street thugs. He might not pull the trigger now, but at one time he had, and enjoyed it. At once, I felt equal parts hatred and kinship with the guy.

"Do we have a deal?" he asked.

"You've made a miscalculation somewhere along the way."

"Oh, have I?"

"You see, you're operating under the assumption that I'm feeling pressure to find a possible target, or uncover a presumably missing corpse. This couldn't be further from the truth. I came to New York to relax and spend some time with my girlfriend. It's true that in the past I worked for a government agency. A fact I am only divulging out of respect to you. But since then, my activities have been isolated to legitimate businesses with my partner."

He slowly clapped three times. A laugh preceded his comments. "You'll never make it as an actor, Mr. Jack. With your background, you should realize that things go much easier when you adhere to honest dealings."

"I'm sure you live your life by those words."

"How I live my life is of no concern to you. The only thing you should be worrying about is your lifespan, Mr. Jack."

I shifted in my seat. The action drew an immediate response from the Old Man. He lifted his hand and let it settle slowly. I eased back again. I could see in his eyes that he felt he had control over me.

"If you have information about any alleged government targets and possible missing corpses," I said, "then the best thing for you to do would be to phone in an anonymous tip, because you're doing nothing but wasting time by talking to me about it."

He slid back and pulled a drawer open. I couldn't see the contents as they were blocked by the desktop. My body tensed. In my current position, it would be difficult to draw my pistol in time. His hands came into view, weapon-free. At least in the direct sense. He set two manila envelopes in front of me.

One was addressed to Detective Reese McSweeney, my new friend who'd accompanied me to the morgue. The other was ready to be sent to Leigh Russo. I recognized the name: She was a news anchor for a local affiliate.

The other item he withdrew from the drawer remained in his hand. He twirled one hundred eighty degrees in his seat and aimed the remote control at the wall. Two panels split in the middle and parted in opposite directions, revealing a wide-screen television. He clicked the remote and the screen lit up.

What followed were several scenes from the morning Bear and I had entered the brownstone to terminate Brett Taylor. Other footage had been mixed in. I saw Neil McLellan facing the window and turn toward the camera. Then he was in the bedroom. The angle made it impossible to tell who else was in there. In a sequence of shots, his expression changed, became confused, possibly scared. A moment later he was dead. The assailant wasn't caught on film. But next was a shot of Bear and me standing over the lifeless corpse.

"It's still a work in progress." The Old Man paused the footage. "I have an expert editor working on it right now. He has enough footage of you two in the building, and in the apartment, to stitch together a compelling time line that all but puts the murder weapon in your hands. But I think when the detective sees you in the apartment with the corpse, she'll put it all together. A shame you lied to her. I really think she likes you. You could have a chance with her, if she never sees this footage that is."

I couldn't wait long to respond, but it was key to process the information first. I had searched the building and hadn't found a camera. Bear ran through it with an RF detector, and we'd found nothing. Where was the surveillance equipment? And how the hell did the Old Man get his hands on it? Was he involved with Taylor in some way? I could only surmise that they had to be working together. Perhaps that was the reason Bear and I had been sent to dispose of Taylor.

"I can see you are struggling with this, Mr. Jack." He clicked off the television and twirled back toward me. "I'm not a fan of coercing people to work with me, but it has and does work effectively."

"You know some of my history, the people I worked for. It should be obvious I have connections that can make things happen. What makes you think that turning that footage over to the police is going to accomplish anything?"

The Old Man said nothing.

I shifted forward in my seat. Our eyes were level. I placed my forearm along the edge of his desk and continued forward another couple inches. "You flip on me and I'll do everything in my power to bring your organization down."

His eyes narrowed to slits and his hands clenched into fists. Presumably, not many men entered the Old Man's place of business and threatened him. Then, as I thought his blood pressure was close to maxing out, the redness left his face and his lips loosened into a smile.

The Old Man laughed.

"I knew I'd like you, Mr. Jack. Balls you have. For a man to come in here, knowing he is outgunned a hundred to one, more than that, and stand up to me like that..." He leaned back in his chair, throwing his arms up and letting them fall behind his head. "You, Mr. Jack, are my kind of man. Now, let's make a deal."

I mirrored his posture and positioning. In high stakes negotiation, he who speaks first loses. I wouldn't talk until the Old Man did. And I had no clue how long that would take. The Old Man didn't get to the position he was in without being a good negotiator.

That's why it surprised me he spoke so soon.

"I can see you need a little more persuading, Mr. Jack. So perhaps you'd like to hear what really happened the morning you were to terminate Brett Taylor?"

CHAPTER 18

I FOUGHT THE urge to jump from my chair. Obviously the Old Man knew more than just about anyone else about the events that morning. He had video footage to back it up, too. And he had connections with at least one of the men, possibly both. He could have been the one to arrange for the corpse to be switched. The body I viewed at the morgue could have been an unlucky sap who'd run across the wrong person in the Old Man's organization.

I could picture him issuing the command. *Just bring me a white male in his thirties.*

"You'd like to know, wouldn't you?" he said.

I nodded, said nothing.

"Then I'm going to need an assurance from you, Mr. Jack."

I held his gaze for several seconds before speaking. "Go on."

"If you use this information..." He paused, laughed, shook his head. "Scratch that. What I am prepared to tell you will solve your problem. Mostly, at least. So, before I give it to you, I need your word that you will perform a minimum of one job for me."

The bomb had been dropped. Not that I didn't see it coming.

"What good is my word to you?" I asked. "You feel there is honor among thieves and assassins?"

"I know there is."

I'd justified everything I had done in my adult life by telling myself it was for the good of the country, and for the safety of its citizens and friends around the world. Now, a potential threat was loose. Brett Taylor had screwed up by getting involved in something he shouldn't have. And now he knew someone was there to take his life. It wouldn't take the man long to figure out that the government had sanctioned the job. It was likely that he had put the nation at risk, and would now be in a position to want to do more damage. And to strike as quickly as he could.

Could I live with doing something on the other side of the law in order to protect my country?

"Mr. Jack?"

"I can't give you an answer right now."

He glanced down at the envelopes on the table. "Are you sure about that?"

"I am."

The Old Man pulled open the drawer and slid the envelopes toward him, letting them fall into the awaiting compartment. "I'm a tough man, Mr. Jack, but I am also fair. I'll give you seventy-two hours to decide. Know that if you decline, or fail to give me an answer within the allotted time-frame, I will be forwarding the video evidence. I know you have the connections to avoid charges, but the news networks will not be forgiving. Your identity, and likely that of the people you work for, will be revealed. You know as well as I do that there are individuals in certain organizations that will not take kindly to this."

I nodded, said nothing.

"I take it you understand the underlying meaning."

"Yes." There was nothing else to say. His offer was take it or leave it, and the "it" was life. I had three days to figure this out on my own. If I did, then I'd likely have enough dirt on the Old Man that he'd keep my secrets to himself. And if I didn't break it in time, I'd have to join forces with him. My stomach knotted for the first time since entering the compound. I knew I'd get out alive, but I felt less free than at any other time in my life.

The Old Man reached for his phone and pressed a single digit.

"Sir," a voice said through the speaker.

"Send in Mr. Charles," the Old Man replied.

We sat in silence, waiting for Charles. If something was going to happen, it would be now, although I doubted it would. A rap at the door signaled Charles had arrived. The Old Man rose and gestured for me to do the same. Then he called out for Charles to enter.

"We good, Boss?" the big man asked.

The Old Man turned toward me. His smile was as fake as the luxury watch on Charles's wrist. "Mr. Jack and I have come close to an agreement. I'd like you to fill him in on some of the benefits of working with me as you escort him back to Manhattan."

Charles nodded. "Nothing would make me happier." The tone of his voice told me there were several things that would indeed make him happier. I hoped that *pounding Jack Noble's face while my goons hold him down* wasn't one of them.

I extended my hand toward the Old Man. "Good meeting you."

He wrapped his frail hands around mine. "Seventy-two hours starting now. Not a second more."

I felt a card against my palm and wrapped my fingers around it as he withdrew his hands. Without looking at it, I stuffed the card in my pocket. Undoubtedly, it contained his contact information.

CHAPTER 19

C HARLES HAD ME dropped off on the east side of the 59th Street Bridge. He hadn't come along for the ride, of course. Left the job of being a prick to his *assistants*.

I hailed a taxi to carry me across the bridge and had him drop me off at the southern end of the Park. From there, I'd walk. I figured the air would do me good, clear my head. Didn't happen. By the time I reached the apartment, things were no clearer than they had been prior to meeting with the Old Man.

Inside, I contacted Bear on a secure line.

He answered and got right to business. "I've picked up a few things on our friend Taylor."

"Such as?"

"Seems he's been pretty busy lately, fulfilling orders that came from outside his normal buyers."

"Who was he regularly working with?"

"Open up a can of alphabet soup and play around with the letters. You'll figure it out that way."

"Gotcha. Same as us, pretty much."

"You could say that."

"What about the extracurricular?" I already knew of one, but didn't want to influence Bear with my knowledge.

"This is where it gets dicey, Jack. I'm hearing he started making himself available to the highest bidder." He paused a few seconds, then added, "And it didn't matter who they were or where they came from."

I would have pegged the Old Man as one of those bidders up until Bear said *where they came from*. He didn't have to elaborate on that point. Brett Taylor had started to take jobs from parties with conflicting interests. I had a feeling that a read through recent news might reveal a few accidents that weren't.

"So are you coming back to D.C.?" he asked.

"I was thinking about it, but considering the place everyone was seen last is New York, I think it's better to remain here. You think you can get up here today?"

"Yeah, I can. Figure driving or flying or riding, I'll be there by seven tonight."

"Sounds good." And it did. I needed a couple hours of sleep. "Let me know when you're close."

I hung up and grabbed a bite to eat before heading to the bedroom. Blackout shades doused the light. My body was ready to shut down the moment I hit the bed. But my mind had other plans. There were too many questions to be answered. How had we missed the surveillance equipment? How had the Old Man come into ownership of the tapes? If he and Taylor had a working relationship, how long had it been established? A closer look at the records on the brownstone would be in order. We'd assumed that Taylor owned it. Perhaps, like the homeless that scattered like roaches, Taylor stayed there with the Old Man's permission.

Then there was the question of Neil McLellan. I wondered if the Old Man really held the key to McLellan's involvement. I couldn't doubt the tapes, but I could question how much the crime boss really knew.

Deciding that answers wouldn't come right then, I forced my brain to shut down, and drifted to sleep.

I woke to my cell phone ringing. Only a handful of people had the number, and none of them would call to shoot the breeze with me. The blackout shades made it difficult to tell how long I'd been out. I reached over for my phone and answered.

"Mr. Golston, this is Detective McSweeney. I'd like to meet with you if you're still in town?"

It took a moment to compose my thoughts. How had I managed to give her this number? The last person I wanted to deal with was a cop. Instantly, I assumed the Old Man had forwarded a copy of the tape to her.

"Mr. Golston? You there?"

"Yeah, I'm here, and I'm still in town."

"Great. Can I see you this evening?"

She stopped short of mentioning where. I had no desire to spend any part of my night in a police station.

I said, "How about an early dinner?"

She said, "It's six o'clock, Golston. People do eat dinner at this time." She mentioned a restaurant that was eight blocks away. We agreed to meet there in forty minutes.

After hanging up with McSweeney, I called and left a message for Bear, letting him know I'd be out until eight or nine. Then I showered, changed, and left the apartment through the back door. Though we had managed to keep the location of the apartment secret, I still felt that the alley was safer, in light of everything. The government might not know where I lived in New York, but the Old Man probably did. Chances were he'd had someone watching me from the moment Charles's guys dropped me off on the Queens side of the East River. Maybe they watched the back of the condo building. They definitely kept an eye on the front. I didn't want word getting back to the crime boss that I'd had dinner with a detective on the same day I met with him.

Even if it was the same detective he threatened to rat me out to.

I stepped into the frigid night air and passed between two dumpsters spilling over with trash. Six months from now, the combination of stench and heat would be enough to knock a man out. But in the freezing cold, it wasn't so bad. About the same as a rotten banana.

The narrow alley cut between six more buildings. At the last, I took a right. It was darker here, with figures scattered along the ground huddled up against the edges of the buildings. I didn't need light to know they watched me as I approached. My size alone was a turn-off to most. And those that considered me a target likely gave up hopes of taking advantage of me because of the way I carried myself.

Once on 5th Avenue, the crowd thickened and I found a group of locals to merge in with. I put my head down and continued on to the restaurant.

It was a small Mediterranean place. Freshly baked pita bread was on every table. Hummus and tabbouli, too. A waiter passed by with two plates - seared lamb that made my mouth water, took me back to a time I spent a week in Greece.

McSweeney spotted me after I stepped through the door. She waved from a table in the back corner. Her hair was pulled back, same as before. She was wearing blue jeans and a light pink polo shirt. Her lipstick matched, but other than that, she wore no makeup. Her blue jacket hung on the chair next to her.

I scanned the half-full dining room. This was a local's place. No tourists. Some of the patrons looked as though they might have come from one of the countries in which the cuisine had originated. None of them posed an immediate threat. A good thing, since McSweeney had planted her stake on the table by taking a chair that allowed her to lean against the back wall, which meant the only option available to me left me with no way to keep an eye on things.

She rose and met me a few feet in front of the table. I shook her extended hand, then we sat down in the configuration that made me most uneasy.

"You're uncomfortable?" she asked.

"I'll get used to it."

"We can switch."

I glanced over my shoulder back at her, then nodded. Clumsily, we changed places. The awkward dance of two people brushing up against each other in public. She left her jacket on the chair that was now next to me. I kept mine on for the time being. Her perfume lingered on both.

"The tabbouli here is excellent," she said, sliding a menu across the table.

"I'll keep that in mind."

"So I guess you're wondering why I asked you to meet me?"

Before I could answer, a dark-haired waitress walked up and set a tray of bread, hummus, and tabbouli on the table. She took our drink orders, then left.

"Anyway," McSweeney said, "I wanted to let you know of a few key developments."

"OK."

"But first, I need you to level with me."

"OK."

"Who are you?"

CHAPTER 20

I FELT THE coldness of the night air moments after the front door opened. Four uniformed cops stepped in. Two remained close to the door, while the other two started toward our table. They split apart, and one started in the direction of the kitchen door. He glanced at me about the same time I looked from the door to him. He placed his hand on his pistol.

"We can do this here, or back at the station," McSweeney said.

I looked at her. She didn't appear to be excited to have placed me in this position. "I should have known you wouldn't give up your seat without reason."

She stared blankly at me and said nothing.

The cops had all frozen in position. They focused on our table and nothing else. I assumed another team was waiting outside. All the patrons of the restaurant had joined the officers and were staring in our direction.

"What is it you want?" I said.

"For starters, your name."

"I already told you."

"You lied to me."

"Why would I have a government ID that says I'm Lawrence Golston if I'm not him?"

She said nothing.

"I already warned you, take me in and you're going to regret it."

"I have a source."

"What kind of source?"

"One who has access to personnel files and can tell me anything I want to know about anyone."

"NSA."

She shrugged.

"OK," I said. "What did they tell you about me?"

"Nothing."

"Good. That's what they're supposed to say."

"No, he didn't tell me nothing because it's his job. He told me nothing because you don't exist."

"Then I'm breaking some pretty big universal laws by sitting here."

"Plenty of Lawrence Golstons exist, but not one working as a government investigator."

"You don't know what you're getting yourself into, Detective."

"Then why don't you tell me?"

"You shouldn't have involved your source." I glanced around the dining room. The four officers remained in position. Without taking my focus off the closest one, I said, "Get them out of here."

"Are you going to tell me what I want to hear?"

I nodded.

"OK." She got up, went over, and said something to the man by the kitchen entrance. The guy nodded several times, then left his post. By the time she returned to the table, the cops had left. "Happy?"

"I'll tell you when we're away from here." The waitress hadn't returned with my drink, so I took a sip of McSweeney's water. "What were you thinking, bringing them in here like that?"

She said nothing.

"And checking up on me with an NSA contact?"

"I didn't say he was NSA."

"You didn't have to."

"He could be DOD or FBI."

"But he's not." I was ready to bail on her and head back to D.C.

"That's not all," she said.

Just what I needed. More questions. "What?"

"We identified the body."

I'd figured she was lying about there being a few key developments, but an ID on the body was huge. Knowing the name of the dead man might provide a clue on who else was involved in this mess. Finding McLellan's body would help, too. But I couldn't ask for McSweeney's assistance with that.

"Let's go," she said. "I don't feel comfortable talking about this here. Not after the scene we just made."

"You made."

"You were involved."

"I was led blindly into a trap."

"Your own fault. You're the government agent."

"Investigator."

"Whatever."

She rose. I fished a twenty out of my pocket and left it on the table. Stepping outside, I scanned the street in search of the team she'd assembled to bring me in. They were nowhere to be seen.

"Don't worry," she said. "I sent them on their way."

I shoved my hands inside my coat pockets. The time in the restaurant had left the deep pockets warm. "Where to?"

"My office?"

I shook my head. "No police stations."

"How about we just walk, then? If you can handle the cold, that is."

"Doesn't bother me."

"Sure about that? You strike me as a southern boy."

"I'm an all-American boy, McSweeney. The country is my home."

I turned and started walking away from her. It didn't take long for McSweeney to catch up. We turned a couple times until we reached a residential street. Pedestrian traffic was light. If we were being followed, I couldn't tell. My phone buzzed inside my pants pocket a few times. I ignored it. Most likely it was Bear calling to tell me he'd arrived.

She broke the silence. "Donald Emmings."

"That's the corpse?"

With her bottom lip protruding, McSweeney nodded.

"How'd you tell?"

"The usual ways."

I didn't press for clarification. I was more interested in who Emmings was, and what connection he might have with Taylor.

"What do you know about him?" I asked.

"He's got a rap sheet going back fifteen years or so. Clean up until he hit twenty-four. Then it was like he decided to take it upon himself to get picked up for every misdemeanor he could. Graduated to felonies before long. None of them stuck, though. Witnesses and judges all bought off. Recently, they were taking a look at him for a double homicide. Three witnesses were able to put him at the scene."

"How'd he end up in the morgue instead of a cell?"

"One witness disappeared, and the other two suddenly forgot what they saw."

"Why'd he end up dead? 'Cause of who he took out?"

She shrugged.

"So was this guy Emmings in the mob?"

"Something like that."

"Doesn't sound Italian."

She smiled. "You watch too many movies."

"What's that mean?"

"It means not all members of organized crime are Italians." She grabbed my arm and pulled me to a stop. "And not all Italians are criminals. Some of us are cops."

"Never would have pegged a McSweeney as Italian."

"Who says it's my maiden name?"

"He must be proud of you."

"Not proud enough to stick around."

"Sorry."

"Whatever."

I said nothing.

"What about you?"

"Proud of you?"

"In a relationship?"

"Sort of."

We continued along the sidewalk, weaving our way around others. Our walk had brought us close to my building. I wondered whether she knew where I lived. If so, she'd know a lot more about me than I wanted her to. That didn't explain the scene at the restaurant, though, unless it was a game aimed at getting me to confess. I wouldn't put it past McSweeney to have been playing me from the beginning.

"So what connection did Emmings have to the guy who lives in that building?"

"You mean Taylor?" she said, daring me to respond.

I shrugged. "All I know is someone lives there."

"So you were really here for Emmings?"

"Didn't say that."

She shook her head. Her ponytail swayed in opposition. "I wasn't lying about my contact. I know who Taylor is, and what he did. And I still don't buy the government investigator bit." A deep exhale sent a trail of vaporized breath streaming over her head. "But, you are obviously here because of some agency or department or politician."

"If what you're saying is true, then it's better for you to keep your distance from me and that brownstone."

"My source says the same thing."

"You should listen to him."

She nodded. "Perhaps I should."

"So why don't you take his advice?"

She stepped out of the flow of traffic and leaned against the glass wall of a corner store. She waited for me to join her. I leaned against the glass opposite her. A thin sheet of ice lined the window. I traced my fingertips along it like they had ice skates attached.

"I want to know what's going on here," she said. "Call it a wild patriotic hair up my butt, but someone is involved in something they shouldn't have been. If I can be a part of bringing them to justice, then I want to do it."

"How do you know that someone isn't me?"

She shrugged and glanced down. "Guess I don't."

"Yet you're still standing here."

"Guess I am."

"Jack?"

Christ, I thought. I hadn't realized how close we were to Clarissa's bar. It must've been slow, because it was too early to be closed, and she was standing behind me. I turned to face her. She could have said nothing else and I would have known exactly how she felt.

"What the hell is going on?" Clarissa said. "Who's this?"

I held my hands up. "Before you get too excited, let me explain what's going on. This is-"

"Save it, Jack. We're done." She turned and merged into a group of Japanese tourists who were heading to or returning from a show. Clarissa failed to blend in. She was a head taller than most of them.

"Jack, huh?" McSweeney said.

I nodded, turned around.

"Got a last name to go with that?"

"Nope. Just Jack is all you need to know."

"Well, Jack, what now?" Her gaze held mine for several seconds. She was serious about being a part of this. I didn't think she realized the implications it could have on her life, though.

"What you need now is to go home and get a good night's rest. Then, when you get up, you need to spend some time thinking about how you really don't want to get involved in this situation. Your contact is right. And so am I. Even if you survive this, you'll never be the same. Your view of the world will never be the same. And you won't be able to do a thing about it."

"What about you and that woman?" She offered a half-smile. "She's your 'sort of', right? Why didn't you chase after her just now?"

"Remember that first algebra question in middle school? The one about the trains?"

"Train A and Train B both heading the same place? Different speeds, distances. How long does it take each to get there?"

I nodded. "That's our relationship. Only we're on the same track and heading toward one another."

CHAPTER 21

A S I WATCHED McSweeney disappear into the yellow light-haze, I made the decision to return to D.C. the following day. I had contacts there that would only talk in person. I also wanted to grill Frank on what had happened. I had a feeling he'd been withholding information from me since the beginning.

It felt as though a thousand eyes followed every step I took. The Old Man had a huge reach, and I couldn't discount him having several members of his crew on the lookout for me. And even though McSweeney had left, she might have someone working undercover, intent on following me home.

So going back to the apartment was out of the question. I couldn't lead either group there. Plus, Clarissa might be waiting for me, and that was an argument I didn't feel like facing.

I found a bank of three pay phones. Maybe the last three in Manhattan. One was missing its receiver. Another its cord. The one in the middle worked fine. I dropped some loose change in the slot and called Bear on his local forwarding number. We agreed to meet at a local bar.

The feeling inside the place was calm and relaxed. I found a corner booth with high backs. No one was seated nearby. Most of the barstools were occupied by what appeared to be two separate groups, seated in different sections of the angled bar. The way they were dressed indicated this was only the beginning of their night. From here, they'd likely move on to some of the trendier nightspots, filling their gourds with alcohol until at least two of them found themselves face down in a gutter, vomiting into the snow's runoff.

Bear entered, drawing the stares of a few patrons. Shock, more than anything else, at the size of the man. He scanned the place in the span of a second or two. I figured his assessment was the same as mine. He strolled over without concern. He smiled at the beer waiting for him and took a seat.

"Tell me you found something," I said.

He shook his head. We'd revealed little over the phone. There was always the chance that someone had breached our systems and was tapping our communications. Frank kept things secret, but that didn't mean word hadn't gotten out that Bear and I were involved in the attempt on Taylor's life. If it got back to the right - or wrong - person, they'd use their influence to begin gathering intel on us.

"Right now, D.C. is like taking last night's Chinese food leftovers and mixing them in with your scrambled eggs." Bear lifted his bottle and took a generous pull. "It's a mess there, Jack. Half the people know nothing. The other half, they know something, but its bullshit, and they're happy to feed it to you."

"Not much better here." I paused to watch as a couple entered through the front door. The man waved at the group on the right side of the bar. After they'd blended into the group, I continued. "I had a run-in with the Old Man. Not sure what to make of that yet."

Bear picked at the corners of the beer bottle's label. "How'd that go?"

"He has a ton of information. So he says, at least. Obviously, I don't know him well enough to tell if he's feeding me a line or telling the truth."

With a corner free from the glass, Bear pulled quickly, then crumpled the label into a ball. He rolled it between his thick fingertips like he was rolling a joint. "What did he say?"

"That he knows what happened, how it happened, and he can pin it on us if we don't cooperate with him." I paused, then added, "If I don't cooperate. He's left you out of this, so far."

Bear's cheeks turned a darker shade of red. It was subtle, and quick, but his anger had been piqued.

"We've got a couple days." I noticed the waitress close by, so I twirled my finger indicating another round of drinks. She set off behind the bar. "He offered an ultimatum of sorts, and he's willing to help us out."

"In exchange for what?"

"Our expertise."

Bear shook his head, lowered his gaze to the middle of the table.

"I know," I said. "Not ideal. But neither is federal prison, which is where we'll be headed. And that's if we're lucky. God forbid we end up in a cellar somewhere with Ted the Torturer going at us."

"I still think about seeing that man water-boarded." Bear flinched.

"I know. Me, too."

The waitress set two beer bottles on the table and collected the empties. Her attempts at small talk went ignored. The guys from one of the big groups at the bar had gathered around a video game. The five of them let out a collective victorious yell as one of them accomplished something amazing in the virtual world.

We'd made the same kind of sound after surviving a ten-on-three attack in Iraq a few years back.

Bear said, "Well, guess it can't get any worse."

"It kind of can."

"Jesus."

"Yeah."

"What?"

"There's a cop."

"There's lots of cops."

"This one's a detective."

"I won't hold it against him."

"Her."

"And?"

"She caught me snooping around the brownstone."

"And?"

"I told her I was a government investigator."

"And?"

"She brought me to the morgue."

"Kinky."

"Little bit."

Bear smiled, said nothing.

"The body wasn't McLellan. Turns out, it was some petty criminal with ties to the Old Man. I'm assuming, at least. No idea what happened to McLellan's body, though."

"So the Old Man isn't trying to pull one over on us?"

I shook my head. "Don't think so. What's he to gain by doing so? He's serious, and we might have to take him up on the offer if we don't get this figured out in the next two days."

Bear held the bottle in front of his face. His eyes focused inward on the neck. He nodded slowly.

"What about your findings on Taylor?" I said. "Did you get any names of who else he'd worked for?"

"Names? No." He set the bottle down, shifted in his seat, extending his left arm out. "Locations? Yes."

"Where?"

"Everywhere you wouldn't want him to be. I got a guy… can't say who, yet… who's putting together a dossier of all the intelligence he's got."

"This could be the source of the job."

"It's not. I can guarantee that. He'd never heard of Taylor until I mentioned his name."

So Taylor had become a mercenary in every sense of the word. He didn't care what he did, so long as he got paid. I was almost certain that he'd taken jobs from the Old Man. And now, Bear had someone promising hard proof that Taylor had worked for those who presented a threat to national security.

"Why the hell would he come home?" I said.

Bear started shaking his head, stopped, nodded. "My thoughts exactly. It was too easy, Jack. We knew his itinerary, everything. Where he was staying, the times of his flights. How often does anyone have that on us?"

"Never. Didn't matter what we did, our plans were known to no one until they absolutely had to know them."

"Something stinks, Jack. And it ain't this bar."

A couple minutes later, my phone rang. A D.C. number I didn't recognize. I took a chance and answered it.

"Jack, Joe Dunne here. I've got some information on McLellan I wanted to share with you."

"OK."

"Someone slipped his body out of the brownstone without anyone knowing."

"You don't say."

"Even put some bum or something in the bed in his place."

"How'd you hear all this?"

"I've got a mid-level contact in a big criminal organization out there. Said he was part of the transfer process. Someone hired them to handle it."

"He give any names?"

"Nah."

"What about his?"

"Can't tell you that, Jack."

"Well call me back when you've got some real information for me."

"Jack-"

I flipped the phone shut and dropped it on the bar.

We sat in silence for the next twenty minutes, both of us running through possible scenarios and outcomes. After finishing another round of drinks, we left the bar. The sidewalks had iced over again, making traveling by foot treacherous, especially after a few beers to upset the equilibrium. Still unsure whether I was being followed, I didn't feel like possibly compromising the location of the apartment, so we checked into a hotel and spent the night in separate rooms. Our next step was clear.

We had to return to D.C.

CHAPTER 22

WE CUT OUR sleep short and left at four a.m. We decided to take my car since no one in D.C. knew about the vehicle, which we kept in New York at all times. The parking garage was seven blocks away. A cab got us there in less than three minutes. The concrete structure offered no respite from the frigid temperature. The wind whipped through the open entrance and exit, but died amid the upward rising slope of the garage.

When we reached the vehicle, Bear inspected the undercarriage, then the engine block. He'd been trained extensively in demolitions and knew a dozen ways to sabotage a car while making it look like an accident. From behind the sedan, he gave me a thumbs up. That was the deal. He got dirty. I turned the key. That way there was no chance both of us would die at the same time.

I gripped the key between my thumb and forefinger, stuck it in the ignition, and closed my eyes. If there was an explosion, I didn't want to see the flames coming. I turned the key. The engine cranked slowly, coughing and sputtering in reaction to being awakened after spending a couple weeks slumbering in the arctic air. I paused, then turned it again. The car roared to life.

Bear stepped through a plume of exhaust that shimmered red in the wake of the taillights. He slapped the trunk twice with an open palm. The vehicle dipped and bounced both times. I still found myself surprised by the force the man possessed even though I had seen it on display more than once.

The clock on the dash read 4:29 when we merged onto I-95 south-bound. The majority of the trip would be smooth sailing. Traffic would pick up around Philadelphia, but not to the point of gridlock. There'd be plenty of stop-and-go once we reached D.C.

Unavoidable.

Outside of New York, cars raced along the interstate's sparsely filled lanes. I notched the cruise control at eighty and stayed in the second middle lane. Bear and I both observed the cars in front and behind. The way I saw it, we had three groups that would be interested in tailing us. At a minimum.

I hadn't gotten the feeling that McSweeney trusted me yet, even after the showdown in the restaurant. I couldn't put it past her to keep track of the guy she'd found wandering around a crime scene and then fed her a false identity. I had half-expected her to show up at the hotel with a warrant for my arrest.

There were any number of agencies that might also have interest in our whereabouts. Spotting them would be easiest.

The wild card was the Old Man. He'd made me an offer and given me a deadline. How close tabs would he want to keep on me? His network - much like the government agencies and law enforcement, if they worked together - was vast.

What it came down to was Bear and I didn't care *who* followed us. If there was someone on our tail, we'd have to deal with the threat. And we'd handle it the same way no matter who it was.

We barreled through New Jersey. Stars disappeared. The sky faded from dark blue to pink to orange. The sun crested the trees outside of Cherry Hill. The interstate grew tighter. I was still able to cruise along at eighty miles per hour, but now I had vehicles no more than a car's length in front and behind me. Watching for a tail became trickier, and much of the job fell upon Bear while I focused on the traffic.

There had been no sign of us being followed so far. But any smart group wouldn't use just one car. There would be a team, and they would work the highway system by having people positioned at various intervals. One car would get off and another would get on, often leaving a mile or two unwatched in order to coordinate the effort. When done correctly, there'd be no chance of the vehicle under surveillance to exit. And they wouldn't have any idea it was going on.

Again, this fell to a group with an advanced network in place. The FBI could do it. So could law enforcement, if they worked together. Could the Old Man? Over the years, I'd heard his moniker mentioned in various circles, but other than the rumors I'd heard, I knew very little about him. People tossed around the word 'network,' but what did it mean in conjunction with the Old Man's organization? Friends? Employees?

On the other side of Philly, Bear spotted a car that gave him cause for concern. A black sedan. Two men occupied the front seat. They were fit and clean cut and wore suits and sunglasses. Feds. Or businessmen. No way to tell, yet. The shoes would be a strong indicator, but we couldn't see them.

I continued on for five miles. The other car remained three to four cars behind. They switched lanes, but always ended up in ours. We approached an exit with half a dozen gas stations and plenty of restaurants. It was a busy area. We got off there.

The exit doglegged to the west, splitting in two. I stayed to the right. There was less of a chance we'd have to stop. I glanced from the road ahead, to the rear-view mirror. Trees blocked my view of the highway the further we angled away from it.

Bear kept his gaze fixed on the side mirror. "That's them."

I glanced up again. The dark sedan was a couple hundred yards back. There were four cars between us and them.

"They just took the right fork," he said.

"I'm gonna stay this course," I said, "and pull into the second gas station on the left. That way we can get out and onto the highway quickly if necessary."

"I think we should split up."

"Not sure I like that idea."

"These guys are obviously Feds. So, it's not like they are gonna capture, torture, and kill us. Worst case, they bring us down to D.C. and lock us up for a while, making it impossible to investigate this mess any further."

"OK."

"If that happens, it's best it only happens to one of us."

"Are you planning on hoofing it the rest of the way?"

"Nah." Bear turned inward and craned his head toward the rear window. "Busy as this exit is, there has to be a rental car place."

"They might pass us by."

"They might not."

The lane we were in continued onto the city highway without requiring a stop. I merged into the far left lane. "Still there?"

"Yup."

"You see anything ahead?"

"Nope."

"OK."

I turned on the blinker and came to a stop. Several cars passed on the opposite side of the road before enough of an opening appeared. By that time, the sedan was right behind us. I turned into the gas station. A thick line of traffic made its way toward us, filling up two of the three lanes. Instead of coming to a stop at one of the pumps, I cut the wheel to the left, cut across the sidewalk, hopped the curb, and pulled into traffic. Brakes sang and tires chirped behind us.

"Christ, Jack."

"Where are they?"

"Still at the intersection. Reverse lights are on, but he's blocked in. Not gonna be able to go backward."

I pressed the accelerator and used the narrow shoulder to push past the five cars between me and the on-ramp. Horns blared. One driver tried to block the shoulder. Must've thought I was a hothead trying to get on the road faster. We reached the crest of the ramp. From there, I had a two-mile view of I-95. Heavy traffic, but not backed up. The shoulder ran out two hundred feet ahead. I pushed it as far as I could before wedging in between a full-size SUV and a minivan.

"How's it look behind us?" I said.

"Haven't seen them yet," Bear said.

I pulled to the left, out of the line of merging vehicles and into the flow of traffic on the interstate. The guy behind us honked and extended both middle fingers. I tapped my brake. His eyes widened and he clutched the steering wheel as if it were the lone branch on the sheer side of a mile-high cliff.

I continued weaving through traffic. As the right lane picked up speed, we joined it momentarily. Bear confirmed that the sedan was still not in sight. I pulled onto the shoulder and sped up to ninety.

"Who do you think it is?" I asked.

"Might've been nobody," Bear said.

"They stayed too close. No way they were nobody."

"Probably right."

At the next exit, I remained in the shoulder lane until the last possible second. The drivers here didn't seem to mind. There were no honks or gestures aimed in our direction. We rolled to a stop, ten cars deep at a red light. Bear remained turned toward me, his gaze focused through the rear window.

He said, "I think that's them."

"Where?"

"Hell of a long way back."

The light turned green. The line of cars began to roll forward. I turned right and drove past the jumbled mess of gas stations, motels, and fast food restaurants. A few miles later we approached a residential neighborhood. I turned in at the entrance and, after a sequence of right and left turns, found a quiet cul-de-sac.

The engine ticked and banged for a few minutes after shutting it off. I glanced at Bear. His forehead glistened with sweat.

"Want to step out for a few minutes?" I said.

He looked around the cul-de-sac. "These people see the two of us walking around, they'll call the cops."

"Since when did you become afraid of the cops?"

"We're in Maryland now, Jack. You know how I feel about this state."

Bear had once been detained in Baltimore. He'd never told me why, only that the experience had changed him.

I dialed Frank's number. He picked up after the second ring, skipping the pleasantries. "What the hell have you two done?"

"Not sure what you're talking about," I said.

"You know exactly what I'm talking about. Cops made you in New York, Jack. You know that?"

I said nothing. There was one obvious explanation, and it made no sense. McSweeney had tracked Clarissa down. In what could only be due to a fit of anger, Clarissa had given me up. Problem was, she'd never do that.

"Where are you guys?"

"Close."

"There's a diner, about ten minutes outside of Langley."

"I remember the place."

"OK, let's meet there."

CHAPTER 23

THE UNASSUMING DINER situated on 193 a few miles from Langley, Virginia, was popular with the local intelligence community. Walk in during the breakfast or lunch rush and there'd be up to seven or eight agents seated throughout the place. The close proximity also meant that a team could be there within minutes of Bear and me sitting down. That didn't worry us, though. We hadn't done anything on foreign soil that was unsanctioned since our days in the Marines.

And back then we were working *with* the CIA.

I pulled into the deserted parking lot and chose a spot close to the restaurant's door, near the lot's designated exit. To the sides of the building an open field ran fifty yards in either direction. Thick woods stood behind it. Maybe thirty years ago, someone would have been waiting back there. If they were watching us now, it'd be from the sky.

"Ever seen it this empty?" Bear said.

I glanced at the dash clock and cut the engine. "At ten in the morning? No."

On principle alone, Frank and the SIS did not get along with the Agency. Or any other group, for that matter. Toes were often stepped on when both sides should have been working together. I shut down the conspiracy side of my brain before it ran rampant with ideas about how the two groups were working together to take Bear and me down.

I opened my door and placed my left foot on the ground. Looking over my shoulder at Bear, I said, "Don't worry. It's not a setup."

"You sound really convinced." He stepped out of the car and slammed the door behind him. His long shadow cut across the walkway and up the knee high brick exterior, and through the glass into the diner.

I waited for Bear to enter, then exited the vehicle and threw a cautionary glance around the parking lot, the diner's perimeter, and across the street. The air was still. The sun's rays powered through the chilled atmosphere. It felt twenty degrees warmer on the walkway next to the building.

Inside, three waitresses in their late twenties or early thirties sat around a table. None of them looked up at me as I entered. One was smoking a cigarette. The habit had already begun to prematurely age her skin. The other women were working on puzzles in the newspaper. Their clothes and aprons showed signs of a busy breakfast rush.

Bear had seated himself at a table in the opposite corner of the dining room, near the back and close to the kitchen. I took a seat across the table from him. Once Frank arrived, I'd switch sides. For now, I was content to let Bear watch over my shoulder for signs that things were about to get out of control.

My gaze continually drifted toward the door separating us from the kitchen. It sat off kilter, tilted an inch inward. There didn't appear to be a draft holding it in that position. Perhaps the back door stood open to allow the cooks respite from the heat of the fryers and griddles and grills.

Or maybe there was something behind the door, a listening device, that required it to be open to eavesdrop on our conversation.

I pointed it out to Bear. He smiled, said, "Come on, man. You really think the CIA is gonna go old school with some antenna-driven listening device when they can just bug the entire joint?"

It was a good point. Paranoia had slipped in through the cracks, and I had allowed it to envelop my psyche, like dirt and dust settling into a worn and cracked leather bag. I doubted I'd ever be able to scrub the feeling away for good.

Footsteps echoed through the empty dining room. I threw a look over my shoulder and saw that the smoking waitress had left her cigarette smoldering in a tin ashtray. Now she made her way toward us. The smell of burnt tar arrived before she did.

"What can I get for you fellas?" Apparently, the habit had prematurely aged her vocabulary as well.

"Coffee," I said.

"Coffee," Bear said.

"Gonna eat something?" She kept her eyes fixed on her notepad.

"Pancakes." Bear couldn't pass the opportunity up.

"Eggs. Scrambled."

She jotted notes onto her pad, then walked away without ever making eye contact.

Bear shook his head and said, "We couldn't have gotten one of the other servers?"

I looked back at the table near the door. The two women still sat there, heads down, pencils in hand, scribbling on the paper.

"Which one you want?" I said. "I'll go talk to her for you."

"You know my philosophy on relationships."

"Who says you need a relationship? A night with one of them might do you some good, Bear. Loosen you up."

He laughed and said nothing. Several seconds later his face slackened, and he jutted his chin slightly toward the opposite corner of the room. I followed his gaze and saw Frank Skinner approach the fingerprint-covered glass door. I rose, switched sides. Frank entered, nodded at us, gestured to the waitresses that he didn't need their assistance. They hadn't bothered to look up to see if he did. Frank crossed the room with the confidence of a man who had stared down the wrong end of a gun and gone on to slay his assailant.

"Don't bother getting up," he said. He unzipped his jacket, sat down and slid to the mid-point in the booth. "You two make a cute couple. You know that?"

Bear chuckled. I said nothing.

"One of you needs to shave, though. A beard works better on Bear than you, Jack."

"Cut the crap, Frank," I said. "Let's get to the point."

It took a few seconds for Frank's smile to fade. He glanced toward the waitresses at the door, then looked at me. "You owe me, Jack."

"I owe you?"

"Yeah."

"For what?"

"Don't ask me how, but I got a friend at the Bureau to cover for you with the NYPD."

"What'd he tell McSweeney?"

"He backed up your claim that you were a government agent, and that he couldn't divulge your reasons for being there, but those reasons were why you were using an alias. He instructed her to drop any investigation into you, and those you know."

"Clarissa."

Frank nodded. "They had her under surveillance, thinking she'd lead back to you."

I shrugged.

"Will she?" he asked.

"Doubtful," I said.

Bear said, "Really?"

I nodded. "Can we move on?"

"We're not here to talk about your personal life." Frank reached inside his coat. For a moment I tensed. My sidearm was not easily accessible. Frank pulled out a five-by-eight notebook and set it on the table. The cover was solid black. The corners of the pages looked worn. Some were dog-eared, adding to the thickness of the book.

"What's this?" Bear asked.

"This belonged to Brett Taylor. For whatever reason, he kept a record of every person he met. Every meeting he held. Every job he was offered."

"How'd we get it?" I asked.

"This is one of five notebooks that an undercover found in Taylor's apartment."

"How long've we had it?" Bear asked. "And undercover for who?"

Frank said nothing.

"Wouldn't he have noticed it was missing?" I asked.

Frank thumbed through the notebook, never letting a page linger in view for more than a second. "I don't know all the details, but he kept these in a secret location that the agent stumbled upon. I think-"

"You think? That's as bad as acting upon assumption."

"I don't need your hyperbole, Jack. Yes, it's an assumption, but we believe he filed these away and only checked on them when he needed them."

"You trust the undercover?"

"Not my call."

"Whose call is it?"

Frank leaned back against the cushioned patent leather booth and crossed his arms over his chest. One hand went to his chin. He rubbed the coarse stubble and gazed at a spot over our heads. He had no intention of answering that question.

The kitchen door burst open. I thought about the crack, and the draft, and wondered again what or who was back there.

The waitress appeared. She set Bear's food in front of me, and mine in front of him. She didn't acknowledge Frank. Bear slid a plate of toast across the table.

"Not hungry," Frank said. "You two finish up and meet me outside. I've got something else for you out there."

CHAPTER 24

I STACKED MY plate on top of Bear's and slid out of the booth. The kitchen door still sat ajar. I stopped in front of it and pushed it inward with two fingers. The room was lined with stainless steel. Pots. Pans. Shelves. Racks. Did they cook in there, or perform surgery? Maybe both. Smoke rose from the grill and was sucked out through a large ventilation hood. The fryers popped. The griddle sizzled.

And the kitchen was empty.

"Help you?"

I let the door fall shut and turned to face the smoking waitress. Her breath was cherry or berry flavored. Reminded me of the gum we stuffed in our faces as kids in Little League dugouts. She held our plates in one hand, and stuck the other on her hip.

"Just curious," I said.

"Well, get out of my way. Got a smoke break to get to out back."

I figured that's where the cooks were. I went outside alone and met Frank at his car. His nose and cheeks were red. The wind had picked up. Gray clouds had moved in and blocked the sunlight. It felt twenty degrees cooler than when we arrived.

"Get in the car," he said.

I looked for Bear inside the diner. Couldn't locate him.

"Give me the keys," I said.

"Jesus, Jack."

"Not getting in without them."

Frank reached into his pocket and retrieved the keys. There had to be a dozen of them, because they made a racket that was audible over an eighteen-wheeler passing by on 193. Frank tossed the entire set over the roof. I snatched them mid-air and stuffed them in my front pocket, then pulled my pistol. Once seated, I set the gun on the dash.

"Is that necessary?" Frank said.

I shrugged. "Is it?"

He shook his head, then leaned toward me, angling his body so he could reach the backseat. He returned with a black leather briefcase. The chrome snaps clicked as he flipped them back. I placed my hand on the pistol. He lifted the lid, shaking his head. Inside the briefcase were several folders of various colors. He pulled out a green one and handed it to me.

I peeled back the cover and leafed through a dozen photos of Taylor.

"Where's this?"

"De Gaulle."

"He's in Paris?"

"Yup."

"Since when?"

"Few hours ago."

"What's he doing there?"

"Fleeing, I suppose."

"He's not safe in Paris, or anywhere in France. And I figure a guy like him knows that."

Frank held out another folder. I took it, opened it, and looked through pictures of men of Middle Eastern descent. Twenty in all. Ages ranging from mid-twenties to late-forties. I'd seen plenty of pictures like these during my days in the Marines, on loan to the CIA, and again with the SIS when we ran counter-terrorism ops.

"Who're these guys?" I asked.

Frank cleared his throat. "Members of a terrorist organization that has yet to claim ownership of anything. We're not sure of their broader affiliation at this time, although you can take a guess at who. We only recently became aware of them. Their leaders come from a few groups you don't need me to name for you."

"Where are they located?"

"Half the guys in that folder are in France."

"The rest?"

"Sleepers. Spread throughout Europe. We believe they're working on a coordinated attack on London, Frankfurt, Venice, and somewhere in the South of France. Vanity attacks, some of them, designed to scare away tourists. Others designed to scare locals. Venice, we actually think they're hoping to destroy the foundation of part of the city."

"Taylor's connection?"

Frank extended the black notebook toward me. I reached for it. He didn't let go. "Go straight to the last page."

There were a list of names, neatly printed in what I assumed was Taylor's hand. Read like an Afghani, Iraqi, and Syrian roll call. There were three dates listed on the page: one day each in October, November, and December, two days before Christmas. There were locations. All in Paris. All busy locales. In addition to the locations mentioned by Frank, the group wanted to coordinate the attack with a large-scale bombing in Paris. And it looked as though Brett Taylor was directly involved.

"This can't be legit," I said.

Frank handed me another folder. It contained a series of photos I recognized as Taylor's apartment. They started at the front door, led past the kitchen and living room, into the bedroom, and to the closet. One moment the wall was intact, the next a false portion had been removed. Hidden behind that partition was a safe. A slender female hand presented itself. There were more photos of the hand in front of the access panel. Next the safe was opened. Cash, weapons and ammo, and ten spiral-bound notebooks, all the same size and colored red and green and blue and black.

"Undercover snapped these. Left them, of course."

"Jesus. Why? He had to have known better than to keep all these records. We've got to go back and get the rest. Find out how long this has been going on."

Frank shook his head. "That safe was rigged, and Taylor apparently had a way of detonating it from anywhere."

"We're sure?"

"Already sent someone in to verify after you and Bear were in." He pulled a photo from another folder and handed it to me. Same safe, opened and containing the charred and melted remains of its contents.

"Shit."

Frank nodded. "Pretty much. Got one more for you."

I took the final folder and peeled it open. The face of a ghost stared back at me. A Syrian man, fresh-faced, but with a heart full of anger and hatred and evil. Looking up, I caught sight of Bear as he exited the diner. He got in behind me. The passenger side of the vehicle sank another six inches. I pulled the keys from my pocket and tossed them back to Frank.

"What'd I miss?" Bear said.

I ignored Bear's question. "Is this-"

"Bashir al-Sharaa." Frank tightened his grip on the steering wheel, turning his knuckles white.

I turned to the next picture. An older al-Sharaa stared back at me. His beard had partially filled in, although it was thin and scraggly on his cheeks and upper lip. Not entirely out of the ordinary for a twenty-eight year old. But the rest of his face had aged considerably in the four years since I last saw him.

"Who's that?" Bear asked.

"Bashir al-Sharaa is a Syrian terrorist," I said. "Four years ago, he was over here on a student visa, in a master's program at George Mason. By all accounts, he came over a peaceful guy. Then he met and fell under the influence of a radical cleric originally from Jordan by the name of Marafi."

Bear said, "Yeah, I remember that name. They shipped him out not too long ago, right?"

"Yeah," I said. "Remember the cell Frank and I took down in northern Virginia? The one that was kidnapping children, then selling them on the black market overseas, then using the money to build up their network?"

Bear nodded. Frank shot me a look that needed no explanation. Bear had been my outlet. He knew about most of the ops I'd run while employed by the SIS.

"This kid, guy, al-Sharaa, was linked to them. A second-tier kind of guy. Frank and I believed that he was going to be part of a coordinated attack on landmarks in and around D.C. We spent four months monitoring him, anyone he came in contact with, collecting evidence. And it went beyond al-Sharaa. We actually had quite a bit on Marafi, too."

"Then that damn Judge Hegland," Frank said.

"What happened?" Bear asked.

"He threw out everything we had. Said we'd gathered it illegally."

"Wait a minute. I thought you guys didn't have to worry about stuff like that. The whole purpose of the SIS was to avoid that."

"Someone tipped al-Sharaa off that we were moving in," Frank said. "It wasn't soon enough, though. We had him blocked from leaving the country. He got caught at Dulles. The cleric Marafi had a snake on retainer who shot holes in everything we'd done. All of it became inadmissible. And I mean all."

"That's right. We couldn't use any of it against Marafi, or the other guys who were planted. Hegland could've thrown the case out and allowed us to start over. Didn't go down that way, though. He deported al-Sharaa and a few of the others. They went back to Syria, Jordan, Iraq, Afghanistan. Couple were UK citizens."

"So what's this al-Sharaa have to do with us now?" Bear said. "Or is it the cleric?"

Frank turned the key in the ignition. "Fill him in on the rest on the way to the airport. He'll want to know why you two are heading to Paris."

CHAPTER 25

F RANK ARRANGED EVERYTHING. Flights, identities, passports, contacts to meet and supply us after we landed in France.

On the one hand, it was a perfectly executed setup. Bear and I could be pulled out of line while boarding and never be heard from again. But Frank wouldn't do that. If he intended to bring us down, he'd do it the old-fashioned way. A gun, tarp, boat, and cinder blocks. Not letting someone else take us into custody. Not giving himself up as the source, the rat. That would lead to embarrassment, pain, and possibly prison. Not the act of turning us over - Frank could live with that. See, Frank knew all my dirty little secrets. The counterbalance to that was that I knew all of his.

That formed the basis of our strained relationship.

I filled Bear in on the latest information while we drove to Dulles. I tried to pry the surveillance photos and the notebook from Frank. He held onto them. Several pages of text penned by Taylor had been photocopied. Frank left those in our possession. Bear read them out loud while I drove.

"This guy worked for anyone who'd pay him dinner money," Bear said. He stated the figures. Taylor earned a hefty sum for the work he did. He sold out his country, repeatedly, for what a small percentage of the population made in a year. For some, our business was a way to make a good living. But the retirement plan sucked, usually involving the words *early termination*.

"He did just about anything," Bear continued. "Assassinations to espionage."

"Wonder how he managed to keep it all under wraps so long."

"Luck. Someone had to have known, though. Why else send in a spy?" After a pause, he added, "Frank wouldn't give her identity up?"

I shook my head. "You expect him to? Would you want him giving me or you up?"

"Suppose not." He rolled down his window. Cold air rushed into the cabin. The smell of wood smoke lingered long after he cranked the window up and the chill had been replaced by hot, recycled air. "What if this is a set up?"

"I doubt it is. But, if so, we deal with it when the situation presents itself."

Traffic picked up outside of D.C., a sea of red taillights rising and falling along the gentle slopes of the Beltway. I didn't stress over the traffic. Our flight was scheduled to leave at six that evening. We had plenty of time.

Bear dozed off while I navigated the crowded interstate. We reached Dulles at one and dropped the car off in long-term parking. Frank had supplied us each with a suitcase and backpack, although none of the clothes inside fit. Appearances only. The more we looked like travelers, the better our chances of clearing security, which was the first real checkpoint for this operation.

We picked up our boarding passes and checked our luggage. The woman behind the counter barely paid attention to us, performing her job as if she were a robot.

We still had four hours to kill. Security looked light, but that was apt to change at any moment. If we came back in two hours, it could be a three-hour wait. After grabbing a coffee, we made our way through a roped-off maze. The last quarter moved the slowest. I presented identification first. The TSA agent studied it and my face for what felt like twenty seconds. He signed off on my boarding pass and waved me through, handing my ID back as I passed. I waited a few feet away while he did the same to Bear. In a few airports, the agents liked to mess with travelers.

Made the day go by faster. I figured he didn't have the luxury of doing so here since Dulles was typically packed to the gills.

The rest of security required no effort. We made our way to the gate, stopping at a restaurant that served burgers and sandwiches. We ate lunch and had a couple drinks. Bear hated flying, so anything that helped settle his nerves, I was all for.

The seating area at the gate was already half-filled. The area across the terminal aisle remained dark and empty. Better for us. We took a seat in the back near the window. Bear closed his eyes and within two minutes was asleep.

Outside, a choreographed dance took place. Vehicles drove from gate to gate with a purpose. Workers handled luggage, refueling, mechanical inspection. Planes taxied off, rolling lazily until out of sight. A constant stream made the journey. Each reappeared a few minutes later. They barreled down the runway a few hundred yards away. The high-pitched whine of the jumbo jets reached the breaking point as the nose lifted and the plane achieved takeoff.

Every few minutes, I'd survey the scene across the terminal. New faces arrived irregularly. Very few left permanently. None posed an immediate threat. Still, I couldn't put it past Frank to have at least one person on board to monitor our actions in the airport, and after departing the plane. It was the smart thing to do.

As departure time crept closer, the seats filled, and overflow was sent into the walkway and spilled into the empty gate where we waited. The team behind the counter grew from one employee to three to five. The flight crew arrived. They spoke with the gate team, and then disappeared into a small room off to the side.

Finally, boarding began. Frank had sprung for first class tickets, so we were among the first to board. Bear had insisted on the aisle. The combination of the large seat and wide walkway afforded him room he would never find in coach. The big man managed to talk the flight attendant into supplying him with enough alcohol to quiet his resurfaced nerves. Maybe it was the thought of seeing a man of his size break down with anxiety and panic that did the trick. Perhaps it was the benefit of first class.

I stared out the window at the artificially lit tarmac. The various crews moved and worked with a rhythm that indicated their jobs had become second nature.

Twenty minutes later, we pulled away from the terminal. The pilot followed the sweeping road leading to our runway. Bear's breathing became rapid, short inhales and exhales. His knuckles paled as he gripped the armrest. Takeoff was always the worst for him, even when sedated. Once in the air, he settled down enough to order another round and eventually fell asleep.

We left the eastern seaboard behind. The twinkle of city lights was gone. With nothing left to look at through the oblong window, I closed the shutter and leaned back in the plush seat. I dimmed the overhead light and joined Bear in slumber.

CHAPTER 26

B EAR AND I stood out. We were conscious of this, and had to remain vigilant because of it. Didn't matter where we went. The two of us together drew unwanted attention. Unless we stood in line with a group of professional football players, we didn't look like others surrounding us. For this reason, I exited the plane ahead of Bear and joined the line for passport control. This wouldn't prevent someone who was aware and looking from putting two and two together. They'd know our travel plans were related. But to the agents who'd made the decision to let us in, we were much more unassuming separate than standing next to each other.

I passed through without incident, then made my way to baggage claim. Seven minutes later, Bear arrived.

"They question you?" I asked.

"A bit," he said. "Nothing major. We're good to go."

Frank had given me a cell phone and three SIM cards, one each for the UK, Italy, and France, in the event we had to travel. Purchasing a phone he didn't know about was one of my top priorities. I inserted the correct card into the cell and powered on the device. Within minutes it rang.

I answered as Frank had instructed. The man replied as I had been told he would.

"Where can we meet you?" I asked.

"Go to long stay parking, the lot nearest Terminal 1. I have a car waiting for you there. It's been parked for three weeks. We've checked it four times. No problems." He gave me the plate number. "The key is hidden in the rear passenger wheel well. There's a prepaid card in the glove box; use that to pay the parking fee. Call me back at this number after you've left the airport."

We took the light rail to the lot and then walked the rows of cars. The mild temperature made it feel like we were in Nice instead of Paris. Eventually, we found the car. Bear laughed at the sight of the yellow two-door Peugeot.

"Can we remove the front seats and sit in back for more legroom?" he said.

"Don't think there is a back, big man."

He reached into the rear wheel well and retrieved a metal box with a magnetized back. Inside was the key. Bear tossed it to me over the roof. It glinted in the morning sun. I snatched the solo key out of the air and unlocked the door. It wasn't the most comfortable vehicle I'd ever sat in, but it had more room than I imagined. At least my knees weren't touching the dash. Bear, on the other hand, barely fit in his seat.

"I'm gonna kill this bastard when we meet up with him," Bear said.

"It's France. All the cars are like this."

He pointed at a full-sized Audi.

I shrugged. "Most, then."

I navigated out of the lot, merged onto the A1 toward Paris. Traffic was thick, but moving. The air blowing from the vents smelled like the street. There wasn't a recycled air option, so we lived with it. I handed Bear the phone and had him call our contact. The man wanted to meet in the 19th arrondissement, at a park off rue Manin. The call lasted less than thirty seconds. Perhaps one, or both, of us were being monitored.

After exiting the A1, I located a corner store, then found a spot to park a block further. We passed a pet shop, a bakery with fresh bread and pastries in the window, and a small café. Inside the store, we purchased four phones and four SIM cards. I felt better with options. Any calls we had to make to anyone other than our contact, we'd use one of the throw-away cells.

From there, we found the 19th, parked a block off rue Manin, and traveled on foot to a road that circled the lake. I called our contact again.

"I'm sitting alone on a bench, east side of the lake. Black leather jacket. Sunglasses. Dark hair. Jeans. I'm holding a loaf of bread. There are four or five ducks near me. Don't think of trying anything. I have four agents watching my position."

After relaying the description to Bear, we scanned the area. The big man pointed at a bench where a lone man sat, surrounded by ducks. We had our guy. Now I wanted to know where his team was positioned. Finding the first member was simple. Obvious. The contact had wanted it that way. The guy was positioned about a hundred yards past the meeting point. The other three members of his team wouldn't be as easy to locate.

The mild temperature and promise of sunshine had lured several Parisians out of their homes and offices. They flocked to the sidewalks and walking trails and the path that wrapped around the lake. I studied each person as we passed. None presented an immediate threat.

We approached the contact from the south. He raised his left hand into the air. He hadn't turned and spotted us, so I assumed that someone had spoken into his ear.

"That's close enough." The man continued to stare out over the lake. "Jack, you take a seat next to me. Your partner can go one bench to the north. A member of my team will meet him there."

I nodded at Bear. He winced and shrugged, and stood his ground for a second. The contact said nothing. Finally, Bear continued on toward the empty bench. I took a seat next to the Frenchman. His hair was close cropped. His neck was red, irritated from shaving. Perhaps he'd rid himself of a beard recently. His aftershave overtook the smells of the park. He continued to stare over the lake.

"Got a name?" I asked.

"Pierre," he said. "And you're Jack. I think that's all we need to know of one another's names at this time."

"Fair enough. Do you know why I'm here? What brought me here?"

Pierre nodded. "We have a common if not overlapping interest. Someone you're looking for has spent some time with men we are monitoring."

"You're DGSE."

He nodded again, turned his head slightly, made eye contact. "Counterterrorism. Most of the time, at least. I've held many positions. Some similar to yours."

I said nothing.

"I'm here to support you with anything you need during your stay. If you need manpower, you've got it. Help crossing the border, I'm there for you. But I won't be able to allow you to complete your job on French soil. However, if you can detain your target, we can take him into custody and transport him out of the country."

"To where?"

"Across the Channel should suffice."

Light glared at me from across the lake. A watch, strapped to the wrist of a man using a tree for cover, reflected the sun. At his feet was a long, narrow case. The second member of Pierre's team. I leaned forward and looked to the north. Bear was seated next to a woman.

"Where's the fourth?"

Pierre flashed a smile. "You spotted the shooter."

"Yeah."

"The fourth is coming up on us, driving a silver van with tinted windows."

Brakes whined and a diesel engine idled. Fumes engulfed us.

"And I suppose you want us to get in the van."

"Only if you want me to arm you and assist you."

I turned toward Bear again. He looked back at me. We both nodded and rose. The four of us climbed into the van. The driver said nothing. He was probably in his fifties. Gray hair, thinning on top. Leathery skin draped over his cheeks.

Pierre sat next to me in the last row. The woman positioned herself next to Bear in the middle row. We looped around the lake and picked up the shooter. No idea what had happened to the first agent we saw. He had slipped out of my field of view a few minutes prior. Presumably, he had a vehicle close by and would tail us.

The silent ride took no more than fifteen minutes, and carried us through a part of the city I'd never seen before. We pulled up to an unassuming weathered brick building that fit in with its surroundings. The block was lined with warehouses and other similar buildings.

The shooter hopped out before the van stopped. He took a few steps away, case clutched tight. The woman was the first to exit through the sliding side door. I followed Pierre out, and Bear stepped down last. Pierre gestured for us to follow him toward an arched doorway that looked like it had been painted over several times in decades past. Red paint flicked off, revealing a coat of brown beneath. A line etched in the second layer revealed that the color prior had been green. Mortar between the bricks crumbled at my touch. The door felt like sandpaper on my fingertips. To the right of the entryway sat a security panel about five feet off the ground. Pierre punched in a code and waved a card past the device. There was a loud click. One of the doors shifted out a half-inch or so.

The woman reached out, pulled the door open. Pierre gestured for us to enter.

The dark hallway gave little away. The outside light only penetrated a few feet. It could've been a cell, or a room with a dozen armed men, I had no idea. Faith alone carried me forward. It smelled old and dry, like chalk. As the door fell shut behind us, a draft hit me from the right. The dim lights at the end of the hall cast pools of light that spread before me. Four antique sofas, two on either side, lined the hallway. There were three wooden doors on the left, and three steel ones on the right.

"Welcome to my paradise," Pierre said. "Head to the end of the hall, and we'll go through the last door on the right."

I led the way. Footsteps echoed off the hardwood floors like a stampede. I heard, and felt, a gentle hum rising. After passing the midpoint of the corridor, it faded. A generator, maybe. Battery room, possibly. Didn't matter. We weren't going there.

Pale light spilled out from the one-inch gap between the metal door and the hardwood floor. I watched for shadows passing at my feet. Saw none. Reaching out, I grasped the doorknob and turned it to the right. The door was heavy, but swung easily on its hinges.

What I saw in the room was not what I had been expecting.

CHAPTER 27

I'D EXPECTED AN old wooden table, a few chairs, maybe a bench, with a single light bulb dangling on a wire hanging from the ceiling. What I found was a room as deep as the hallway and at least twenty feet wide. Three rows of monitors lined the left wall. There were six pods in the room, each with a computer equipped with a dual- or triple-monitor setup. Three of the pods were occupied by analysts. They didn't look up from their work to inspect the group entering the room.

I assumed they already knew we were there.

The wall to the right was drywall or plaster from the floor to about waist high. The rest was glass, possibly bullet-proof. It looked in on three divided rooms. Each of the rooms had a table, two chairs, and a bench. The benches had three eyebolts. Perfect for handcuffs or chains. None of the rooms was occupied.

Bear stopped next to me and looked at the monitors. His eyes shifted a millimeter at a time as his gaze traveled from screen to screen. They displayed live feeds, maps, data in the form of names and addresses and phone numbers.

Pierre squeezed between us. "Follow me."

He continued, passing between the glass wall and the pods. Anyone seated stopped working and minimized their screens as we walked by. The woman who'd been with us since the park took a seat in front of a computer. She waited until we had passed before unlocking it.

At the end of the room was a door, painted the same as the rest of the room. The handle was thin and long and silver. A security panel was fixed a few inches away. A small red light remained lit on the bottom of the panel. Pierre swiped his card in front of it and the light switched from red to green. Pierre grabbed the handle, pushed it down. The door swung open. Using his body as a prop, he gestured for us to enter the room.

Bear went first this time. He took a step in, then moved to the side. A large antique desk filled most of the space. The wood was dark and rich. The top was clean, and the items present were organized into logical groups. A laptop rested in the middle with its lid closed.

"Please, sit," Pierre said, letting the door fall shut as he passed in front of us. He walked around the desk and took a seat. With his cell phone clutched tightly in his left hand, he used his right to lift the lid of his laptop. For a few minutes, his fingers danced on the keypad. He said nothing and gave no indication that he realized we were still in the room with him. The fan above us hummed rhythmically and cyclically.

"Why'd you bring us here?" I asked.

Pierre stopped typing. He blinked at the screen, and then closed the lid. The chair creaked as he shifted his weight to the right and leaned back.

"We've got a job to do, Pierre. And we're on a major time restriction. I'd appreciate it if you could give us the info we need so we can be on our way."

The Frenchman smiled. "You're not going anywhere."

This time Bear shifted in his seat. I knew from experience that he could launch an attack from his new position; he'd done it in a back office meeting with a target in Brazil a few months back.

Pierre gestured with his hand. "Easy, easy. It's not like that. I'm not detaining you. Everything you're going to need is here in this facility. We have a room for each of you here. Weapons, communications, all of it's here."

I said, "We'd prefer to stay in a hotel where we can operate freely after you give us our starting point."

Pierre pulled a drawer open, reached in, and pulled out a folder, which he placed on the table between us. It was brown and scratched and bound by a string that wrapped around a sewn-on button. It looked like something that had been in the building since early last century. Pierre reached up and switched on a task lamp. Focused light washed over the middle of the desk. The lines etched into the folder stood out. Faded ink revealed dates: 1918, 1937, 1944, 1959, 1968. Pierre unwound the frayed string and peeled back the cover like he was opening a five-hundred-year-old tome. The light reflected off the glossy image within. One by one, the Frenchman then arranged ten six-by-nine black and white photos. Head shots. The first nine were of seven men and two women. Six of the men were Middle Eastern. One of the women was. The remaining man and woman were Caucasian. I recognized them all from the pictures Frank had shown me.

Bear said, "That's al-Sharaa."

Pierre glanced up. "Know him?"

I nodded. "I'm the one responsible for him being deported."

"I'd thank you, but in doing so, you made him my problem. He's the one leading this cell."

"Trust me, Pierre, I'd have rather sent him to a dungeon to answer questions until his heart and lungs gave out."

"Then what happened?"

"Bureaucracy."

Pierre studied me for a moment, and then slid the tenth picture, face down, across the table. I reached for it and flipped it over. I didn't have to study it long.

"Is that your Brett Taylor?" he said.

Bear nodded. So did I. "That's him."

The Frenchman crossed his arms and smiled wide. "Then I know exactly where he is."

CHAPTER 28

PIERRE SAID NO more. He collected the pictures into a pile at the center of the table and shuffled them until they merged into an organized stack. We all stared at the photo on top. Brett Taylor. Finally, Pierre placed them back in the folder, closed and bound it, and returned it to the drawer.

Bear said, "If you know where he is, we need you to tell us so we can apprehend him. This guy can't be on the street any longer than he has been."

Pierre said, "I understand your concern. Taylor's going nowhere, though. And I'm afraid I misled you. I'm not certain of his current location. But I know where he'll be in two days time. Until then, you'll have to remain here, under our care."

I said, "I appreciate your constraints on time, but we have our own, and two days is too long for us to be doing nothing."

Pierre said nothing. And despite our additional questions, the Frenchman revealed no more. Eventually, I stopped trying. Frank would hear from me soon and we'd work it out from there.

Pierre escorted us out of his office and through the long control room, which was now deserted except for a single analyst working at a pod with a triple-monitor set up. She stopped and locked her computer until we passed. We exited into the dim hallway, crossed it, and went through another badge-controlled door. The room we stepped into reminded me of a foyer in a house or apartment building. There were stairs in front of us that went up and down. To the right was a door. Only a wall to the left. I glanced back. A badge was required to get out.

"Upstairs," Pierre said, taking the lead. "You join a short list of foreign associates designated worthy of staying here with us."

"Don't really consider ourselves as staying," Bear said. "Feels more like being held against our will."

Pierre stopped on the landing, turned, held out his hands. "Then feel free to leave. And realize that once you do, you will get not one ounce of support from us. Your passports and the fake names you flew in on will be flagged in the system. Your faces will be plastered throughout our intelligence community as individuals hostile to France." He paused. We didn't move. "Now, I'd prefer to think of you as guests of our unit. I think you'll find the provisions and accommodations more than suitable. Again, please follow me."

We weren't in a position to rock the boat.

Yet.

So we continued on.

At the top of the stairs was a single door. Pierre unlocked it, and then handed me the key he used. A sign of trust, perhaps. Telling me that he wouldn't invade our space. Of course, there had to be another key. There always was.

Beyond the door was a small living area with a kitchen and an island separating the rooms; two bedrooms; a bathroom with a stand-up shower I doubted Bear would fit in. There was a small television. No phone. No computer. I pulled out the cell phone Frank had given me. No signal. I'd wait until after the Frenchman left to check the other phones.

"Sorry," Pierre said. "Situations typically dictate that this area be silent. No outside communication is allowed. It won't be for long. Forty-eight hours max. I promise."

"We don't know each other well enough for you to promise me anything," I said.

Pierre shrugged. "So be it. I think you'll find I'm true to my word, though." He then exited the room through the front door, leaving me and Bear alone.

"I'm not liking this, Jack."

"I hear you. It's not ideal, but they aren't holding us in a cell, so I say we roll with it for now."

I switched the television on. The picture was grainy, with static and a roving vertical band that was tinted blue. I pulled back the blinds to get a view of what lay beyond the building. The only view I had was of a brick wall where a window should have been.

"No way out." Shaking his head, Bear rose and stepped into the kitchen. After rooting through the fridge, he returned with two beers. "Might as well have a drink."

I took the bottle, cracked the top, and drank close to half of it on the first pull. It went down smooth. I could handle a few more.

Bear adjusted the dial on the television. He settled on a French twenty-four hour news station. I was born linguistically challenged, but the big man had a knack for picking up foreign tongues. He sat on the couch and watched the feed intently.

While he caught up on world events, I investigated the apartment. Searched the bookshelves, mattresses, dressers, other furniture. As expected, I found nothing. It wasn't as though they had to bug the place in a hurry. They owned it, which meant any surveillance equipment was built in. Could be in the walls, TV, appliances, pictures. Too many places, so why worry?

I realized the situation was the same at the brownstone - we'd been looking for visible and traditional equipment. However, someone had gone through, installed it within the structure of the building, and used technology that we weren't equipped to sniff out. When everything was done, I wanted to go back to that building and perform a thorough search, perhaps with some new equipment. My contact Brandon could help with that. He knew people from every agency, and was into bleeding-edge technology himself.

"Hey, Jack. Come take a look at this."

I stepped back into the main room. Bear pointed at the television. There was a picture of one of the women from the photos Pierre had shown us earlier. The feed cut from the picture to a scene on a street. A blood-soaked sheet covered a body. A pale and slender arm stuck out, the hand clutching a small caliber pistol.

"What are they saying?"

Bear cleared his throat. "The woman and a companion were dining on a café terrace when a group of men approached. The woman and her associate remained seated while the men surrounded them. There was some shouting, and a few shots were fired. One of the men collapsed. The others carried him to a waiting van. As the men left the scene, onlookers saw the woman on the ground, and her friend face down on the table. Both had blood pouring from holes in their heads."

"Who was the friend?"

Bear shrugged, pointed at the television. "They're only talking about the woman we saw in a photo earlier."

I picked out a few words uttered by the reporter, but not in any kind of organized manner needed to make sense of them. The news channel began showing still images.

"These are from CCTV," Bear said. "They've started incorporating some of the same things you find over in London and South Korea with the cameras." He paused, then added, "They didn't say that. My observation only."

I studied each picture for as long as it remained on the screen. I recognized faces from the pictures Frank and Pierre had shown us. Absent was al-Sharaa. Expected, considering his role within the group. One picture stood out. It was taken from the direction the men had approached from, and swept past the café terrace. The photo had caught a man exiting a store, looking to the left.

Staring at the unfolding scene.

"Christ," I said.

"What?" Bear said.

"Brett Taylor." And then the picture changed again to a crowd of people gathered around the two dying women. "We've got to get a hold of that photo."

"How?"

"Pierre, or Frank... I don't friggin' care how we do it. We need it in our possession so someone can analyze it. And we need every photo snapped from that same camera before and after that moment."

Bear kept his focus intently on the television screen. "Don't see what difference it would make, Jack."

It made every difference. "That photo along with others would put together a timeline. Which direction he went after exiting the store. Which direction he came from to enter it. What he was doing prior to going in."

The newscast cut to a commercial, allowing Bear to re-channel himself. "I got you. Sorry. Was still looking for anyone else we might know in the footage."

I waited for Bear to continue.

"So, you think he might have come ahead of time, maybe as a spotter for the terrorists. He saw the woman dining on the terrace and called it in after slipping into a store."

I shrugged. "Possibly. It's that, or he was dining with the woman and her friend, or her associate, whoever she was, and left to get something from the store. It was sunny. Maybe he went in and bought those sunglasses he was in the process of putting on."

"In which case, he was pretty lucky, again, that he wasn't around when the guns showed up."

"There's one thing that doesn't jibe, though, Bear."

"Pierre - and Frank for that matter - thinks all of these people were working together."

"They might have been. Perhaps the woman was working with someone-"

"The associate."

"-and giving up secrets."

Bear rose and walked past me on the way to the kitchen. He opened the fridge and fished out two more beers. He cracked them open and discarded the caps into the garbage can. They bounced around the unlined can a few times.

After taking a pull from the bottle, Bear said, "What the hell we gotten ourselves into this time, Jack?"

I shrugged, laughed, said, "You surprised? Frank's been dragging me into these kinds of messes for a couple of years now. It was one of the driving forces that led me to resign my position in the SIS."

It had been a surprise that they let me walk away and rejoin the civilian world. Of course, the release did not come without strings attached. Although Frank technically *asked* me to do jobs for him, there was no option to decline. The guy kept a file on me, and if he ever decided to turn it over to anyone outside our shadowy world, I'd go away for a long time. And so would he, because I'd roll over on him, too. It created a tenuous relationship, at best.

Bear set his bottle on the table, then leaned back, throwing his thick arms up in the air and letting them come to rest behind his head. "So, what do we do now?"

"I guess we wait for Pierre, unless you know of a way out of here."

"I think we're probably safest right here."

I laughed. "When did safety become a consideration?"

Bear joined me. "I guess never." He lowered his arms and crossed them over his chest. "Christ, Jack, I dunno. Don't like this. Don't like it one bit."

Before I could respond, the door behind us whipped open and cracked against the wall.

CHAPTER 29

BEAR AND I hopped off the couch and spun to face the man who'd burst into the apartment. We both held our beer bottles like projectile weapons, ready to launch. Liquid poured from mine, half landing on the floor, the other half on my shoe.

Pierre stood in the doorway, arms out, raised in front of his chest as if to thwart our attack. Out of breath, he coughed while trying to inhale. I wondered if he'd sprinted from another location.

"We have to go now," he said.

"Go where?" I said.

"We have to move on them." Pierre took a step in, chest heaving, rapidly forcing air in and out. "They'll be gone by midnight, and I'll have wasted two years on nothing."

"Why'd they kill the French woman?" I asked.

Pierre shook his head. "I don't know. How do you figure she's French?"

"A guess."

"The pictures on the news, you have access to them?" Bear asked.

"Yes, and I'm having Laure pick them up right now. She should be here any minute."

"It'll be all the pictures?" I walked around the couch, set the empty bottle on the kitchen counter. "We need to see what happened before the incident."

The Frenchman had caught his breath. His voice was still tight, terse. "I'm sure we can get them, but I don't know what good that would serve."

I glanced at Bear. The big man gave me an almost imperceptible shake of his head. I decided to keep the ace up my sleeve and not tell Pierre about Brett Taylor's presence at the café. It was only fair, as it was obvious Pierre wasn't sharing everything he knew.

"We need to be armed," Bear said, "if you expect us to take part in anything tonight."

"I've got everything you need downstairs. Body armor, sidearms, suppressed HK MP7s, night vision, communications." Pierre assumed our involvement. He turned and exited the room.

We followed him down the stairs and across the hall into the situation room. Bodies filled the pods. Fingers danced across keyboards. The monitors that lined the wall blurred with data. One of the interrogation cells was occupied. A lone Middle Eastern man sat hunched over the table, hands tied behind his back. His lips trembled with prayer. His body rocked a few inches back and forward. The other cells would be occupied in time. The only question I had was where would they place the overflow.

Maybe they didn't plan on having any.

Pierre waved us over to where he was standing. A woman waited next to him. She was tall and lean, with strawberry blonde hair that didn't match her olive complexion. One of the two had to be fake. She said her name was Laure.

The four of us moved to Pierre's office. After he'd taken position behind his desk, Laure placed photos on the table. I anxiously awaited the picture of Brett Taylor exiting the store while a group of alleged terrorists surrounded one of their own. I wanted to see where Taylor had been when the shots were exchanged.

She dropped the last picture and said, "This is everything they had at the station."

"No, it's not," I said.

"Beg your pardon?" her English was crisp, neutral in accent, like she'd spent a lot of time in Washington D.C., or some other melting pot area.

"There's one missing."

"I'm afraid you are mistaken."

"I saw it on the news broadcast. The men had surrounded the woman and her associate. They stood around the table, hovering over their prey, right before the shots were fired."

"What does it matter?" Pierre said. "We know what happened then, as well as right before and after. I agree with you, Jack, that we need to see the events that unfolded prior to the group's arrival, but we don't have that evidence at this time. I'll get someone on it."

The time wasn't right to mention Taylor's appearance, so I said nothing. When we had the pictures, I'd bring it up. I switched the topic to the plan for tonight's activities.

"We were still in the planning phase," Pierre said. "We have the layout of the house, and we know the identities of most of the residents in the surrounding area. But..."

"What?" I said.

"Across the street, and two houses to the right..." He pushed away from his desk. "We're unsure about them. Could be spotters."

"How much extra manpower can you get?" I said.

"Another ten." He shot Laure a look. "Maybe fifteen."

"Send a team into each house, through the back. Lock them down."

Pierre continued to stare at Laure. She shrugged. After a moment, they both nodded.

"I'll get everyone activated." She brushed past me on her way out. Her shoulder felt like a stone knife against my chest.

Pierre slid forward and began tapping on his keyboard. A few strokes and clicks on his mouse were followed by the whirring of his printer. The machine lit up and began spitting out paper. After it finished, Pierre rose and gathered ten or so sheets and brought them back to his desk. In the same manner that Laure had laid out the photos, Pierre spread the papers on his desk. When he was done, we were staring at the blueprints of a house.

"Three stories and a basement," he said. "Exits in front and back. Fire escapes from every rear window. Obviously this is a row home, so no way out on the left or right side."

"Unless they own the houses to the side and broke through."

Pierre shrugged. "Unlikely, even if they own them. Those are brick firewalls."

"Man can break through brick," Bear said.

"So we watch the neighbors' back yards too," Pierre said. "We'll already have a team on the street waiting in case any of them flush out through the front." He traced a line through the front door to where the street would be located.

"What's behind?" I asked. "Another line of row homes?"

"A little backyard," Pierre pointed with his pencil, then used the device to create a line approximately ten to twenty feet from the house. "A fence." He shaded in the area behind the fence. "An alley." He looked up. "Then, a mirror image."

I said, "We need to know about the houses on the next street."

Pierre nodded. "We're on that."

The three of us remained silent for the next couple minutes, all staring at the papers aligned neatly on Pierre's desk.

"How many are we expecting to be there?" I asked.

Pierre drew in a sharp breath and exhaled through tightly pressed lips. "I won't have an answer to that until it is time to move. Best guess? I'd say six to eight heavily armed men, two to four of whom are prepped to be jihadists."

"The ones to carry out the attacks in Paris," I said.

Pierre nodded, said nothing.

"So we don't give 'em time," Bear said. The big man clenched his fists and released them. "Shoot fast. Shoot to kill. We already know the sons of bitches are guilty as sin."

Pierre looked from Bear to me. He held my gaze for a moment before redirecting his focus toward the door. I looked back to check for someone's presence. There was no one there.

"What is it?" I said.

"This is why you're here." Pierre glanced down. Shadows darkened his face. "My team and I are support only."

"I'm not following you."

"We don't have everything in place, you see. We can't just go in there and take them out. Arresting them will only result in their expulsion from my country. And, as you can imagine, that is unacceptable. We let them walk, that's a win. They'll triple their ranks. And they'll ride back in with explosives strapped to their chests, prepared to detonate them in the most congested areas of our major cities on their first day back."

I said nothing. Bear cleared his throat, but remained silent.

"Under the cover of dark, two American secret agents infiltrated a house known to be associated with a terrorist cell. The Americans neutralized the men. DGSE became aware of the operation only after it was carried out. They are looking for the American operatives at this time."

"You serious?" I said.

Pierre nodded once, letting his gaze bounce from me to Bear.

"You want us to go in and carry this out for you? Kill seven or eight trained men?"

"They'll get away, Jack. Bashir al-Sharaa will get away again. Do you want these bastards leaving, reconfiguring themselves, then coming back even more powerful? That's what happens every time. It emboldens them. Think of all the innocents that will suffer because of this. We know they're preparing to strike. We have a chance to put an end to them. And the intelligence we'll gather from their house will allow us to take out another twenty or thirty terrorists."

"And what about the next one after that? And the one that follows them? As long as you leave the head, Pierre, you're totally screwed, because these people are going to run you over if this is how you act. Why not let them flee? Follow them. They're bound to lead you to the next level."

"It's not my choice." Pierre's ears turned a shade of red I hadn't seen before. His cheeks came close to matching it. He didn't speak. Probably couldn't, with the way his breathing had gone ragged and inconsistent. Finally, he calmed enough to continue. "Do this for me, and I'll place every resource I have on finding Brett Taylor. And when we do, I'll place my own gun to his head and pull the trigger. Tonight, we can solve each other's problems. Are you with me?"

CHAPTER 30

THE LIGHT OVER Pierre's desk flickered. Shadows grew and retreated. Stale air forced from an overhead vent cooled my damp forehead. Bear, still seated next to me, mumbled something that sounded as though he thought we should reject Pierre's offer. The big man was free to go. I had the chance to right a four-year-old mistake by killing al-Sharaa. I was willing to see this through for that reason alone.

"I'm in," I said.

Bear groaned, turned toward me. "Dammit, Jack."

Pierre slapped his desk and rose, barely able to contain his rejuvenated energy. "We should get moving while there's still light."

Bear slid back until his chair slammed into the door, sealing us in. He pointed a finger at Pierre. Started to speak. Paused. "Jack, I don't think this is a good idea. We're here for one reason, and one reason only. Getting caught up in French DGSE's operations is only going to lead to trouble for us. I know why you're doing this. It's still a bad idea."

Pierre settled into his seat, slowly, as if he were a balloon with a slow leak. For a moment he stared at the planner laid out on the corner of the desk. Then his focus shifted to me. Both men held their breath, waiting for my response.

"We've got one thing to do, Bear, and that's take down Taylor. I don't care how it goes down. The one thing I know is that I don't want to see is

Taylor leaving France alive. We escort him to the UK, who knows who he's got waiting and watching there? We do this now, and the situation is over. Done with Taylor, McLellan, Skinner, all of them."

Shaking his head, Bear said, "How do we know he's gonna hold up his end of the bargain? And how do we know he's not gonna have us thrown in jail or subject us to endless interrogation after we do his dirty work?"

I looked at Pierre. The man's face was solemn, tight. "We'll have to trust him."

Bear grabbed a handful of his own hair and pulled back, laughing. "Jesus Christ, Jack. I've heard everything now."

"You have my word as a Frenchman." Pierre leaned over his forearm, halfway across the desk.

"Fuck the French," Bear said. A moment later he offered a weak apology, then added, "We need additional assurances, Pierre."

"We're running out of time." The Frenchman tapped at his watch without breaking off the stare between him and Bear. "You tell me what assurance I can give you that is suitable, and I'll do it."

Bear rose and took a step toward the desk. His knees rapped against the metal casing. He started to extend an open hand toward Pierre. "You come inside the house with us."

If there was one area of the operation that concerned me, that was it. For all we knew, Pierre was operating in coordination with Langley, and this entire operation was a set up aimed at framing Bear and me. We'd be operating illegally in a foreign country. A DGSE team who had been monitoring us would be in place. They'd bust and detain us, before sending us off to a CIA field office. Or maybe they'd prosecute us in France.

The only thing that moved was Pierre's eyes. His hands remained flat on the desktop, his back rigid. How he responded would tell us everything about any ulterior motives. His gaze shifted from Bear, to me, back to Bear. Slowly, he rose, pushing off the desk. Standing erect, he extended his hand and grasped Bear's.

"I will enter the residence with you. But fair warning, should you two do something stupid prior to leaving France and get pinched, I could be forced to testify and recount the events as I witnessed them." Pierre's eyes widened after making the threat. I glanced down. The muscles on Bear's forearms bulged. His fingers were pale. The tips of Pierre's were red, ready to burst.

"Easy, Bear," I said. "He's just covering his team and himself. That's all."

The relief in Pierre's face was instantaneous the moment Bear released the man from his grip. Pierre held his right hand with his left and massaged the pain away. He said nothing. A gesture toward the door was his signal that it was time to leave.

In the situation room, we met with Laure and the two male agents who were to accompany us. One of them, a man who introduced himself as Jean, led Bear and me to another section of the building. He armed us each with an HK 9mm pistol and an HK MP7 equipped with a suppressor. We donned body armor. Earwigs and microphones were provided for constant communication. Since the operation would take place in the dark, the man presented us with night vision goggles.

Pierre, Laure, and the other male agent were waiting for the three of us at the rear of the main hall. Pierre nodded, pulled a panel off the wall, and reached inside. A moment later, a hidden door opened to a courtyard, where a black van with tinted windows idled a few feet away. Jean exited and took the driver's seat. The rest of us piled in. There was no sense of rank or authority inside the vehicle. We said little during the thirty minute drive. This was a kill mission. What was there to say?

As we neared, Pierre received a phone call. He listened and said nothing. After hanging up, he broke the silence. "We've got teams in place at the suspect houses, as we discussed. Snipers are positioned out of view. They can provide support if necessary, but only as a last means of defense."

"Visuals on the men at the house?" I asked.

"It's been under surveillance for a while now. Eight men are present."

"Taylor?"

Pierre said nothing. He gave no indication whether his intelligence indicated Brett Taylor's presence at the terrorist's house.

"Pierre? What about Taylor?"

The Frenchman threw a cursory glance toward his team, then said, "Let's take care of this first, Jack. Then we'll handle the other situation."

The van stopped in the middle of a residential street. Porch lights illuminated the front stoops that lined the road. Cars were packed tight to one another along the curb. Cracks in the drawn blinds and curtains gave a glimpse inside the family life of many of the street's tenants.

"Let's go," Pierre said.

Laure slid the side door open. She, Jean, and the other male agent exited. Bear followed. Pierre grabbed my arm, halting me.

"We don't think Taylor is here right now." His gaze drifted toward his advancing team. "But we do have a location to follow up on. We'll go tonight, after we finish here."

I nodded and broke free of his grasp. Sliding out of the van, I breathed in the crisp, wood smoke-laden air. Clouds lined the dark sky. The last traces of the sun lingered to the west, the direction we walked. Fire fueled me. Anticipation of taking out al-Sharaa overruled every emotion. No matter what I did, who I helped, who I saved, the failures stuck with me. Tonight, I had the chance to erase one of my worst ones.

Pierre and I caught up with the others. We joined five additional agents, three of whom I recognized from the situation room. One of the men stepped forward. He had blond hair, and pale blue eyes, and skin that seemed translucent under the street lamps. A scar ran the length of his left cheek, blending into the crow's feet that surrounded his eye.

"We're one block south. There's an alley about six meters from here, between two fences. That will deposit us directly across the street from the target house. Teams are in position in the two houses we had no ownership information on. They've locked them and the occupants down. Snipers are in position. Should you need them, call. Same with us. My team is going to position one block north. Pierre and his team will remain on either end of the alley."

We'd caught the attention of a few residents, who watched from their windows and porches. Probably figured we were cops about to bust someone for drugs.

The blond man continued: "You can abort at any time up till you make entry. After that, well, you know the drill. Give us five minutes to get into position." With that, the man and his team slipped into a van and disappeared into a right turn.

"You didn't tell him," I said to Pierre.

He shook his head.

"What?" Laure asked.

"I'm accompanying them into the house."

"You know what you're risking?"

Pierre nodded at her. "It's the only way, Laure. If I don't do it, they skate."

Bear pulled me aside. "You still sure about this?"

I shrugged. "Sure, why not?"

"Up to eight men. Close confines."

"These guys are experts at blowing themselves up, Bear."

He clasped his hands behind his head. "You know that's not true. These guys've been trained in camps. You've seen the propaganda videos. We witnessed this type of fighting in Baghdad."

"I know, Bear. I know. And we left undefeated. For what it's worth, I bet on us. Add in a power outage and night vision, odds are heavily stacked in our favor."

Pierre's phone rang. He answered it, nodded a few times, and hung up. "They're in position. Laure, have the grid shut down the moment we reach the end of the alley."

She nodded, then directed two other two men to take position at the alley's entrance.

"Pierre," I said.

"Yeah?"

"Silence that phone. I don't want any surprises once we enter that house."

We walked down the narrow alley and stopped shy of the end. The street in front of us looked like a mirror image of the one we'd left behind. I let my eyes go unfocused by staring at a point to the left of a light. I watched, waited, on alert for any movement within my field of view.

Pierre gestured toward the house. I scanned the rooflines, spotted one sniper. Wondered where the others were.

Jean approached and joined us.

"What the hell are you doing?" Pierre asked the man.

"My OCD won't allow for a group of three to enter that house. It has to be done in pairs."

Pierre shook his head, and then rubbed his eyes with his thumb and forefinger. It killed the man to deviate from the plan. As far as I was concerned, this whole thing was a deviation.

"Do not shoot unless fired upon," Pierre instructed Jean.

The terrorists' front porch light was on. The window to the right of the door was bright. The other was illuminated, barely, with flickering blue light. A television. Soccer, maybe, or cricket. I pictured al-Sharaa, with his sparse beard and thin mustache, leaning back on a couch, watching the game. The upstairs lights were off. Of course, that was only half the house, and it didn't mean the rooms were unoccupied. On cue, someone spoke over the comm system.

"Upper levels are dark in the rear."

So we had as close to confirmation as we would get that the terrorists were gathered downstairs. Or hanging out upstairs in the dark. The more of them in one room, the better. I could take down three before they could react; Bear could do better. The trick for me would be to keep the al-Sharaa tunnel vision at bay.

Laure's voice boomed through the earwig. "Going dark now."

At that moment, street lamps and houselights shut off like dominos in rapid succession from one end of the block to the other. The element of surprise was ours. Inside the terrorists' house, men calm enough to detonate themselves would grow apprehensive. Some would search for flashlights, using their cell phones to guide them. One or two might reach for a weapon, believing that there was no such thing as a random power outage. But mostly, they'd be out of sync with each other. Eliminate comfort, disrupt routine - that's how you bring down a group like this. But they'd only be that way for a moment or two. And that's why we had to act immediately.

CHAPTER 31

THE COLD WINTER wind barreled down the street, hitting us from the side. I became aware of the sweat that lined my body for the first time. I blinked away the tears filling my eye as a result of the gusts. The night vision goggles afforded no protection. Setting the chill aside, I climbed the porch steps and looked through the cracks in the curtains. A sea of green lay before me.

No trace of anyone.

Bear joined me, with Pierre and Jean following close behind. The plan was for them to cover us as we entered.

Getting in was easy. The door was unlocked.

I went in low, clearing the first visible area. After Bear entered, I moved past the door. I had to trust that Pierre and Jean would act accordingly. A feat more difficult due to the necessary silence. We'd never worked together, but tactics were tactics, and training was training. They'd done this before.

Room by room, floor by floor, we investigated the house. And we found it empty.

The thought of Bashir al-Sharaa slipping out of my grasp once again gnawed at my gut.

Returning to the first floor, Pierre spoke into his mic. "Teams, any activity on the street or behind the house?"

Four responses. All negative.

"The basement," I said.

We found the entrance off the kitchen. I split the blinds on a rear window and surveyed the backyard. It wasn't much of a space, running the width of the home and about ten feet deep, enclosed by a wooden privacy fence. The grass was dead. A couple old tires were propped against the fence. No people. No dogs. Empty.

Jean pulled a stun grenade from his pocket. He reached out for the basement door.

"What the hell are you doing?" I said.

"If they're here," Jean said, "they're hiding down there." He aimed his finger like a gun toward the door. "And I intend to neutralize them."

I grabbed his wrist and pulled him back. "You don't know what's down there. I once walked into the basement of a suspected terrorist's house and found a dozen abducted kids living in a dirt pit."

Jean yanked his arm away. "I'm going."

I grasped the MP7 in both hands, stopped short of aiming at him. "It'll be the last thing you do."

The man took a step back. He looked toward Pierre and spoke in French. I translated what he said as, "Are you going to let him do this?"

Pierre nodded and extended his hand. Jean relinquished control of the grenade.

As a parting shot, the man said, "I'll go last, and you'd better duck if I have to shoot." He retreated to the corner. The night vision goggles shielded our eyes from view. Despite that, I felt Jean's stare burn through me.

"We ready?" Bear said.

"Go," I said.

He reached out, grabbed the handle, and pulled the door open. We waited, outside of view, for a moment. I peeked down the stairs first. With Bear covering me, I traveled halfway, lowered myself, and scanned the rest of the basement. The draft blowing up the stairs had told me what I would find.

Nothing.

"It's clear." I pulled a flashlight from my utility belt and switched it on.

The stairs creaked under Bear's weight. I panned the light across the room, freezing the beam on the open hatch in the corner.

"The hell is that?" Bear said.

"Escape hatch," I said.

Pierre hurried down the stairs with Jean close behind.

"Christ," the Frenchman said. "How?"

"They must've received advanced warning of the raid," I said.

Pierre cursed in French, then said something to Jean. He spoke so quickly I couldn't decipher any of it. Before I could ask Bear, Pierre brushed past us with his flashlight out and switched on. He walked to the hatch and illuminated the hole in the floor.

"We need to follow it," he said.

"I think the better idea is to wait until you get another team in here and send them down," Bear said. "No telling where that leads, if anywhere. These guys could be long gone, man. That might be a trap."

Pierre activated his mic and relayed instructions in French. From what I translated, he wanted a team to start combing through the house, looking for computers and any paper documentation.

"I'm going down there," he said. "Switch to channel four, and I'll relay everything I see."

Bear and I adjusted our comms and watched as Pierre descended into the hole.

"I'm down about ten feet," Pierre said. "It goes one way, further than my light can illuminate. It's maybe six feet high, three feet wide. Uneven. Smells stale." His breathing grew loud and ragged.

"What is it?" I said. It was no use. He had his mic activated, shutting us off.

A few tense seconds passed, during which time Pierre's breathing became labored. Finally, he spoke. But the words were garbled.

The line went silent.

"Pierre?"

Ten seconds passed. Nothing. Another ten. I called for him again. A burst of static blared through the earwig.

"I'm here," he said.

"What's down there?" Bear and I had inched our way forward and were now hunched over the hole in the floor, fingers dug into the cool, damp dirt, staring down into the darkness.

When Pierre spoke again, we heard his voice through the tunnel and the communications device. "You three need to get the hell out of here."

"What is it?" I said.

"Explosives!"

I emerged from the house, arms waving, yelling for Laure to call the local police and fire department, and to start evacuating the neighborhood. Pierre hadn't responded to my attempts to contact him while rushing up the stairs and out of the home. I switched back to the original comm channel and heard him frantically barking orders in French.

Within minutes, blue strobes were bouncing off the clouds. Police cars parked sideways at the end of the street, blocking access. Cops emerged from the darkness, running toward us. Soon they would go door to door, rousing people from their lazy evenings and directing them away from the detonation area.

Only they didn't make it in time.

The fireball blinded me, and the force of the blast knocked me back. I was unconscious. Perhaps stunned. My skin burned. My nostrils, mouth, and throat felt scorched. Regardless, when I pushed myself off the ground and wiped the dirt and ash away, I saw a pile of rubble where four homes had been strung together. To either side were standing structures, engulfed in flame. The smoke and wall of fire made it impossible to tell what the street a block over looked like.

Pierre stood a few feet away, his hands wrapped behind his head. Looked up at the orange sky. Yelled. A primal sound. I didn't need a translation to feel the pain. The team in the house next door hadn't escaped. Pierre had lost five men.

CHAPTER 32

THE VAN APPEARED out of no where. Perhaps the driver had traveled on the sidewalk, or maybe he'd pushed park cars out of the way with the bumper. I didn't know. Hadn't seen. He stopped in front of us. Laure got in, asked us to grab Pierre. Bear and I dragged the Frenchman to the van and lifted him onto the middle seat. Tear tracks snaked their way down his soot-covered face, which remained in a state of distraught rage the entire trip back to his office.

We pulled through the security gate, into the square courtyard. Laure slipped out first. She opened the rear building door and waited for the rest of us. Pierre kept his gaze fixed on a spot on the ground always a foot ahead. That was the only way I knew how to get through something like this: keep taking that next step.

Laure, Bear, and I entered the situation room. She went to one of the pods, tapped on the keyboard. Six monitors on the wall flickered to life, each relaying a separate news feed. They all ran footage of the explosion's aftermath. It looked like a terrorist bombing because it had been one. Bodies covered with crimson stained sheets lined the street in front of the home. A charred foot stuck out from one. The fires had spread. Several houses stood ravaged and gutted. Men and women wept openly in the street, mourning the loss of neighbors and loved ones and people they had never met.

Pierre entered the room and came up to me. Said, "Speak with you for a moment, Jack?"

I followed him into his office. He rounded his desk, fell back in his chair, letting his head rest against the padding. For a moment, he stared at the ceiling and his eyes misted over. Finally, he glanced at me.

"Sorry for getting you into this. I used you, and in doing so, put your life in danger."

I leaned back against the wall and crossed my left leg over my right. Stuck my hands in my pocket. My fingertips traced the piles of dirt that had ended up there when I was knocked back.

"I... Bear and I knew the risks going into this. Had the targets been there, it could have been worse for us. That was a chance I was wiling to take in exchange for your assistance helping us bring Taylor in."

His eyes rolled back in his head. He brought his hand to his face and shielded them. "I lied."

I took a step forward. "About helping us?"

The first admission of guilt out of the way, Pierre looked at me. "I'd help if I could, Jack. But the truth is, we know nothing of this Brett Taylor. He's not associated with these terrorists. Someone tossed out feelers, and we went with our story because we thought it would mean American intelligence sharing information with us. Hell, they knew about these men." He paused and allowed a thin smile to form. "Instead, it brought you and your large partner to me."

"Fair trade." I hid my anger. "At least I had a moment where I thought al-Sharaa would be stopped."

Pierre laughed, briefly. His somber demeanor returned. "I figured we'd do the dance for a while, then that'd be it. You'd lose interest, or your real purpose for being here would be revealed. Then, the cell decided to leave after today's incident. You and Bear provided me the opportunity to prevent that, so I took it."

"And now five of your men, not to mention who knows how many citizens, are dead."

Pierre's eyes misted over as he nodded. "I'm sorry, Jack. I deceived you for my own gain."

"No honor among thieves. That's what they say, right?"

Pierre said nothing. The distant gaze had returned. His thoughts obviously turned toward the men he'd lost and the families he would have to face, knowing it was his slip up that had cost their loved ones their lives.

I turned and reached for the door handle.

"Jack?"

I stopped, but didn't look back. "Yeah?"

"If there is anything I can do to help, anything at all, don't hesitate to ask."

I looked over my shoulder. We shared an awkward stare for a moment. Then I said, "I think you've done enough."

A moment before the door fell shut, I heard Pierre sob. Tonight would be a long one for him. He'd take solace somewhere. A line, a bottle, a woman. Or perhaps a bullet, if he didn't have the fortitude to carry on.

Bear and Laure were the only ones occupying the control room. The ghosts of the slain remained in the shadows. The others had yet to return.

Bear met me halfway across the room. "How's he doing?"

"Pretty shaken up."

"Imagine so."

"He lied to us."

"What?"

"About Taylor. They've got no intel on him. Nothing at all. The whole thing was a song and dance to see if we were holding back information on the cell they'd been monitoring."

Bear turned away, toward the monitors on the wall. For a moment his expression became one of remembrance and sorrow. The blast, the shockwave, the death. He looked back at me. Anger crossed his face.

"So what now?" he asked. "Call Frank?"

I shrugged. Said nothing.

"He might be in on it, Jack."

"I don't think he'd have gone to this much trouble. Why send us away from his target?" I thought of the mentally weakened man hiding in the back office. Pierre would be easy to get information out of; he had little to hold onto at the moment. "We can go ask him, but I think it's a waste of time. I'm willing to bet that Frank thought Pierre could help us out."

"Let me handle him." Bear pushed past me and walked toward Pierre's office. His heavy footsteps competed with the resting computer towers. Outside the door, Bear looked back, and added, "Who knows what kind of moment you two shared in there."

I suppose it was meant to be funny, but neither of us laughed.

Laure looked down as I turned toward her. Her fingers pecked at the keyboard. I wondered how much she knew. Was the whole set up Pierre's doing? Or was his team involved?

I approached her. She ignored me. Behind her, I asked, "How well did you know them?"

Laure's hands froze over the keyboard, each arched at the middle knuckle. She turned her head to the side. Her damp cheek answered my questions. A tear fell from the corner of her right eye, gliding easily down a path that had been made by several tears before it.

"I see." I grabbed her shoulder, squeezed, then walked across the room, toward the entrance, where I pulled out a chair and waited.

Eight or nine silent minutes later, Bear exited Pierre's office. He walked past Laure, stopped in front of me.

"Anything?"

Bear shook his head. "If there's more, he ain't telling me."

I didn't think the Frenchman would. Any other secrets he held would go to the grave with him. Or the review board.

"But," Bear continued, "he has arranged for a car to take us to the airport. And a friendly agent is going to accompany us past security."

"You believe him?"

"I listened in on the call. We're clear to take off." Pierre's door opened. Bear looked back. The Frenchman nodded. "And we called a friend back home. VIP treatment awaits."

"Last time someone told me that..."

Bear waited a moment for me to continue. "What?"

I shook my head. It didn't matter if we were detained. I had enough favors to call in that we'd be out within twenty-four hours. Of course, that was about all we had left, due to my deal with the Old Man. So it'd be slightly more than a minor nuisance to deal with.

"We good to go, Jack?"

Were we? I doubted it. Did we have a choice? No.

Bear asked again.

"Yeah," I said. "We're good."

Pierre said something softly across the room. He closed his cell phone, stuffed it in his pocket and walked toward us. "The car will be here in two minutes." After a pause, he added, "Jack, I just want to -"

"Save it, Pierre. You want to make this up to me, then be ready to do anything I need when I call on you."

He nodded and turned away. "Laure, please see our guests out."

CHAPTER 33

OUR PLANE DEPARTED before midnight. As Pierre had promised, getting through De Gaulle required no effort. An escort led us to our gate and waited with us until we boarded. He said nothing. Made no eye contact. Sat two rows away from us.

The entire time, I expected a group of heavily armed men to appear and arrest us.

It never happened.

The first hour of the flight required a certain level of intestinal fortitude. The plane dropped forty, fifty feet at a time as we hit air pockets. The pilots did their best. Didn't matter to Bear as he nearly ripped the armrest out from between us. Nothing was going to calm him. At least, not until the plane settled.

And it did.

I slept the rest of the flight. Bear might have, too.

Eight hours after departing, we landed at Dulles. It was dark out, and would be for another three hours. Bear's contact met us at the gate and provided an escort through the empty airport. Customs agents backed down upon viewing the man's credentials. I didn't recognize the man. Bear wouldn't reveal the guy's identity. Loyal to a fault.

After his contact left us, Bear took off to rent a car. Not knowing who else might be aware of our arrival, we figured that was the best option.

Twenty minutes later we were on the Beltway. The most dangerous time to drive. Double- and triple-shifter workers were on their way home, as were the partiers. Both groups straddled the interstate's dashed lines in hopes of arriving home alive. Early risers, meanwhile, were kicking off their day with yoga, a jog, oatmeal, whatever kept them fueled. Two people from different groups could live next door to each and never know the other.

"Know where you're going?" Bear asked.

I nodded, said nothing.

"Been there before?"

"Twice."

"When was the last time?"

"Summer before I left SIS. Frank held a barbecue for the team to celebrate his latest promotion. He'd become my boss, but we still worked as partners. After I left, he never partnered up again. Focused on running the show."

"So you're sure he still lives there?"

"Can't be sure of anything, Bear. If it's not him, we'll exit quietly into the dark night."

"Poetic."

"Close."

A red sports car with blacked out taillights drove past us doing at least 120. The sound was similar to a fighter jet passing overhead at low altitude, minus the intensity, of course.

"Wonder what his hurry is?" Bear rolled down his window for a moment. Air rushed in and undid the effects of the heater. A white Lamborghini flew by, faster than the previous car. He cut into our lane. The next two minutes were spent riding in exhaust that smelled like rotten eggs.

Five miles later, I exited the interstate and made the series of right and left turns that led to Frank's neighborhood. The area consisted of several three-thousand-square-foot homes on small lots, with maybe ten feet between each house. The front lawns were minimal. Backyards non-existent. Frank had purchased before prices spiraled out of control. He'd also been married with two kids at the time. Now it was just him inside that large house. Despite the equity, he refused to sell, thinking only of the investment he was making with his mortgage payments.

"That's it on the right." I continued past the brick-and-siding colonial, made a right, and parked after driving another hundred feet. There were no houses facing the side street. No one to look out their window and wonder who the two goons getting out of a rented sedan were.

I opened my door, stuck one foot out. Bear hadn't moved. "Ready?" I asked him.

He shook his head. "Don't get a good feeling about this."

"Why?"

"For starters, we're both unarmed."

I hiked my shoulders an inch. "He's not a good enough shot to hit both of us."

Bear didn't smile. "My place isn't twenty minutes from here. I got an armory there."

"And it's probably under surveillance."

"Maybe not."

"You want to hinge our futures on maybe?"

"I dunno, Jack. You willing to do so on probably?"

I pulled my leg into the vehicle and shut the door. "Frank's kids were born on April 4th and May 5th."

"So?"

"Four-four-five-five. That's his pin for everything."

"How do you know?"

"Just trust me." Frank had given me access at one time another to his ATM pin, password for his computer, and the gun safe he kept under his desk at SIS headquarters. "He's got some new lock for his back door. It's electronic. Guess he was testing it. Anyway, I bet my half of our bounty for this job that will be the code."

"And if it's not?"

"Then we risk our necks going to your place for a couple pistols."

"Fair enough."

The big man opened his door and got out. We headed down the alley that ran behind the two rows of homes, which was wide enough for the garbage trucks to fit through. A dog barked as we passed the second set of homes. By the time we reached the fourth, the canine had quieted.

We stopped behind Frank's house and lay low for a couple minutes. The alley remained still. No doors opened. No windows slid up. Bear peered over the privacy fence. He confirmed that there were no lights on inside Frank's house. There hadn't been in front when we drove past a few minutes prior. The gate was unlocked. I entered first. The yard was barren except for a shed in the rear left corner. The grass was dead and crunched underfoot. Might as well have been setting off fireworks in the dead of the night.

The moon provided enough light to see the keypad when we reached the backdoor.

"Fancy," Bear said. "Mind if I give it a try?"

"Have at it."

He reached for the door handle. After pressing the first number, the pad lit up bluish-white. He punched in the rest of the code. A click indicated my guess had been correct. Bear opened the door and waited. The only sounds we heard were the ticking of a grandfather clock and water dropping from a faucet, presumably from the kitchen to the left of the door. Other than that, nothing. No sirens. No dogs.

No Frank.

I entered the blackness of the house first. Bear came in a moment later and quietly shut the door. My eyes started to adjust, and I forced my memory to reveal every square inch of the place. I didn't get far.

It sounded like a foot scraping across concrete. A burst of flame appeared above the kitchen table and settled into a spiraling tendril, illuminating Frank's face as he inhaled the fire through a cigarette.

"I was wondering if I'd see you two tonight," he said, rising and flicking the light switch on. Positioned next to an ashtray on the table was his pistol. He picked it up, pointed it in our direction. "Set your weapons on the floor."

"We're unarmed."

Frank forced a laugh. "Don't screw with me, Jack."

I pulled my shirt up and turned in a circle. "Like I said, we're unarmed."

"What the hell kind of thinking is that? You break into a house-"

"Didn't break in," I said. "Code worked just fine."

Frank set his pistol on the table. He regarded us for a few minutes while drumming his fingers on the wood top. Then he rose, grabbed his pistol, and tucked it behind his back into a holster in the waistband of his sweatpants.

"Go ahead and have a seat." Frank walked to the counter and turned his back on us. "I'll start some coffee."

The brewer bubbled in the background. The aroma of fresh grounds thankfully overtook the smell of three men sitting around a kitchen table at four in the morning.

"What were you doing up?" I asked.

"Got a call, not too long ago. A name we'd flagged a year back popped up on the radar. A little digging revealed an escort had led the man through the airport. When you didn't call first, and when I realized you were traveling back under a different name, I figured you knew."

"Knew what, Frank?"

He averted his eyes to the coffee maker, took a drag off his cigarette, then rose. "Looks like there's enough for a cup."

I stood and blocked his path. "Don't avoid the question. What do we know?"

He placed his hands on the table and lowered back into the seat. "You have to know that I would have never sent you in there had I been aware. It's just..." His voice trailed off and he looked down at the table.

"Frank," I said.

Bear shifted uncomfortably in his seat.

"Jack, Riley, trust me, if I'd known that McLellan had been issued a kill order, I never would have sent you in."

CHAPTER 34

C OFFEE DRIPPED INTO the pot at irregular intervals. The final
drops. Weakest of the bunch. It smelled good anyway. My mouth
watered at the prospects of having a cup. I stared into the bloodshot eyes
of the man across from me. His breathing, like the dripping coffee, had
become sporadic at best. Restrained panic. Years of training had made it
second nature to beat back the symptoms of anything that could interfere
with the operation and situational awareness.

"So, there weren't two groups out after Taylor?" I said. "Someone
wanted us, so the other guy was there to do us after we did our target?"

"That's one possibility," Frank said. "The other is more likely: that you
two mean nothing in the grand scheme of things. And if someone was to
get busted on the initial hit, better it be you guys than their guy. Only
problem is, he got there first and was under-prepared for what he faced."

"We know he didn't walk in after Taylor arrived," Bear said. "I was
following Taylor, and Jack had his eyes on the building for hours prior."

Frank shrugged. "We can't say anything with certainty. You didn't see
Taylor leave, either. Maybe there's another way in and out. Hell, we can
assume as fact that there is. Maybe McLellan was there already. Christ, he
could have been dead when Taylor arrived, prompting him to skate. Have
you heard from Agent Dunne lately? Maybe he's got something."

"He called me, but didn't have any information I didn't already know." I paused, then said, "Let's move forward a bit. Taylor was never involved with the terrorists. Pierre admitted that to me. Where'd this intelligence come from?"

"You know how things are," Frank said, shaking his head. "There are some things I can't reveal."

"Was it the same source that arranged the hit?"

Frank leaned back and said nothing. That was indictment enough.

"We could have died."

"I'm sure the French would have been grateful for your sacrifice."

"Screw you, Frank."

"What do you want me to say?" He crossed his arms over his chest, glanced between Bear and me. "You idiots didn't have to go charging into a house that may or may not have been occupied by terrorists."

"I'd say by the big-ass charred hole in the ground," Bear said, "there were most definitely terrorists there."

Frank looked away, shrugged. "Does it really matter now?"

I said, "It matters insomuch as I want to know what the hell Taylor's crime was to warrant sending us in."

"Some French operator tells you Taylor had nothing to do with those terrorists, and all of a sudden I'm a liar?"

"So help me, Frank. If I find out you used us on this one-"

"What, Jack? What are you gonna do? Tell on me? Call up your local senator and complain? Give me a break, man. For every one thing you got on me, I got three on you. If I go down in flames, you'll be the pile of ash they burn me on top of. Besides, you wanted to do it for the chance to nab al-Sharaa once and for all."

"I'll destroy everything that ever meant anything to you."

Frank rose quickly, knocking his chair back and the table a half foot forward and into my gut. It ground against the floor, emitting a high-pitched scratching sound. He reached around his back, presumably for his pistol, but left his hand out of sight.

"Are you threatening my kid, Jack?"

"I said anything that meant something to you. We all know your wife and kid never meant anything to you."

Frank brought his hand around. It was empty. He aimed a finger at me.

"Get the hell out of my house. Go, before I do something stupid. If I hear anything new, I'll contact you." He walked across the kitchen and opened the back door. "And don't think about coming back here. Next time I'll shoot on sight, and I'll aim to kill."

Bear got up and placed himself midway between me and Frank. "Jack, let's just go. We'll follow up later when heads have had a chance to cool off."

"Get your evidence together, Frank," I said. "You've got one hell of a case to make."

Frank didn't back down as we approached and subsequently exited. Perhaps being the only armed man in the room had given him confidence. He knew at that close of a distance, it didn't matter. We exchanged one last glance before I stepped out and he slammed and locked the door, disengaging the electronic lock.

We went back the way we came. Across the yard, through the gate, down the alley. The sky was still dark, the car was still parked next to the curb on the side street. Bear checked the undercarriage and under the hood while I waited a hundred feet away. I started the car with him a safe distance back. Neither of us blew up. I had to give that to Frank. He knew we were coming, and that we were probably going to be pissed, and he didn't call in back up.

I drove to Bear's position. He slid into the passenger seat and leaned back. His eyes shut, but I knew it would be pointless. Adrenaline was a sleep killer.

"What do you want to do now?" Bear asked.

"Breakfast, I guess. There's a Waffle House nearby."

He shrugged. "Not in the mood for waffles."

"Then get bacon and eggs. Christ, does it really matter?"

He laughed, but both of us were too tired to care, and this was shaping up to be a long day.

CHAPTER 35

W E SETTLED ON a local diner. The kind of place that opened at five in the morning and served breakfast and lunch only. The glasses they served the water in looked like they'd been in use since the seventies. The silverware too. The bathroom smelled like it hadn't been cleaned in as long. We ate quickly, drank a cup of coffee each, and grabbed another to go.

Back in the parking lot, I placed the cardboard mug on the car roof. Steam slipped through the lid and blended with the smoke escaping from stacks across the street. The air was thick with industrial exhaust.

Bear exited the restaurant. Keys dangled from his hand, banging together with every step he took. The door locks clicked. As I gripped the iced-over passenger door handle, my cell phone rang. I glanced at the display: a New York number that I didn't recognize.

Ducking inside the sedan, I answered.

"Hello, Mr. Jack." The voice was old, distinct, with a slight Asian accent. "I'm sure this call comes as no surprise to you."

"Yeah, I've been waiting by the phone all morning."

The Old Man chuckled. "I am going to enjoy working with you."

"Who says we're going to be working together?"

"Well, if not, then I'll enjoy torturing you."

The car dipped as Bear sat down behind the wheel. He turned the key in the ignition. The large engine roared, and cool air that smelled like corn chips blew full force from the vents.

"Going somewhere?" the Old Man asked.

"What is it you want?"

"To see if you are ready for some assistance. Things got nasty over there in France, didn't they?"

I said nothing.

"Regardless, I know where your man is now. I can tell you the reason everything happened."

How much did the Old Man know? How much of my hand could I reveal to him? Not much, probably.

"And what do I have to do in exchange for that information?"

"Just a little job, Jack. You and your large friend. One job. On the house, of course." He paused, then added, "And trust me, you'll want to know all the details behind this botched operation. It might help to extend your lifespan another few months."

"How much time do I have left to decide?"

"Well, six hours if you're going by the terms of our original deal. But, to show you how generous I can be, how about we call it a day from now?"

"Talk to you tomorrow." I hung up and shoved the cell phone into the glove box, wishing I hadn't forwarded my primary dial-in number to it. Something told me when it came to the Old Man, it didn't matter. I had Brandon to help me gather sensitive information. The Old Man presumably had a dozen Brandons.

Bear stared at me for a few seconds, but said nothing. He eased the shifter into reverse and backed out of the parking spot. A couple miles down the road, he asked about the call. When I told him it was the Old Man, and the two options presented, the big man shrugged. Bear feared no one. I always joked that it'd be his downfall. And it might be, if we couldn't manage to locate Brett Taylor and get to the bottom of everything.

Going to either of our apartments wasn't an option. If Frank didn't have someone there, then the FBI or maybe even the CIA or Homeland would. We felt strongly that we'd be marked after what happened in France. So we stayed north of DC and checked into a motel outside of Laurel, Maryland after buying new clothes.

I crashed in the full bed closest to the window and managed to sleep for three hours. Bear only said he was going out. I didn't hear the door shut. After waking, I showered and put on the new jeans, undershirt, sweater, and hiking boots I'd purchased that morning. A week's worth of stubble littered my face. It wasn't enough to change my appearance. At the same time, I didn't feel like shaving, so I left it. It might come in handy a few days later when it filled in a bit more.

Sunlight sliced through the slit between the drapes. A long finger of light stretched across the table and the bed nearest the window. I crossed the room, parted the curtains, and looked out over the rear parking lot. Silent and still. Behind the lot, a highway teemed with cars. People on lunch breaks.

I grabbed my phone and jacket and exited the room. The building blocked the sun, but not the wind. The cold air belted me across the face. I headed left to the stairs, then descended to ground level. A short walk later, I found a spot sheltered from the wind and in full view of the sun's rays.

A call to Bear went straight to his voicemail. It was too early to consider something happening to him, so I pushed the thoughts aside and assumed his cell battery had died. Before I managed to stuff my phone into my coat pocket, it rang. Another New York number I didn't recognize. At first, I thought about ignoring it. Curiosity got the better of me, though.

"Jack? This is Detective McSweeney. Are you in the city right now?"

I hesitated.

"Jack? Are you there?"

"Sorry, yeah, no, I'm not in the city."

"How soon do you think you can get here?"

"What's this about, detective?"

She clicked her tongue a couple times. "I really don't like discussing these things over the phone."

"And I don't like discussing them inside an interrogation room."

"Fair enough," she paused. "But I doubt it's going to come to that."

"Doubt leaves a possibility of it actualizing."

"Did you do something that would get you arrested, Jack?"

"I've done a lot that could get me arrested."

"You sure you want to tell that to a cop?"

"Detective, this'll go a lot smoother if you tell me what this is about."

She sighed. "We were having so much fun, though."

I said nothing. The wind managed to find my hiding spot. I turned away.

"OK, I'll get right to it then. Neil McLellan. Friend of yours?"

CHAPTER 36

I T DIDN'T MATTER where I went. The wind found me. The cold
wormed its way inside my jacket and under my clothing. But I forgot it
was fifteen degrees out when I heard McSweeney mention McLellan.

"Jack? Does that name mean anything to you?"

I lied. "Never heard it before."

"You sure about that?"

I nodded, then asked, "Who is he?"

"A corpse that was bobbing along in the river. They left the chain too
long. DNA matched what we found inside Taylor's home. Which is odd,
because it also matched Emmings, the John Doe, at the morgue. In fact,
what they are telling me is that these two were a perfect match."

I raced through the possibilities. For the DNA to match that closely,
the two men would have had to have been identical twins. Which, judging
by the way they looked, was impossible. At least highly improbable. The
evidence that had been presented disputed that claim as well. The logical
explanation was that someone had tampered with the lab results. Plausible, considering who all was involved.

"I'm trained to notice things, Jack."

"Such as?"

"Such as your face when you got a good look at the corpse of the Doe.

Surprise - confusion even - overcame you, just for the briefest of moments. But that moment was long enough. I couldn't figure out why at the time. I thought then that you were lying about not being able to make the vic. But it makes sense now. You really didn't know him."

"Any reaction I had was probably due to the smell, detective. Don't read too much into it."

"Yeah, well, don't forget I have a friend on the inside who can tell me pretty much any secret I want to know. If you have a connection to McLellan, it's best you let me know now."

I paused while an eighteen-wheeler drove past, half of its wheels falling prey to the same pothole. I made a mental note to contact Dunne and see if he had any input.

"You don't want to do this, detective." Whether she was feigning confidence, or really had balls the size of church bells, she was entering into territory that she wouldn't be able to back out of. "There are people involved in this... People who can make you disappear. No one can protect you. Not me. Not your department. Not your friend on the inside. Sometimes, there is no escape once you pass through the looking glass."

Her voice lowered, sounding huskier, like she had pulled the phone closer to her mouth, and maybe cupped it with her other hand. "So you do know more than you've let on."

"As I've said, I can't discuss what I may or may not know. What don't you understand about that?"

"Where are you, Jack?"

"Not in New York."

"Can you get here soon?"

"Possibly."

She assumed the close. "Call me when you get in. I'll meet you anywhere, and I'll do it on your terms. No more shadow teams. This will be entirely on me, not the NYPD."

"I'll think about it." I held the line open for a few moments, then closed the phone and ended the call while she was mid-sentence.

I wove my way through a maze of walkways toward the front of the motel. Wrappers and cans and cigarette butts littered the asphalt gap between the sidewalk and parking spaces. Our room was on the second floor, in the middle of the U-shaped building. I glanced up in time to see a man in a dark trench coat stepping over the threshold. I stopped, stepped back, and scanned the parking lot. A black sedan was parked on the other end of the lot, close to the manager's office. It looked familiar. A couple days ago we'd suspected a black sedan of following us. Problem was, a lot of government-issued sedans looked the same. I glanced up again. The door to my room was closed.

There had to be a second man. They wouldn't send a single agent to deal with us. Hell, I doubted they'd send only one team. To do so, and then have both of them enter our room, waiting for us to return? They had to know Bear and I would be together.

Unless they already had Bear in custody. Which could explain how they'd found this location at all. Aside from the call from McSweeney, I'd been silent.

I pulled out my cell. At that moment, I realized it had been on the entire time. Perhaps that was how they knew. I dialed Bear's number and scratched my knuckles against the brick wall while it rang. Four times. Five. Six. It kept ringing, never diverted to voicemail.

"C'mon, Bear. Answer."

I dialed again. It rang a dozen times. Where was he? Why wasn't the call going to the messaging system? I took a deep breath and forced myself to relax. Could have been a problem with any of the servers the call routed through. No reason to panic. Because panic would lead to mistakes. And mistakes weren't acceptable when a hit team was nearby.

I tried a different number. Frank Skinner answered immediately.

"What'd you do, Frank?"

"Jack? What're you talking about?" He slurred his speech, sounded like he hadn't slept.

"I got two spooks residing in a rented motel room, and a partner I can't find. What the hell did you do?"

"Nothing, Jack. Jesus." He paused. "After you left, I erased the encounter from my security footage and made myself forget about seeing you."

"Yeah, well, somebody knows we're here."

"You think we're the only ones who might've been monitoring for your reentry?"

Aside from the racing sports cars, I hadn't noticed anyone on the highways last night.

"Who else knew we were gone?"

"That doesn't matter, Jack. You became a blip on a radar when you came home. And obviously, someone wants to talk to you. Maybe you should go see what they want?"

The door to the room opened. A shadowy figure appeared. The man said something, turned back, and let the door fall shut.

I said, "Yeah, I think I'm gonna pass on that. Do some digging and call me back with what you find out."

After hanging up, I retreated further into the shadows, keeping the room in view. How long would they wait? Would they get a call from Frank, or whomever Frank called, and come looking for me outside? It was times like these that being unarmed was a bad idea. In fact, being unarmed at anytime was akin to asking for the chair or the needle. In my world, shadows were everywhere, and they hid the kind of secrets people killed over.

Five minutes turned into ten, then twenty. There was no sign of movement upstairs, or anywhere else in the motel, or its parking lot. Frank hadn't turned me in. Not yet, at least. Or, if he had, they were waiting for me someplace else.

I tried calling Bear again. By the eighth ring, I was ready to smash my phone on the concrete walkway.

And then Bear answered. I told him about the two agents camping out in our room, and the possibility for more.

"I'm five minutes away. Secured us a few helpers. So, if you wanna head up to the room after I get there, we can."

I thought about it for a moment. The room layout gave the men hiding in there the better position. We would have to go through the bottleneck. They could take us one at a time, and there was little we could do to improve our chances of survival.

"Let's skip town. Head back to New York."

"Like that's gonna be any better?"

I didn't think it would be, but everything centered around there. It would be where Taylor would return to. It was where McLellan's corpse had turned up. If we were going to solve anything, it would be there.

"If this is gonna end," I said. "It'll be in the city."

CHAPTER 37

I SPENT THE first hour of the drive looking backward. Couldn't have described one car in front of us. I was more concerned about a black sedan and two government agents who had somehow tracked us down to a motel north of D.C.

The following hour I remained vigilant, but not obsessed. Bear watched, too. Between the two of us, if we were being followed by a single car, or a tag team of two or three, we'd spot them. As it was, nothing stood out. Of course, if they were tracking us another way, which I feared, it didn't matter. They'd find us after we stopped.

"We should ditch our phones," I said.

"Think they're monitoring them?"

"Perhaps." I glanced out the window at the dirty piles of snow that passed in a blur the same way the times I recalled either placing or receiving a call in the past three days. "Can't hurt."

"Maybe a new rental, too."

"Think they tagged it?"

"Where?"

"Outside of Frank's would be my guess. He knew we were coming. Wouldn't put it past him to have someone waiting outside for the sole purpose of getting something on this vehicle to track it."

Bear scratched at the growth of hair on his chin. "Possible, I guess."

The next exit had everything we needed. Food, convenience store, and a car rental place. Bear parked in the back of the store lot, and then headed across the divided highway on foot to get a new rental. I went inside and took care of phones and grabbed drinks and food. Wasn't the best stuff, but it'd do.

I tracked down Bear at the rental place and waited outside, watching for anyone resembling a Fed while he finished up. Ten minutes later, we were in a new sedan stopped in the middle of a U-turn in front of the convenience store where the old vehicle was parked. The store's front doors popped open, and a man stepped out. Short, stocky, older. Looked familiar. His shoulders squared up to us. We straddled the median, squared up to him. Sunglasses shielded his eyes. I couldn't tell where he was looking. He walked toward a Ford Mustang.

The break in traffic Bear waited for appeared. We whipped around the median. I spun in my seat to reestablish visual contact, but the guy was gone.

"What is it?" Bear asked.

"That guy," I said, "he looked familiar."

"From where?"

"That's the problem, man. I don't know."

"One of the guys from the motel?"

"Only saw one."

"How'd you know there were two?"

"When the one guy was getting ready to leave, he said something, or the other guy said something, and the guy in the doorway stopped and shut the door. Besides, no way someone comes after us while flying solo."

Bear stuck his fist out in between us, expecting me to do the same. "You know that's right."

"Anyway, keep an eye out for a Mustang, a red one."

We never spotted the Mustang, but that didn't prevent my mind from chewing on the man I saw, trying to place him. I'd seen lots of guys like him, from the moment I stepped foot on Parris Island, South Carolina, for recruit training. Half the guys in our platoon looked like him. Half the guys in the field working for the CIA looked like him. Almost every Spec Ops guy I ever encountered looked like him.

I called Joe Dunne and left him a message. I figured he'd written us off as being any help to him.

The sun was setting by the time we reached New York. Reds and purples rippled across the sky, fading deeper with every passing second. We pulled into a public garage and ditched the car on the third level. Bear wiped the interior down, erasing any sign of us ever being inside.

We weren't far from the apartment, but I didn't feel comfortable returning there. Sure, it had cash and weapons, but Bear had secured those earlier that day while I was at the motel. Going back to the apartment posed a great risk. The Old Man most likely had it staked out. McSweeney probably did too. I didn't doubt that she knew my identity by this point. If her contact was any good, he'd have figured it out.

"So where to?" Bear asked, stepping over the waist-high concrete barrier on the ground floor of the garage.

I continued to the opening and met him on the sidewalk. We merged into the crowd moving east. There were few people I trusted. Bear was one. The other, while possibly pissed at me, was our only hope at that time.

"Clarissa's," I said.

"She ain't gonna let you in, man. Maybe me, but definitely not you."

"I'll take my chances." We crossed the street, continued toward the bar. "Besides, she's not ready to kick me to the curb yet."

"How can you tell?"

I shrugged. "Just a feeling. Our story isn't complete."

"Whatever." The big man stepped ahead and pulled on the bar's front door.

Soft chatter rose up the six steps that led to the dining room. There were two couples seated at one corner of the bar. Four booths were occupied by unrelated parties. Clarissa stood behind the counter. I crossed the room. She looked up when I placed my hands on the counter.

"Jesus, Jack," she said. Her eyes misted over. "What the hell happened in France?"

"What are you talking about?"

She wiped her eyes with her sleeve as her cheeks reddened. The concerned look on her face turned to one of anger. She stormed toward the kitchen. Looking back at me, she kicked the door open and gestured for me to follow her in.

"I could care less how classified whatever you were doing is or was," she said before I fully crossed the threshold. "You were on TV, fifty or a hundred feet from a man-made crater. They said the bomb was detonated by a terrorist. What the hell is going on?"

I wanted to ask her about the footage she saw. Frank hadn't mentioned it. Pierre hadn't called about it. Instead, I tried to calm Clarissa down. "Look, you're right, I can't talk about that. But it's over, and I'm OK, and so is Bear."

Clarissa looked down at the floor in an effort to hide her tears from me. One dropped, creating a tiny lake on the tile between us. She brought her palms to her face and wiped the rest away. Looking up, her eyeliner smeared along the ridge of her cheekbone, she said, "And this detective. She won't leave me alone."

"McSweeney?"

Clarissa nodded. "And she knows a lot about you, Jack. Too much."

"Like what?"

"Your last name, for starters. She knows you were in the Marines, said your files were classified, but that she knew our connection."

"What'd she say about your father?"

"She knew he was murdered. Said things that I'm pretty sure the public shouldn't have access to."

"Such as?"

"She knew what my dad did, a few details of the program and who you co-oped with. I don't think she realized his murder was connected."

"McSweeney's got a source, a relative or something, working in the NSA. At least I think it's the NSA. They have access to files. Could be any other agency, really, or even someone inside the Pentagon. High enough up, it all blends together."

"What do I do about her, Jack?"

"You tell her where I live?"

"She already knew." She wiped her face again with her sleeve, turning the cloth from white to black. Glancing down at it, she said, "I look like a clown now, don't I?"

"I didn't want to say anything."

Clarissa hit my chest. "Bastard." She smiled, seemingly forgiving me for all past transgressions, if only for a moment.

"As far as McSweeney goes, play her game for now. It might get us further with her."

"OK. Help yourselves to whatever you want behind the bar. I'm gonna clean up. Back out in a sec."

Bear had already helped himself, and a few of the patrons. He'd gone so far as to tie a white apron around his waist. In less than a minute it had three stains. He nodded as I approached, leaned back against the wall.

"Having fun?" I said.

Bear shrugged. "What'd she have to say?"

"The detective knows too much." I took a second to look around the room. Nothing had changed since we walked in with the exception of one person leaving the bar to pick a song on the jukebox. Amos Lee started serenading us through the ceiling-mounted speakers.

"What kind of stuff?"

"Everything. What it really means is that her source knows everything and is feeding it to her."

"Who do you think it is?"

"You know how classified this stuff is. So, pick an acronym and you might be right."

Clarissa returned to the bar, all makeup washed away from her face. It made her look less jaded, more pure. Maybe even more attractive.

"What are you staring at?" she asked.

I said nothing.

"You want to stay at my place tonight?"

"Both of us?" I glanced at Bear, then back at her. "Probably better off in a hotel."

"You know," Bear said, "with all that's going on, and that detective sniffing around, it might be best if we're around her. I think she's good alone here, in public, but at home, maybe we should be there."

Bear had a point. We had at least three, maybe up to five, different groups to deal with. Between the Old Man and his organization, Frank and the SIS, and whoever McLellan worked for, someone might stoop low enough to go after a person we cared about.

Clarissa made the ideal target on several levels. Past, present, future; it was all there.

Not only would we stay with her, I considered cashing in a favor and getting an ex-Special Forces friend to be her bodyguard for the next forty-eight hours.

"So about the Old Man," Bear said. "You really thinking about caving to him?"

The thought had played on my mind as well. "Thing is, Bear, battling him would be the same as taking on a small country. Alone, or with little support." I nodded in his direction.

He nodded back, said nothing.

"He's got his hands into everything, and everywhere. I don't know how far he's penetrated the government, but just the fact that he has makes this difficult. He's got ins with the FBI. I'm sure the CIA, too. Probably a contact or two at the Pentagon. No doubt his local politicians have pockets lined with the Old Man's money. Possibly some at the national level. Is this who I, we, want to go to war with?"

Bear thought it over for a moment. His fingertips worked their way through the growth on his face. We both hadn't shaved the same number of days, yet his beard was three times as thick as mine. Hell, I looked like an out-of-work coffee house barista. He looked like he belonged in the woods, chopping down trees.

"We don't want to go to war with him, no," Bear said. "But do we want to work for him?"

"If you'd have asked me that a few days ago, I'd have said no, absolutely not. But after what we've been through, and the obvious fact that someone we should be able to trust to not stab us in the back has gone and done just that..." I paused and watched Clarissa as she crossed the floor to deliver a round to a table of guys in their early twenties. They were all dressed alike. Chinos and designer shirts. Expensive gel held their spiked, disheveled hair in place.

"I get what you're saying, Jack."

I glanced at the ground and traced an imaginary line with the tip of my foot. "Let's just say that, when it comes to compromising my values and working with the Old Man, the line has grown so thin, I don't know if it even exists anymore."

The bells hanging on the front door jingled as it opened. I looked up, first catching Clarissa's eye. She looked toward the door, then avoided me as her head spun the other direction. Slowly, my gaze drifted, taking in every person at every table in the second it took to sweep the room.

And then I saw McSweeney.

CHAPTER 38

THE DETECTIVE WAS dressed in blue jeans and an off-white sweater. She had unzipped her leather jacket, but left it on. Her hair fell across her shoulders in waves. This was the first time I'd seen it down. The soles of her boots rapped rhythmically against the floor as she crossed the room toward me. Men seated behind her, unable to resist the allure of her footfalls, turned away from their dates to get a glimpse of McSweeney. Her jacket brushed open as she moved, revealing her holstered Glock. She looked from me to Bear, sizing up the big man. Then, with a gesture that lasted a second, she tossed a glance and a nod in Clarissa's direction, confirming what I feared earlier.

Up to that point, there had been two people I knew would never sell me out. Now Bear stood alone.

McSweeney swung her left leg over a barstool, rose over the padded seat, and then settled onto it. The air in the padding hissed out. She seemed comfortable, almost to a fault, for a woman who faced two trained killers. Ones she had to presume were armed.

"Get you something?" Bear said sarcastically.

McSweeney smiled, shook her head, said, "Jack, don't blame Clarissa for this. I had her in a pretty bad spot. If she didn't do this for me, she'd be facing some serious consequences."

I heard the kitchen door swing open and shut. The swishing grew faster and higher pitched with each successive pass through the door frame.

"I need answers from you," McSweeney continued. "Tell me who these men were, and what all of you were doing in the same location."

"Which men?" I said.

"Don't play dumb, Jack."

"Hear from the FBI recently?"

"What's that got to do with this?"

I shrugged, said nothing.

"I hear from them quite often, but not over this. Yet, at least." She sipped from the glass of water Bear had set in front of her. "Back to my question."

"Can't your source tell you this?"

She looked past me, toward the mirrored wall, and shook her head. "Current intelligence isn't their strong suit."

"No, I suppose they're only good at raising the dead." I paused. She said nothing, so I continued. "You know how many people have access to the information you've been given?"

Shrugging, she reestablished eye contact with me.

"A handful," I said. "There are people running the Pentagon that don't know some of the things you've been told."

"Jack, I'm simply trying to get to the bottom of a-"

"What you're trying to do and what you are actually doing are two separate things. You've dug yourself a pretty deep trench, and if you're not careful, someone's gonna bury you in it, McSweeney."

Her cheeks reddened. I couldn't tell if that meant she'd grown embarrassed or angry. I certainly wasn't the first possible *witness* that gave her push back. Perhaps she thought the information her source provided gave her some kind of an edge or leg-up on me. Fact was, no one in local law enforcement gave me reason for pause, because my contacts always trumped them.

"You want my advice, detective?"

She stared at my forehead, said nothing.

"Take your file and bury it so far in the archives that the cold case unit would need thermal underwear and arctic parkas to come close to sniffing it." I paused to allow her a chance to react. She didn't. I continued. "You don't want the attention that will go with figuring out who these men are. Take me, for example. You've learned things about me that you don't need to know. That you shouldn't know. Not because I'm afraid of you finding out, but because it puts your life in danger should someone ever try to find me. These kinds of people will scour the bowels of the city in an effort to get any shred of information about me. Your name comes up? It's not a knock at the door in the middle of the night you'll be receiving. You'll end up with a bag over your head, in the back of a trunk, driven out into the woods to be tortured until you tell them what little you think you know. Then you're dead. Is this what you want?"

McSweeney said nothing for a few minutes. Every so often, she made eye contact with me for a second or two, then broke it off.

Two spiky-haired men rose from their seats and crossed the room. They took seats three down from McSweeney. One looked in her direction every few seconds, apparently hoping she'd do the same. Bear brushed past me, placed his hands on the bar, and leaned toward the guys. They ordered a few drinks and continued to occupy the stools. The only danger they posed was overhearing something that put them at risk.

Presumably sensing this, McSweeney reached into her pocket, pulled out one of her business cards, and scribbled something on it. She flipped the card over so the writing faced the bar top, then handed it to me. Before releasing it from her grasp, she said, "Meet me in one hour."

"And if I fail to show up?"

"I'll have you arrested."

"And you know that'll be a waste of time and taxpayer dollars, right?"

"Yes." She hopped off her stool, zipped up her jacket, and added, "And I don't care."

The two guys rotated toward the front of the establishment and watched her leave.

"Don't bother, guys," I said. "She's a cop."

After McSweeney left, I headed for the kitchen, ignoring the calls of the two morons still perched at the bar. Clarissa waited for me near the rear door, twirling an unlit cigarette between her fingers.

"Thinking of taking up the habit?" I said.

"Jack, listen, I'm sorry. I didn't have a choice. She knows about-"

I silenced her with a gesture. "Forget about it, Clarissa. It doesn't matter. I think she'd have put the pieces together at some point." The draft switched directions and blew toward us from the bar. The front door must have opened, and now air was being sucked through the back. Burger-scented smoke from the grill blew past, and my mouth watered.

Clarissa stared up at me, her eyes dark green in the dim light. "Am I in danger?"

"You usually are."

"Shut up." She smiled, briefly. "More so than usual?"

I nodded. "I'm calling in a favor now. He'll be by your side every moment I'm not."

Pushing past me, she squeezed my hand, then made her way back to the dining area. After she disappeared from sight, I stepped out back. The deserted alley smelled of trash and grease and wood smoke. Conflicting, for sure. I pulled out my cell phone and called a ghost. A man from my past, who had done the things I had done, and been in some of the same places I had been. Born into a family with the last name Kolinski, we called him the Russian, though in reality, he was of Czech descent. Our conversation was short. He agreed without requiring explanation and told me he'd be at the bar within ten minutes.

I bummed a smoke off a cook, enjoyed the chilled and stagnant alley air alone for a few minutes, then returned to the kitchen. There, I updated Bear while Clarissa attended to two new groups of patrons seated in booths. It was better that she was busy tonight. Left her little time to worry.

A few minutes later, the door opened. The Russian stepped in. His black leather jacket accentuated his bloodless face and pale blue eyes. He'd have made an excellent villain in an eighties war movie. These days, they'd probably cast him in a vampire flick. With a casual sweep of the bar, the Russian sized everyone up, stopping for a brief second on the two men who could possibly pose a problem. Same ones I'd made a note of when returning from the kitchen. He stared at nothing as he approached the bar and took a seat at the end closest to the front door. Bear walked over, nodded, acted as though he had never seen the man before.

Kolinski ordered a beer, but barely took a sip. Every so often, he'd slide the mug away from himself, then tilt it so that the liquid spilled onto the splash rail behind the bar. Twenty minutes and a beer-and-a-half later, he got up and went to the restroom.

I followed him in. His lingering cologne gave way to the odor of urinal cakes.

"She's the dark redhead?" he said, gaze fixed on himself in the mirror. He looked paler under the fluorescent lights. I wondered if he'd glow in the presence of a black light. Would his veins stick out like streams cascading down a mountainside? At least he had a reflection, though that hurt his Hollywood prospects a bit.

"That's her," I said. "Name's Clarissa. Just keep doing what you're doing, then when it's time to leave, stay with her."

"What kind of trouble's she in?"

"She's not." I turned on the faucet and ran my hands under the icy water. "I am."

"Say no more."

I withdrew my hands from the stream of water, shook them into the sink, and then grabbed a paper towel. "I appreciate this, Kolinski."

He shrugged and scratched at the small scar on his neck. A reminder of our past. Five years ago, we were running the same Op in Iraq. Kolinksi had been captured by a small group of terrorists who weren't even related to the men we were tracking. Certain members of our three-department team were willing to let him die. Not Bear and me. We tracked the small cell down. Arrived at the last possible moment. While they had a camera running and a knife the size of a machete pressed into Kolinksi's neck, we fired off six quick shots, dropping all six of the terrorists in under three seconds.

"Think nothing of it," Kolinksi said. "I owe you. Can't think of a better way to pay you back than being in the presence of a beautiful woman for an evening."

We stepped out of the bathroom. Clarissa waited alone in the dark hallway. I introduced her to Kolinski, then Bear and I left the bar.

CHAPTER 39

B EAR LOOKED UP the address McSweeney had given and told me it
was close enough for us to walk. Despite that, the frigid temperature
warranted considering a cab. But we had time to kill. On top of that, I'd
reached the point where the cold didn't bother me as long as I didn't plan
to sleep outside.

The sidewalks were packed with groups of people coming and going
from the theater, restaurants, and bars. A new smell littered the air every
few steps. Occasionally, it was steak. Far too often, I caught a whiff of the
stench of the sewer as it rose through the grates and mixed with the
melting snow.

The directions took us off the main thoroughfare. I was fine with that.
The Old Man had eyes everywhere, and by this point he had them trained
to look for Bear and me. Getting away from the crowds took us away from
the Old Man's lookouts.

When we arrived at the building on East 77th Street, the wind had
stopped. The light over the glass door flickered. Bursts of orange faded in
and out. There was no doorman. In his place, a call box. I punched the
button for apartment 4C, then announced myself. The door buzzed a
second later. Bear pulled it open and held it while I walked inside.

Once shielded from the street, we both repositioned our pistols for
easier access. A set up like this felt, quite simply, like a set up. The

rational part of my mind tried to downplay the notion. After all, why would McSweeney go through all this if she wanted to arrest me?

Ice traveled down my spine as my gut knotted. At once, my chest, back, brow were lined with a thin layer of sweat. The answer danced on the tip of my tongue, but the phrasing wouldn't come. Only logical answer was that she didn't intend to arrest me. It would be worse.

Bear said, "What if her source had her arrange this?"

I glanced toward the door and the cone of view it provided of the street. Empty. Not a soul in sight.

"My thoughts exactly."

"Well, be ready to shoot first and bail if necessary."

I considered this for a second, then nodded. Together, we continued through the foyer and found the stairwell. Unlike the lobby, the concrete chamber that ran the height of the building was not heated. Compared to outside, it felt like Miami Beach, though. I welcomed the lack of wind. Dull fluorescents lighted the stairwell. The combination of that and the painted concrete gave the stairwell a greenish glow.

Four flights of stairs later, we stood in front of a metal door labeled in stencil, FOURTH FLOOR. The paint had faded over the years. Left the demarcation looking grungy. I pulled the door open. Bear shifted his pistol to his coat pocket.

The hallway was brightly lit and ran the width of the building. It appeared to dead end at the far end. I figured there had to be another stairwell down there. Ten evenly spaced doors, five on the left and five on the right, stood before us. The first to our left was labeled A. On the right was B. In front of C's door, a colorful welcome mat, flowers and birds, occupied a few square feet of flooring.

"Think this is her place?"

I nodded.

"Pretty ballsy leading us here."

For a moment, I felt I could let my guard down. That meant remaining vigilant was more important than ever.

I positioned myself in front of the door. Before I managed to rap my knuckles against it, McSweeney answered. She had on the same jeans, same sweater, but had ditched the coat. Her hair was pulled back again. She nodded at Bear. Smiled at me, briefly.

"Thanks for not making me drag you in," she said.

"Never would have come to fruition," I said.

"You're a little too cocky, Mr. Noble."

I recalled Clarissa telling me that McSweeney had uncovered my identity.

"Oh, it's not me," I said. "But when Bear's around, I know I'm safe."

She arched an eyebrow as she cast her glance toward Bear. "Yeah, he's even harder to get information on than you."

Bear chuckled. "Good reason for that, too. You know what they say about sleeping bears."

"I thought that was sleeping dogs?" she said.

"Whatever," I said.

"Get you guys a drink?"

Bear declined.

"Water's fine," I said. "What's this all about, detective?"

"You can call me Reese now. We're not in public, so you don't have to defer to my authority."

Bear laughed again. "She's sharp, Jack."

"Yeah, your kind of woman."

"This is fun, guys, but I can assure you, I'm right for neither of you." She handed me a glass of water, took a sip from her own cup. Then she said, "And it's about time we got to the real reason you're here."

"About time," I echoed. "It's your show, Reese. Start talking."

She set her glass down on the counter. A ring of condensation quickly formed around the base. McSweeney crossed her arms over her chest, just below her breasts. She shifted her gaze from me to Bear and back.

"Before I tell you, I need you to promise that you will hear us out."

I glanced around the room, looking for the other part of *us*. Didn't see anyone. My senses became aware of sounds and signs of movement outside my field of view.

McSweeney continued. "All of this will be recorded. If things don't go the way I've planned, then my partner will find an envelope inside his desk. That envelope will lead him to a secure web address where he'll be able to witness tonight's events. You will be..." she paused a beat, smiled. "Scratch that. You already are on camera. So know that any action you take will be used against you for purposes of prosecuting you. During the process of that, all of your secrets will come to life."

"We're out," I said.

"Wait," she said.

"Why?"

"You have to stay, Jack. You two are the only ones that can help us."

"How do I know you're not gonna use whatever happens here anyway?"

She lowered her head, looked at the ground. "Trust me, once you see who's here with us, you'll realize that I have plenty of motivation to get that envelope and destroy its contents."

"Jack," Bear said.

I turned toward him. Shrugged.

"Let's just get this thing going." He waited for me to nod, then said, "Reese, go get him."

"I'm already here."

I looked up at the man standing in the shadows at the hallway's edge. He held my gaze, no trace of fear on his face.

"Son of a bitch," I muttered as I pulled out my pistol.

CHAPTER 40

THE MAN WE'D been sent to terminate, the reason we went to France and had our facial hair singed, the guy who'd been working with or for those terrorists, with or for al-Sharaa, stood less than fifteen feet away from me. And he didn't flinch as I drew my pistol and aimed it at him. In fact, he squared up, as though he'd prepared himself to take the fatal shot with no fight.

Or maybe he trusted Reese.

"Jack," she said. "Don't do it."

I took my eyes off the target for a second and swept over the room. McSweeney had positioned herself a few feet back. She held her Glock out, aimed at Bear. The big man had one hand in his pocket, where he'd placed his own sidearm, and the other up in the air. His eyes darted wildly between McSweeney and Taylor.

Brett extended his arms to the side. Fingertips brushed against plaster walls. He took two steps forward. "Listen to her, Noble. It's not worth shooting me. Not here."

I kept my pistol trained on him, said nothing.

"Just give me ten minutes," Taylor continued. "And if you aren't satisfied, I'll leave with the two of you, and you can do what you need to. Just not here."

"Turn around," I said.

Taylor complied. He even lifted his shirt as he twirled in a circle for me to show he was unarmed. "Happy?"

I nodded at Bear. The big man pulled his other hand from his coat and placed both on the kitchen island. McSweeney, in turn, lowered her weapon. I did the same, directing the barrel toward the floor, ready to rise up if Brett acted in any way threatening.

"Taylor," I said. "Come in here, opposite Bear, hands on the counter."

He did as instructed without any sign of resistance. He perched atop a stool, further placing himself into a position of weakness. Any action he attempted would require him to get off the swiveling seat. That would add a second or two. Not much to most people. A lifetime to us.

"Guns away, Reese."

She counted down from three and holstered her weapon, as I tucked mine in the waistband of my pants. We both kept our palms on the handles, neither willing to give up yet. The first to move would be in a disadvantageous position. McSweeney gave in. She directed both hands, palms out, toward the ceiling. At shoulder height, they held firm. She took a step toward the island.

A long silence persisted after I joined the other three. We stood around the kitchen island, like four friends enjoying a drink after a long week. The sound of our breathing, out of sync, rose and fell. Finally, Bear spoke.

"What are we doing here?"

Taylor started to speak. I cut him off. I wanted to hear from McSweeney first.

"You know who this man is, right?"

She nodded.

"And you're aware that we were sent to terminate him."

Again, she nodded.

"You understand that order is not given lightly, and it means this man is a threat to national security."

McSweeney remained still this time. Her eyes glassed over, but that was the only outward sign that my words had affected her.

"So what's he doing in your living room?"

"Jack," Taylor said.

"Shut up," I said without taking my focus off McSweeney. "Reese, answer the question."

She said nothing.

"I don't care what the cameras catch," I said. "We'll be long gone before your partner sees anything."

Her voice trembled as she replied. "This is one of my sources. And..." She paused, wiped her eyes, took a deep breath. Exhaling, she said, "He's my brother."

Brett stood at one end of the island. Reese at the other. I glanced between them, my head on a swivel. Same eyes, similar lips. Hair color didn't mean anything, but theirs matched. The faces were similar enough. She might've been telling the truth.

But it didn't add up. Why wait until now to reveal this?

"You said your maiden name was Italian."

"It is," she said.

"Where the hell does Taylor come from?"

"You think that's really my last name, Jack?" Brett said. "Do I look like a Taylor?"

My head rotated toward him. "Do I look noble to you? What does it matter whether someone looks like their last name?"

"Stop it." McSweeney glanced at her brother, who nodded. Permission, I presumed, to reveal a secret he'd sworn to take to the grave. "We were orphaned as kids. Somehow they managed to keep us together, most of the time. Every once in a while, he'd end up at one foster home, me in another. When that happened, we'd act up, get kicked out and put back in the program. The case workers, bless them, would go out of their way to place us at the same orphanage, or if we were really lucky, another family who could take on two kids. After a few years, we were adopted by the same family. They insisted we take their name. Neither of us cared much about our history or ancestry, so we did."

I said, "So, maiden name, you meant it changed then, when you were a kid? Not when you were married?"

"Yes and no. Look, I don't want to involve them. They took us in when I was eleven and he was twelve. Raised us as their own. You don't need to know their name."

Taylor wasn't Brett's last name. Hell, Brett might not be his first name. Who was this guy, that the government had given him a new identity?

Bear said, "Enough of the genealogy lessons. Now let's circle back here. It doesn't matter who's related to who. They don't send us to the front door of a boy scout's house. You sold your country out, Brett. The question is, how bad? How deep were you in with those terrorists over in Paris?"

Brett seemed taken aback for a second. I could sense him calculating, determining where Bear was going with the line of questioning.

"We saw you in the footage," I said. "Coming out of a drug store in Paris. Right as they shot the woman and her associate."

His face darkened. He averted his stare. His right hand briefly clenched into a fist.

"Who was she?" I asked.

"She was my asset," he said. "A junkie with nothing to lose, so I used her and got her inside that cell. And it's my fault she died. We were so close, so friggin' close to taking them down. Another month, maybe two, they'd have led me right to the next man in their chain of command, and then they would have been worthless to me. So, anyway, I return home, tailed by the big man there, and I find a dead guy in my apartment. The man, well, it was easy to tell why he was there. Question was, who stopped him, and where were they when I got there?"

"So you didn't kill McLellan?"

"That's what I just said." He looked up at me. "Did you?"

"I'd never seen the guy until I found him dead in your bed." I thought through the list of things the Old Man had said to me about the evidence he had. Did he have conclusive proof of McLellan's assailant?

"Why were you guys sent?" Brett asked.

"I used to think it was because you were involved with a terrorist cell in Paris. A group that once had and might possibly maintain connections in the U.S."

Brett shook his head, stared at the counter. "I've been trying to bring them down for eight months, Jack. Like I said, we were there, close. The attempt on my life meant I had to speed things up if I was going to succeed. I had a feeling that's why you were sent. Why that other man was sent. My haste, that's why Angela died."

"You can't blame yourself for that," McSweeney said.

"I can," Brett said, "and I do."

"It's pointless," I said. "She knew what she was getting into the moment she agreed to work with you. No different than any of us."

"It's a lot different than any of us. I signed up for this. I let them erase my life so I could do this. You two, you enlisted, you accepted your special assignment in a top secret division. You joined the SIS of your own recognizance, Jack. There's not one contract you two have taken on since going independent that your arms were twisted to get you to sign."

Brett leaned forward. There was something about the way he looked at me. Not desperation. Something else, more powerful.

Conviction.

And a need to have someone in his corner. I was familiar with how far that would drive a man.

"Why was McLellan sent, if we were already on the docket?" Bear said.

Brett nodded as he considered this. "You know, in our line of work, the right hand often doesn't know what the left is doing. But, I think this goes further than that. I think whoever sent him, and this was my first instinct, was someone who had a stake in the terrorist cell."

"Someone over here?" I said.

Brett nodded.

"In the government?" Bear said.

Again, Brett nodded.

"Reese," I said. "You and Brett go in the other room for a few."

"Why?"

"I need to talk to Bear."

She reached for her pistol.

"Keep it on you," I said.

The pair went to the other side of the apartment. There, they talked softly while staring out a window into the diffused darkness. Beyond them, a glow of orange haze rose from the street.

I leaned back against the stainless steel fridge. It felt cool against my back. Heat rained down from the vent above. Both sensations met somewhere in the middle.

"Thoughts?" I said to Bear.

"We can do our job now and be done with this mess. We had an order to take him out. Someone up high had to sign off on it. Nothing bad will come of it if we do it."

"If everything he's said is true, and I don't have a reason to doubt him, then we'll be killing an innocent man."

"Innocent is a relative term."

"Innocent in our eyes. He does what he does for our country. It's not like he's a psychopath killing everyone in his wake. It's not like his actions have led to mass death and destruction."

"What if his story about the terrorists was made up? What if he was sitting with that woman who got shot, and got up to call in those bastards to take her out?"

"What if he didn't? What if he was there to gather intel on that cell? Jesus, Bear. We can play the *what if* game all night if you want."

Bear leaned his head back, inhaled and exhaled deeply and loudly. He directed his gaze to the other side of the room, said, "What happened to that line that you couldn't find, Jack? Good and evil and all that drivel. If that were the case, and you believed that mumbo jumbo, we could just do him and be on our way."

I glanced at Taylor and McSweeney, two people that up until a little while ago, had no connection other than a dilapidated old brownstone. They stood the same way, arms crossed, left leg rotated outward and bent at the knee. The sibling story seemed plausible. It grew on me. How strong was the bond formed in foster homes? How far would a sister go to save her brother? Deep enough down the rabbit hole to take on the shadowy side of the government?

"I'm straddling the line, Bear, and from where I stand, he's innocent."

"So what now?"

"I think we need to find whoever issued the command, and get the real reason they wanted Brett Taylor killed."

CHAPTER 41

B EAR REMAINED IN the kitchen, near the apartment's door, while I crossed the room toward Brett and Reese. Taylor made eye contact using our reflections in the glass. McSweeney looked back over her shoulder. She forced a smile, sad and concerned, but wouldn't look at me. Beyond them stood two large apartment buildings. One glass and steel, the other old brick. Half the windows in each burned with artificial light. A testament to the city and all it had endured, and the progress it had made. Yet so many things were still the same.

"Brett, I need to ask you a few more questions."

He nodded. "Anything."

I stared at McSweeney and said nothing. After a few seconds, she took the hint and excused herself.

I filled the empty space she left behind. Stared down at the empty street. "Do you have proof, and I mean hard evidence, that can clear you?"

Brett remained silent for a beat. I studied his reflection. His eyes didn't dance around. He wasn't working up a story. Brett had to decide how much he could reveal to a man who had been sent to kill him. Say the wrong thing, and I'd use it as a reason to carry out the order.

"There are some things," he said slowly, "hidden in my apartment. I'm sure you can appreciate that's the last place I want to go right now." He glanced at me. I gave no outward reaction. "Other than that..."

"Your computer?"

"Wiped it in France. They were close behind from the moment they shot her. Left me with little choice. Uploaded what I could, cleared the system, and ditched the machine."

"What about your boss?"

Brett looked down. His gaze followed a cab that passed by. "I think he's the one who recommended my termination."

"You think he's involved with the terrorists."

"Didn't say that."

I backtracked the conversation. "You said you uploaded some of the data. Can you access that?"

He shrugged. "Suppose so, but honestly, I have no idea what made it and what didn't. I'm not even sure how far it got in the transfer process."

I needed more from him. "Face me, Brett." He turned, leaned against the window with his left shoulder. I mirrored his posture. "Tell me what happened. From finding the body in your apartment to ending up in Paris and arranging a meeting with your asset."

He remained expressionless, though his gaze drifted toward the kitchen. He studied McSweeney or Bear for a few seconds.

I didn't take my eyes off the man. His gestures and expressions could tell me more than the words he uttered.

Finally, he turned his head forward, and, with a slight nod, proceeded to tell me about a day that had lasted over thirty-six hours. He'd been in Paris and told to return on short notice. I didn't mention to Brett that Frank Skinner had known about Brett's departure before he did. He had looked forward to getting back to his apartment, sleeping for a few hours, then driving down to Cherry Hill, New Jersey for a meeting with his boss.

"Of course, that didn't happen. When I first spotted Bear, I figured something was up. I guess he's not the typical shooter, but something about him was obvious. Then, when I got to my place, the building was eerily vacant. Normally when I come home, there are at least a few people lingering inside. I never say anything to them. Don't need to. A glance is all it takes. They clear out eventually. Frankly, as long as they don't approach the third floor, I don't care. Anyway, none of that matters." He stopped, smiled. "First thing I do when I come home is check my grand-parents' apartment."

"Your grandparents?"

"Yeah, the other unit on the third floor. I've left it as they had it."

I thought back to the room stuck in time. The furniture and photos depicting the happy family. "If your grandparents were around, why were you in an orphanage and foster homes?"

"Didn't find out about them until I was eighteen and getting ready to leave for the Army. I'm sure if I had, they would have put me up, and prob-ably taken Reese in too. Anyway, they owned the whole building. Shortly after I left the Army, my grandmother passed. I was the only family they had left, so they left the building to me."

I wondered which one, the boy or the girl, had gone on to have him, then abandon him.

"You said that none of that other stuff mattered. The empty building…?"

He straightened up. "I entered the apartment, and it was apparent right away that something was wrong."

"Why?"

"Things out of place, not the way I left them."

I nodded.

He continued. "And then, you know, there was McLellan, in my bed. Dead."

I took a chance. "You speak as though you knew him."

Brett took a deep breath. His upper lip stiffened. Slowly, at first, he nodded. "I did."

"Why was he there?"

"Maybe to kill me. Perhaps to warn me. Possibly to trap or eliminate you."

"That was his job, then, to kill?"

"It's one of the tasks we performed."

"You worked for the same department."

"We did. Same boss, even." He again glanced toward McSweeney. Doubts swirled around the legitimacy of the sibling story. "McLellan had been my partner at one time. We met in boot camp when we were eighteen. Became friends. Ended up in the same company later on. Both were selected for the same special assignment."

"Sounds familiar."

"I know your history."

"Did she know from the beginning?"

Brett said nothing.

"Did McSweeney know about the McLellan connection from the beginning?"

"No, she didn't."

I had no way of knowing whether it was the truth. Brett gave nothing away. Like a pro poker player, he'd trained himself to hide his tells. Would he lie? Yes, if it had to do with McSweeney. He'd cover for her, and I couldn't fault him for that. At this point, it didn't matter anymore. McLellan was dead - and with him, any knowledge to be gained from why he was there. There were three people who might be able to fill in the blanks: Brett's boss, Joe Dunne, and Frank Skinner. I got the feeling that these men knew each other well.

"So what happened next?" I asked.

Brett explained there was a secret exit in the basement of the brownstone. When I told him I searched the entire room, he smiled, and said there was no way I would have found it.

"Anyone else know about the exit?" I asked.

He shook his head.

"I was watching your building. I saw you go in. Never saw McLellan enter. Never saw his killer enter or leave."

"It could have taken place hours before you arrived."

"The body was too fresh."

Another deep breath. "He was my partner once. My friend until his last breath. Of course he knew about the entrance."

"Then that means whoever killed him, came with him."

Brett looked away, said nothing. He didn't have to. And at this point, we could only speculate on why the two men were sent to his apartment, and why only one of them left. We also had no idea of the identity of the other man. Brett had names, but we didn't have the resources to conduct a proper investigation.

"Either that," I said, "or you pulled the trigger."

He remained silent as his cheeks and ears darkened.

"Were you expecting him to be there?" I asked.

Brett shrugged. "Not really. We had plans to meet later that day and review some of the intelligence I'd gathered."

"What were you planning on doing?"

"Cutting off the head of that terrorist cell, and using it to get to the next link in the chain."

He proceeded to give me a high-level overview of the organization, and explained that it was planning to splinter into three new groups. They aimed to eventually return to the U.S.

Brett explained that he'd hastily set up a meeting with Angela, his asset, in Paris, and traveled there under the guise of a French citizen returning for an emergency. I was sure that somewhere in this was the connection between Pierre and Frank. Presumably, Brett had showed up on Pierre's radio; and Frank, armed with details of the reason for the hit and aware of Brett's previous whereabouts prior to returning to the U.S., was in touch with the Frenchman.

"She was seated outside the café. I had a visual before I entered the store. The woman she sat with was another member of the cell. I thought that maybe she was willing to turn as well, in agreement for some kind of immunity. Angela was supposed to come into the store. When she didn't show at the predetermined time, I knew they'd been compromised in some way. As I exited, the shots were fired. I watched them bleed out from across the street."

And that explained why I'd seen Brett in a still picture taken from the video surveillance.

"I got back here, obviously, to lie low and piece this thing together. At that point, I filled Reese in on all the details. She knew the type of work I was involved in, but she had no idea about Paris and what was going on there. She told me about you, the government investigator. Together, with help of a couple friends, we determined your identity."

"It was a risk sending McSweeney out after that."

"She did that on her own. Said she trusted you."

"I was sent to kill you, and I lied to her."

"Despite that, I'm still standing here."

"For now."

Brett smiled, genuinely, and glanced again toward McSweeney. "So what now, Noble?"

"No one's going to let their guard down while they think you're at large, Brett. And my concern is that they'll continue to play up this story that you were engaged with the terrorists. They'll feed this to the local authorities, FBI, Homeland. You know how the list grows. All that, rather than working to bring that cell down before they recoup and find a new place to operate from. They still have sleepers in place. For all we know, they have dates picked and will proceed no matter what. With the cell broken, almost all chances at gathering signals are gone."

"So you believe me. You don't think I'm working with those bastards over in France?"

"Crazy as it sounds, I believe you. But I'd like to see some kind of proof. I was told there were notebooks, penned by you, that had names and plans and dates. Unfortunately, they were burned. Same person that found them did it."

"Why would I keep information like that?"

"It was in a safe in your apartment."

"I kept cash, IDs and passports, and backup weapons in that safe. No notebooks."

"Someone's been framing you for a while."

Brett said nothing.

"The Frenchman," I said. "He admitted to me that he fabricated the story of you working with the terrorists in order to gain my confidence and get the big man and me to do his dirty work." I paused. "Why would someone want you dead?"

"Why not?" Same thing I would have said. "I've pissed off more powerful people than most. Lots have reasons to kill me."

"I think there's only one way to figure out who is behind this thing. Brett, how'd you like to be a dead man?"

CHAPTER 42

I SPOKE WITH Pierre that night before falling asleep. Two a.m. my time, seven his. He was still distraught, but coping with the losses his department had suffered in the bombing. He confirmed that he had no evidence Brett Taylor had any involvement with the terrorists. In fact, after we left, he'd investigated further in an effort to occupy his mind. Another department in his agency had been tracking Brett for a few months and were fully aware of the work he was doing. Why they hadn't shared this with Pierre, the Frenchman couldn't say. Al-Sharaa was his op. Everyone knew that. If they had information that could help Pierre and his agents, they should have shared it. So the information he'd uncovered backed up Taylor's story. According to Pierre, Taylor had enough to bring the cell down, but held off because he was close to getting an asset within the next level of the organization. Before hanging up, the Frenchman pledged his support, if necessary. If we had to run, he had a place to hide. If we needed firepower in France, he had the guns.

And I felt I could trust him to come through for us.

I managed three hours of broken sleep. Story of my week, it seemed. My legs refused to settle down. After today, there would be time for rest. Either on an island, or in a cell.

At seven, while finishing my second cup of coffee, my cell rang. I snatched it up and walked to the back of the apartment. I peeled back the curtains and looked down at the street. People trudged up and down the sidewalk, adorned with heavy coats and gloves and hoods in an attempt to keep the arctic air at bay. The pale gray sky indicated a strong chance of snow today.

The phone rang a sixth time. One more and it'd go to voicemail. I didn't let it.

"Good morning, Mr. Jack." There was a lightness to the Old Man's voice this morning. Perhaps he felt he had me pinned down. "Have you made your decision? Are you in with me, or the state pen?"

"It's over," I said. "We got him last night. Found him hiding in a dive of a bar. Took him for a ride he didn't survive. Disposed of the body up north."

"Lies," he said. "I've had men on you since day one."

"Then where am I now?" No one had followed me home, other than Bear, and at fifty yards, he would have spotted a tail.

The Old Man hesitated a beat too long.

"Don't bother," I said. "I know I wasn't tailed."

"Do you think killing him the best course of action?" He spoke quickly, slurring words. The call wasn't going the way he'd expected. "After all, I still have the footage that shows you killed McLellan."

"Push that all you want, but since we got our man, anything you give up will be buried. Collateral damage. Anyway, that guy was just a spook. No one's gonna miss him. No one important, at least. You seem to have an idea how these things work on the inside, so you know what I mean. He might have one backer, someone who wants to see justice done. But a lone voice carries no weight in a room full of hot air. It floats on the currents of bureaucracy and gets absorbed into the sea of deception."

"Eloquent."

"So's this." I paused, took a sip of coffee. "I will not be working for you. If you try to push that footage, it'll be the biggest mistake you've ever made, and I'll go back on a promise I made and personally ask for a position in whichever agency will have me spearheading the effort to bring you and your organization down. I will attack you non-stop, ruthlessly, until you're backed into a corner with nowhere to go through but through me. And I can guarantee you, you won't make it past."

The Old Man remained silent for several seconds. I imagined the thoughts going through his head. When was the last time someone had dared to speak to him like this? Had anyone ever? Certainly if they had, they weren't alive to tell about it. A burst of laughter broke the silence.

"Do you know how bad I want you right now, Mr. Jack? My God, with you on my payroll, we'd be unstoppable."

"Don't hold your breath." I hung up, tossed the phone onto the couch.

"Sounds like it went well," Bear said.

I shrugged, jutted my chin in Brett's direction. "Old Man thinks he's dead. One down, one more to go."

The next phase would be tough. Frank wouldn't accept our word that Brett had been neutralized. He'd want proof, and a photo wouldn't suffice. Brett didn't particularly care for the idea of giving up his finger, and though Reese said she could get one from the morgue, we settled on delivering Brett's phone as proof. He left some sensitive material on it, things probably known by whomever Frank was working with, as well as some info that could clear Brett's name as a traitor and turn him into a private martyr. We wiped the rest of the data on the device.

Bear started a fresh pot of coffee. We sat around the table in silence, waiting for it to finish brewing. It was as though we couldn't think through the rest of this without a fresh mug in front of us.

"We've got a place," I said, "about an hour north of the city, in the country. I want you two to go there."

Brett waved his arms and shook his head. "She's going, but I'm not. I'll be with you two."

"Can't let you do that," I said.

"And I can't hide out. I need to be out there, trying to solve this. Clearing my name."

I looked at Bear. The big man shrugged, indifferent.

"You realize if we so much as get pulled over, the whole thing is ruined, and the three of us are likely headed for a cell in the kind of place they reserve for people who they plan on making disappear?"

"Travel separate," Brett said. "You find out who was behind this, and I'll take it from there."

"We ride together until we are thirty miles from the meeting point. I know Frank. He's a distrustful bastard, and he's going to want to meet with me alone. He'll push for the office, but I'll talk him out of it. After he departs, so will I. Opposite directions. He'll insist. We'll need a way to follow him. Plan A will be a bug."

"If that fails?" Brett asked.

I pointed two fingers at him and Bear. "You two will follow him."

"He'll spot us," Bear said.

"I've got an idea for that," I said. "And besides, it might not be necessary. A trackable device can follow him places we can't."

"It will be, and you know it, Jack. Ain't no way that man's gonna let you get a bug on him."

"Maybe in him?" Brett said.

"A beacon?" Bear said.

"Sure, why not?"

"Well, for one, and in general with this bug technology, we'll need someone capable of tracking."

"I can get that," I said.

Bear shook his head. "Two, we need to get it on him, or for him to ingest it. This ain't the year 2107, man. There aren't nanobots or something ridiculous like that we can drop into his OJ. You ever seen one of those things?"

"Sure," Brett says. "Could mistake it for a pill."

"A horse pill." Bear leaned back, arms crossed. "You can try it, but we need to be ready to follow him."

The plan was to get him somewhere we could control, some place with food. We'd add an agent to his coffee to bring on a headache. From there, the waitress would offer him some ibuprofen. A long shot, for sure. Still a shot worth taking. It would allow us to maintain a safe distance between us and him.

First, I had to arrange the meeting.

Frank answered on the second ring. Apprehension lined his voice. "What's the update?"

"We got him."

"Where?"

"New York."

"He went home?"

"Close enough."

"Where's the body?"

"Disposed of it."

"What proof do you have? Photos?"

"Too risky. It was dark. Alley. Flash would have drawn attention. Got his phone, though."

"Come back to SIS. Bring the phone."

I said nothing.

"Jack?"

"Not inclined to walk into your office again," I said. "Not after what's happened."

Frank exhaled. "This isn't the time for this crap, man. Get down here now."

"New Jersey."

"What about it?"

"Let's meet there. Outside Cherry Hill."

"Not a chance."

"Then I'll box this phone up and ship it UPS."

"Don't be a jackass."

I waited for his counter, and knew exactly where he'd want to meet.

CHAPTER 43

CLOGGED ROADS MERGED with the packed interstate. Morning rush hour added at least forty minutes to our drive. We'd built that into our planned meeting time. The traffic dissipated after crossing the state line, and by the time we passed Newark, we had no trouble keeping the speedometer at eight-five.

We used the time for last minute planning. Solidifying the story. The little details that would make the difference between Frank believing me, or having me detained. I knew he would spend the morning checking with any available sources. Fortunately, there wouldn't be too many he could talk to. This was messy. A high-level operative had been framed and targeted. The fewer minds in the know, the better for all involved parties. With the charges alleged, people would start digging for proof and answers. I figured three people knew about the op. Obviously, Frank was one. Determining the identity of the other two would be crucial to Brett's welfare if they learned he was still alive. One failed attempt would not dampen their intent. They'd keep coming, using every option available to them, until Brett was dead.

Bear arranged for a friend in Winchester, Virginia to meet us thirty miles west of Langley with a pickup truck. When we arrived at the location, a warehouse for a gravel distributor located off Highway 15, the man was nowhere to be seen.

Heavy trucks arrived with empty cargo holds. They left with their large open containers weighed down with a couple tons of broken rock. The cracked asphalt leading away from the warehouse absorbed the pounding. Their tires spit up dust and tiny rocks into the air. A cloud of dirt seemed to constantly envelop the parking lot.

None of the drivers paid much attention to us as we occupied a spot in the small lot near the showroom entrance. Brett remained relaxed, his eyes closed, head back, arms crossed at the chest. Another day at the job. Bear's head remained on a swivel. He monitored the road, north and south, looking for his associate.

"Call him again," I said.

Bear pressed the phone to his ear, held it there a dozen or so seconds. "No answer. Again."

I said nothing.

"If they bugged my line..." He scratched his beard in an effort to coax his thoughts. "What you think?"

"I think they'd be on us before him. They would have already been here, ten agents or cops or whatever, guns drawn. We'd be on our way to Langley, or wherever they wanted to take us, by now."

"So you think I'm worrying?"

"I think that until we see those dump trucks replaced by government issued sedans, we're OK."

Brett smiled, kept his eyes shut and said nothing.

"There he is."

Bear pointed toward a red dual-wheel GMC pickup barreling down the road from the north. The truck slowed as it drove past the entrance, then made a U-turn. A few moments later, Bear had visual confirmation of the man behind the wheel.

"Yup," Bear said. "That's Jeremy."

The big man opened his door and stepped out, one arm in the air. The pickup pulled into the exit, one rear wheel riding over the curb. Not the first time a vehicle had done so, given the crumbling concrete.

A guy the same size as Bear hopped down from the cab. The large truck rumbled like a thunderstorm ten miles out. The two men embraced in a half-handshake, half-hug. Words were spoken between them. Smiles exchanged.

I didn't know much about the guy, other than he was from a part of Bear's life that occurred before the military. A time the big man rarely spoke about. They'd grown up together, at times, and kept in touch.

The man backtracked toward the warehouse. He said something to Bear, nodded at me, pointed at his truck, said, "Take care of her, or you're buying me a new one."

Bear stepped on the chrome running board and slipped into the cab. Looked at home behind the wheel. He twirled a finger and pulled out of the lot. I followed him down the road. We took 15 north for a few miles, then pulled off again.

Brett had moved to the front passenger seat.

"Why'd you let all those homeless stay inside your building?"

He considered the question, shrugged, said, "They acted as kind of an advanced warning system. I got to know many of them. A lot are transient, but there are some who remain in that one area year-round. They'd tell me if someone was snooping around, which happens frequently, as I'm sure you can imagine."

In our line of work, it was not uncommon for people, friendly and not, to be checking up on us.

"So, in exchange for that kind of intelligence, what do I care if they stay warm in apartments I didn't use? I'm not sure why they scatter when I get back. Like a bunch of mice when the cat comes home, I suppose."

"Roaches when the lights flicked on."

"There's that, too, I suppose."

Bear turned onto a road that appeared part dirt, part gravel, and part asphalt. A cloud of dust kicked up behind the four rear wheels and enveloped the sedan.

"What about that grisly ex-SEAL?"

Brett glanced up as though he were searching a mental database of his occupants. A few seconds later, he shrugged. "Not sure who you mean?"

I gave a description of the guy I'd encountered outside the brownstone, the references to Panama, and recounted our journey through the building. The intimate details the man knew of the place. How the ebb and flow of homeless worked within the structure.

"Sorry, Jack, but that doesn't ring any bells or tick any boxes. If I had a picture, perhaps. Maybe I just never got to know him."

A few minutes passed. Bear pulled off the road into the parking lot of what appeared to be an abandoned restaurant. A pole rose twenty feet into the air. The sign that had once adorned it had gone missing. The building's windows were shattered. Beyond the jagged openings, the skeleton had been picked bare.

"You sure he was an ex-SEAL?" Brett asked.

"Looked the part. Said he'd been in Panama. The way he spoke about it - it was the way that only guys who lived through it can. No video or movie about the event can capture the horror, the panic, the rage."

Bear rapped on my window, took a step back, then gestured for us to go to the truck. We met him there. Situated on the passenger seat was a box filled with communications equipment.

"Who the hell is your friend?" Brett said.

Bear shrugged with a smile. "We go way back. He's a hobbyist, mostly. Bit of a prepper. Somewhat of a snoop." He turned to me. "Jack, no dice on the beacon."

"That was a long shot anyway. Nearly impossible to control that situation, and it would rely on others working for us, or Frank trusting me enough to ingest a pill I handed to him."

"Yeah, not gonna happen."

"Right."

"But we do have this." Bear fished around and pulled out a small box. Inside was a transmitter with a wire and earpiece. And what looked like a SIM card. "Let me see Brett's phone."

I'd kept the phone in my possession. No point in leaving anything to chance. I handed it to Bear. He proceeded to dismantle the back, and then removed the battery and pulled the SIM card, which he replaced with the one from the box.

"Here." Bear handed me the device with the wire and earpiece. "Wear that and turn it on." He walked about fifty feet away. Facing away from me, he brought the phone to his face. "What d'ya say, Jack?"

I heard it through the earpiece. "You're kidding me."

Bear turned, smiled. "Supposedly works up to ten miles away. I know there's more advanced stuff out there, but as long as he's got the phone within a few feet of him, and we stay close enough, we'll hear every word that comes out of his mouth."

"Can it track him?"

"That's where we're at a disadvantage."

"Except he probably won't be too concerned about a red pickup."

The three of us finalized our plan. I would continue on alone, with Bear and Brett close behind. They would pull over a mile west of the diner, at a strip mall, and wait for me to get to the diner. Once I confirmed I'd been seated, they would move to an empty lot off a deserted road while monitoring the conversation.

CHAPTER 44

F OUR CARS. ONE van. Three by the front door. Two parked around the side. Probably belonged to one of the cooks and the waitress. Any other employees must've been dropped off or carpooled.

I pulled into a snow-crusted parking spot near the corner of the building, away from the entrance and remained in the vehicle for a minute. Battling the glare on the diner's windows, I made out which tables were occupied. Couldn't determine much past that, though. Whether they were old, young, Feds, male, female, I'd have to get inside to tell.

The corner of the building spent most of the day shielded from the sun's rays, and the crunched snow had iced over. I maneuvered carefully around the back of the vehicle, opting to walk along the dried asphalt instead of on the hazardous sidewalk.

I cast a sweeping glance around the dining room as I entered. The waitresses were in the same positions as the last time I'd been there, gathered around a table, smoking, doing crossword puzzles, wrapping silverware in old linens. Different crew this time. Guess it didn't matter.

One rose and forced a smile. She looked like she'd been there since five a.m. and traffic through the place had been non-stop. Her smile turned genuine when I gestured for her to stay put and told her I could seat myself.

I found my usual booth in the corner near the kitchen unoccupied. I sat with my back to the front door at first. There, I ran my hand under the table and the seat. Then I switched sides, slid the table six inches away from me, and performed the same check. There were no obvious listening devices at the table. No guns or other weapons fixed there. The rest of the restaurant, that was a different story.

And one that was out of my control.

Frank could lead the conversation. I would attempt to steer it where I wanted it to go, but there was only so much he'd reveal inside the place. He was as paranoid as me, believing that the Agency had employees posing as cooks and waitstaff and hosts.

I spotted the blue Cadillac as it approached from the east. It slowed and pulled into the lot, where it parked in the closest available spot near the door. The glare off the windshield made it impossible to identify the occupant. The kitchen door whipped open. Grease and batter and bacon followed the waitress. She traveled in a line away from me that blocked my view of the vehicle. By the time visual was restored, the door was swinging shut. I caught a glimpse of the man walking toward the back of the car. He had on a dark gray overcoat and a hat. I lost him as he stepped behind the van.

I pulled the phone from my pocket and set it in front of me. "I think he's here," I said softly, with my left hand covering my mouth in the guise of combing down my stubble. "He might not be alone. Be ready to move." The device offered no response. I could only hope that Bear and Brett had heard me clearly.

Frank entered the restaurant. One hand remained in a pocket; the other worked the buttons of his overcoat. His eyes followed the same pattern mine had, sweeping across the room, dividing it into quadrants. He locked in on me. Waved off the waitress without looking at her. A few quick glances were cast in his direction as he crossed the dining room. An elderly man looked up from his soup and pondered Frank's presence for a moment before once again burying his face in the steam rising from the bowl in front of him.

"Jack." Frank stopped three feet from the table. He still had his hand in his pocket. I left one of mine on the table, lowered the other out of his line of sight. He smiled, nodded, withdrew his hand. It was empty. He shrugged off his jacket and hung it on the end of the booth.

"Good to see you, Frank."

He lowered himself onto the cushioned seat and slid in a foot. The vinyl groaned. The table rose and dipped. "Yeah, sure it is." He reached for a menu, opened it up. Staring at it, he said, "Order yet?"

"No. Just got here." I suspected he knew that. "Who's in the van?"

"What van?"

"Wrong answer."

The kitchen door opened and a young waitress stepped out. She walked over, smiled, asked, "What are we eating today?"

I ordered bacon, eggs, and coffee. Frank opted for coffee only. The woman tapped her pen against her pad and set off for the other side of the dining room where she entered the meal into a computer.

"Back to the van," I said.

Frank fidgeted with an unlit cigarette.

"Tell them to leave."

He said nothing.

"You want this?" I held up the phone. "Then we keep this meeting between the two of us."

"Give me a break, Jack. I know you got that behemoth around here somewhere."

"You see him out there in the parking lot?"

Frank shrugged.

"That's what I thought. Now get your team out of here."

Frank pulled out his phone, pressed a button on the side, and spoke his instructions after the device made a quick chirping sound. A few moments later, the van's headlights cut on and the vehicle backed out of its spot. The driver navigated to the edge of the lot and turned left, heading east. They wouldn't go far. Just enough to be out of sight and in a place where their communication equipment would still work.

"Happy now?" he asked.

I'd pissed him off, but he had to have expected I'd react that way. He kept a unit in plain sight, even had the balls to walk up to them before coming in. It was as though he'd wanted me to see it.

That last point stirred panic within.

"Hand it over," he said, pointing at the phone.

I spun it around in my palm a couple times, then set it on the table. With a flick of my finger, it slid across the laminate tabletop. Frank stopped it in its path.

He sat there for a long moment, staring at the phone. Did he suspect it to be bugged? Would he have any idea how we did it? With one hand, he picked it up and flipped the phone open. His thumb moved up, down, left, right, pressed and held buttons. Frank's expression changed. He arched an eyebrow.

"What is it?" There was nothing left on the phone that would have provided anything other than confirmation it had belonged to Brett Taylor. Yet, Frank looked like he'd discovered the lost treasure of the Grand Canyon.

"Seems you proved the case against this guy. Bet your new buddy in Paris would like to see this." He turned the phone around and extended it midway across the table.

I leaned forward. The screen was small, which made the text on the picture nearly impossible to read. What I could make out was written in French.

"Taylor had someone manage to take a photo of Pierre's plans," Frank said. "Probably showed this to that terrorist he was linked with."

My heart pounded against my chest like a stampeding bull. I had to fight to pull air into my lungs. My face burned. No one ever accused me of being a technophile, but I'd been through every file and folder on that phone and had never come across that image.

"You all right, Jack?" There was no concern behind Frank's words.

I looked over his shoulder. The van that he'd parked next to raced past.

Frank smiled. "Think you can screw me over?"

CHAPTER 45

T HE ELDERLY MAN looked back at us. His spoon hovered where his lips were before Frank's profane outburst. The waitress stood frozen, carefully balancing my food in one hand and two mugs in the other. Even the parking lot and road beyond it were still.

Frank kept both hands in view. So did I. The moment one of us moved, the other would as well. The results wouldn't be pretty for either of us. One dead, one alive. Maybe both wounded, bleeding on the table and floor, scrambling to get to the parking lot.

After the old man had returned to his soup, and the waitress dropped off the plate and the mugs, I countered Frank's assertion.

"I'm not sure what you're talking about, Frank."

He shook his head. "Everything I did for you, and you want to stab me in the back?" He pulled the back off the phone, removed the battery. "Where is it?"

"What?"

"Whatever you did to this phone."

I said nothing. Half my concentration had left with the van. Had they been able to trace the signal to its source? I had to get this over with so I could get to them.

"We picked up on your link in the parking lot. Don't worry. We jammed it as soon as we had a car close to the other end of the signal. Bear hasn't heard any of this. I expect by now he's in cuffs, crammed in the backseat. The van was just to figure out what all they might have picked up on."

"That photo's fake."

"What does it matter? Huh? It's on Brett's phone. The one you willingly gave me. That picture gives us everything we need to take him in. Guess we could do your job, but you'd probably turn on us for that. That's a mess neither of us needs right now. This way, he'll go through the legal channel and get what he deserves."

"You know he's innocent."

"I couldn't care less whether he's innocent or if he's feeding secrets to Bin Laden. We had an order to take him out. That order was handed to you. You decided against completing the operation. I don't know what he told you, or why you chose to disobey, Jack. I'm not gonna, though."

The rest of the diner carried on as if nothing was happening. They had no clue an innocent man would soon be in the bowels of a federal penitentiary, waiting for his death sentence to be carried out. But none of that would happen until they had beaten him to within an inch of his life in an attempt to extract whatever secrets might remain.

And perhaps he had them. Presumably he didn't, though. Maybe he would fabricate some. Wouldn't be much of a stretch for a guy who's seen as much as Brett to create a few story lines that would waste millions in taxpayer money while the Agency tracked down leads made of vapor.

"Here's what's going to happen," Frank said. "In ten minutes, I'm going to get up and walk out of here. You're going to finish your breakfast; you know, clog up those arteries with that slop you got there. Then no sooner than five minutes after I leave, you'll get up and go. If you're lucky, or I should say, if Riley is lucky, you'll find him wandering on the side of the road."

I studied his every movement in search of a tell that said he was lying or trying to intimidate me. I saw nothing to indicate either.

"And then, Jack, you two will disappear. I don't want to hear of you guys accepting another government job ever again. I don't care what you do. Go back to the Keys where I found you. Start a dive shop. Run a bar. Couldn't care less. But don't ever let me hear of you taking on another job. I will personally make sure it gets so jacked up that you end up buried."

How far would he go? When motivated, Frank could be as heartless as a dictator hell-bent on genocide. Our past meant nothing if it got in his way.

He slid to the end of the table. And for a brief second, while worming out from behind the table that I'd intentionally moved six inches earlier, Frank looked back toward the door.

And I made him pay for it.

Getting out was effortless. Frank must've sensed it. He twisted and went into a defensive position. Too late, though. A quick strike to the solar plexus neutralized him. I cocked back and drove the same fist into the side of his red face. His eyes rolled back and he stumbled to the side. One more strike connected with his nose. Cartilage snapped against my knuckles. Blood sprayed diagonally toward the kitchen door.

There were cries from the other side of the restaurant. Someone yelled out to call 9-1-1.

Frank was down on both knees, bent forward. Despite the punishment he took, the bastard hadn't let go of the phone. And there was too much unrest in the diner for me to wait any longer. One of the waitresses frantically pleaded with the police to hurry. I recalled that the station was only a few blocks away. If I didn't leave now, they'd have me pinned. And the one guy who could hand over my get-out-of-jail card was bleeding all over the floor in front of me.

So I bolted for the door and left Frank, and the phone, behind.

The old man with the soup rose and tried to block my path. He moved at the last second, tripping over his chair and falling. I didn't look back. Two waitresses rushed over to help him. They shouted something at me. I didn't bother to respond as I could barely understand the words.

Tunnel vision had set in.

I burst through the door and navigated a slick section of sidewalk and asphalt. The car roared to life as I turned the key in the ignition. Lukewarm air blew from the vents. I threw it in reverse and hit the gas. The car worked against me at first, but I corrected and exited the lot.

The next mile was the longest of my life. The speedometer said eighty, but it felt like I was crawling. The turn off approached. The brakes locked up and tires squealed. I pumped the pedal and decelerated rapidly. Snow lined either side of the road, probably iced over. If I hit it, I might end up rolling several times through the field. After making the turn, I stayed to the middle of the dirt-packed road. It wasn't far to the spot where Bear and Brett had positioned themselves.

Now I wondered whether they would be there.

The red pickup loomed in a distant clearing. It stood alone, all four cab doors open. I pulled off the road and exited the vehicle. I swept the area, right to left, back again. There was no sign of anyone.

Components from the box Bear's associate had provided littered the ground next to the passenger side of the truck. I knelt down to inspect them. Looking ahead, I saw blood on the seat, dash, and floor. I scanned the ground for shell casings. Didn't see any. Didn't mean shots weren't fired. The guys sent here were pros. They would have policed their brass and left without a trace.

For the most part.

They knew I'd make my way here, and Frank had probably told them to put the fear into me.

Banging arose from behind the truck. I positioned myself in front of it, gun drawn, checking underneath for anyone who had remained behind. There was no one there. I shifted to the driver's side, peeked around the corner. Nobody. Did the same from the passenger side. Same results.

"Someone there?"

The deep voice managed something indecipherable. It sounded rougher than normal, but there was no mistaking who it was. I rose and hurried to the back of the pickup. Bear tried to lift himself off the bed floor. His face was bloodied. It poured from his mouth, nose, and a gash on his forehead.

"Christ, Bear. What the hell happened?" I held out a hand and helped him up.

He shook his head. Blood flew left and right. "We lost the signal. Lost isn't right. Static overtook the line."

"Yeah, it was Frank."

"I know." He leaned back, pinched the bridge of his nose. "Bastards didn't try to hide it."

"How many it take to do that to you?"

Bear shrugged. "They clipped me from behind. Three or four strikes with a blackjack and I was down. Don't remember climbing up in this truck, so I figure they hauled me up here."

"How many were there?"

"I only saw one. A big blond bloodless bastard."

"Any shots fired?"

"Not that I heard, but after they cracked my skull, I didn't hear much."

"Frank said they'd take Brett in, let the courts handle it. He somehow downloaded what I assume are fake documents to the phone. Guess they'll use that. Wouldn't be surprised if they make one or both of us testify, using the threat of false charges against us if we don't."

"You know where they'll take him?" Bear used the rail to pull himself toward the lift gate. He sat on the edge for a few moments, eyelids clamped shut, head down. He took a couple steadying breaths before dropping one foot to the ground.

"There's holding cells in the lower levels of the SIS building, but Frank won't go there. He knows I've got the layout committed to memory."

"So that leaves whoever put him up to the job, then."

"Probably."

With every step Bear took, he regained a little balance and strength. Using his shirt, he wiped blood from his face. A fresh stream of crimson spilled from the gash in his head.

"We need to get you to a hospital," I said.

He shrugged. "I can manage."

"Not a good idea. At the very least, you need to be stitched up."

"Jeremy's a paramedic. We need to bring his truck back anyway."

"Why am I not surprised?"

Bear laughed, then winced. He climbed into the cab and started the truck. He had a possible concussion, but there wasn't anything I could say to keep him out of the driver's seat, so I got into the sedan and led the way.

I used the first minute or two to walk through the likely sequence of events and where they might take Brett. I'd need help moving forward. From who, though? Frank had always been my closest ally, and now we were done. Perhaps Reese's contact could help. Maybe even Joe Dunne, if I could reach him, and depending on how bad he wanted to figure out what had happened to McLellan.

A short drive later, we were on the road to the warehouse, bracketed by trucks with empty cargo beds. We turned into the lot and parked near the main structure. Jeremy must've been waiting, because he was jogging toward us before I had the car in park. Panic spread on the man's face. No doubt he'd caught a glimpse of Bear.

"What the hell happened?" Jeremy yelled.

I intercepted him and calmed him down as Bear lumbered over, a fresh sheet of blood spilling from the largest wound. Jeremy led us into the building through an unmarked side door. He called his wife and asked her to bring him some supplies. While waiting, he cleaned Bear's wounds using the warehouse's first aid kit.

I gave him an overview of what happened to his equipment at the diner. Bear filled him in on the rest.

"So it was for nothing," I said.

Jeremy stopped, shook his head. "Not exactly."

"How so?"

"That receiver has a hard drive. It should have recorded everything since the moment you began transmitting."

"But we missed everything," Bear said, explaining that all he heard was static.

"Did they run the interference through the phone with the chip?"

"No," I said. "They had a van outfitted with communication equipment."

"So they just broadcasted some interference. You get the right guy, someone with serious audio capabilities, he can probably clean that up for you."

There was a sharp rap on the door. An attractive brunette stuck her head in.

"Jesus," she said. "What happened to him? Drop a load of gravel on his head?"

"Something like that, babe," Jeremy said. "You bring it?"

She set an orange and gray backpack on the table, kissed her husband on the cheek, cringed at the sight of Bear's wounds, then left. Stepping into the hallway, she said, "Don't be late for dinner tonight. I hate when you're late."

We remained silent for a few minutes while Jeremy threaded the stitches through the gash on Bear's forehead. The big man kept his eyes closed and his breath steady. The muscles on his arms stood out. He hated needles almost as much as he hated flying. The cotton stuffed in his nose turned from white to solid red, and the flow of blood from his lip slowed to a trickle, wire holding the split together.

"So," Jeremy said, applying the final stitch. "You got anyone who can do it?"

"The audio?" I said. "Yeah, I got a guy."

CHAPTER 46

B EAR PULLED THE soaked cotton from his nostrils and tossed them out the open window. They twisted in the air before riding the currents on their way to the ground. He leaned back in the seat with his eyes closed.

"If they ever find a dead body near there, you're screwed. They'll have your DNA."

He laughed, winced. I noticed him press his thumb against his upper teeth.

"They loose?" I asked.

He shrugged. "Maybe a bit."

"Your buddy good with dentistry, too? We can go back."

Another laugh. Another wince. The frigid wind rushed in through the gaping hole. It made him comfortable, so I didn't complain. He kept his eyes shut, left his mouth partly open. Blood began pooling on his upper lip.

"Dammit," Bear said. He reached for fresh cotton and shoved a strip in each nostril. Then he shifted in his seat and stared at me for a moment.

"What?"

"Where we going?"

"An old friend."

"You don't have any friends."

"Acquaintance, then."

"This acquaintance got a name?"

"Brandon."

"He really exists?"

"Partly."

Bear smiled. No wince. He must've been satisfied with the answer. He shifted again, stared out the front windshield, then closed his eyes and leaned his head back. In a day or two it'd be as though nothing had happened. His body had amazing regenerative capabilities. I'd seen him banged up worse than this and then back on his feet within seventy two hours.

I turned my thoughts to the guy we were going to visit. Few people knew Brandon, much less where he lived. I'd been there once, at his request. Brandon had pissed off the wrong guy. Someone with access to as much, if not more, access and information than he had. The other guy had one advantage over Brandon. But once I got involved, he backed down.

We took I-95 north to Baltimore, then 83 to Harrisburg, Pennsylvania. Not the first place you'd look for a guy with ties to several undisclosed agencies, but it was where he felt most comfortable. The downside was the travel time. Every minute we were on the road was a minute less Brett had to live. But I couldn't mail the device, and uploading it was tricky. Brandon insisted that we bring it to him personally.

During the drive, as Bear slept, I debated calling McSweeney. I figured she was a wreck by this point. If things had gone well, we would have updated her three hours ago. The danger with telling her what had happened was that she might push it internally. Or worse, pull some FBI agent's card out of her desk drawer and place a call to them. Hell, maybe Dunne had contacted her, too, since she worked the case. She tells him, he brings someone else in on it. Too many names I didn't know would be a bad thing. If the wrong person got involved, we were all screwed.

Brandon's house was close. We were still in the sticks when we exited the highway about ten miles before city limits. The roads hadn't been cleared. Packed snow had turned to ice. I navigated the treacherous stretch slowly until I found the turnoff to Brandon's place.

The driveway snaked through a hundred-foot-thick cropping of trees.

Cameras were mounted throughout the woods. They swiveled and tracked us as we drove past.

Brandon called to verify we were the ones on his property. I answered affirmatively. We kept the line open.

As we reached the clearing, one of the four garage doors rose. The rattling and banging penetrated the closed windows of the car. I flipped on the high beams and came to a stop at an angle. Light flooded the empty garage, illuminating the three visible corners.

"Go in, Jack," Brandon said. "No one in there."

After confirming it for myself, I switched to regular headlights and eased into the garage. Bear kept watch over the darkened corner of the garage.

The heavy door closed with more rattling and banging. I lowered my window, then cut the ignition.

"All right," Brandon said. "Up the ramp, and through the door. I'll meet you in the kitchen. That'll be the first room you come to off the hall."

"The fridge and stove wouldn't give it away, would it?" I said.

"Just get in here, man."

I ended the call by flipping the phone shut. We exited the car. Entered the house. It smelled like my grandmother lived there. Potpourri and cookies. It left me feeling calm for all of three seconds. Then reality set in again.

Brandon waited at the end of the hallway. He'd been confined to a wheelchair for the better part of twenty-five years. His slight frame provided evidence to the fact. The stubble on his head represented a week or so of growth, much like my beard. He wore silver-rimmed glasses with lenses thicker than Coke bottles. He had enough strength to manually maneuver the wheelchair, but he preferred to use the electronic controls.

"Quit staring," Brandon said. "It makes me uncomfortable."

I hit Bear across the chest. "Yeah, quit staring."

Brandon laughed. Bear shifted on his feet and looked for a wall to back into.

"Just messing, man," Brandon said. "Come on, we got work to do."

The kitchen was part utilitarian, part computer lab. He'd hung a television on the wall, tuned to CNN. Dishes piled up next to and in the sink. A clothes basket was stuffed with shirts. Half were folded, the other half discarded. It was obvious Brandon spent the majority of his time in the room.

"Sorry about the mess," he said. "Hard to find good help who won't snitch to the authorities once they find out you're hacking into government databases." His smile had a way of making me forget about his condition. "Anyway, hand over this contraption you were telling me about."

I nodded at Bear. The big man reached into his pocket and pulled out the small black box. He set it on the table in front of Brandon.

"You look like a ravaged side of meat, by the way," Brandon said. "How's the truck that hit you doing? Still standing?"

Bear smiled, looked at me, said, "I like him."

"Yeah, he's a keeper."

Brandon ignored the banter. He focused on the device, connecting it to his laptop with a USB cable. A button press scooted him forward a couple inches. His toothpick legs disappeared under the table and he began tapping on his keyboard. A moment later, the laptop's speakers emitted a hissing sound.

"That's all we heard," Bear said.

"Just a minute," Brandon said. "Gotta rewind a bit." He paused. "OK, there."

A car door opened. I muttered something, slammed the door shut. Wind. The ambient sounds of the diner. The wait staff, kitchen, others eating, silverware attacking food and clattering against plates. The device picked up on all of it, even my knuckles rapping on the table.

Then there was static. Solid static for the rest of the recording.

"Neither device was physically altered, right?" Brandon asked.

We both said no.

"So, basically, then," Brandon said slowly, "what they did was add another layer to the channel." He tapped away at his keyboard. I leaned over and saw what appeared to be an audio editing program. Lines and waves mirrored the sounds coming through the speakers. "And there we go. Let's just rewind back to the point where we picked up the interference."

And from that point on, we heard every second of audio crystal clear.

"You computer hacking genius," I said. "Can you make copies of that and put them on disc?"

"Yup."

"Multiple discs?"

"How many you want?"

"Five."

"Five?" Bear said.

"One for each of us. McSweeney. Safe deposit. Feds."

"So I guess this stuff is important?" Brandon said.

I laughed. "Quit pretending like you don't know. In fact, why don't you tell me everything you do know?"

Brandon ignored me, focusing instead on creating the discs I requested. After he finished, he looked at me. "You wouldn't be able to handle everything I know. But I did manage to home in on a download that took place at a diner located conspicuously close to Langley, Virginia. A place I hear is popular with the Agency's employees."

I nodded, said nothing.

"You might find it interesting to know that the originating server is located on a farm on Capitol Hill." The printer next to him roared to life and spit out a piece of paper. Brandon leaned over and snatched it. He folded the paper, then grabbed a pen and scrawled something on the back. "You want additional answers, this guy might be able to help. But I'd only use it as a last resort."

I took the paper, unfolded it. Staring at the string of random letters and slashes, I asked, "What's this?"

"The directory path of where that document is stored. That's why I said last resort. Tell the wrong person, that entire path and all its contents might disappear. If so, this guy can find it. He has the access, clearance, and knowledge. Likewise, he would also be the guy to make it disappear. For all we know, he has a standing order to do so should anyone mention it."

"Can't thank you enough," I said.

"Keeping my name out of this is thanks enough," Brandon said.

"So this does everything but tell us where Brett is right now."

Brandon's expression changed. "Hey, you said you used a chip with the phone to communicate with the recorder, right?"

"Yeah, but we were told it wasn't long-range."

He bit his lip for a moment. Then, as he excitedly wagged a finger, he said, "So all they did from that van was a full-spectrum disruption."

"What?" Bear and I had the same reaction.

"I bet everything within a couple miles was affected. Static on the radio, CB radios, that sort of thing. That's why I was able to peel it away from your recording. They didn't jam that frequency, they just overlaid it. But for these devices, the phone and this box, to talk, they had to be programmed to do so."

I watched Brandon reconnect the device to his computer. He entered a series of commands and muttered something to himself.

"Hell yes," he said. "There you go. They didn't go far, man. Look." He pointed at a dot on a map located about eighty miles south of his house.

"Can you drill down to a specific address?"

"Sure can. In fact, look at this." He changed a setting, and it went from a traditional map overlay to a satellite image. He zoomed in, revealing a small house tucked away in the woods. "They're holding him there."

I started toward the garage. "Bear, let's go. Brandon, call me with the exact address and directions."

CHAPTER 47

I T TOOK EVERYTHING I had to resist the urge to pin the gas pedal to the floor and ride the shoulder. Any time wasted was time we couldn't afford, and getting pulled over could result in a long delay. So I settled into the left lane and followed the fastest car. I figured we'd cover the distance in about an hour. Too soon for them to put an end to Brett.

Assuming they hadn't yet.

And that was my assumption. If they wanted him dead, they would have killed Brett and Bear. And waited for me.

I believed Frank. He planned to turn Brett over and then distance himself from the mess the op had become. But first, he wanted information from the man.

With the windows down, I choked down as much exhaust as oxygen. The cold air kept us sharp, alert. Perhaps a bit frostbitten, too. Bear adjusted the side mirror so he could watch behind us. He also kept an eye on the shoulder and lanes ahead.

About thirty minutes in, my phone rang. I rolled up the windows while Bear answered and put the phone on speaker.

"They're moving," Brandon said.

"Can you confirm that visually?"

"Not without someone noticing I'm hijacking a top-secret satellite."

The phone was on the move; that didn't mean Brett was. We could always track the phone. Hell, we could split up and one of us would follow it. But if we were wrong, and Brett remained behind at the house, he could die because we didn't check.

"Brandon," I said. "Keep tracking that phone. We're going to the initial location. If the signal comes to a stop, let me know."

"You sure about this?" Bear asked after we'd ended the call.

"I'd rather be wrong about this than about Brett being with the phone."

Twenty minutes later, we were off the interstate and speeding down a country road. Bear followed along with a map and GPS unit that Brandon had provided.

"We should pull over here."

"How close?"

"A mile through the woods."

It was twenty after three. That gave us less than two hours of light to work with.

I pulled the car to the side of the road. Inside the glove box was a white hand towel. I wedged it between the rear window and door frame. Made the car look legit, as though it had broken down or run out of gas and its driver had bailed.

We slipped into the thick woods and walked northeast. Bear corrected our path as necessary. The cropping of trees stopped, forming a ring around a cabin and expanse of uncut lawn. The place wasn't big, maybe could accommodate a small family for a weekend or a pair of couples on a retreat. The driveway was packed dirt. A black sedan with government tags was parked in front of the house. Looked like the ones we'd seen on I-95. And a thousand others.

Bear covered the front while I used the woods to shield myself and continued to the rear of the property. The darkened windows hid any sign of life from within the house. If someone was in there, they weren't making any noise. Could be a good thing. Absence of screaming reduced the chances that Brett was being tortured.

Or maybe he had a high tolerance for pain.

An hour passed. The sun seeped into the trees. Its rays fought to reach us through the tangle of branches. The cold penetrated my clothing, and my arms and legs shivered involuntarily. Large muscles spasming due to a trick my brain played to warm me up as it diverted energy toward major organs.

I worked my way back to Bear's position, slowly and methodically, watching the house, the lawn, the woods. It felt good to move again.

"Nothing," Bear whispered when I arrived.

"Same back there."

"Let's just bust in."

"It'll be dark in fifteen. Do it then."

I wondered if Brandon had called my silenced phone. Had the signal stopped transmitting? Or had it reached a new destination? We'd find out, hopefully, in about half an hour.

Darkness fell over us. A glance to the west revealed a few final traces of pink and red clinging on, but ultimately losing the fight. As the last traces of the sun faded, a light switched on inside the cabin.

Bear said, "Payback time."

CHAPTER 48

I WAS THE first to approach the cabin, and did so from the side. Bear covered me from within the woods. Though the distance wasn't great, the blackness that had enveloped the area prevented me from seeing him - which meant anyone inside the house wouldn't be able to make him out either. The lights from inside the cabin illuminated the area in front. I lowered to the ground and continued on my stomach. The soft, wet ground soaked my clothing, freezing my skin that much more.

The soft murmur of chatter filtered through the structure. Two voices, low and deep. I eased closer to the cabin, inched toward the window. Inside I saw a man dressed in dark pants and a white undershirt, his jacket slung over an unoccupied chair.

I squatted and slid to my left a couple feet. Rising, I heard something fall to the floor inside. Another man bent forward to retrieve it. I was struck by his age as he rose. He could have been the other guy's father. As he turned, the light hit him favorably.

He had short blond hair, combed back. It was thinning, and his red scalp poked through. Ice blue eyes locked in on his partner, and didn't divert. His face looked like bloodless, pounded iron. I dubbed him 'the Norwegian' in my head.

Had he and the other man been in one of the cars that had tailed us?

I lifted my arm and gestured toward Bear, signaling for him to come to my position. Both of us squatted down and took position under the window.

"Any of those guys look familiar?" I whispered.

Bear rose, slowly, and turned at the waist. A few seconds later we were face to face.

"Yeah, I remember seeing both of them there. That squat old bastard is the one that busted my face. I guess there were more. You see more in there?"

"No. Sleeping." I paused a beat. "Or left with Frank."

"Assuming Frank came here."

I had no doubt the man had. He'd sold me out. Exactly how far would determine his fate.

I rose again and studied the two men. They were both sitting on kitchen chairs in the middle of the room, hands wrapped around twelve-ounce Pabst cans, eyes fixed on the soft blue glow of the television. The Norwegian smiled. Two of his front teeth black. Must've liked what he saw on TV. The other guy's eyes drooped. Long day. Tired, presumably. No way they had Brett in there. They were too relaxed. Or comfortable. A deadly sin, in my book.

But why stay out here?

Frank, and I assumed Brett with him, was coming back. That was the only explanation.

Bear agreed after I ran the theory past him. We decided to neutralize the two men inside, then question them separately.

The big man handled entry. With the men in a relaxed state, the crash of the door startled them. They were slow to react and reach for their weapons. Sentries on their mark would have put three holes in Bear the moment the door cracked open. As predetermined, Bear discharged a round at the Norwegian. A scream followed the deafening roar of Bear's pistol. The older man grabbed his shattered kneecap, lost his balance, fell to the floor.

The other guy, who I figured to be an FNG in the SIS, managed to rise. His beer can flipped through the air, spilling out a cycloning stream of cheap alcohol. The FNG reached behind his back.

I fired.

His leg bowed backward, body bent forward, hands grasping at his bloody knee. Before he managed another move, I closed the distance between the two of us and delivered a nose-crushing blow to his face. He fell backward, landed sprawled out on the floor, half-conscious. I stripped his weapon, and then turned toward Bear.

He had the Norwegian in a stranglehold, weakening the older man to the point of passing out.

Casting a sweeping glance around the room, I spotted a pair of handcuffs, a length of rope, a knife, and a blackjack. Blood coated the knife's blade. More blood and a clump of hair were matted to the end of the blackjack's metal rod.

I grabbed the weapon and flicked it, extending the business end. As I stepped over the presumed FNG, I slammed it against his head. He gasped, a gargled choking sound, and his head fell to the side. The Norwegian watched through bulging, bloodshot eyes. I slammed the weapon against his upper arm, causing it to give, and his body to collapse.

"Back off, Bear," I said.

The big man didn't move.

"Don't want him dead," I said. "Yet."

Bear looked up at me, squeezed harder on the man's neck.

The ex-SEAL's eyes rolled up. His beet-red face slackened.

"Bear!"

The Norwegian was gone. Bear let go.

The older man clawed at the floor, then sucked down a mouthful of air.

Not dead. Yet.

CHAPTER 49

THE ROOM SMELLED like human waste, and with good reason. Turned out the FNG had defecated. Bear got a laugh out of it. Not the first time he'd scared the shit out of someone.

We got little out of the young guy. Slightly more out of the Norwegian. We kept them in separate rooms. After a little encouragement, both admitted that Frank and another guy who went by the name of Riggins had left with Brett. Neither had any idea where to. Even after taking his fingertip with the bloodied knife, the Norwegian wouldn't reveal the location.

When the FNG restated he didn't know with the blade pressed to his finger, I didn't believe him. The older man was a mercenary, but this guy worked for Frank. He knew. Sawing through the gristle at the first knuckle yielded screaming, but no confession. As his fingertip fell to the floor he threatened me with legal action, then passed out again.

"They don't know, Jack." Bear hoisted the man over his shoulder and carried him to the back room. He tied him to the bedpost and then returned.

I stepped away from the pool of blood and fingertips that were drowning in it, then checked my phone.

"Christ."

"What?"

"Bunch of calls from Brandon."

"Any messages?"

I checked. "None."

"So, call him back."

I did. "What's going on?" I said after the man answered.

"I got an address for you. Signal's been there for about as long as you've been at that cabin."

"How do you know how long we've been here?"

"What need do I have for a GPS, Jack? Think, man. I've been monitoring you through that."

My paranoia level rose by a factor of ten. Brandon and I had an agreement of sorts, but he chased the money. No matter what.

We all did.

"So where's this place?" I asked.

Bear inched closer. A streak of blood dripped from his hand and pooled on the floor. It wasn't his this time. I didn't think so, at least.

Brandon said, "Looks like an office building in D.C."

I covered the mouthpiece. "If they've got him at SIS headquarters, he's as good as dead." I removed my hand and gave Brandon the SIS address without telling him what was at the location. "That where they are?"

"Uh, nah. That's not it."

I said nothing while Brandon tapped softly at his keyboard.

"You're not gonna believe it, man, but this signal is coming from the Cannon House Office Building."

"Capitol Hill."

"Yup."

"Quaint. Can you pinpoint the exact office?"

"Sorta," Brandon said. "That building is five stories, I think. So I can tell you pretty much where in the building, but I can't get altitude off this signal. So you'll have to narrow it down."

"Print off the floor plan and mark the exact spot, Brandon. Got that? I need the exact location. I'll be levying some serious accusations here. I need to be right." I gave him a number that would ring to the fax machine in my apartment.

"Doing it now."

I ended the call.

"Got no more use for these guys," I said.

Bear nodded, said nothing.

"Your call, big man. They jumped you and left you for dead."

"Didn't kill me, though."

"Their mistake?"

The men were clinging to the last thread of consciousness. By now, their shock-ridden bodies prevented them from feeling the full pain of their wounds. The tradeoff to that was they'd soon pass out. Bear went up to each of the men. They became visibly panicked as he approached. Bear leaned over, whispered something to them, then returned.

"Let's go," he said.

"You sure?"

"They ain't worth the bullets."

Outside, the cold air chilled my sweat-soaked clothing as though I'd walked into a freezer after exercising. The ground beyond the cabin clearing was frozen and crunched under the soles of my boots. Wood smoke from a nearby home filled the air. Good thing we were in the woods, considering we discharged two rounds. Neighbors probably attributed it to hunters.

We didn't bother trekking through the woods to get back to the car. The need to conceal ourselves had passed. The driveway led to the road. We jogged to the car, reaching it in less than ten minutes, and got back on the highway.

As the lights of D.C. polluted the sky, Brandon called again.

"They're on the move, Jack."

"Stay on the line with us," I said. "We're probably fifteen minutes from the city."

"Hey, Jack. What's at that address you gave me earlier?"

"Can't say."

"Why can't you say?"

"Because." I paused, glanced at Bear. "Why do you need to know?"

"The signal stopped there about thirty seconds ago, and now it's disappeared altogether."

I crossed into the next lane, riding the shoulder, tempted to pull over.

If they'd brought Brett to SIS, he was done. Whoever Frank had gone to see had green-lighted the termination under the new circumstances. Would they do it there? Or hold him until it was time?

The lanes in front of us were thick with traffic, but not congested to the point of causing a slowdown. I pushed the speedometer to ninety and weaved my way forward.

"How'll we get in?" Bear said.

"Not sure."

"How many people will be there?"

"No clue."

"If half the staff is there, how are we gonna get down to the cells?"

"Chances are we won't."

"Mind dropping me off so I can get some dinner, then?"

I glanced between Bear and the road. "This is what it comes down to? Gonna back out on me now?"

Bear flashed a smile. "Just messing. Till death do us part, my man. Till death do us part."

CHAPTER 50

THE UNASSUMING BUILDING looked like most on the street. Brick and glass. Old. It had two halves, two lives. At one point, a law firm had rented most of the offices. The others had been split between a mail order firm, and a B-movie production company. A few years back, everyone had been ordered to vacate, and the building had been condemned.

The companies moved out at once.

And the SIS moved in.

The main level and upper floors, though perfectly suitable for use, remained empty. The hive of activity occurred underground. A secret entrance in the rear opened up to a parking garage. To get to it, two card-controlled gates had to be opened, and then knowledge of how to get into the garage was required.

Few had this information. And no one ever found out about it because after the second gate, everything was covered. Someone might look out and see a car driving down an alley, but they wouldn't see anything past that. To them, it would look like the vehicle entering a covered parking deck, not the secret garage of a clandestine government agency.

We were parked across the street, about two hundred yards away. There was no sign of life in the building. There never was. It had become an empty mausoleum. Soon, though, it would have a corpse to house, and a soul to trap. Below, a life was close to being extinguished.

"What're we gonna do?" Bear said. "There's no way down from that main floor is there?"

"Can't access SIS from the main floor. There's a way up, but it's only accessible from my old office."

"Why don't they just get a regular building?"

"Because 'they' don't exist." I rolled my window down to let in some air. "And that's our ace, Bear."

"Gonna expose the secret government agency you used to work for?"

"Time to call Frank."

The desire to call him had been eating away at me the entire drive. But making contact too soon would have done no good. They'd move, and we'd lose them; unless somehow, someway, Frank had Brett's phone. He wouldn't, though. I knew that much. I presumed the cell was locked inside Frank's bottom desk drawer. He'd ship it off to be destroyed before the week was over. Maybe Brandon would pick up on the signal then. Definitely not tonight.

Now that we were close and could maintain visual contact, we had to take our shot.

I called Frank.

He picked up on the third ring. "Don't bother, Jack. Nothing you can say will stop this. And, honestly, I'm looking forward to hearing your reasoning behind keeping that traitor alive, but that's a talk for another day. And when we have it, you'll be bolted to the floor while trying to dodge my fists."

"Your little trick didn't work." It was all I needed to say.

"What're you talking about?"

"I've got the entire conversation recorded."

Frank laughed. "And what are you going to do with that, Jack? Call up CNN?"

"Yeah, and every other network. A single email will deliver the file to all of them, plus reporters at the *Times*, the *Post*, the *Wall Street Journal*. And then I'll go on camera and detail every op you and I ran together."

Frank started to answer, paused, said, "You'll screw yourself."

"They gotta find me first."

"You're not serious."

I said nothing.

Neither did Frank. For a few moments, at least. "What do you want?"

"I want you to call up whoever ordered this hit. You're gonna drive out and pick them up. Then we're all gonna meet and have a little talk." I paused, then added, "And you better have Brett with you, and he better be alive."

"He's alive, but this isn't going to happen."

"You know as well as I do that once this gets out there, an investigation will follow. It might not be public. Doesn't have to be, though. It's all going to fall back on whoever ordered this. You know how this works. Every witch hunt needs a witch."

"All right." Frank paused for a long beat. "I'll call him. Where do you plan on meeting?"

"How about the diner?"

"See you there in an hour."

Bear and I remained in the car, focused on the alley that ran between SIS and the building to its right. Only way in. Only way out. Finally, headlights swept across the concrete and asphalt. The wide cone of illumination narrowed. The vehicle came into sight, pulled past the curb, and eased into the street, turning away from us.

I made out two heads at different heights. Frank in front, Brett in back. Presumably. Could have been another agent. We'd find out soon enough.

I eased away from the curb with my lights off. Couldn't stay that way for long, so after twenty seconds, I switched them on. Frank was about three hundred yards ahead of us. Too far. I pushed the speedometer to fifty and closed the gap down to about a hundred feet. After we left the city I could increase the distance again, and allow a car or two to get in front of us.

There were no surprises in the route Frank took. He left the city by way of I-395 and then exited onto I-66. From there he drove to Highway 7.

"He's going to the diner," Bear said. "Nowhere else."

"Not unless the order was issued by Langley."

"You think CIA's involved?"

"Not sure, Bear. Maybe Brett stepped on some toes along the way. Hell, look at how many people you and I have pissed off. The process these things go through, all the committees, the sign offs. Man, for all we know, someone intended a bullet for each of us long ago, it just never got approved."

"Tell me another bedtime story, Jack. That one made me feel nice and fuzzy inside."

Bear laughed, and so did I. Perhaps it was the tension rising to a boil. Maybe relief that he hadn't been killed. They probably thought the blackjack had done him in. Should have used a bullet. Five, for that matter. Only thing that saved the big man was the location. Too close to the listening public to put him away. And his size made it a pain to toss him into the back of a car so they could attempt to finish the job later.

Frank's brake lights blossomed like two exploding cherries. The vehicle in front of us decelerated quickly and turned right into a residential area. I cut our headlights after Frank's car slipped out of view, and then hit the brakes.

"Quick," I said. "Look at the GPS and tell me if that neighborhood has a back entrance."

Bear pulled the device out of the console and activated the screen. I turned right on the same street Frank had. Taillights shone like pin pricks. Still in view, though, and on the same road.

"Doesn't look like any other way out," Bear said. "Just some side streets that connect, like a rib cage. Only dead end is the road we are on."

I kept the car in the middle of the road, avoiding the pools of orange light cast from the street lamps. The further we went, the more homes I noticed that looked freshly built. The lots were unlandscaped. Nothing but dirt and maybe a malnourished tree or two. They'd put hedges and bushes around the houses, but little else. Then we came to a wooden skeleton that rose from a tumultuous grave of rock and sand and dirt. There were six of these, three on each side.

Then nothing but tall grass on either side of the road.

Frank's taillights lit up. Exploding cherries again. The car abruptly turned to the left, its headlights doused. The interior flashed for a moment, the result of the dome light. Didn't last.

"He knows we're here," Bear said.

I brought the car to a stop. "Wonder when he spotted us?"

"Keep going, man."

I eased off the brake. The car rolled forward. Bear lowered his window. A crosswind blew cold smoke-flavored air through the grasses. Sounded like almost-muted cicadas.

Frank's door glinted as it swung open. His silhouette rose. It was hard to determine his subsequent movements, but I was able to tell that he opened the rear door, at which someone fell out. Frank stepped back, turned sideways, extended his arm.

"Hang on, Bear."

As my left hand switched on the headlights and turned on the high-beams, my right foot slammed the gas pedal down. We covered two hundred yards in a matter of seconds. The vehicle fishtailed most of it. I kept the high-beams on, moved my foot to the brake, and slowed down rapidly. I didn't have to worry about friction between the tires and pavement. We were on dirt now. Sliding was the concern.

The only movement Frank made as the car barreled toward him was to force Brett to get off the ground. The man stumbled forward and had to use Frank's sedan to pull himself up.

We came to a stop. Bear and I stepped out, using the doors as shields.

"Cut the lights, Jack," Frank said. He kept his pistol aimed at Brett.

"Survey," I said to Bear across the roof, and then I called out, "Ditch your gun and I'll get rid of the lights."

"You don't get it, man." Shaking his head, Frank laughed. Then he lowered his arm, an inch, maybe two. A bright flash of light exploded, accompanied by the sound of a quarter hitting a tin trash can. Brett let out a stifled yell and collapsed. One hand remained attached to the fender. A small pool of blood formed next to his left knee.

A knee for a knee, I thought. Hopefully Frank would stop there.

"Doesn't have to be like this, Frank," Bear said.

"Shut up, you overgrown lumberjack." Frank lowered his weapon further. The trajectory would carry the bullet into Brett's head. "Jack, cut the damn lights, or I'll do him right here, man."

I knew Frank well enough to know it wasn't a bluff, so I leaned into the car and killed the headlights. For a moment I saw nothing but blackness. Slowly, my eyes adjusted. Brett hadn't moved. Neither had Frank. Dogs barked in the background, their howls stretching for miles like a line of falling dominos.

"What are we doing here, Frank?" I stepped out from behind the cover of the door - not that it would have done much more than take some velocity off the bullet.

"Think you're so smart, Jack. C'mon, man, I have the entire street wired at SIS. I saw you two pull up to the curb. Was watching you the entire time we talked."

"Why not take me, then? Why come all the way out here?"

"Because I need to know if what you claim to have is the real deal before I decide what to do with you."

Bear spoke loud enough for me to hear, and no one else. "Someone's out there. Fifty yards to the left."

I moved forward cautiously, and aware of the blackness to my left. "Frank, get in the car and drive off. Leave Brett there. Promise to leave him alone, and this all ends. No need for anyone to die. No need for careers to be ruined."

Frank turned his pistol on me. I knew Bear had him covered now, which left the field wide open.

"Close enough, Jack."

In my left hand was one of the CDs. I lifted it into the air. "It's all on here."

"Toss it over."

"Let Brett go."

Frank lowered his pistol, and said to Brett, "Walk about ten yards, then stop."

I flung the CD toward Frank as though the disc were a frisbee. It deflected off his hand and bounced on the ground a couple times. The man made no advance toward it.

"Jack!" Bear yelled as a bright flash of light blinded me.

CHAPTER 51

DIVING TOWARD THE ground, I pulled my pistol and fired a round in the direction of the light. Momentum carried my body in a roll to the left. The beam dissipated, but in front of me, all I could see was a bright red artifact, burned into my retina. A bullet crashed into the ground next to me. Shots were fired from behind. They made more sound when they hit the side of Frank's car than when they were fired.

I scrambled to my knees, my feet, ran to the left and into the knee high grass. Another shot meant for me burrowed into the dirt. Bear continued his assault, being careful not to hit Frank or Brett. He fired to provide me cover.

"Cease fire," I called out.

Frank dove into his car. Bear fired a couple more shots. Brett, presumably realizing this was his opportunity, staggered with a pronounced limp, and managed to reach the field on the opposite side of the road.

With the red glare down to the size of a small halo, I scanned the field and caught a glimpse of someone running away. Obviously an SIS agent that Frank had planted out in the undeveloped land. He'd known we were outside SIS, and he'd planned on leading us here, where he had someone waiting.

Bear took position behind the car. He stopped firing and concentrated on covering me and Brett.

Frank started his car, then scrambled out of it. He stayed low and collected the CD off the street. Guess the evidence was important to him, after all. The engine revved, and then the vehicle lurched forward. Tires spun in the dirt as Frank pulled away.

I knelt in the grass as he passed. His pistol, aimed at me, glinted in the traces of light that found us.

But he didn't shoot.

Instead, he gunned the engine and fled.

I rose up and sprinted across the street. Bear was already in position at Brett's side. After surveying the blackened expanse beyond the development for signs of any other SIS agents, we lifted Brett and carried him to the car. He gritted his teeth and groaned as we placed him in the backseat.

By the time I had the car started, Frank had driven out of sight. Didn't matter. I knew he'd go back to the SIS building. Or Langley if someone there was involved in this mess. Either way, not places we could get into. And we couldn't worry about that. Brett needed medical attention. He could be in danger of losing his leg, depending on how much damage the bullet did.

I called Brandon. He located a hospital in McLean, Virginia, fifteen minutes from our position. The only problem was a gunshot wound would require the hospital to bring in the police. We couldn't just drop Brett off. The moment the call hit the scanner, Frank would have a team en route to collect.

Brett said, "Take me to Langley."

Bear said, "You CIA after all?"

Brett shook his head. "Can't get into that."

I said, "And we can't pull up to the gates of the CIA."

"Give me your phone then." Brett sat up and pulled himself forward. The pain spread further across his face with every inch he moved. He took my phone and placed a call. The conversation that followed was brief and to the point.

We drove to the hospital in McLean. There, we met the man Brett had called off to the side of the emergency room. He had on jeans and a heavy coat. His hair was neat and short and didn't move in the wind. His hairless cheeks were red. He didn't bother to introduce himself before opening the back door and helping Brett out. He didn't have to.

Joe Dunne glared at me. My mind, already racing because of what had transpired earlier, tried to piece the puzzle together. What connection did Brett have to Dunne that he would call the FBI agent in a situation like this?

"I'll be in touch, Jack," Brett said. "Either directly, or through Reese. Put an end to this."

With that, Brett and Dunne headed toward the ER entrance. The wide glass doors spread apart, and the men disappeared into a flurry of action.

Bear leaned back, took a deep breath, turned toward me. "What the hell?"

"I'm trying to wrap my head around it, Bear. I really am. Maybe Brett had worked with him a time or two. He didn't live around here, so I'm thinking it might be the only number he knew."

Bear nodded. "Sounds plausible to me." He paused, scratched at his beard. "But something ain't right."

"Brett was comfortable calling him. Dunne has the creds to keep the police at bay." I made a three-point turn in front of the ER and started toward the exit. "We have to head up north. Get those files from Brandon."

"Not comfortable going home?"

"Frank knows where I live. Probably has two guys sitting in my living room, waiting for us to walk through the door."

"You think we'll figure out who it is?"

"Yeah. Do I think he'll admit to it? No."

"We'll probably never know the story behind this."

My gut told me Bear was right. At this point all I wanted was confirmation that the job was scrubbed. The command revoked. Our names erased from the case file before they burned it.

Ten minutes later, I called McSweeney and recapped the events, up to the point of us leaving Brett at the hospital with Dunne.

"Thanks for seeing this through, Jack."

"No problem. And he called the guy who met us at the ER. Seemed comfortable with him." I left out the fact that the guy was FBI and investigating her case.

"He should." She paused, then added, "That was my ex-husband. His name's Joe Dunne. He's a good guy, we just had..."

"Philosophical differences?"

"Guess you could say that. I'm a New York cop, he's FBI."

"Like putting together a Baptist and a Catholic."

"I suppose."

"Bound to happen at some point, Reese. Better you found out sooner."

She said nothing, despite the fact that I'd called her by her first name.

"McSweeney, do something for me?"

"Sure, what?"

"Go check up on Clarissa. I trust the guy we left her with, but, you know."

"I do."

"Thanks."

"Think nothing of it. Hey, how bad are the philosophical differences between the two of you?"

"That's not a conversation we're having. Call me and let me know how she's doing."

We continued north on the route to Brandon's. Along the way, Bear and I didn't speak. I barely managed a thought beyond recounting everything that had happened over the past few days. There had to be something I was missing, but no matter how many times I replayed it, I couldn't find the one thing that would tie this together. Even the odd triangle with Dunne, Brett, and McSweeney seemed insignificant. Chances were she knew he'd been involved in the case the entire time. They'd played me from all ends.

I supposed this was where Brandon's expertise would come into play. Hopefully, he'd managed to isolate the specific room that the signal had come from. Even if not, narrowing it down to five offices would help. All we had to do was take those names and start drilling down. Committees, constituents, service records. Something would give the guy, or gal, away. And the thread would cinch tight.

I pulled off on the same exit on I-83, short of Harrisburg. The roads were still covered in ice. The driveway still snaked through the woods. I didn't see the cameras this time; it was too dark. But I knew they were there, swiveling to follow us through the woods. As we pulled into the clearing, the garage door opened. I drove in, cut the engine, and Bear and I got out. The door to the house was open. Brandon was waiting for us in the kitchen.

The man smiled. It looked forced. At once, he went back to staring at his computer screen, biting his bottom lip on the right side. He tapped at his keyboard, but not in any kind of pattern. A single key, repeatedly.

"What's wrong?" Bear said.

Brandon shook his head. He forced air through sealed lips.

"Tell us," I said.

He wheeled back a few inches and turned to face us. "Better I show you, because I don't think you'd believe me if I told you." He backed up some more and maneuvered around the kitchen table. "Come over here."

Bear took the opposite side. I stood at the head of the table. Laid out on it was a diagram of the Cannon House Office Building. There were markings in various spots. Coordinates, I presumed.

"Good work," I said.

Brandon said nothing. He reached for another sheet of paper. It was folded. He took his time opening it. Once unfurled, he sat it on a space above the blueprints. On the printout was a general diagram, an outline of the building. There was only one mark made on the paper.

"That dot is where your signal stopped and transmitted for fifteen minutes and change." He dragged his finger across the printout. "It went from this entrance to this exact spot. Stayed there. Then it exited the same door it came in through."

"Great," I said. "Tell us which offices line up with that spot and we'll take it from there. We can even bring the GPS, and you can watch from here and let us know if we're even a hair off."

Brandon shook his head. He leaned over to his left and reached down. The process was painfully slow, with the man grunting as he forced his weak body to contort into positions it hadn't formed in months or years. He returned with a clear piece of plastic.

"Bear," he said. "Grab a marker off the counter."

Bear did.

Brandon placed the plastic over the outline printout. "Now use that marker to trace the outline of the building and put an X on that signal marker. Then transfer it to the blueprints."

Again, Bear did as instructed. After he finished the tracing, he slid the plastic diagram on top of the blueprints.

"I'd say that lines up," Brandon said. "Agree?"

I nodded. So did Bear.

"So take a close look and tell me what you see."

"Shit," Bear said.

"Shit," I said.

"Shit is right," Brandon said.

CHAPTER 52

"A STAIRWELL?"

I couldn't believe what I was looking at. Everything we planned hinged on knowing one of the five possible offices Frank visited with the phone I'd given him after the man had Bear left for dead and abducted the guy we'd been sent to kill. Instead, we had nailed down a stairwell.

"What the hell was he doing there for fifteen minutes?" Bear asked.

Brandon shrugged. "Too far away for anything to have been recorded. And, really, how much would this guy discuss in a stairwell?"

"Could have gone to the roof," I said. "Even the top floor landing. No one would be coming down. You'd hear every single person that entered. Their footsteps would echo up. Wait till they exited, then resume."

"Where was Brett during this?" Bear said.

"The trunk, maybe. One of Frank's associate's houses. Don't know."

"So what can we do?" Bear asked.

Brandon backed up until his chair hit the wall. "Don't know how much I can help you guys from here on out. You get some signals, or a bug on Frank, I'm your guy. But I already searched everything that's come through the past few days and there is nothing on any of y'all."

Bear said, "How can that be?"

"Got me, man. Almost like whoever is really behind this is off the grid."

He wheeled back, pivoted, and slipped past me. "You know me, Jack. I can find water in a rock in the desert. But this time, there's nothing but sand out there."

I said, "Nothing you've done is going to get you in trouble, right?"

"Me?" The light from the open refrigerator shone down on Brandon. He smiled wide. First time all night he looked confident. "They'll be searching Indo-China for me. Or Siberia. The UAE. Hell, Mobile, Alabama if I want them to." He aimed a frail arm in the direction of his computer. "I route my traffic all over the world. Can make it look like it originates from pretty much anywhere. None of it ever leads back to Harrisburg."

"OK." I glanced at Bear. The big man looked worse than earlier. The adrenaline had worn off, and every time he spoke, he winced or flinched. It was counter-productive for him to even stand at this point. He needed to heal. "My man here had a rough day. I can leave him here to watch out for you if need be."

"I'm good," Brandon said. "I see someone on my monitors that I don't like the looks of, they got a nasty surprise coming."

"He's good, Jack," Bear said with a slight edge to his voice. "Besides, I trust Brandon to take care of himself more than you."

I smiled. A weak effort at best. No one liked being frozen out. Bear was no exception.

"When's the last time either of you slept?" Brandon said.

Neither of us answered. I'm not sure either of us knew. A span of days like we'd had made it feel as though a month or more had passed. I'd reached a point where my actions were on autopilot. This was good and bad. I could trust myself to get out of just about any situation. The problem was that I couldn't trust myself to not get into the situation to begin with right now. Poor decision making was a concern.

"Crash here for the night," Brandon said. "You're safer here than anywhere else."

"Unless they bugged me when I went down," Bear said.

Brandon rolled his eyes as he made a production out of sweeping an arm out in front of himself. "Bells'd be ringing and chimes'd be chiming if you were bugged, my man. Trust me, you're clean."

We decided to stay, get some rest, then start the day around five a.m. I found a bottle of Bud and nursed it on a broken-in leather couch that practically swallowed me whole when I flopped back on it. I found the TV remote on the coffee table and switched the television on. None of the news broadcasts had anything to say about the events of the day. Didn't expect them to.

As my eyelids grew heavy enough to remain closed, my phone buzzed inside my pants pocket. McSweeney.

"I checked on Clarissa."

"How is she?"

"Good. Seemed calm. That bodyguard you sent over is vigilant, to say the least."

"He give you trouble?"

"A bit." She paused, and then added, "Even called in my badge number to make sure I was legit. Anyway, I offered to stick around, too, but she declined. Can't blame her, I guess. I'd feel plenty safe with that guy around."

"He's good at what he does. Always has been." At that moment, my mind slowed down. One less thing to worry about. Clarissa was safe.

"I'm gonna close this case, Jack."

Make that two things.

She continued. "In fact, I'm going to walk it to the back of the storeroom and bury it under all the unsolved cases from the sixties. No one will look in there. Not with all the crap we've got going on in this city now."

"I appreciate that," I said. "There are things we still don't know. You sure you don't want to get to the bottom of it? Doesn't your brother? Your ex?"

She sighed into the phone. "I'm sorry about that, Jack. I knew he was working the McLellan angle. And before you ask, no, he didn't give me any of the details. He always withheld information from me, both in our professional and private lives. He kept too many secrets. Probably the biggest reason we didn't last."

"No worries, Reese. What about your brother? He seemed adamant about figuring this out earlier."

"Not anymore. In fact, he's the one that told me to do this. Said he just wanted to put it behind him." She took a deep breath, exhaled into the phone. It sounded as though a hurricane force gust had taken over the line. "He's going to get out. Take his money, cut his losses, disappear. That's what he told me. He also wanted me to tell you not to worry. He won't seek revenge on you for taking the job, or on whoever ordered it. I don't know if that's Joe's influence on him, or what, but he honestly sounded at peace with the decision."

Discussing this over the phone made me uncomfortable, but the connection was secure. The number she dialed in on would route through a server that, if the computer determined another party was on the line, or any kind of monitoring had been put in place, it would disable the call.

"Let him know that if he needs anything, I'm here to help. And I still want to figure out how and why this went down the way it did."

She laughed. "He knew you'd say that. Not the help part, but figuring it out. Jack, he insisted that you let it go."

I said nothing.

"OK. Anyway, give me a call sometime, if you're in the city."

We ended the conversation there. I tried to actively replay the conversation in my mind, but it was pointless. A few minutes of staring at the television was all it took for my eyelids to grow so heavy I couldn't lift them. But then, trapped in a place between sleep and wakefulness, I thought about the recent revelations. What I knew. What I didn't. Working backwards, certain things stood out to me.

In the span of a few hours, Brett had gone from telling me to end this to having his sister tell me to drop it. Why? What had happened in the time after we left him? Had his ex-brother-in-law provided him with new information? Was it something we could use?

The only way to find out what was going on was to talk to Brett directly.

Frank's visit to a Cannon HOB stairwell bugged me. Did it mean anything at all? Meeting in the stairwell led me to believe that whoever he went to see played a big part in this. Or it was a routine visit. If the former, could I get Frank to sell them out?

Brett's involvement in the incident in Paris - and on a larger scale, with the terrorist cell - still nagged at me. Too many things that didn't add up.

And the fact it led to al-Sharaa seemed too great a coincidence. Too perfect, too easy. At best, I had access to half the files that would clarify things, assuming I could get a contact in the CIA to help me out. Would Pierre give up what the French had compiled? Maybe he'd divulge a little information, but he had bigger things to worry about now.

Finally, why had McLellan been at Brett's apartment? Had the ex-SEAL come with him? Or was the older guy already there? Maybe someone had sent him in for clean up, and he arrived afterward? I'd settle for knowing the truth about McLellan. My gut told me he'd had an order to kill someone. Was that someone Brett? Or me? Or perhaps us both?

In the end, it was he who'd lost his life.

Anything I had been told about the events up till now had to be discounted. Brett's request I drop it, leave it, seeped down. Was it worth it to investigate any further? I supposed I needed to talk with Frank again. So long as the man had plans on continuing to go after Brett, Bear and I were in danger of being targeted as well.

Morning, I decided, was when I would make my decision.

CHAPTER 53

ICE PELTED THE the windows like dozens of pebbles had been tossed against the glass. The sound roused me from my sleep. I opened my eyes to darkness interspersed with the soft, pulsing blue and green glow of lights emanated from Brandon's computer equipment.

I reached out for my phone, swung my feet out, and sat up.

Four a.m.

Bear was stretched out on the other couch, his legs extending a good foot past the armrest. He snored lightly every fourth or fifth breath. The floorboard creaked the first step I took. The big man didn't notice. Not like him. But, after what he'd been through, his sleep was deeper than normal.

I went to the kitchen and started a pot of coffee. Eventually the thoughts I'd fallen asleep to circled back around. A decision was nowhere closer than it was four hours ago. I'd start with Frank, and my message would be simple: We end this now, or I'll go live with the biggest tell-all the shadowy side of D.C. has ever seen. It'd be the kind of thing that would make hardened men weep themselves to sleep at night. I'd end it there if he agreed and provided confirmation that the job was terminated. I wouldn't be bothered by unanswered questions.

The coffee ready, I grabbed a mug, made my way through the garage, and stepped outside, using the overhang to shield me from the falling frozen rain. Each drop hit the pavement, scattered a few feet, like kicked-up gravel. Each breath of cold air awakened me further. Each sip of the hot liquid in my mug loosened up my throat and chest, allowing me to breathe deeper.

I spent twenty minutes out there, staring into the darkened woods, wondering if anyone was staring back.

As I turned to head back inside, I received a call.

The display said unknown. Against my better judgment, I answered.

"Hello, Mr. Jack," the Old Man said.

"Don't you sleep?" I said.

"Sleep is for those who don't want to get ahead in life, Mr. Jack."

"I think you've made pretty big strides. You can afford to nap for a while."

"Indeed." He paused, then added, "Aren't you tired of chasing your tail?"

"Never met a dog that tired of doing that."

"You consider yourself a dog?"

"Better than considering myself a cat."

The Old Man cackled.

"Look, I rescued the guy, made the girl happy, lost a friend, but also made a new one. All in all, a good day's work. I think I'm done with this. You can do what you will."

Through the thickness of trees, I made out headlights. They held steady maybe fifty yards ahead. Couldn't tell if it was a car or truck or van. They passed, and for a moment the red from their taillights was visible. The falling ice steadily pelting the ground made it difficult to focus on the rumbling engine. The vehicle could have continued on, or it could've stopped.

"Come see me, Mr. Jack. I have the answers you seek. These are answers that you want. Even if your Mr. Skinner agrees to call off the job, this will not end for you, not unless you know what I know."

"I don't like to play games. If you've got something to tell me, then do it now."

"I've already said more than I care to over the phone. From Harrisburg, it should take you no more than four hours to get here, even with traffic.

I'd suggest you leave now. Failure to arrive by nine a.m. will result in me pulling the plug on my Jack Noble experiment."

"The hell are you talking about?"

"Brett is no longer the target. You are." With that, the Old Man ended the call.

I stepped out from under the protection of the overhang and wrapped my hands behind my head and looked up. Frozen rain stung my face, numbed my skin. Above, the clouds had parted, leaving a jagged oval, like a hole in the ice on a lake after someone had fallen through. That was how I felt. The ice had cracked a day or two ago. I stepped in the wrong spot and was trapped underneath.

Smothered.

And now I was on my own.

CHAPTER 54

ALMOST FOUR HOURS later, I was driving through Queens. Navigating by memory. Looking for the first signs of the Old Man's compound.

The guys on the street corner were the first confirmation that I was close.

I didn't have to wait long to make a decision. The Old Man knew I was there. From what I knew of his organization, he had the reach to make something major happen within a half hour if he wanted to. I didn't want to put Bear at risk in his current state, and after all Brandon had done for us, including putting us up for the night, the worst way to repay him would be to allow a bunch of gangsters to descend upon the man's house.

I knew there was a chance the Old Man was bluffing. Fine. So be it. He could show me what he had in person, and we'd go from there. For whatever reason, the guy had a hard-on for me. Who was I to refuse him?

An hour after leaving Brandon's, I gave Bear a wake-up call. He'd been pissed I'd left him there, but after I relayed the conversation I'd had with the Old Man that morning, Bear understood. He resigned himself to watching over Brandon, so long as I promised that any further action would involve him.

And I was sure there would be more to do after this meeting.

Charles's Cadillac sped toward me. I rolled to a stop. He slammed on his brakes. Smoke wafted in through my open window. For a moment, it smelled like I sat in a chemical factory. He pulled up next to me, rolled down his window.

"Didn't think you'd show up, Jack."

"Nothing better to do this morning."

Charles regarded me for a moment, nodded, said, "Follow me."

I made a hasty three-point turn in an effort to keep up with the fleeing Caddy. He sped away from where I estimated the Old Man's compound to be located.

We headed south, over a bridge, eventually reaching Rockaway. Charles turned into a deserted public beach access parking lot. Sand skated along the pavement, rising, falling, shifting, ever-changing. I pulled into a spot three down from where he'd parked.

He exited his vehicle, lifted both hands in the air, and walked around the back of the Caddy. Twenty-four feet of asphalt and loose sand separated us.

I glanced in the rear-view. Two cars drove past. Old beaters. One blue, the other rust. Neither stopped. The sidewalk was empty. Nothing but cracked concrete with brown grass poking through. The store across the street stood deserted like a graveyard with its caretaker stuck inside a bulletproof box.

Charles didn't move. He'd stuffed his hands in his pockets and crossed his left leg over his right. He was a little shorter than Bear, but wider, thicker. Reminded me of a bull.

I opened my door and slid out. We squared off. Him at his car, me at mine. He made no outward signs of aggression. Finally, after thirty seconds of enduring angry, biting sand and frigid winds, Charles gestured with his head toward the beach.

A weathered wooden walkway stretched from the parking lot through the dunes to the beach. Sand had accumulated on the planks like snowdrifts, inches high in some spots. I turned away from Charles and set off toward the ocean.

The walkway rose upward, taking me eight to ten feet higher. As I walked past the first dune, I saw a lone, fragile figure walking along the edge of the water. Waves broke, flinging a frothy head into the air. After the salt water retreated into the mouth of the ocean, the foam clung to damp sand.

Seagulls hovered near the Old Man. At least a couple dozen of them, squawking like a bunch of teenagers in the mall. I noticed a worn canvas bag dangling from the Old Man's left hand. He reached into it with his right, pulled out a handful of its contents, which he tossed into the air. Gulls raced toward the fragments of food, fighting in mid-air for the rights to it. Pieces fell to the ground, and the birds descended upon them. They knocked one another away, usually allowing a waiting gull to swoop in and scoop up the prize.

And on it went.

The Old Man looked back, spotted me, turned while raising the bag into the air. With his other hand, he gestured for me to join him.

I journeyed into the fray, keenly aware of the location of the birds. With so many this close, it'd be hard to avoid the errant droppings that fell.

The Old Man dumped the contents of the bag on the ground and began walking northeast along the shifting shoreline. The waves crashed, and water and foam rolled over his tennis shoes and the bottom of his sweatpants. The Old Man didn't care. He kept walking.

I started in the same direction, increasing my pace until I caught up to him. He glanced over, smiled, looked back down at the ground and continued on. Gusts of wind whipped up off the water, sending sea foam into the air. It fell back to the earth like thick snow.

He stopped, faced the sea. I watched as he lifted one arm over his head, then the other. The Old Man held the pose for a few seconds. As his arms fell to his side, he spoke.

"Are you ready to work with me?"

I positioned myself next to him, facing the sea, back to the road. Uncomfortable, but he hadn't brought me out here to kill me.

He turned his head, smiled briefly. "Well?"

"I'm not in the mood to discuss that. I need answers." A pod of porpoises passed in front of us, maybe forty feet out. Like sea serpents, their sleek, dark bodies rose out of the water and slunk back in. "You said I was the target now." I paused to allow the Old Man to speak. He nodded, eyes focused on the ocean. "Who targeted me and why? Was Frank Skinner behind this?"

The Old Man filled his lungs with salty air and exhaled slowly. His right hand gripped his left wrist behind his back. He turned to the left and began walking at a slow pace until I joined him.

"Excuse me, Mr. Jack, I just don't like staying in one spot too long unless I'm at home." He smiled, presumably for my benefit, because there was no life or charm associated with the gesture. "Consider the contract on Brett Taylor's life to be null and void."

"You said he wasn't the target anymore."

"And you believed me."

"So this had nothing to do with me."

"Wrong, Mr. Jack. It had everything to do with you."

"You're making no sense." I fought to keep an even tone. I hated being jerked around, much less driving four hours for the privilege.

"I have many friends here, and abroad." He performed a sweeping gesture across the ocean. "Partners across the Atlantic were having trouble with a nuisance. They asked me to help. A little digging uncovered that the man was former military, Army in fact, and former CIA. He'd done quite a bit in twelve years. I knew that in order to kill a specially trained individual, you needed a highly skilled team. Now, my guys are good, but I didn't want to involve them in this, as it was tantamount to espionage."

"So you called a friend in the U.S. government."

The Old Man nodded.

"And would this friend happen to work on Capitol Hill with an office in the Cannon HOB?"

The Old Man's silence answered my question, and now Frank's reason for being at the building was clear.

"Can you give me a name?"

Again, the Old Man said nothing.

"So, I get the job. But then it's botched. There's a dead man in the bed, who turns out to be associated with Brett. Brett's not there, and we can't figure out how he got out and the other guy got in. Come to find that there's a way to enter through the basement."

"We'll discuss Brett first."

The Old Man reached into his pocket and pulled out a pack of cigarettes. After several failed attempts to light it in the heavy winds, he snapped the smoke in two and flicked it toward the water. A seagull dove down and snatched it from the grasp of the sea.

"With the US government failing me," he said, "I used leverage I had with Brett's asset and had her set up a meeting with him. In fact, I provided her with false documents. And then we tipped off my associates. Things should have worked themselves out the natural way."

"Only they arrived at the worst moment, and then did the stupidest thing possible."

The Old Man nodded several times. "Irregardless, now. They've hunkered down and you likely won't hear from them for a year. Maybe more. And that's according to them. I think they've screwed themselves, and will likely dissolve and return to whichever country they were from, or join up with another fledgling group."

"You supported terrorists." I decided against mentioning al-Sharaa.

"Terror doesn't pay, Mr. Jack. I've got no ideological dog in this fight. No, I supported criminals doing my bidding. The rest of that stuff was their own doing."

"But they used your money."

The Old Man hiked his shoulders an inch. "I'm not going to tell anyone what to do with the money they receive for a job competently completed. Buy a car. Buy a bomb. Makes no difference to me."

Perhaps the line wasn't as thin as I'd thought.

"What did they do for you?" I asked.

He said nothing.

"Forget it. It'll come back to haunt you."

"I love when people say things like that, Mr. Jack. I've been doing this for over forty years, employing those who get the job done, and offering services to the highest bidder. It has made me wealthy beyond anything you and most people can comprehend. I don't feel the least bit bad about it, either. Generations of my descendants will be provided for, if the world manages to hang on for that long. So what if someone puts a bullet in my brain? I'm old. I'm ready to go."

I stopped. "You know what, I didn't come here to listen to your philosophies on life and how it relates to what you've accomplished. You said I was targeted. I want to know by who."

The Old Man turned a few feet in front of me. "Let's go to my car, Mr. Jack. I've got something you'll want to see."

CHAPTER 55

THE BLACK LEXUS sat alone in the sand-covered parking lot. Every gust of wind brought a new wave of biting particles. They slapped us across the face and went on to settle on the ground and his car, replacing those that had blown away.

He gestured for me to take a seat on the passenger side. I glanced around the lot, across the street, then got in. The Old Man opened the back door. He reached for a leather bag. The zipper slid effortlessly, and he reached in and pulled out a folder. A moment later he was seated next to me.

"I think this will answer your questions."

He backed out of the spot. Tires spun on sand, caught the pavement. With a chirp, we lurched forward.

I opened the folder, which contained several five-by-eight pictures. Some were black and white. Others in color. The first was of Brett's empty apartment. What followed was an exact sequence of events. At least, according to the Old Man it was.

McLellan had entered first. According to the timestamp, he was alone for two minutes before someone else appeared. Through four pictures, all shot in the main room, the new guy had his back to the camera. He was short and wide and the kind of guy who'd bled and killed and didn't take shit off anyone.

A few pictures later, a third man showed up. I expected this. What I didn't count on was recognizing the jacket and hoodie combination the man was wearing. The photos tracked him through the house. None showed his face.

Until he went into the bedroom.

"These aren't doctored?" I said.

The Old Man shook his head. "I'm putting everything out in the open for you, Mr. Jack. I want you to see that I have your best interests in mind. I want you to accept my offer when I make it."

I wanted to open my door and fall out. I was trying to figure out what the hell happened in Brett's apartment. The Old Man's sole desire seemed to be to court me.

Three men had been in the apartment.

McLellan.

The ex-SEAL I encountered at the brownstone later.

And Brett Taylor.

In the next picture, two of them stood in Brett's room. I had no idea where the ex-SEAL was at this point. Hiding, presumably, because Brett wasn't to know the man was in Brett's apartment.

It appeared Brett and McLellan were having an argument. The time-stamps on the pictures were sporadic. Some were twenty seconds apart, others two minutes. The sequence went from the two men facing off, pitting McLellan with his back to bed, to McLellan on the bed with an obvious mortal wound.

"Tell me you've got audio for this," I said.

The Old Man said nothing.

"Do you?"

"You told me to tell you I did. I don't like to lie to my associates, Mr. Jack. There is no audio."

"Full video then?"

"Only what you see there."

"The older man, the SEAL, where was he when these last shots were taken?"

"I can only presume he was elsewhere in the building."

"Who was he there for?"

The Old Man said nothing. I couldn't tell if he was withholding information, or simply didn't have an answer.

"Take me back to my car," I said.

The Old Man slowed, and then whipped the wheel in a circle. "Whatever you were offered for this job, I can pay you that on a monthly basis, Mr. Jack."

"What?" My mind had been going through the sequence of events in the pictures, trying to place words with expressions. Searching for a reason the three men were together, and why one had been left dead in Brett's bed. And why Brett had lied to me about his presence in the apartment when it happened.

"There is no way you are this dense," the Old Man said. "I want you on my payroll. I'm willing to pay you a million dollars a year to work your way up to be my right-hand man. Within months, you'll be practically running my operation, set to take over when I finally retire." He paused, smiled, then added, "Or someone manages to put a bullet between my eyes."

We pulled up to a red light and still intersection.

"I've got no interest in being a criminal."

The Old Man laughed, a cackling, maniacal sound right out of an old horror flick. "You think you aren't one now? Killing for the government makes you some kind of hero, right?"

"I don't go after choir singers."

"Neither do I. It takes bad men to do bad things, Mr. Jack, no matter what side of the law they're on. If there is even a side. As far as I am concerned, there's no more difference between good and evil than there is space between us right now."

I didn't want to admit that we agreed on the topic. Still, I had principles to adhere to. "Look, I appreciate the offer, but-"

"Now is not the time to make any decisions. You've got to figure out what happened there, after all."

We pulled into the lot. My car stood alone amid a sea of brown sand.

"Do you know where Brett Taylor is now?" I asked.

"I told you, I called that off. He is no longer my concern. I'd suggest you forget about him too, Mr. Jack. Besides, he did you a favor."

I pushed my door open and dropped my right foot on the ground, stopped, looked back. "What about me? You said I was the target now."

"It turns out my overseas associates had another contact here in the States that they contracted. I suppose they wanted one party to handle the killing. The other would take the fall if it came down to that."

"Which was which?"

"Who got there first?"

McLellan.

I shrugged. "He's dead. Brett's off the grid. Already encountered the ex-SEAL, and he's not getting around for a while."

"Most definitely not. He was found dead in a cabin in the woods this morning."

"Would you happen to know any additional details?"

The Old Man shook his head, said nothing.

"Of course you don't."

"Anyway," the Old Man said. "You see, I no longer have an interest in assisting my former associates. But this other party does. And their target now is you."

I exited the car. Before my door had shut, the Old Man was pulling away. I heard the vehicle stop and idle. His window rolled down. I looked back.

"I'll be in touch, Mr. Jack, about that job. In the meantime, let this go. No good will come of you digging any deeper. You either need to get away, or join me. I can provide the protection you need now."

The Lexus faded into the cold, gray haze. I waited there, in the deserted parking lot, half-expecting Charles to return or a team of SIS agents to appear and shoot me, or escort me back to D.C. I couldn't decide which would be worse.

The breeze momentarily died down. The sounds of waves crashing and gulls squawking took its place. If I could tune out the cold, I'd have stayed there the rest of the day. With every second that passed, I slipped into an almost comatose state. There was nothing worse than losing. Except for tying.

And that was precisely what had happened.

There were no winners or losers here, except for McLellan and the ex-SEAL. Brett would always be looking over his shoulder. And so would I.

I couldn't leave it alone. I had to find him. The story had a missing piece, and it lay with Brett.

And whoever else the terrorists had contacted to take him, and now me, out.

CHAPTER 56

BEFORE EXITING THE parking lot, I called Bear and updated him on my meeting with the Old Man, the new evidence, and the confusing story it told. He didn't have much input, and wanted time to think it through, perhaps call a few of his contacts. We planned to meet up later that evening. But first, I needed to head into the city.

During the drive, the Old Man's advice about letting the thing with Brett go kept playing on my thoughts. Aside from the other party now targeting me, what could he have held back? I assumed there was more to Brett than I'd been told. Maybe McSweeney, too. The brother-sister angle hadn't sat well with me. The chemistry wasn't right. Though it had been seventeen years since my sister, Molly, had been murdered, I could still recall the way we acted together. Even my brother Sean and I, though we had our differences at time, there was a bond there.

Perhaps I was overthinking it.

Maybe after paying a visit to Clarissa, I'd find McSweeney and simply pose the question to her.

After ditching the car in the parking garage, I walked to my apartment building. My intention was just to pass by, not go in. Someone could be waiting inside my place, gun aimed at the door, hoping I would show up. I made a quick check of the perimeter, noticed nothing out of the ordinary. Didn't mean it was safe, though, so I kept going.

I hadn't called Clarissa on my way in. Wasn't that I wanted to surprise her; I wanted to catch anyone who might be watching her off guard. If she expected the visit, they could become aware of my pending arrival.

Since the bar was closest, I went there first. The front door had cracked since the snowstorm. The split ran about head-to-waist-high on the right near the hinges. I reached for the knob and found it unlocked. It took a few seconds for my eyes to adjust to the dim lighting. A shaded, slender figure hopped over the bar and rushed toward me.

I smelled her perfume before her arms wrapped around my neck. Her lips pressed against mine. Peach Schnapps and gum. Reminded me of younger years.

"You doing all right?" My hands closed around her waist.

Her grip on my neck tightened and she said nothing.

Had something happened with the Russian? Had he tried to hurt her? I swept the room, spotted him perched on a bar stool near the kitchen door. He hoisted a sweaty glass of water to his lips, took a sip, and then nodded.

"Clarissa, what's going on?"

"McSweeney showed up a while ago, a bit frantic. Said all she had was a bag packed. All she had time for, apparently. She wanted me to go with her. Said I was in danger." She paused and bit her bottom lip. Her eyes darted back and forth, focusing on me, then the door, then another spot.

"All right, calm down and think. Did she say why?"

Clarissa shook her head, tight and terse. "No, she just repeated that I was in danger and should go with her. And, you know, if you had called and said to do it, I'd have gone. But, I barely know the woman. And besides, I feel safe with that guy over there."

I glanced at the Russian again. He'd returned to acting like he wasn't paying attention.

"OK, we'll get this figured out. All right?"

She nodded.

"Go ahead and get back behind the bar. Let me talk to him for a minute."

She took the long way, rather than hopping back over. I gestured toward the Russian. We met at the other end of the bar, away from the sole occupied table and talked.

I showed him a picture of the ex-SEAL from the brownstone. Though they were twenty years or so apart in age, their paths might have crossed at some point. He took a long look at the picture, frowned, and handed it back.

"I can say he looks familiar, but from where, I don't know. If you want, I'll pass it around and see if anyone knows him, of him, or his last known location."

After debating how much to tell him, I said, "I've got that last part, and he's not moving on from it."

The Russian lifted an eyebrow and leaned forward a couple inches.

I nodded. "Ran into him yesterday, but it wasn't me. Not saying I didn't leave him in bad shape, but certainly not enough for him to end up with a toe tag. Someone came along later. I only have a general idea who, and I think it's someone hell-bent on clean up."

The man didn't press for details. He'd left behind this world some time ago. If I'd asked for additional help, perhaps he would have considered it. As it was, he seemed content to stick to acting as Clarissa's bodyguard.

And I was content to let him.

I knew what I faced in the Old Man and Frank; the real danger was the unknown. What other contact did al-Sharaa have in the U.S. that would be willing to assassinate a target for him? I understood the Old Man's motivation. Did money drive the other person, or was the catalyst ideological?

McSweeney's words to Clarissa meant something. For her to be afraid, it had to be someone, or some group, that could operate without fear of the NYPD. The only way to know for sure was to find the woman.

Once again, that led me back to Brett.

I spent another thirty minutes at the bar, at Clarissa's insistence. She had the cook whip me up a burger topped with fried eggs. I wasn't hungry, but I ate it anyway. I downed three cups of coffee. One before the meal. One during. One after. Figured that'd be enough to keep me going through the four hour drive ahead of me.

I paid her for the meal. She made a show out of not accepting it, but did. Then I left.

Before heading to the garage to get the car, I decided to stop by McSweeney's apartment. I had to wait ten minutes in the cold before managing to catch the door as someone exited. I took the stairwell to her floor. The carpet on the landing felt spongy under my feet, and I detected a hint of mildew in the air. A drop of water hit my hand as I reached for the door. It had fallen from a pipe that ran along the ceiling.

I stopped in front of McSweeney's apartment and pressed my ear to the door. The old paint grated on my skin like sandpaper. I heard nothing. I reached for the handle. Surprisingly, it was unlocked.

I wasn't sure what I expected to see. A bookshelf toppled over, perhaps. Her clothes strewn about, maybe. Furniture overturned, for sure.

There was none of that.

There was nothing at all.

CHAPTER 57

I STOOD IN the empty apartment, aware that just a few days ago it had been fully furnished. A quick call to Brandon confirmed for me that Reese McSweeney was a detective in the NYPD, and that she hadn't shown up for work in two days. Even her partner hadn't heard from her. Was this premeditated? Had McSweeney planned to flee?

I continued through her barren apartment. It smelled of lemon and pine trees. Reminded me of Saturdays as a kid, when my mother had my brother, sister, and me clean the house. She had knick-knacks on every shelf. It was my job to take them off, clean each individually, and then dust the shelf. If I didn't put them back in exactly the right place, there'd be no television for me that weekend. And I hated missing my Saturday after-noon wrestling.

The discoloration of the hardwood floors was the only sign that there had been furniture in the place. I moved from the living area to her bedroom. Traced the position of the bed. Her dress blues still hung in the closet, along with a pair of jeans and a sweater. Nothing else. I pulled them off their hangers and searched the pockets, hoping for a note or receipt or anything that might give a clue. Came up empty. Why had these items been left behind? Someone on the run wouldn't have packed every-thing up; they'd have left far more behind. And nothing had given me the impression that McSweeney had been planning to take off.

Maybe that was it. She had disappeared; but not by her own doing.

I gave the closet a once-over, looking for any false spots on the wall where a cut-out existed. A place where a safe had been installed. Finding nothing, I left the room, wiping my prints from the doorknobs. I checked the bathroom and linen closet off the hallway. They were as barren as the rest of the place. I made sure to wipe everything down in the living room and kitchen, and then I left.

The stairwell door opened a second after I shut McSweeney's. I stood there, facing the door, and knocked. A slender, raven-haired woman in her early twenties approached. She made eye contact as she passed.

"Excuse me," I said. "Have you seen the woman that lives here recently?"

"Wasn't friendly with her." She spoke with an Eastern European accent. "But there were movers here yesterday. Guess she found a new place."

Perhaps she had.

I waited until the woman disappeared into the safety of her apartment. She cast one last glance in my direction as she slipped through the opening. Afterward, I made my way to the same stairwell and descended to the main level.

The car wasn't far away, but I had another stop I wanted to make before leaving. The brownstone. I wasn't sure when I'd be back, and the scene would never be as secure as it was at this moment. Not saying it had been kept pristine, but every day that passed meant someone else could have trampled on possible evidence.

I hailed the first taxi to approach. A man with a short gray beard and a bald head and a cigarette dangling from his thin lips asked me where I wanted to go. I had him drop me off four blocks north and east of the brownstone.

The path I walked took me past the café where Bear and I had sat in the freezing weather, drinking lukewarm coffee, moments before we were to do our job.

Moments before everything changed.

It had all started at the café.

Things seemed uncertain at that time. They always did. And it was the same state of constant flux I'd grown accustomed to. But this, now, I had no idea where the next few moves I would make would take me. That didn't sit well.

A short walk later I saw a scorched skeleton rising from the ground, squished between two renovated buildings, amid smoldering ruins and ashes and rubble.

My head swung like it was attached to a swivel. My gaze didn't linger long on any one spot. And it was pointless. If whoever had burned down the brownstone had a spotter, they wouldn't be visible on the street.

And so I turned, and looked up to the same spot where I had waited days ago, across the street from the now-burned-down brownstone. A shadowy figure backed away from the window. I reached behind my back, wrapped my hand around the pistol's grip. I moved toward the door. Walking, jogging, running, jumping past the stairs. Inside the mold and mildew hit me. My nostrils itched and my lungs burned. I ignored the sensation, knowing that in a few short seconds, it'd pass.

I heard the sound of soles squeaking on linoleum. It came from above. I took the stairs two at a time, then paused on the landing. A door slammed shut on a higher floor. I passed by the second floor and continued on to the third. The dim hallway stretched out in front of me, four or five apartments on either side. Pale light peeked out from under the doors. I approached each slowly and cautiously.

All I wanted to see was the glow emanating unblocked from under the door and a pinprick of light through the peephole. Every door but the last on the right met the requirements. I almost didn't notice. At the final second, the dot of white disappeared for an instant. Someone could've passed by, on their way from one room to the next. But when I looked down, I noticed the last two inches on both sides of the space under the door were darkened.

Someone was standing there, inches from me, on the opposite side of a dented hunk of solid-core wood, and they weren't moving. Were they waiting for me?

This all happened in a couple of seconds. I never stopped moving. The door to the other stairwell approached. I wrapped my hand around the knob.

The door behind me cracked open.

I held my pistol down by my thigh. Turned my head to the right, slightly, so that I could see the door in my peripheral vision. Yellow-white light bled into the hallway. A shadow filled some of the space. They took a deep breath, as if to steel themselves. An exhale, grunt, hand gripping the doorframe, black barrel of a pistol emerging.

I spun, back pushing through the heavy hallway door.

He grunted, emerged from the apartment. I didn't attempt to identify the man. My focus remained on the pistol, which he angled at me while contorting his body.

I held the sidearm waist-high, and instinctively fired. The suppressor muffled some of the sound, but not all. If anyone in the adjoining apartments was near their front door, the sound might be enough to give them cause to investigate. Or just call 9-1-1.

The man shot back, but missed. Plaster exploded to my left and rained down on me. The deafening sound echoed throughout the stairwell and hallway. My ears sang.

I fired again. Both shots had hit him. Crimson blooms formed at his lower gut and dead-center on his chest. He fell, landed sideways. Ragged and sporadic breathing followed.

A door opened. An old woman poked her head out. Curlers weighed down her blue-tinted hair.

"Get back in there."

She froze at the sight of a pistol aimed at her face.

"Now," I said.

She complied. I returned my attention to the dying man on the ground.

"Who are you?"

The man said nothing.

I rose and placed the heel of my shoe against his stomach. "Who the hell are you?"

His eyes rolled back in his head.

I leaned over and searched his pockets, all the while keeping my eyes up, focused on the open doorway to the apartment. Did he live there? Or had it been the only one he found unlocked? I considered tempting fate and investigating, but after coming up with a wallet and cell phone, I left the man to die and made my way down the stairs.

CHAPTER 58

THE TEMPERATURE WAS in the mid-forties. Might as well have been ten below. The sweat that coated my face, back, and chest cooled and felt like ice melting on my skin. The sidewalks were deserted. I heard no sirens. That old woman was probably cowering behind her door or under a table. Eventually, someone would walk out of their apartment and find a man dying or dead in the middle of their hallway.

I wasted no time moving, heading back the way I came, past the café. I took a look inside in an attempt to determine if Clarissa's friend was working. Didn't see her. Perhaps she had seen what, or who, had started the fire at the brownstone. I had no shortage of potential candidates. Brett could have come back and done it himself. Not likely, but possible. Maybe McSweeney on her way out of town. Frank, the CIA, the Old Man, or anyone else with a vested interest in not being indicted could be responsible.

There were better things I could spend my time worrying about. That's what I told myself. The fact that someone had been watching over the remains of the building, and then attempted to kill me, told me that I needed to keep pursuing the investigation. Were they looking for me, though? Had they expected that I would return? Maybe the shooter had been there to watch for anyone suspicious. But he'd fled when I spotted him. He hadn't made an attempt on me until I passed by his hideout. Could have let me go. Instead, he attacked.

He'd been waiting for me. Maybe not only me, but I was on his list.

I pulled his phone out and checked the contact list. Empty. I navigated to the recent calls list. One number. I didn't recognize the area code. Could have been Maryland. Maybe Montana. One of those that I was confused by every time I saw it. And it really didn't matter. Presumably, the number was a forwarder and routed around the country. Like mine. Like Bear's. Nothing like Brandon's. But then, whose was? The timestamp indicated the man had called the number around the time I was outside the building. Further evidence he'd recognized me and reported my presence.

And whoever he reported it to had authorized him to strike if I came closer.

I only had one shot at this. After my call, they'd know their man was down. They'd abandon the number, their position, everything.

The café provided shelter from both the wind and prying eyes. And it was empty except for a portly red-cheeked guy behind the counter who didn't seem to care I hadn't approached him for a cup of coffee.

And I could have used one about then. But this was more important.

I called Brandon on my cell and asked him if he could link up to the phone I had taken off the man in the apartment building. He had me sort through various menus and read to him combinations of letters and numbers that made little sense to me but had him giggling like a child watching cartoons.

"All right, Jack," he said. "When you redial that number, I'll capture every step of the way. You just need to hold the line for twenty seconds. You got that?"

"I think I can manage to count that high."

"Good. How're you gonna keep them on the line?"

"No clue, Brandon. Not a single friggin' clue." I glanced up at the counter. The guy had taken a seat on a stool and paged through a magazine. I couldn't tell which one. "OK. I'm gonna dial now."

"Wait, wait, wait," Brandon said. "I'm not quite ready."

I approached the counter. The guy looked up from his magazine. I spotted a blonde straddling a motorcycle on the page it was opened to. The man's cheeks grew redder.

"Help you, sir?" he said.

"Restroom?"

He aimed a finger down a narrow hall, waited for me to pass, then went back to his stool and his literature.

"All right," I said. "How about now, Brandon?"

"Yup, I got you, your location, so on. Go ahead and make that call."

I placed my cell on the sink and grabbed the faucet. It felt grimy, pitted, like it had powdered cleaner caked on it. I turned it, then cupped my hands under the cool stream of water that fell into the sink. I splashed some on my face. My lips parted, allowing some into my mouth, swishing it around, then spitting it out. I cut the water, grabbed a paper towel, and dried off.

After a deep breath, I highlighted the number and pressed send. There was a delay as the call routed through multiple switches, possibly including a government server.

Finally I heard the half-burst of a static-laden ring. Another, a full one, followed. On the fifth ring a man answered.

"Got an update?"

I hesitated while attempting to place the voice. It didn't draw a match. Instead of answering him, I groaned.

"Vogel?" He paused, presumably waiting for me to answer. I didn't. "What the hell's going on?"

Again, I answered with a groan. The countdown in my head continued. We were halfway there.

"Vogel, Christ, stay where you are. I'll get the team over there now."

"Wait," I said in as gravely a voice as I could muster.

"What?"

I grunted a few times, took a deep, wheezy breath, then choked. Quite a production, and in all, it ate up five more seconds, which meant the twenty Brandon required were up. Best to add a few more to be on the safe side.

"I can't keep this line open," the man said. "Stay put. I'll have someone there in a couple minutes."

The call ended. A phone icon flashed several times on the screen, then disappeared. The time stared back at me. I grabbed my cell off the sink.

"Tell me you got it?"

"I got something," Brandon said. "It'll take me a while to figure this out. That call went all over the world, but if anyone can trace it, I'm the guy."

"Love your confidence, man."

"Always said I'd be making millions in the big leagues if my body hadn't been so ravaged."

I smiled, said, "Call me when you know something. Also, look up this Vogel guy. Can't be many with that last name in the community. I'm gonna make my way to the car and get moving."

For a moment, I stood in front of the sink, regarding myself in the mirror. With a nod to my reflection, I tucked both phones in my pocket and exited the restroom. I ordered a cup of black coffee from the red-faced guy, then left the café through the front door.

Two police cars were parked further down the street, across from the burned-out brownstone. Blue strobes reflected off the buildings. I didn't see the cops on the street. There'd be plenty after the body was found. And who knows who else would show up after Vogel was identified. That didn't matter. Forensics did. In my haste, I hadn't wiped down every surface I'd touched. In a day or two, I might be named as a suspect. It all depended on what restrictions Frank had removed from my files.

The garage was close, but I figured the less time I spent on the street, the better. I grabbed a cab and ignored the middle-aged Irish woman's attempts at conversation. She dropped me off in front of a hotel I had no intentions of staying at. I entered the lobby, walked past the desk, and exited in the rear. The abandoned alley led me to the parking garage.

I peered through the tinted windows of a passenger van. I had a view of the area surrounding my car. I gave it thirty seconds, then started toward the vehicle. A parade of footsteps resulted in a long succession of echoes throughout the structure. Sounded like an army approaching. But only one man was creating them.

Me.

Brandon called back before I'd managed to merge onto I-95. I activated the speaker and set the phone in the console.

"OK, Jack. I've got some information on Vogel. Wasn't easy, either."

"Tell me what you know."

"Kind of atypical, I think. Joined the Navy at eighteen, SEALS not long after. Left at twenty-six to finish his degree, which he'd started working on during his enlistment. All online, apparently. At twenty-eight he enrolled at Georgetown Law. Finished at thirty-one. Shrugged off several potential employers. Immediately got a job with the FBI."

"The FBI?"

"That's what I said. Why?"

"Those guys usually end up CIA or cops, if anything. Just wondering why he chose to be a Feeb."

"Well, if you want to go unkill him, you can find out."

"What about family?"

"Wife, kid, divorced before he was done with the Navy." He paused, and I said nothing. "This guy was all over the place with the Bureau, man. LA. Dallas. Denver. Chicago. D.C."

"Which office does he work out of now?"

Brandon's phone beeped a couple times like he'd hit the keys while shifting the device from one ear to the other. "None, man. He bailed on the Bureau. He was up for a leadership position. Didn't get it. Quit."

"How long ago was that?"

"Sixteen months."

When it came to the FBI, I had no contacts other than my new friend Joe Dunne, and I wasn't going to call him for information on Vogel. They hated the power given to the SIS in the wake of 9/11. Outside of SIS and the CIA, I had to rely on Brandon for intelligence. And it appeared that was the case once again.

"OK, Brandon. Keep digging on him. Find out what his parents did. What his siblings do. If he remarried. Who his last boss was."

"Yeah, yeah. I got it, Jack."

"Any luck on that trace yet?"

"Looks like it dead ends in Northern Virginia."

"Where?"

"I've got three locations."

"Gonna make me guess?"

"Yeah. No. Sorry. Was looking at something else." He muttered something I couldn't comprehend. "OK, forget that. These are the locations. Remember that server on Capitol Hill?"

"You're kidding."

"Nope. That's location numero uno. Next up is the walled fortress we call CIA located in beautiful, and heavily bugged, Langley, Virginia."

"And three?"

"Quantico."

"Shit."

"You can say that again."

"What are the chances this call is bouncing between all three places?"

"I don't like dealing in chances, man. When I get the spaghetti tangle figured out, you'll be the first to know."

"We definitely need more about Vogel's time in the FBI. Focus on cases he worked and people he brought down. And detail his movements from the past sixteen months."

"I'm on it."

"All right, sounds good. I'm making my way south. Might come by there this evening."

"Yeah, get down here and collect Bear. He's getting restless, man. And I ain't got enough food in this house for him."

I pictured the big man limping around the house, raiding the fridge, feeling like he wasn't doing anything to help. It would be driving him crazy.

"OK. I'll call in a few hours." I pulled the phone away, then stopped myself from shutting it. "Brandon, you still there?"

"What's up, boss?"

"See what you can find on a Special Agent Dunne, maybe out of the D.C. office. All the same stuff you're looking for with Vogel."

"He's got some connection with that detective, right?"

"Yeah."

If he even existed.

CHAPTER 59

A N HOUR INTO the drive, I rolled down the front windows. I'd never been able to just have one open. Wreaks havoc on my ears. Something about the pressure makes me dizzy. The cold air, laden with gas fumes, acted like a jolt of mainlined caffeine, only with a pungent aftertaste. It cleared my head, and I began the process of sorting everything that had happened since we took Brett at the back of that new development.

The waters were muddied. More so than ever.

Why had an ex-SEAL, ex-FBI Special Agent, been hiding across the street from the skeletal remains of the brownstone? Who fled when he saw me. Could've stayed holed up in a room. Instead, he attempted to take me out. There was no doubt in my mind that Vogel knew my identity. Otherwise, he'd have let me walk and gone on to live another day.

That meant he'd had a standing order to kill me, or had received an order from whoever was on the other end of the line. This added some validity to the Old Man's claims that I was now the target.

Presumably, if I had carried on down the sidewalk, he would have radioed in my position and either followed me or another team would have picked me up. The fact that no one else showed up in the beginning, to my knowledge at least, meant there'd been no other team nearby. Or Vogel had broken protocol and failed to notify his local team. Of course, it could also have been perfect timing on my part. Maybe they'd been running up the other stairwell, or stuck in the elevator.

What he'd failed to do and where they were didn't matter anymore. Vogel died. No one had come to his rescue.

A car horn blast snapped me back to the moment. I'd drifted halfway into another lane without realizing it and had come close to taking away an elderly woman's front fender. I figured it was a good time to get off the road for a bit. At the next opportunity, I exited, hung a right, and drove until I found a place where I could buy a cheap disposable cell. Ten minutes later, with the phone connected to the cigarette lighter so I could keep the device powered on, I called Frank.

As expected, he didn't answer. I left a message informing him my next call would be in fifteen minutes.

Instead of jumping back on the interstate, I continued driving further into a residential area. An empty parking lot at the community park looked like an inviting place to conduct matters of espionage, so I turned into the gravel lot and backed into a space. Crushed rock gave way beneath the weight of the vehicle with the sounds of small waves breaking.

Seated in the vehicle, facing the road, my stomach tightened with every car that passed. None turned in. They all kept going, on their way home, back to work, to get the kids from school.

Things I didn't understand.

Fifteen minutes had passed. I dialed Frank's number again. This time he answered.

"What do you want, Noble?"

"Noble? What happened to Jack? Two of us no longer friends?"

"Friends don't try to kill each other over a shared target. They don't kill each other's associates either. C'mon, Jack, those guys left Bear alive."

"They left him to die. We left your guys missing a fingertip and with holes in their knees. Someone else did them."

He responded with silence. For a moment I thought he might have disconnected the line. A cough let me know he hadn't.

"Look, Frank, we did what we did to get answers. Plain and simple. No different than some of the things you and I did together."

"Why, though, Jack? You had an assignment, an order. A goddamn executive order and you didn't follow through. Christ, you went so far as to help the guy. And you went rogue on me. And being the one who issued the assignment to you, it falls upon my shoulders to clean this whole mess up. That meant taking Brett in myself. I should've had a bullet put in his brain the moment they found him hiding in a field a mile from that diner. Bear's, too. But, no, I figured if you had a reason to pause, maybe I should as well. So I wanted to question him."

That explained why Frank had taken Brett to SIS, but not Capitol Hill. Had the man done enough to convince Frank the way he had me?

"So we chatted, a bit. He said little. Wouldn't mention names, anything like that. It was the setting, I'm sure of it. You know how it is in the bowels of that building. But by that point I decided I didn't need to hear anymore of his BS. We were going to take him out, finish the job, and I was going to let you decide whether you and your overgrown friend lived or died."

"The sniper in the field, he was there for Brett."

"Yeah." Frank paused. It sounded like he took a drink. "Anyway, I wanted it to be a little dramatic, and it was. Things got out of hand. The plan was to turn him over, believe it or not. Create some plausible deniability on my part, if need be. Then, after I'd left, boom, down goes Taylor. We're all national heroes." He paused, and then added, "I didn't plan on us trading shots like that. Anyway, where is he now?"

I said nothing.

"Doesn't matter. The job was called off."

I didn't bother to feign surprise. Nor did I mention the second party. "Where's that leave us?"

"I don't know, Jack. I honestly don't. At the moment, I can't imagine the two of us working together again. Word'll get out what happened. It always does, and you know that. Chances are, you're going to be black-balled in the community. Probably need to watch your back for a long while."

I debated telling him about my experience in the building across from the brownstone. That was the thing about Frank; it didn't matter if we were at odds with one another. Despite his ruthless approach to life, the guy had something about him that I trusted. That created a problem. I put it at a thirty percent chance he was in on the attempt at the brownstone. If anyone out there figured I'd return to the scene, it'd be Frank. Maybe he didn't plan the hit, but he could've given input.

So I had to keep the information to myself. For now.

Frank continued. "If I hear anything, specific or otherwise, I'll let you know, Jack."

He was feeling remorse over the situation too. Understandable, considering the things the two of us had been through together as partners in the SIS. I hadn't gone out to that development with plans on shooting him. Only if he left me with no choice. Had it really come to that?

"Appreciate that, Frank." The words were sincere. I meant it. And at the same time, my gaze darted left and right on the lookout for someone Frank might've sent. "One more thing."

"What?"

"Who do you know at the Cannon House Office Building?"

I expected he would deny knowing anyone there. Instead, he laughed.

"You serious? Christ, Jack, I deal with about three dozen people there. I spend a good amount of time there each week these days, meeting with those political dicks. That's management for you." He paused, then added, "Why?"

"Got a source that puts you there same day, an hour or so after you acquired Brett."

"Who?"

I said nothing.

"Doubt it was who I went to see, otherwise you wouldn't be asking what I was doing there. Tell me who it was."

I still said nothing.

"That meeting was classified and has nothing to do with you. In light of what had happened that day, I didn't want to go, but had no choice in the matter. Can we leave it at that?"

We couldn't, but I agreed anyway, and we hung up. It'd help if I could nail down who he'd gone to speak with. Instinct told me all of this would come to a screeching halt if I managed that. Logic told me instinct had a fatal flaw.

A car finally pulled into the lot, continued past me, and parked at the other end. I watched, waited. A woman, probably in her late thirties, stepped out. Her foot sank in the gravel. She opened the back door and a young boy and girl both climbed down. The girl waited by the woman. The boy sprinted across the lot and climbed the split-rail wooden fence.

I found my way back to I-95, then detoured north of Philly on I-76 toward Harrisburg. The path to Brandon's house was different from this direction. Here, the roads were clear, most of the snow having melted. Until I got to Brandon's street.

But I didn't notice the snow and ice and slush, or the car sliding and veering to the right and nearly coming to rest in a snowbank.

I was too busy focusing on the plume of smoke rising from within the woods.

CHAPTER 60

THE SMOKE WAS thick and gray and rapidly overtaking the blue sky. Though some distance away, I had a sudden acrid taste in my mouth, and a strong, pungent odor filled the car.

A map formed in my head. My location. The road. Brandon's house. And that was roughly the fire's position.

I fought back the instinct to race forward in the car. This was no coincidence. If I was right, and that was Brandon's house, someone had set the fire deliberately. Pulling the car to the side of the road, I called Bear. There was no answer. I tried Brandon next. No answer.

I exited the vehicle and raced through the woods. The snow was deep, affecting my speed. The odor grew stronger. Though I couldn't see the smoke, I could taste it. My eyes stung, and my throat tightened. Eventually, the view grew hazy. By the time I reached the clearing surrounding Brandon's home, it was like I was standing in the middle of a storm cloud.

My breaths were short and wheezy now. Oxygen was hard to come by; the raging fire was consuming it faster than I could. The heat two hundred feet away from the blaze was intense. The roar of the fire and the crackling of wood consumed by flame drowned out all other sounds.

I pulled my shirt over my nose. I had no idea if it would help, but it produced a feeling of calmness. And that was how I would survive the situation.

The adrenaline coursing through me began to wane, a byproduct of reality setting in. Staring at the rising flames, I felt the first pangs of doubt that I'd find Bear and Brandon alive. There was no way I could get into the house. Fire jutted from every window. The roof had dissolved. I expected the place to collapse at any minute.

Hunched over, I scanned the front lot and saw no signs of movement. If the two of them had been in the kitchen, a rear escape would have been likely. So I made my way along the edge of the clearing to the back of the house. As it came into view, there was an explosion, similar to what I'd experienced in Iraq five years prior.

And like then, I dove to the ground, covered my head while debris rained down all around me. After a few seconds, I looked over and saw the shell of an oil tank consumed with fire. Flames danced along the grass.

Past the spreading blaze and rising smoke, I saw two forms on the ground. Lifeless shapes. One large, one small.

I raced toward the bodies, shirt covering my mouth and nose, angling away from the growing fire. The wail of sirens approached. Could've been the ringing in my ears matrixing into a sound I hoped to hear. I didn't veer from my path to the bodies.

The way they were lying before me, Bear face down, Brandon a few feet away from Bear's head, perpendicular to the big man and facing the trees, it looked as though the big man had carried Brandon out of the house.

I knelt next to Bear. As I felt along his neck for a pulse, my eyes scanned the thick woods. After a short distance, it all looked the same: skeletal trees intertwined into a tangled mess. Bear's heart beat fast and strong, but he was unconscious. I checked his body, found no wound. Moving to Brandon, I once again scanned the area and saw no one.

The wailing in the distance was definitively sirens, about a mile away. Not close enough for their strobes to be visible.

I dropped to one knee next to Brandon. My head spun. Oxygen was in short supply. I had to be careful, or I'd be on the ground next to the two of them. If there was another explosion, that could spell death for all three of us.

Blood flowed from a gash on Brandon's forehead. I touched his wrist. He opened his eyes. They fluttered back in his head for a moment, and then his gaze settled on me. He tried to speak, but his hoarse voice produced nothing coherent.

"Save it," I said, leaning in close to ensure he heard me. "I'm gonna move you back, out of the smoke."

He blinked a couple times and gave me a slight nod.

I rose, turned back toward Bear, still unconscious. Had it been the smoke? Was it choking him now? I didn't know if I'd have the strength to move him in the current conditions. Perhaps by the time I returned from carrying Brandon, Bear would have regained consciousness.

Emergency vehicle strobe lights fought through the smoke surrounding the house. Maybe I wouldn't have to carry Bear. I decided to hoist Brandon over my shoulder and carry him to the rescue crew. The clearing to the right of the house was wide enough that I could stay out of the thickest smoke The wind assisted by blowing most of it to the other side.

I dropped to my knee again, next to Brandon, and performed a quick assessment to verify nothing was severely broken, then worked my arms under the guy's upper back and knees. My brain signaled that it was time to lift and rise.

But the blackness stopped that from happening.

CHAPTER 61

M Y HEAD FELT like a tire iron had split it in two. That was the first thing I noticed. The second was that my arms were behind my back and I couldn't separate my wrists.

The air felt cool, still, and damp. My left eye wouldn't open. Forcing the issue produced a stabbing pain and flash of light, and both eyelids clenched shut, resulting in additional discomfort. I sucked in a lungful of mold-ridden air. My chest burned as I held it in and counted back from eight. Exhaling, I allowed my right eye to relax and open.

The room appeared to be carved out of the earth. It was dim, the only light coming from two windows that peeked out a half foot or so above ground. They were coated in grime below the surface. I could make out trees in the distance. Not much else. The walls were slick with condensation. A leak produced a droplet of water every five to ten seconds. It splashed like it was landing in a puddle and not on a barren floor.

Pain shot through my neck as I angled it downward. My shirt was missing. So were my pants. They'd left my socks and underwear on. Guess I should've been thankful, but I wasn't. Not at that moment.

Turning to the right produced a tingle down that shoulder and into my arm. That corner of the room was dark. Oblong shapes pressed against the wall. Rakes, maybe. An axe, perhaps.

I barely managed to turn my head to the left. Pain raced down my spine, leg shoulder, arm, all the way to the tip of my pinky finger and toe. I feared a fractured vertebra. Panic rose, and I drew in another moldy breath of air and held it. As the tension lifted, I wiggled my toes and fingers, and clenched my hands into fists. I tried to draw my arms to the side again, but the lashing that bound them together at the wrist dug in. This produced no additional pain. Possible diagnoses played on my mind. It could be as simple as a pinched nerve.

I'd go with that.

Millimeter by millimeter, I turned my head left until my chin hung above my shoulder. The pain stopped when my head did. Dried blood caked my shoulder. It had flowed in rivers, now barren, down my back. From a wound on my head, I figured. With my left eyelid clamped shut, there was only so much I could see. As I swept back to neutral position, I noticed a bundle of cloth moving against the wall. Chains rattled. They ran the length of the wall, attached to an eye bolt near the ceiling, then disappeared into the dirty sheets on the ground. Slender and pale feet poked out from the linens. A woman groaned.

"Who's there?" I marveled at the grotesque sound emitted from my mouth.

The lump rose a few feet. The sheet fell away, revealing a head of dark, matted hair, thin black eyebrows, brown eyes. Her left cheek was bruised and swollen. Other than that, her face appeared untouched.

"McSweeney," I said. "What the hell happened to you?"

She clenched her eyes shut and slowly swung her head side to side. The sheet continued to slide. They'd left her with a shirt, which had tinted brown from the dirt she slept on. She drew her knees to her chest and wrapped her arms around them. Each hand grasped the opposite forearm, drawing the chain tight.

"Your brother, ex, what happened to them?"

She lifted her head. Opened her eyes. Tears cascaded down both cheeks. They fell from her chin and landed on the dirty shirt. She took a couple of deep, shaky breaths, and settled down.

"I haven't seen Brett," she said. "They won't tell me what he did with him."

"Tell me you know what this is all about."

"I was going to say the same to you." She offered a smile. The left corner of her mouth retreated. From the pain, presumably, of her cheek.

"What happened to your face?"

"Fell down the stairs." She looked away. Her gaze swept the floor.

She didn't have to say anything else. I knew what she meant.

Shadows raced across the wall like fleeing spirits. I turned my head. The move was met with resistance and pain, knifing through my spine and shoulders. Two feet walked past a window. Another set followed a couple seconds later.

"We're about to get visitors," I said. "Get back under those sheets and don't come out. I don't care what they say or do or what sounds you hear out of me. Stay under there."

"They know I'm here."

"That's fine, McSweeney. I don't want them finding any reason to beat on you too."

"Why won't you call me Reese?"

Before I could tell her it was because I hadn't thought to, the door opened. Wind barreled through the small room, diesel fumes riding the gust. The back of my throat thickened with mucus after being inundated. Wherever we were, these guys had driven here to pay us this visit.

The first thing that appeared from behind the wall was the barrel of an M4 Carbine, a standard among FBI SWAT teams as well as the armed forces. I recognized the man in possession of the rifle. Short, squat, thick, older. His cropped hair glistened with sweat. Odd, considering the temperature. The ex-SEAL that I had encountered outside the brownstone. And then seen getting into a Mustang near I-95. He took a few steps into the room, raised the weapon, and aimed it in my direction. Then he held still.

"For Panama," he said.

Joe Dunne, the man who'd contacted me for information on McLellan. The guy I'd seen for mere seconds outside of a hospital in McLean, Virginia, followed the ex-SEAL. Joe cast a glance at me, then went over to the pile of sheets on the floor. They rustled as he peeled them back. The man whispered something to McSweeney, too low for me to make out. Then he kissed her. She choked back a sob. Joe whispered something again, still inaudible, but the tone was enough that I could tell he was angry.

Perhaps he'd flipped. Why? I supposed I was about to find out.

His slow footfalls echoed inside the chamber. Step by step he approached, looping around behind me. Unable to see out of my left eye, I scanned the floor back and forth with my right. Perhaps his shadow would give him away. The footsteps stopped. A foot, maybe two, behind me. I could push off the floor, explode back. Maybe neutralize him by landing the perfect reverse headbutt.

The ex-SEAL smiled as he white-knuckled the M4. Had he read my mind? Or was I as transparent as a piece of plastic wrap?

The glinting wire passed in front of me. Instinct told me to bring my arms up. That couldn't happen. The thin steel ligature wrapped around my neck and closed in. I kicked back, but that only served to get me off balance and allow Joe to draw me in closer. I tried to kick, but couldn't get close. I caught a glimpse of his face, beet red, lips curled back, teeth bared. Strands of spit hung from his lips. He grunted maniacally.

The edges of my vision darkened. I hadn't drawn a breath in close to a minute. Could have been longer. Wasn't keeping track. My shoulders, arms, torso, all went limp.

Then Joe Dunne let go. He stepped back, and I crashed backward. The resulting slamming of my head onto the floor put me under once again.

CHAPTER 62

I WAS SEMI-UPRIGHT, slumped back in the chair, when I came to. The base of my skull rested against the wood railing on the back. The dull pain in my head was exacerbated by the light Joe Dunne was aiming at my face. It was the kind of device used when you wanted to see a thousand yards away in the dead of night. His voice was the only reason I knew it was him.

He cut the light. Everything turned red. I couldn't see the end of my nose. Joe laughed and snapped his fingers in front of my face. If I could've located them, I would have bitten one off. Since that wasn't a possibility, I tried the next best thing. Only I found my legs bound to the chair, so the sweeping action only served to jerk the chair forward a couple inches.

Joe's hand came out of nowhere and slapped backhanded across my face. It stung, but did no damage. He taunted me, daring me to move again.

I did.

He struck again, a little harder, still backhanded.

The retinal-burned image of the light shrank and darkened and hollowed out. A pinprick at first, the space in the middle expanded. I saw Joe, a couple feet away. He leaned forward. His gaze met mine.

Rising, Joe said, "Want to tell me what that disabled brainiac friend of yours was doing pinging my computer non-stop?"

I met his stare, held it, and said nothing. An educated guess would place Joe's office inside Quantico. One of the three possible destinations for the call I'd placed from the Brooklyn café's bathroom.

Joe smiled, glanced down, dropped to a knee, and then brought his hands up swiftly. Held between them was the light, and he cut it on before I managed to close my eye. Even with my lids shielding them, the beam burned. I felt the heat radiating across my cheeks, chin, lips, and forehead.

"Come on, Jack. This is the easy stuff." He switched it off. "Answer my question."

"Piss off." I opened my eyes. The light-etched image had returned, and I couldn't locate him.

He slapped me. Open handed. A move that would do nothing more than sting for a few seconds, but meant to humiliate me.

"Why don't you lean in closer so I can spit in your face?"

Joe laughed. The light-burn had faded again, leaving the man visible in a dark shade of crimson. I watched as he wiped his face with his left hand. Then struck me in the mouth with his right. A dead-on shot that split one of his knuckles. And knocked my front right tooth loose. I drew from my reserves and spit, sending a wave of white-hot pain through the nerves in my gums, and bloody saliva out in a mist. Some of it managed to strike his shirt. Most of it fell on my chest and stomach.

"God dammit." Joe struck me again. The blow loosened the other front tooth. Split another of his knuckles, too. Blood flowed down Joe's fingers and dripped to the floor. I imagined a puddle forming at his feet. I wanted it to grow into a pool.

"It really doesn't matter," Joe stepped back and shifted toward the sink. He turned on the water, ran his hand underneath. The basin turned a pinkish color. When he spun around, a wet towel engulfed his hand like a misshaped boxing glove. He continued. "About your friend, I mean. The only one I wanted was you. Well, friends of mine do. Bullet in the brain for the others, I told my guys. They did. The big freak and the little freak, both of them. Left for dead."

I made no outward show of emotion, although at that moment my stomach clenched and twisted, and my heart pounded against my chest wall. Felt as though it was a bull trying to take down a brick wall.

"What did he want, Jack?"

"Fuck you." The blood in my mouth spilled over my bottom lip, down my chin, dripped onto my chest. I added, "You should have seen Vogel beg for his life as his blood spilled onto the floor."

Joe stood stoic, expressionless. What would his next move be? Slowly, a smile spread. "God, I wish that whore ex of mine was around to see you die."

I hadn't realized they had moved her when I was unconscious.

"What'd you do with her?"

"Not so much what I did, it's what I'll do, if you don't give me a few answers." He unwound the wet towel, pulling it tight with every reverse revolution. "I'm not gonna lie to you, Noble. You're not leaving here alive. So, if you want to hold all this knowledge in, that's your prerogative. But, if you do, Reese is going to join you in that grave she's digging." He nodded toward the window.

I turned my head in that direction. The pain I felt throughout my body doubled in intensity from earlier. Through the grime, I made out a pile of dirt, and Reese standing in a pit wearing only her shirt. She heaved a shovel up and down, flinging earth behind her. Clumps stuck to her arms and bare legs. As my head spun back toward Joe, the towel whipped in my direction. It caught me on my cheek with a thunderous crack. It felt as though my face had split open. I waited for the warm flow to start. It didn't.

"Ever been water-boarded, Jack?" He drew the towel wide. I took in the look on Joe's face. He seemed excited about the prospect of torturing me not with pain but mental anguish. He wound the towel up a couple times around each hand. His next step, presumably, would be to fix that towel across my face.

"Why me?" I said in an attempt to buy a few minutes. "I never had any beef with you. I don't remember your name from my days in the SIS. Did I step on your toes one day? Take a case away from you?"

"You think this is over something that happened three or four years ago?"

I said nothing.

"Actually, it is." He circled behind me, tilted the chair back, turned it, and set me down. "Come on in here."

Words formed on my lips, but the breath needed to say them couldn't escape my tightening throat.

The bearded Syrian man that appeared had looked like a teenage boy the last time I'd seen him in person. Of course, Bashir al-Sharaa had been in his twenties then, living in the U.S. on a student visa, committing low-level crimes for a group of terrorists that financed their intentions by running a kidnapping ring. He'd done this while he waited for his own number to be called.

"I see there is no need for reintroductions, Mr. Noble," al-Sharaa said.

"What are you doing here?"

"Joe called to advise me that he had a place for me to stay until I got back on my feet. It seems that a couple infidel meddlers ruined what I had built in Paris these last four years. Not all of it, though. I still have sleepers in place, and, Insha'Allah, they will perform their tasks in beautiful harmony on the predetermined date."

"You know about this, Joe?" I said. "You're just going to sit here and let it slide? You're FBI, man. You took an oath."

"An oath that gives trash like you the right to make a living killing people. And for money, at that. At least Bashir here has a plan, a purpose, and meaning behind what he is doing. He did then, too, when you kicked him out of the country."

"How the hell do you two know each other?"

"While you were busy trying to take down Bashir, I was getting to know him. He was feeding me information, and I, in turn, was keeping people off his back. Then you butted in."

And then I realized what had happened. Joe Dunne and Bashir al-Sharaa had remained in contact. A twisted bond had formed between the men. Instead of al-Sharaa converting to our side, Joe had taken on some of al-Sharaa's ideals. The Old Man had told the truth about two parties being contracted - Joe had been the other party. He wasn't investigating McLellan. There was a connection between the men; Joe had hired him to take out Brett. What better way was there to do it? Bring in someone the target trusts, and they'll willingly turn their back while you plant a knife to the hilt.

A smile crossed al-Sharaa's peaceful face. "Sometimes, I don't know whether to hate you or thank you for having me deported, Mr. Noble. In a way, your actions are directly responsible for my rise to power, and the countless ones you will certainly call innocents that will die at the month's end."

"If it had been up to me, you'd have had two bullets in your heart, and one in your brain."

Al-Sharaa swept in and delivered a backhand across my face. "How I wish we were in another country. I'd saw your head off on live TV. Not that anyone would care enough about you to tune in, of course."

"You're still the same scared kid you were four years ago. Hell, you weren't even man enough to handle those kids your associates kidnapped."

He stood there, fists clenched, ready to strike. He didn't. A shadow fell past me and landed on al-Sharaa.

"Ready for this, Jack?" Joe said.

CHAPTER 63

BEFORE I COULD respond, Joe lunged forward and wrapped the towel around my head. No movement I made stopped him and al-Sharaa from securing it. Joe stepped to my left and disappeared, while al-Sharaa hovered over me, staring me in the eye. A moment later, Joe leaned the chair back until my feet were off the ground and I was at greater than a forty-five-degree angle.

What came next is something I'd never want repeated on anyone.

Joe covered my eyes with a black cloth, long enough that turning my head couldn't dislodge it. I heard metal on metal, rotating. Then a stream of water splashed into something empty, deep and hollow, at first. The pitch rose as the container was filled. The water cut off. Single drops splashed against the basin every second. Joe grunted, presumably heaving the bucket up and moving it toward me. The liquid splashed over the rim. Errant streams hit the dirty floor in a torrent.

Then the room fell silent.

Except for our breathing. Rapid and ragged. Me facing the unknown. Joe in anticipation. Al-Sharaa elated at torturing me and exacting his revenge.

Without warning, the first drops of cold water hit the towel spread over my nose and mouth. It sounded like raindrops hitting a tent. It stopped after a second. The wetness spread. I tried to draw in one last breath, but couldn't. Panic doesn't describe the feeling that set in. The water returned, hitting harder, flowing faster. The dampness spread to my cheeks and neck, but I only noticed that for a second. It was the flooding of my mouth and nose and throat that hit hardest. I couldn't control my body's natural instinct to draw in air. It only served to bring me further down. I felt smothered, as though I'd been thrown into a pool of water, and then wrapped in cellophane.

"How's that feel?" Joe shouted.

I tried to yell back, swore I had, but I didn't. There was no way I could. Not while choking. Slowly dying. I saw blackness on top of the black cloth.

Then Joe yanked the towel and scarf off me. The light blinded me, but that was the least of my concerns.

I continued to drown.

Joe pushed me forward. Spasms forced the water out of my lungs. I coughed, spit up, vomited. The expelled water fell on me, on the floor. My chest, arms and legs were coated in the regurgitated fluid.

"Ready to tell me?" Joe stood behind me, my hair clenched in his hand.

I said nothing. Don't know if I could have if I'd wanted to try.

"What about me?" al-Sharaa delivered a kick to my stomach that, in my weakened state, I couldn't defend against the strike.

Joe yanked back on my hair. The chair tipped and again I was staring up at the dark mold that lived on the ceiling. For a brief moment, at least. The scarf fell upon my eyes. The wet towel was dropped on my face, then removed.

"Last chance," he said.

I tried to curse at him, but only managed a grunt.

Without warning, the first of three waves hit me like a waterfall, thunderous and powerful, but without the rush that comes from standing next to one of nature's most powerful sights.

I endured the torture, five to ten seconds at a time, though it felt like minutes. My mind was at odds. People had lived through this kind of torture, day after day, and lived to tell about it. I knew it was only a tactic, aimed at getting me to talk. At the same time, there were myriad ways death could be induced, from suffocation to stress-induced myocardial infarction.

How far would Joe and al-Sharaa go?

I focused on the image of McSweeney, waist-deep in a dirt pit, hauling the shovel up and down, flinging earth behind her. Her shirt, hair, and soft skin muddied. The ex-SEAL's lips curled up in a smile as he watched her sweat. She wasn't digging her own grave; it was meant for me. And Joe had no intentions of dragging my lifeless body from the cellar and dropping me in a hole in the ground. The bastard would want me to kneel in my own grave first, freedom all around me, no path to escape. One last chance, Jack, to save yourself. Talk.

I'll make you eat your tongue, Joe!

I was at the breaking point. That place where consciousness floats. My oxygen-starved lungs were ready to explode. I'd been through drown-proofing in training years ago. Part of the regimen I went through had us experience passing out underwater. This felt similar, but different. Perhaps it was the towel, the smothered feeling. Knowing that only a piece of wet fabric separated my nose and mouth from the air and oxygen my brain, heart, and lungs craved.

Joe pulled the towel away. He didn't bother with the scarf. It fell off on its own. My body lurched to the right, then fell to the left, still attached to the chair. I couldn't brace myself for the fall. Didn't matter, because I was too numb to feel the collision with the floor. But I heard the sound of my cheek smacking against it.

My body convulsed, spasmed, and forced the water out. It exited in a manner of ways, from coughs, to heaves, landing six inches away, a foot, and dribbling out, forming a pool around my face.

Joe stepped over me. His boot set down in the puddle next to my mouth. For a moment, it remained there. And he didn't say or do anything during that time.

My swollen left eye pressed against the dirty floor. I couldn't feel the pain associated. Exhausted, I forced myself to keep the other eye open, focused on that boot like it was the key to my salvation.

The hard rubber sole lifted a couple inches in the air. I expected it to rise up further, then smash down on my head like I was a cockroach.

Instead, it moved away. I saw its partner, and in tandem, they exited the cellar.

Al-Sharaa knelt down, placing his knee in my water vomit. He stroked my head, leaned in further. "I will behead you before the sun sets on this day."

And then he left the room.

CHAPTER 64

M Y FACE FELT cemented to the gritty floor. Dust filled my nose, throat, and lungs with every breath I took. The only thing I could smell was bitter mold. I don't know how long I lay there, stuck to the chair. Exhaustion prevented me from finding a way to free myself from the confines. Even if I managed to release my legs, where would I go with my arms bound at the wrist? Instead of freedom, I focused my energy on staying awake and remaining aware of my surroundings.

I heard two distinct male voices. Couldn't tell from which direction, though the muted tones told me they were not in the cellar with me. Joe and al-Sharaa, and presumably they were speaking of their plans for me.

I pried my cheek from the floor, craned my head, and managed to get a view through the window. Mostly trees, dead branches, and pine needles. And a shovel blade as it rose high to toss back a scoop of dirt. I smiled for the first time in a while. Reese McSweeney was still alive. When Joe had left, dread filled me that his intention was to kill her. The elation faded as I considered he only kept her alive so that I could watch her die.

Or worse, he planned to force me to kill her.

That wouldn't happen. I knew my death would follow, so if placed in the position, I'd make every attempt to take Joe or al-Sharaa or the ex-SEAL out before they got to me. Maybe Reese would make it out alive; maybe she'd die. Not by my hand, though.

The cellar door creaked open. A flood of light pushed past the dividing wall, only to disappear as the door fell shut again. Hard-soled boots hit the floor. Joe entered the room, carrying an M4 Carbine. Maybe it was time. He stood over me, looking down and smiling, in perfect position for me to strike him in the groin if I had one free arm or leg.

"The great Jack Noble," he said. Then he took a few steps back and rested the rifle against the wall. I tried not to stare at it. My last bastion of salvation, only eight feet away. Joe took a step forward, then stopped. "You'd like to get your hands on that, wouldn't you?"

I refused to answer his rhetorical question.

Joe continued toward me. He didn't stop in the same spot. Instead, he stepped over me. A few seconds later I was hoisted off the ground. My exposed skin peeled a thin layer of grime away from the floor. The chair's two right legs groaned under my weight as they settled. I hoped the chair would split in two.

It didn't.

The man turned his back on me, grabbed the bucket, and walked to the sink. He whistled an old tune. I couldn't make it out.

"Ready for round two, Jack?" Joe glanced over his shoulder.

The sound of rushing water sent a chill through me. Muscles responded by tightening.

I lowered my chin to my chest and stared at the ground, still wet. We were doing this again, and there was nothing I could do to stop it. He had me defeated in every sense of the word. And he knew it.

Joe set the bucket in the sink and let the water run. He turned toward me, leaned back against the porcelain sink and crossed his arms over his chest. Was the calm demeanor a show? Had he done this so many times that it had become second nature?

The sound of the water filling the bucket rose to a higher pitch, notifying us that the container was nearly full. Joe reached behind his back, and, without taking his eyes off me, switched the spigot off. He knelt down and picked the towel up off the floor, half of it stained dark with dirt and blood. He tossed the towel at me. It hit my chest, fell to my lap.

"What do you want?" It came out as a whisper.

"What's that, Jack?"

Managing a slightly louder tone, I repeated myself.

Joe started toward me. Heel, toe, heel, toe. Each step deliberate. He stopped and leaned over, hands on his knees. "I'm gonna tell you something, Jack."

A moment passed. "What, Joe?"

He motioned with his finger for me to come toward him. "My bad." He laughed and shuffled forward a couple inches. "We've got no more use for you. Anything you could have told us was just relayed to us. That's what happens when you've got too many canaries singing, my friend."

At that point, I considered trying to rationalize with the man to let Reese go. If I served no purpose, then neither did she. Kill me, but let her walk.

"By who?" I asked.

Joe looked down and shook his head. Maybe he was making a production out of telling me. Perhaps he had no intentions of revealing the source or the information. It could have all been a lie. None of that mattered.

What did matter was that his head was inches from mine, and instead of paying attention, he was relishing in the power he had over me.

Supposed power.

I drew my head back, slapped the base of my skull against the wooden frame. Joe inched up, wrinkled his brow as he lifted his gaze from the floor to my abdomen and chest to my eyes. His widened as I whipped my head forward with every ounce of strength I could muster. He tried to move back, and in doing so, set himself up for a better strike.

My forehead met the bridge of his nose. Thick dense bone versus cartilage and a small flap of skin. Skull crushes nose every time, and this was no exception.

Joe stumbled backward. My momentum carried me forward. I planted both feet on the ground and regained my balance. The man remained doubled over. I hopped the chair into position. As he looked up, I delivered another strike with my forehead, but this time his cheek and eye took the brunt, likely resulting in an orbital bone fracture. Bad for him, and me. Bone on bone left me off balance. Not a good sensation when using chair legs for support.

Joe fell to the floor. Unable to maintain my balance, I stumbled forward as well.

Blood poured from Joe's wounds. It mixed with the dirt and dust on the floor and formed a dark crimson pool. He clawed at the floor.

I forced myself to a kneeling position. The back of the chair dug into my upper spine. Fire raced through my nerves as the wood pushed against my damaged vertebra. I fought against the pain, and walked on my knees. Joe had managed to get to his side and had pushed off the floor with his elbow. I shuffled toward him, and once in range, drove my shoulder and the side of the chair into his chest and arm. The wooden frame cracked under the force. So did Joe's ribs. He groaned in pain. I got to my knees, rose up. The back of the chair wasn't digging into me anymore. The damage to the frame allowed it to move freely. I drove my forehead into Joe's face again. The collision between solid bone and his nose and mouth worked in my favor. His front teeth were smashed in. Blood coated his nose, lips and chin. His eyes rolled back.

Adrenaline energized me. I kicked and straightened in an effort to split the damaged chair. It only took a few sequences before it broke. I got to my feet. Joe writhed in pain on the ground. I kicked him in the gut and head until he stopped moving. Then I dropped to my knees, my back to the man, and searched his pockets, where I found a set of keys. I brought them over to the sink and set them on the ledge. Fixed to the keychain was a small pocketknife. I drew my hands to my right hip and angled my torso so that I could watch while sawing through the cord that bound my wrists. Numb hands made the job difficult, but I succeeded.

The rope fell to the floor. I rubbed the flesh covering my hands in an attempt to restore feeling.

I grabbed the M4 and crept toward the opening. Six concrete stairs led up. Sunlight knifed through the gap in the cellar door, and dust danced in solid beam. Then something blocked the light. I backtracked, rounded the wall. Joe lay motionless on the floor. The door opened. A single set of foot-steps fell on the stairs. Closer. Nearer. A shadow breached the divide.

I brought the M4 up, in reverse, stock in my right hand, right arm extended out. The blow was timed perfectly. I aimed at the spot where I expected al-Sharaa's mouth to be.

Instead, I hit the ex-SEAL in the throat. His mouth twisted open, but he was unable to yell, as the strike had crushed his larynx and possibly his esophagus, judging by his darkening face. I drew back again, delivered another strike. This one crushed his upper lip and teeth. The man was doubled over in front of me. His blood spilled to the floor and pooled between us. I dropped the rifle, grabbed the back of the man's head, and drove my knee into his face three times.

He fell to his knees. I twisted his limp body around. He flailed his arms up in an attempt to grab or attack, but the weak blows bounced off me. I wrapped my hands around his chin, opposite sides, then pulled. The guy's thick neck snapped, and his lifeless body crashed to the ground.

I grabbed the rifle and headed for the door again. I peeked through and saw nothing but a carpet of dead leaves and the skeletal remains of trees rising up from the forest floor. I pushed the door open, stuck the barrel of the rifle through, and then emerged, dividing the land in front of me into quarters.

At about seven feet high, the structure provided me cover. I followed it to the right, in the direction of Reese McSweeney. The wind whipped around the corner, negating the effects of the sun. My body, uncovered and damp with sweat and water, started to shake. I had no control over it. I clenched my arms, legs, chest, abdomen, all several times. The contractions warmed my muscles, and the trembling momentarily stopped.

I fought off the instinct that told me to run. I refused to leave McSweeney behind with al-Sharaa. And who knew if someone else would show up later?

The shovel made a slapping sound and penetrated the earth. Dirt hit the ground like fat raindrops. I inched toward the corner, the M4's muzzle below my chin. Reese's head poked out of the dirt pit. The shovel swung up, dove down. She worked fast, as though she could tunnel away.

I didn't see al-Sharaa. But I caught a whiff of a menthol cigarette. He must've been leaning back against the cellar wall. I backed up and took a deep breath to clear my head. I had one shot, one chance, to end this. If I missed, then Reese would die.

And so would I.

CHAPTER 65

DISCARDED SMOKE SATURATED the wind. Leaves lifted up and blew past, circling one another. Reese's shovel continued its cycle of rising and falling. She grunted with every pass. But she was alive, and my job was to keep her that way.

I felt like my feet had sunk six inches, and the ground held me in place. My body, breaking down. There wouldn't be a better time than now to do this. Things would only get worse, in fact. Every second I was exposed to the elements, I reduced my chances of making that shot a successful one. But I remained there. Frozen.

And then al-Sharaa spoke.

"That's deep enough. Kneel down."

The ex-SEAL must've been coming to get me, and al-Sharaa was expecting us back.

Reese McSweeney choked and sobbed, and then composed herself enough to plead for her life. It wouldn't do any good. Al-Sharaa was going to behead her, or watch over her until Joe came out to finish the job, whether Reese knelt or not. She'd buy herself, and me, a little time if she refused to yield.

"Get down," he yelled.

Defiant till the end, Reese screamed back at him, unleashing the primal sound of a warrior. The shovel thumped against the ground. The blade clanked against the earthen wall.

Al-Sharaa laughed and told her goodnight.

I stepped out from cover and sighted al-Sharaa. It was something I should have done four years ago. He must've seen me in his peripheral vision. His head turned, body followed, gun came around last. I squeezed the trigger and put a round dead center in his chest. It stopped him cold. I fired again. Hit close to the same spot. The man dropped to his knees. I took a few steps forward, keeping the M4 trained on the stain spreading across his chest. I lifted the barrel a touch and depressed the trigger one more time. The final round went clear through his head. The sound of the shots echoed throughout the woods, sending dozens of resting crows into the air, the mass of them like a black, swarming cloud.

Reese screamed my name. She clawed wildly at the dirt ledge. The action only served to bring more of it down upon her. She slipped and fell. I hurried over and found her on her back at the bottom of the pit. She clenched her eyes while driving her elbows into the ground, lifting her chest in the air.

"Just relax," I said. "It takes a second for the wind to come back."

She pulled in swallows of air before exhaling forcefully. Slowly, she sat up, got to her knees, then her feet. I shifted the M4 to my left hand, reached down with my right. Reese grabbed hold with both of hers. Still weakened from the waterboarding, I stepped back, using my weight instead of muscle to pull her out.

I felt one hand let go completely, and the other unfurl from my grip. Her stare darted past me. Her eyes widened.

"Look out," she shouted.

I glanced back. Joe staggered toward me, aiming a pistol at my head. I released Reese from my grip and started to turn, tossing the M4 in the air while bringing my right arm up to catch it. But unless Joe was blind, I didn't stand a chance.

Simultaneously my eyes shut and muscles locked, bracing for impact. The sound of his sidearm discharging ripped through the air. The M4's stock grazed my right hand, and my fingers closed in around it. My abdomen burned. I couldn't tell exactly where the bullet hit, or what damage it had done. I unleashed a primal scream of my own, intent on sending a surge of adrenaline through my body that would allow me to ignore the wound and bullet that had torn through my flesh. I didn't need to put it off long, just enough to send a deadly shot in Joe's direction.

I opened my eyes and located Joe as I fell to the ground. He fired another round. It slammed into the dirt near me. He continued toward me. One foot up, the other dragging. I brought the M4 to my shoulder, managed to sight Joe, and then squeezed the trigger. But nothing happened. It had jammed. A bloody, toothless smile formed on Joe's face. Blood spilled out over his chin and onto his chest. He stopped and extended his arm. The man took his time, presumably because he wanted this to be the final shot before he moved on and ended Reese's life.

Summoning every last ounce of energy I had, I reversed the M4, wrapping both hands around the scalding muzzle. The flesh coating my fingers melted. I swung the stock at Joe's knees. I couldn't get there, though. White-hot pain seared through my abdominal wall with every movement I made. I refused to give up, to lie there and be put out of my misery like a dying deer. I dropped the M4 and reached into the waistband of my underwear, where I'd stored Joe's knife keys. I couldn't get the blade to retract from the knife's housing.

Another loud crack was followed by pain radiating throughout my arm. The bullet had hit midway up my forearm, shattering the bones. I released the knife from my grasp.

Joe stood a few feet away now, laughing.

I lay there, on my back, trying to keep from dying. My right foot hovered in the air over the pit Reese McSweeney had dug. They almost got me in it. I doubted Joe was going to try and push me in before delivering the fatal shot.

He sent a wad of saliva and blood and pus in my direction. I closed my eyes and didn't see where it hit. The pain in my arm and abdomen made it impossible to feel anything else. I didn't notice the cold, damp ground under my exposed back and legs. Couldn't feel the breeze as it whipped over and past me. Never noticed the leaves as they danced across my body.

But finally, I heard the shot that ended a life.

And then I heard Reese calling out. And following that, a man shouted back.

"Jack," they both said, one after another.

Reese's voice remained trapped in a dirt pit. But the man's voice got closer with each successive word.

I opened my eyes. Joe's body laid a few feet away. His eyes were stuck open. He'd been covered in blood to begin with, so it was impossible to tell where the fatal bullet had landed. One of a couple places. And it didn't matter where, only that it had happened.

"Jesus, Jack." Brett hovered over me.

I licked my lips and forced a swallow. "Get Reese out of the ground."

"We're on it."

I tried to look over, but pain prevented it. Reese called my name. It was soft, gentle. I looked up. She stood next to Brett. They leaned against each other for support. In the filtered light, they looked nothing alike. He said something to one of the agents that had accompanied him, and the man led her away. Two others knelt by my side and assessed me. Meanwhile, I managed to ask Brett a question.

"How'd you know?"

"They were keeping me nearby. I guess they own all this land. For whatever reason, they didn't kill me. I think al-Sharaa wanted to bring me back to Syria or Iraq, do the whole thing on film as punishment for my role in forcing them out of Paris. The man they left watching over me didn't lock the room on his way out. He paid for it, too."

"That's some pretty amazing luck."

Brett smiled. "Seems I'm full of it this week."

"What about those guys?"

"Used the dead man's phone. Led them to me."

One of the men pulled on my broken arm. A jolt of pain ran up through my shoulder. After it subsided, I said, "You were watching the whole time?"

"We just followed the sounds."

"Bear," I said. "He was hurt. Another contact of mine, too."

He nodded, said nothing.

"What've you heard?"

Brett looked away for a second. His jacket rippled in the breeze. He glanced at me, shook his head. "Sorry, Jack. Not good news."

I closed my eyes and let my head fall back.

And the wind engulfed my body.

CHAPTER 66

THE FIRST CONSCIOUS thought that streamed through my mind was, "Where the hell am I?"

The steady beeping that had been there while I arose from a deep, sedated sleep increased in pace. I had a faint recollection of the events that had transpired, but no idea when they'd occurred. The images that flashed in my mind's eye caused sensations of panic. The beeping sped up. A steady alarm rang out.

A flurry of activity occurred around me. Two women and one man, dressed in scrubs, silenced the machine and took readings manually. One touched my abdomen. I tried to lift my head, but a device kept me from doing so. With good reason, too. The half-inch I managed on my own hurt like hell.

The man left. One of the women followed. The one in pink remained behind. She explained I was in the hospital, recovering from wounds suffered and three surgeries to repair a broken arm, lacerated kidney, and fractured vertebra. They had kept me heavily sedated for five days with a combination of anesthesia and narcotics. Pain medication.

At first, I had no memory of the bullet that had penetrated my abdominal wall. Nor the one that shattered the bones of my forearm. It wasn't until a doctor by the name of Jovanovich came by and explained my surgeries that the images played out in their entirety.

"McSweeney," I attempted to say. My throat was drier than the desert surrounding Dubai.

The nurse in pink scrubs placed an ice chip in my mouth. Cold water laced my parched throat. I might as well have swallowed fire. Eventually, the burning subsided enough that I tried again.

"Reese McSweeney," I said. "How is she?"

Dr. Jovanovich exchanged a glance with the nurse. His face showed no sign of recollection.

The nurse spoke up. "We don't have a patient by that name. However, we were told to contact a Mr. Taylor the moment you came to, and I'm going to do that now. Perhaps he can answer your question?"

Forgetting about the device around my neck, I tried unsuccessfully to nod.

"Some swelling around your C-3 and C-4 vertebrae," the doctor said. "Should go down in a few days. We'll be holding you for observation during that time." He aimed a pen toward my head. "Took a few nasty blows. Already had a dentist wire your teeth. Considering the damage elsewhere, I'd say you lucked out that they were still attached." He jotted something on his chart, and then added, "Must've been a scary event for you."

I allowed another pool of chilled water to slide down my throat. "What's that?"

"Getting mugged and beaten and shot like that by those street thugs. I know plenty of people leave here and go right to their shrink for meds. Find a support group. It takes a while, but just remember, what you went through was a once in a lifetime event that happens very rarely. Chances of you going through it again are very slim."

It hurt to smile. I did anyway. This wasn't the first time I'd woken up in the hospital. Would it be the last? Too soon to make that determination.

"Anyway," Jovanovich said. "I'll let you get your rest. I'll be back in the morning to check up on you."

I fell asleep before the door shut. My dreams were plagued with a feeling of drowning, the sensation of being smothered. I woke, gasping for air, the beeping behind me fast enough to set off the alarm. The nurse raced in. After she determined there was nothing wrong, she sent another stream of IV-administered codeine coursing through my veins. Within minutes I was under again. Suffocating in my sleep.

Darkness filled my vision the next time I opened my eyes. No feelings or sensations this time other than a disruption to the space surrounding me.

"How're you feeling, Jack?"

The light next to the bed switched on. I shifted a couple inches to the left and tried to smile at Brett Taylor. He stood next to the bed, dressed in tan slacks, his hands in the pockets. He'd left his blue shirt unbuttoned at the collar. I figured his sports coat was hanging up in the car.

"Reese?" I asked, hoarse.

Brett's face grew tight. He nodded several times while exhaling heavily. Finally, he said, "They're putting her into the witness protection program. She'll be shipped off to God-knows-where."

"Protection? Why?"

"Fear of retaliation. The true facts will never be released. Joe Dunne was a popular man in the Bureau. Reese wasn't liked by her own partner, much less the FBI. To them, she's the reason this happened. Last thing anybody wants is a group of men with the knowledge of how to commit the perfect crime actually doing so. Know what I mean?"

I dipped my chin an inch. Progress.

"I wanted to take her away from here. Establish a base somewhere outside the country. They wouldn't have it."

"Who is 'they'?"

Brett waved me off. "Anyway, I doubt you'll be able to follow up with her. She's being held in an undisclosed location, being debriefed by every agency under the sun. They won't tell me where. But I have a close contact who's watching over the proceedings, and he says she's being treated fairly. I'm hoping he'll allow us one more visit before she goes."

"Don't think she'll reach out to you?"

Brett shrugged. Smiled. She would, and he knew it.

I took a deep breath, steeling myself for the next question. "What about Bear?"

I waited for Brett to tell me that Bear's body had been shipped to wherever the big man's next of kin was located. I only knew of a step- or half-brother in Montana. Instead, Brett said, "He pulled through. Going to take a couple weeks, but he's going to be all right. Once I can sign you out of here, we'll go see him."

The vice that had gripped my heart and lungs released. I swore the beeping slowed down at the same time. "Any word from Frank Skinner?"

Brett shook his head. "We had a long talk. My feeling is he'll go to the grave before he gives up whoever issued the job to the SIS. I mean, I guess I can respect that. Kind of have to, right?" He paused a beat. "Anyway, he said that you've effectively been blackballed. No one is going to want to work with you after this. While I thank you, they think you've lost your edge. Doesn't matter that you were right, trusting me back there in Reese's apartment. You failed to complete an op, and they don't trust you anymore."

I would have shrugged if I could.

"Frank said he'd try to throw you a bone here and there. You know what that means. Worst kind of jobs. Off the grid type stuff. Foreign soil, sand. But, who knows, maybe in time they'll ease up and welcome you back into the community."

"What about you?"

"Me? You don't have to worry about that. I still have a group of terrorists to eliminate. It felt good to nail al-Sharaa and put him in the ground, but there are others. And I want to get the next level. So, with all that's happened, I see myself disappearing into France to take it from there."

"Pierre," I said. "Reach out to him. He's seeking vengeance, and I know he'll offer you unlimited support."

Brett nodded, then reached into his pocket and pulled out a piece of paper. He set it on the table next to the bed, under the light.

"That's a numbered account," he said. "About a million dollars in there. Should be enough to keep you on your feet while you wait this out or look elsewhere for opportunities."

"I can't take your money."

"You could have taken my life, but you didn't, Jack. You lost out on whatever they were going to pay you, too."

The only way I could get that kind of cash was to accept the Old Man's offer to work for his organization. That wasn't going to happen.

"Maybe you can get away. Some place tropical. Might enjoy it enough to just disappear there. A million dollars goes a long way in a country like Dominica."

I said nothing.

"Well, think about it. Either you use it, or the money goes to waste."

With that, Brett turned and walked toward the door.

"Brett?"

He stopped, placed his hand on the door frame and looked back at me. "Yeah?"

"Mugged? Really?"

He laughed and said, "They'd have never believed the truth."

CHAPTER 67

TEN DAYS LATER I was walking down 5th Avenue, Midtown Manhattan, amid a crowd of Japanese tourists. I'd been out of the hospital for five days. My first stop after being released was to see Brandon. He'd lost everything in the fire except for his life and his brain. His computer equipment and gadgets, his wheelchair, all was gone. Worst part was he had no insurance to cover any of it. The smile on his face when I handed him a slip of paper revealing a numbered account with a million dollars on it was thanks enough. The only stipulation I had was that he used the bleeding-edge tech he would build to locate Reese McSweeney for me. I had to know that she was safe. Out of reach for anyone that might be delusional enough to support Joe Dunne. I wanted her to know that she could count on me anytime, anywhere.

Following my visit to Brandon, I located Bear. While Brandon had been spared in the clearing behind his house, Bear had taken a bullet to the brain. Guess the ex-SEAL and Joe Dunne were more worried about the guy with working legs. Bear had spent six days in a coma and suffered partial memory loss. When I tried to discuss the details of our ordeal, starting with him on the flight with Brett Taylor, Bear had no recollection. Doctors said the gap might be filled later, but he seemed to have lost about a month's worth of data.

Probably better. I knew I'd like to forget what we'd gone through.

The doctors also said they had left the bullet where it had embedded itself. Removing it would have left Bear's brain at risk of hemorrhaging. As long as he limited contact to his head, and stayed away from heavy-duty magnets, there was little chance of the left-behind bullet doing any damage.

At 6' 6", most people didn't bother to aim for his head, so I figured he'd be all right.

He had to remain at the facility another four weeks before they'd let him leave. Despite his initial protests, I talked him in to staying.

From the recovery center, I hopped a flight to Tampa Bay, Florida, and drove north a bit. There, I spent a couple days with my family. Time in a boat, on the gulf, under the sun fishing does wonders for the soul. As I departed, my mother begged me to stay longer. She always feared she'd never see me again. It wasn't in the cards. After a visit to the cemetery to talk to my deceased sister Molly for a half hour, I hitched a ride to the airport with my brother Sean. Normally we'd talk little during such a trip. This time he pushed for answers on why I was wearing a cast and looked as though I'd gone fifteen rounds in a heavyweight fight. I fended him off until we reached Tampa.

I picked up a pay-as-you-go phone at a stand inside the airport, found my gate, and napped for two hours before boarding the 757 bound for New York.

I'd only been in town for a couple hours now. Most would want to head home, get a shower, nap, change, whatever. Their greatest desire, I supposed. I had one too, and it meant I had somewhere else to go.

And so, as the Japanese tourists turned at 45th Street, I continued on another few blocks, approaching my destination.

"Noble."

I knew the voice, unfortunately. So, I stepped to the curb where Charles stood waiting.

"What do you want?" I said.

"Why's everyone always think it's me? I don't want nothin' with you, Jack. The Old Man would like to have a word."

"Tell him I'm a bit busy right now."

"Tell him yourself." Charles pointed across the street. "He's waiting in there."

"You don't scare me."

"That's good to hear. But, before you think about doing something, I've got five guys within fifty yards. All of them got itchy fingers, too."

"Tell them to start wiping with toilet paper."

Charles shook his head. "I don't know why the Old Man has got such a hard-on for you."

"Well, if he spends most of his day with you, just look in a mirror. You'll figure it out."

"Yeah, yeah. All right. Enough." He opened his jacket enough for me to see his shoulder holster and the pistol it held. "Get across the street and talk to him for a few."

The situation was unavoidable. I figured now was a good a time as any to get this over with. I crossed 5th, maneuvering around the vehicles stopped on the road, and entered the boutique. A middle-aged woman waited by the door. After I entered, she turned the lock and slipped out of view.

"Her husband's a degenerate," the Old Man said. "Owes me a lot of money. She just cut the debt in half by letting me use her store."

"I'll spare you the time of saying anything else. I'm not interested in whatever you offer."

He smiled and stepped toward me, the same slow pace as during our walk on Rockaway beach. "That's typical. Usually, when I make an offer, it'd mean you owe me. But, in this case, you owe me nothing, Mr. Jack."

"Great. I'll be going then."

"Just a minute of your time. That's all I ask."

Charles and three other men gathered across the street. They talked and laughed and smoked. Outside the store, two other guys had stopped and positioned themselves in front of the door. Whether to keep me in or customers out, I wasn't sure.

"OK," I said. "A minute."

The Old Man gestured for me to follow him to the sales counter. On it sat a folder.

By this point, I was weary of opening folders. They always contained trouble.

Fortunately, the Old Man grabbed it and did the honors himself.

"I won't pay you for this job, Mr. Jack."

"Even more enticing."

His smile returned. "I think you'll take it anyway."

"Why are you so sure about that?"

"Because I'd like you to kill a certain member of the House of Representatives that I've recently had the displeasure of working with. Sources indicated that he's planning a nasty tell-all. He needs to be silenced. Interested?"

I reached out for the paper. The Old Man released it.

"It needs to look natural," he said. "Can you handle that?"

"I can handle anything."

"So you accept?"

I said nothing. Turned toward the door and started walking. The lady rushed forward and unlocked it for me. Charles pulled it open. He tried to make a joke, but I had a foot on the asphalt before he got the second word out. I crossed 5th again, rounded the stuck vehicles again. They might have been the same ones. For once, I hadn't paid attention.

Back on the sidewalk, I resumed my walk another two blocks. I folded the paper six times, so it fit in the palm of my hand. Barely noticed it was there. At the same time, it felt like it weighed six hundred pounds. I'd always said that the difference between good and evil was a thin line. So thin it almost didn't exist. I realized at that moment I'd been lying to myself. The gap was great, and I'd straddled it since the age of eighteen. Justification was easy: what I did was for the good of the country. But accepting the job from the Old Man had dragged me clear to the side I never envisioned being a part of.

And I didn't think twice.

The bastard deserved to die.

I altered my route to make it look like I was heading back to the apartment. Along the way, I stopped into a Starbucks and kept my back to the counter, watching the street. One café americano later, I started toward my real destination.

The crowd was thick enough to get lost in. The rise of footsteps, voices, engines, horns, and exhaust choked the air. I barely noticed any of it. One thought occupied my mind. It drove me forward, four blocks, finally coming to a stop in front of the sunken, split, weathered door that led to a bar.

Jack Noble's story continues in *Noble Intentions (Jack Noble #4)* - sample & link below!

Want to be among the first to download the next Jack Noble book? Sign up for L.T. Ryan's newsletter, and you'll be notified the minute new releases are available! As a thank you for signing up, you'll receive a complimentary copy of *The First Deception (Jack Noble Prequel) with bonus story The Recruit: A Jack Noble Short Story.*

Join here: http://ltryan.com/newsletter/

I enjoy hearing from readers. Join us in my private Facebook group https://www.facebook.com/groups/1727449564174357 or drop me a line at contact@ltryan.com. I read and respond to every message.

If you enjoyed reading *Thin Line*, I would appreciate it if you would help others enjoy these books, too. How?

Lend it. This e-book is lending-enabled, so please, feel free to share it with a friend. All they need is an amazon account and a Kindle, or Kindle reading app on their smart phone or computer.

Recommend it. Please help other readers find this book by recommending it to friends, readers' groups and discussion boards.

Review it. Please tell other readers why you liked this book by reviewing it at Amazon, Barnes & Noble, Apple or Goodreads. Your opinion goes a long way in helping others decide if a book is for them. Also, a review doesn't have to be a big old book report. If you do write a review, please send me an email at contact@ltryan.com so I can thank you with a personal email.

Like Jack. Visit the Jack Noble Facebook page and give it a like: https://www.facebook.com/JackNobleBooks. And then join us in my private Facebook group: https://www.facebook.com/groups/1727449564174357

"Momma!" the little girl called out in a frightened voice.

Jack Noble looked over and saw her standing alone. She looked to be eight or nine years old. He watched people walk by the crying child, paying no attention to her. His first thought was to ignore her like the faceless others who didn't notice or care that a little girl was standing in the middle of the sidewalk alone and lost.

"Momma? Where are you?" she said through sobs.

Jack jogged over and knelt in front of the child. "What's your name, sweetheart?"

"Mandy." She wiped tears away from her big blue eyes. "Can you help me?"

Jack looked around at the crowded street and then at his watch. The old man would be there soon. The instructions were explicit; he had to be at the corner of Main Street and Roosevelt Avenue at 9:30 a.m. The old man did not like it when people were late.

Jack looked at the little girl. "Didn't anyone ever tell you not to talk to strangers?"

She stared back at him.

"C'mon, Mandy." He hoisted her onto his shoulders. "Can you see her?"

Mandy looked up and down the street. "No. I don't see her nowhere."

"How long have you been lost?"

"I dunno. A long time." Her crying had stopped.

Jack turned in a tight circle so Mandy could scout the crowd.

"I can't see her mister."

Jack pulled her down from his shoulder and held her against his chest. "Where do you live?"

"23423 52nd Street, Apartment D." She rattled the address off fast, like a robot, and he knew the address had been drilled into her by her mother or father.

"Do you know your mommy's cell phone number?"

As quickly as she offered up her address, the little girl gave him her mother's cell phone number.

Jack reached into his pocket and pulled out his cell phone, dialed the number and waited for it to ring.

"We're sorry, the number you have dialed has been disconnected. Please check the number and try again," a recorded operator told him.

He dialed again, but the same message played.

"Shit."

"Oh, you said a bad word," Mandy said.

He smiled at the girl, but his smile turned into a look of concern when he saw the white Mercedes getting closer. The old man was here, 9:30 a.m. on the dot. He looked around to see if anyone recognized the little girl. People walked by, eyes ahead staring off into the distance like zombies. It was always the same in every big city he visited. Everyone walked around with blank stares, looking straight ahead. They didn't give a care about him or his problems.

The Mercedes pulled up to the curb. The rear window rolled down. An old Asian man peered at him through thin glasses. "Hello, Mr. Jack."

Jack nodded back at the man.

"Do you have the documents with you?"

Jack held up the briefcase for the old man to see. "Right here."

"Is today bring your child to work day?"

"Condescending much?" Jack continued to look around for someone, anyone, who recognized Mandy. "I need you to give me a couple minutes here."

"There are no minutes to give, Mr. Jack. Our agreement was 9:30 a.m. It is now 9:30 a.m."

"Just give me a minute. She's lost. I need to find a safe place for her."

"I can assure you my car is the safest place for her." His sly, yellow smile was enough to put Jack on alert.

"Just give me a minute," Jack said.

He knew the old man wouldn't blink an eye at the little girl if she weren't with Jack. And if he turned her over, then the old man would drive five minutes out of the city and drop her on the curb, if he didn't kill her first.

"You have 30 seconds, Mr. Jack. Fail to return in 30 seconds and... well, I don't have to tell you what's to come. Do I?"

"No. I'm well aware of that." In six years he had done at least four dozen jobs for the old man. Jack knew the only reason the crime boss continued to give him assignments was because Jack didn't screw up. He didn't attract attention, and he most definitely didn't tell the old man to wait.

"You are wasting time, Mr. Jack."

Jack took off down the sidewalk. He recalled seeing a police officer stationed a block away. Dealing with a cop wasn't ideal. There was always a risk that Jack's face was plastered on a wanted poster somewhere. But if he wanted Mandy in a safe place, there was no other choice.

"Officer!" Jack yelled.

The police officer turned to face Jack with a look of indifference smeared across his face.

"Officer, this little girl is lost. I need you to take her. She knows her address and her mom's cell phone." Jack pushed the little girl towards the cop. She turned and reached back for Jack, apparently not wanting to leave his side.

"Whoa, whoa, wait," the policeman said. He held out his hand and shook it in Jack's face. "What the hell is going on here? You can't just dump a kid on me."

"I know how it looks, officer, but she's in danger. Just take her back to the precinct until her mother shows up."

The cop eyed Jack's six foot two inch frame up and down. His gaze lingered a second too long and Jack got the feeling the cop didn't care too much for him. He watched the policeman's eyes stop at the handcuffs attached to Jack's left wrist. They widened when the cop seemed to realize that the other end was attached to a briefcase. The cop backed up.

"What the hell is attached to your wrist?"

Jack checked to see how many people were around. It was crowded. He was in New York for Christ's sake, of course it was crowded. He preferred not to make a scene with this many people nearby, but he didn't have much choice. He looked back at the cop. The pudgy officer had his hand on his gun. Jack knew at that moment he had no other choice.

Jack slowly raised his left hand and distracted the officer by pushing Mandy toward him. The moment the cop looked down at the little girl, Jack's window opened. He reached into his pocket for a stun grenade, or flashbang as he called it. In one fluid motion he threw the flashbang at the cop's feet, pulled Mandy back, and turned so he wouldn't be blinded by the light.

The cop didn't have time to react. *BOOM!* The flashbang exploded with a burst of bright light that instantly and temporarily blinded anyone who saw it. The explosion was loud enough to upset the fluid in the inner ear, disrupting all sense of balance and direction. The officer fell back and hit his head on the sidewalk. Hours later neither the cop nor any of the bystanders would be able to describe Jack. The only thing the cop remembered was the briefcase.

Jack lifted Mandy in a fireman's carry and ran. He scoured the street for the Mercedes, but it was gone. It looked like the old man hung him out to dry.

Again.

Jack cursed out loud.

Mandy giggled.

"You think this is funny?"

She stopped laughing and pushed with her hands to get off of his shoulder. Jack tightened his grip as he looked for the Mercedes. He spotted it parked a block and a half away. He was almost out of breath when he finally reached the car.

"Mr. Jack," said the old man, "I would have thought that someone in your line of work would be in better shape."

"Dirty cigarettes," Jack said.

"You know, those will kill you." The old man reached into his shirt pocket and pulled out a cigarette, lit it with a wooden match, and threw the match out the window toward Jack.

"When?" Jack asked in a sarcastic tone. He set the girl down and ran his hand through his brown hair. "Let us in," he said, "we'll get this sorted out on the way."

"Mr. Jack, you are late. Not only that, you have attracted the attention of the police. This meeting has been compromised." He rolled up the window and the Mercedes pulled away.

"Wait!" Jack said. "Let us in. I've got what you want right here."

The Mercedes stopped and the old man stuck his head out the window, looking back at him. "Another time, Mr. Jack." The old man paused and lowered his sunglasses so Jack could look at his cataract covered eyes. "I'll be in touch soon."

The Mercedes sped away and Jack heard the sounds of sirens approaching. The cops would be here soon. He had to get moving or it would only be a matter of seconds before they found him.

"It's time for plan B, Mandy." He lifted her back onto his shoulder.

"What's plan B, Mr. Jack?"

"I'll let you know as soon as I do, sweetheart."

Jack jogged half a block and ducked into an alley. He pulled out a map of the area that was marked with the locations of places he considered safe houses. Over the last decade he had performed enough favors he could always call on someone when in a tough situation.

Clarissa's apartment was on a block away. She was a friend. Truth be told, she was more than a friend. There were two people Jack trusted with his life and Clarissa was one of them. She would hide him for the night, no questions asked. He might even be able to pawn Mandy off on her. He looked at the little girl and laughed at the thought of Clarissa taking care of a kid.

"What's so funny?"

"Other than your face?"

"Hey! That's not nice!" Mandy stuck out her lower lip in an exaggerated pout.

Jack laughed. "I'm teasing sweetie. Only teasing."

They hid out in the alley until dark. Clarissa's apartment wasn't far away, but he didn't want to risk the cops spotting them. He didn't want to kill a cop in front of Mandy. He might be a killer, but he did have some morals.

"Who is it?" Clarissa asked from the other side of the door.

Jack held Mandy against his chest. She was asleep, had been since before they left the alley. He quietly replied, "It's Jack."

"Jack?"

"C'mon, Clarissa. I'm in trouble. Need your help."

The door opened and Jack was greeted by the gorgeous red head. There weren't many women who could look him in the eye, but at five foot ten and wearing heels, Clarissa could. She motioned with her hand for Jack to come in. As he walked past her, he noticed how great she smelled. She always smelled great. Not cheap like most of the other strippers he knew.

"Who the hell is this?"

"Her name's Mandy. She's lost." Jack paused a beat. "I was waiting for an associate and spotted her. She was standing there, crying for her mom. No one would help her."

Clarissa raised a curious eyebrow. "Ahhh, you've gone soft, baby."

"Shut up."

"So, what, you went up to her and?"

"I offered to help. Figured her mom was in a nearby store. You know something simple like that."

"I'm guessing you assumed wrong then?"

"Yeah, very wrong. Worst thing is I missed my meeting, which pissed off some very bad people." He unlocked the handcuffs and set the brief-case down.

Clarissa cast a curious eye toward the briefcase. "So why are you here? You need me to hide you?" She laughed.

"I also pissed off the cops." He looked up at the ceiling, his hands clasped behind his head.

"Let me get you a drink."

Jack nodded.

"What do you want? I got beer, whiskey, tequila."

"One of each," Jack replied. "Hey, you got somewhere she can lie down?"

"Sure, go ahead and put her in my room for now." Clarissa pointed to the back of the apartment with one hand as she filled shot glasses with the other.

Jack walked over to the couch and picked up the sleeping girl. It had been a long day for the child. She opened her eyes and stared at him, lips drawn tight and her eyebrows furrowed. He waited for her to ask him a question, but before she could open her mouth, her head fell forward on his shoulder and she went back to sleep. He stroked her hair as he took her to Clarissa's bedroom. Jack laid her down and covered her up with a blanket.

He walked back to the kitchen and went straight to the counter where his shot glasses were waiting. He threw back a shot of tequila and grimaced at the burn and aftertaste. He'd only had three jobs go bad. Two of those three had been because of tequila.

"I've never seen you that gentle with anyone," Clarissa said. She placed her hand on his shoulder and gave it a soft massage, then dragged her nails lightly across his back.

He picked up the second shot glass and held it to his lips. "I screwed up." He drank the whiskey, slammed the shot glass down and then cracked opened the bottle of beer. "Big time."

"More?"

"Yeah, one of each." He slid the shot glasses across the counter.

Clarissa poured his refills. "How bad can it be?"

Jack said nothing. He drank his shots in succession and returned to his bottle of beer. "We'll only be here tonight."

"Jack, you know you can stay as long as you need. I don't mind. Even with the kid, it's cool with me." She put her arm around his shoulders. "As much as you have done for me, it's the least I can do."

"It's the old man," he said.

Clarissa looked down at the floor, toward the briefcase. "I'm guessing that briefcase has something to do with it?"

Jack nodded and said nothing.

"What's inside?" she asked.

"Just some papers." He paused. "It's better you don't know."

"Will he try to kill you?"

Jack thought about it for a moment, shrugged. *Would he kill me?*

"If he wanted me dead he would have killed me after I botched the deal."

"So why don't you go to him tonight and complete the deal?" Clarissa asked.

"The cop on the corner. He saw enough of me to be able to identify me. Plus, the old man said he'd be in contact. Better to just wait it out."

"You want to turn on the TV? Check the news?"

"Nah, that garbage's depressing."

They both laughed but the moment was short lived, interrupted by a shrill scream. Jack raced to the back of the apartment to check on Mandy.

"Mommy!"

Jack sat on the edge of the bed and stroked her hair. "Shhh," he whispered, "we're going to get you to your momma. I promise." He sat with her until she fell back to sleep.

Clarissa greeted him with a smile when he returned to the kitchen. He smiled back. She looked good tonight. Hell, she looked good any time of day. But tonight she seemed more vibrant than usual. Even though he had ten years on her, they'd always had a connection. Things had progressed further the last few years, though, and that scared Jack. In his line of business it didn't pay to be close to anyone.

"Another drink?" she asked.

Jack nodded.

Clarissa brushed against him on her way to the fridge.

Jack followed her, waiting behind the opened door. The air escaping from the refrigerator felt cool against his flush face.

She stood, turned and stopped inches from him. Bit her bottom lip.

He lifted his hand, brushing strands of her hair behind her ear. Leaned in and kissed her neck. His hands worked down her sides. Steady fingers unbuttoned her jeans and slid them off her waist. "For a stripper you wear some pretty boring panties."

"Exotic dancer," she said in between nibbles on his ear. She wrapped a leg around his.

"The little girl," Jack said. "She's sleeping in the other room."

Clarissa waved off Jack's protest. "I'll be quiet."

"But you know I can't be," he said with a wry smile.

They found the couch and fell into one another.

Visit https://ltryan.com/pb for purchasing information.

ALSO BY L.T. RYAN

Visit https://ltryan.com/pb for paperback purchasing information.

The Jack Noble Series

Bear Logan Series

Rachel Hatch Series

Drift

Downburst

Fever Burn

Smoke Signal

Firewalk - December 2020

Whitewater - March 2021

Mitch Tanner Series

The Depth of Darkness

Into The Darkness

Deliver Us From Darkness - coming Summer 2021

Cassie Quinn Series

Path of Bones

Untitled - February, 2021

Blake Brier Series

Unmasked

Unleashed - January, 2021

Untitled - April, 2021

Affliction Z Series

Affliction Z: Patient Zero

Affliction Z: Abandoned Hope

Affliction Z: Descended in Blood

Affliction Z: Fractured (Part 1)

Affliction Z: Fractured (Part 2) - October, 2021

ABOUT THE AUTHOR

L.T. Ryan is a *USA Today* and international bestselling author. The new age of publishing offered L.T. the opportunity to blend his passions for creating, marketing, and technology to reach audiences with his popular Jack Noble series.

Living in central Virginia with his wife, the youngest of his three daughters, and their three dogs, L.T. enjoys staring out his window at the trees and mountains while he should be writing, as well as reading, hiking, running, and playing with gadgets. See what he's up to at http://ltryan.com.

Social Medial Links:

- Facebook (L.T. Ryan): https://www.facebook.com/LTRyanAuthor

- Facebook (Jack Noble Page): https://www.facebook.com/JackNobleBooks/

- Twitter: https://twitter.com/LTRyanWrites

- Goodreads: http://www.goodreads.com/author/show/6151659.L_T_Ryan

Made in United States
Orlando, FL
19 July 2022

19965434R00211